Kenyon Dobson is a writer who builds. Or perhaps a builder who writes? In the swinging 60s he attended college in Blackburn and Liverpool. Previously, in the not so swinging 50s, he was educated at Queen Elizabeth Grammar School in Blackburn. Here he learned to put pen to paper, but was alarmed by the distinct lack of girls! He soon made up for lost time, however, and today has six children. His first novel *Jacob's Trouble* was published in 1992 by Endage.

THE GOD OF THIS WORLD

Kenyon Dobson

Book Guild Publishing
Sussex, England

First published in Great Britain in 2007 by
The Book Guild Ltd
Pavilion View
19 New Road
Brighton, BN1 1UF

Typesetting in Baskerville by
Acorn Bookwork Ltd, Salisbury, Wiltshire

Printed in Great Britain by
Athenaeum Press Ltd, Gateshead

A catalogue record for this book is available from
The British Library.

ISBN 978 1 84624 142 0

Contents

1

Origins

'... for then there will be great tribulation such as has not occurred since the world's beginning until now, no, nor will occur again.'

– Jesus Christ

Plymouth Hoe, England. The Near Future.

When that day comes, as soon it must, the old man's daughter, Ellen, along with her husband, Tony, and their children Stephanie and John, will actually be sitting on the lawns of Plymouth Hoe enjoying a lunch of greasy beefburgers and crispy fries. The day will be clear and calm and the family will be warmed by the early autumn sunshine.

The day will hold the sound of children's laughter, an infectious, excited laughter, coaxed from the mouths of the young by the travelling fair which will, on that day, have descended on the Hoe. Finger-gripping rides, not-so-finger-gripping rides, side shows, a-prize-every-time stalls, fast food bars, candyfloss. Stephanie and John will be excited.

And Ellen herself will be feeling a sense of excitement. Yes, in spite of the frightening international situation with its wars and rumours of wars, Ellen Jones will be thinking of her own pleasant childhood in Lancashire rather than morbidly allowing her mind to dwell on matters possibly dangerous. She will be remembering times past, times when her own father and mother had on various occasions taken herself and her brother to travelling fairs.

Ellen will be remembering the almost forgotten joys and eager excitement of her own childhood and so intense will be her recollections that at the critical moment, at the moment of death, her eyes will be gazing out to sea, seeing but hardly noticing one of His Majesty's destroyers ploughing a liquid furrow through the still waters of Plymouth Sound.

The thermonuclear device will explode directly above her at a distance of less than a quarter of a mile. Death will be instantaneous. She will be given no time to avert her eyes from the sea so as to gaze lovingly upon her family. There will be no time to say goodbye. She will not live to see the incineration, the vapourisation of husband and children, of those so dear to her heart, for in an instant the earth will scorch, the sea will boil and turbulently steam, and the city of Plymouth will perish along with all flesh.

I will not personally be present to witness the destruction of the old man's daughter and her brood, although some of my friends undoubtedly will be present. They will, I feel, take great satisfaction in observing the beginnings of the war, in observing in cities across the globe the agonies of those who will be at a little distance from the centres of the grand explosions, in observing the agonies of those who will not die so quickly! What a day it will be! The day of my inspiring! But, as I say, I will not be present in Plymouth, nor will I be present in New York City where the old man's son will meet his end.

*

New York City. The Near Future.

New York City will not be incinerated when suddenly World War Three violently erupts upon a largely unsuspecting world. New York City will escape total destruction because American missile defensive systems will be capable of shielding the city from a direct attack. These defensive systems, however, will not save the city from great devastation. The aggression will come from space, from orbital nuclear weaponry, and against this weaponry there will be no adequate defence.

The missile directed against New York City will be deflected from its course to explode at ground level some ten miles to the north-west of the city. David Brooke, the old man's son, will witness the explosion from the windows of his offices in Brooklyn Heights.

He will see the brightest of bright lights, the whitest of lights suddenly and silently permeating the entire building, the entire city. The light will fade and in the eerie ensuing silence David Brooke will look out to see the sky to the north-west a fiery red. In silence he and his colleagues will gather at the window to observe the turbulent boiling sky. It will then become apparent that above and around the fiery sky a cloud will be forming, a dense, fear-inspiring, mushroom-shaped cloud.

'My God!'

These words, these almost whispered words, will be the last words ever to be spoken in David Brooke's office.

The blast and heat will come in from the north-west with terrifying speed. Within a matter of seconds it will traverse from the outskirts of the city to Brooklyn, blasting and burning everything in its path. From the office windows David Brooke will see buildings blasted apart by a wall of fire which will descend upon him with such speed that his brain will find it impossible to fully comprehend that the moment of his death will suddenly and cruelly have arrived.

The blast and heat will hit, destroying Brooklyn Heights, blasting and searing frail flesh.

Well now. Poor Uncle Sam!

Not only New York, but Chicago, Philadelphia, Washington, Dallas, Los Angeles, San Francisco and all major cities along with missile sites and various other military installations. All will burn! And they will burn in one co-ordinated strike lasting less than one hour!

The United States of America will become a blackened smoking ruin with a suddenness that will prove to be unbelievable and American response to European aggression will be negligible, if the destruction of Paris combined with a rogue detonation over the Italian Alps can be classed as negligible.

If you would care to look at an American dollar bill you will find upon it these words: 'In God We Trust.'

But as a nation, the United States does not place its trust in God. Because, in their might, they trust the more! Yet might will not deliver them.

My followers shall witness the nuclear destruction of the United States. I myself will see the destruction of Great Britain, specifically of the county of Lancashire, for there I intend to be, in order to taunt the man, William Brooke, yes, my enemy, who will, at the outbreak of tribulation, have grown old.

Rest in peace, Uncle Sam! Rest in peace, John Bull!

But I will give no peace to William Brooke.

*

Brinscall, Lancashire. The Near Future.

The old man will sleep late on that day, on the day when the world will suddenly change, never to return to its old ways. The old man will sleep and he will dream of times past, of the times when his wife, his beloved Jessica, had not yet died, of the times when Ellen and David were yet young children. In this dream the old man will weep, his deeper feelings stirred by the recollection of good times forever lost, yet on awakening he will not remember this dream, for a later dream will stamp itself on his memory, consigning the earlier dream to the cupboard of forget-fulness, a later dream, a sinister dream, a frighteningly unnatural dream!

William Brooke will stir restlessly in his bed. Beads of sweat will trickle down his wrinkled face wetting his whitened beard. His mouth will twitch as he begins to dream of very unpleasant things and the trapped wind in his intestines will in its own way contribute to the unpleasantness of his dreaming. Yet the main contributor to this unpleasantness will be the person standing unseen at the foot of William Brooke's bed, the person bombarding the old man's subconscious mind with dark and unnatural thoughts, the powerful person composed not of flesh and blood but of spirit, the person of Satan, ruler of the demons and of this world, the person of the Devil himself.

The old man will see terrible visions. He will hear the Devil's voice.

'Fire!'

In the old man's mind a chilling vision will begin to form.

'Fire! Ascending to the heavens! Fire and black billowing smoke!'

The old man will find himself looking out of his own bedroom window, looking up over the moor which lies to the south of the village of Brinscall. His eyes will focus on a particular hill, and though in reality this hill cannot be seen from his bedroom window, he will in his dream see it clearly. With fear in his heart he will see the hill begin to grow, to rapidly force itself upwards so that it will

5

quickly become a mountain towering high, high over the moor, high over the village. He will see this mountain pulsating. He will see it glowing the colour of blood.

'Fire! To burn your feeble flesh! To take you to your death in agony!'

Suddenly, to the old man's horror, the pulsating mountain will violently explode, spewing fire and thick blackened smoke high above the already great height of the mountain. In terror the old man will see fire every-where above him, covering the whole sky, shutting out all traces of the blue, and he will see this fire begin to fall, to fall towards the village, towards his home, to fall with increasing speed towards him.

'Flee! Hide! It comes to devour you! To burn your naked flesh!'

In panic, the old man will find himself fleeing down the steps of his stairs. He will be naked and, despite his choking fear, he will yet be aware of the deterioration of his once strong and firm body. He will see his wrinkling flesh, he will be conscious of wasting muscles, of the shrivelled penis between his naked legs. Also, he will actually feel the aches and pains in his joints and he will feel a greater pain in his intestines where the trapped wind will be struggling to escape. Yes, mingled with the old man's terror will be the awareness that his failing body will be hindering his frantic efforts to escape the rapidly approaching fire.

'Hide yourself! Quickly! The fire is almost upon you!'

Through his downstairs windows the old man will see the air outside turn red – bright red. He will hear a sound resembling thunder – a dreadful roaring – and he will hear screams, the screams of his neighbours. He will feel a sudden and sharp rise in temperature, he will actually feel a burning of his aged and naked flesh.

'Quickly! Under the stairs!'

The old man will struggle to open the door to the cupboard under the stairs. Feeble hands against a strong-springed door handle, hands trembling with fear, refusing to go where the brain will be instructing them to go. Amid the thunder and screams, a sound of rushing wind, the bright redness outside beginning to permeate the downstairs rooms and the windows in these rooms beginning very unnaturally to buckle inwards.

'Hide! Hide! Conceal yourself. The devastation is upon you!'

The cupboard door will suddenly open and the old man will go inside, shutting the door firmly behind him. He will sit upon the floor trembling uncontrollably. In the darkness he will see a faint red glow beginning to form on the walls and ceiling of the cupboard and also upon the door. The glow will quickly intensify and the old man will actually feel heat upon his flesh. He will see thick smoke oozing into the cupboard through the gaps around the door and in a fit of sheer panic he will come to realise the hopelessness of his situation. He is being roasted alive! He is choking to his death!

And then it will occur to him that he might be dreaming.

In his bed he will open his eyes but he will not at once realise that he will be staring at his bedroom ceiling because the power of the dream will still hold him. Clammy sweat will cover his body and the heat of this sweating will focus his mind on the fire in his dream. In his head he will hear the Devil's voice, mocking, taunting.

'Go back to the cupboard, old man. Your wife and your children are burning there!'

He will see his wife, he will see his young children, and they will be in the cupboard burning and choking. He will hear them scream out to him, imploring him to save them. Yet somehow he will be able to remember the death of his wife and he will be able to remember that his children have grown. Again it will occur to him that he is dreaming and again he will attempt to awaken, to come to his senses. But the dream will hold him for a moment longer.

'So, old man. You have remembered that your wife is dead! You have remembered that your children have grown!'

Once more the old man will open his eyes. He will now realise that he is in his bed, though the power of the voice of the dream will still be holding him. With horror he will come to know that someone, something malignant, will be standing at the foot of his bed, but try as he might he will be unable to raise his head so as to look towards the foot of his bed. In fact, he will find himself unable to move at all. He will feel a great terror, a greater terror than that engendered by his dream.

'Yes, old man. It is I! And this day your children are to be reunited with their mother.'

Paralysed, William Brooke will feel a great weight pushing down upon his chest, forcing the breath from his body. In great and all consuming terror he will cry out loud for deliverance. He will utter only one word and that word will be the name of God.

'Jehovah!'

Instantly the power of the Devil will be broken and William Brooke will find himself able to move. Instantly his fear will vanish and his full senses will return. He will know that he has been the target of a demonic attack and he will look towards the foot of his bed and he will know that the Devil has departed, at least for the time being.

He will give thanks to God for his deliverance, yet he will know on that not-too-distant day matters sinister and cruel will be afoot and that the work of the Devil will be about to come to its head.

Now, in case you are thinking that I can sometimes be cruel, let me put you straight. I am always cruel! Be in no doubt. I am the personification of cruelty because I am the originator of cruelty.

I am also the originator of a few other things – like murder, like lying. The son of God himself has labelled me a Manslayer and The Father of Lies! But am I telling you the truth now? You will decide.

Still, let us see what will happen to the old man, William Brooke, on that day which, according to the same son of God, is destined to 'come in on all those dwelling on the face of the earth'.

The old man will arise from his bed on that day with the emotions engendered by his vision still gripping him. He will wash his hands and face, he will brush the remains of his teeth, and all the while his mind will be tortured by the intensity of the dream. Yet by late morning, after the old man will have eaten, the reality of the vision, of the attack upon him, will somehow seem to be less real. Had he really been subjected to a form of demonic attack? Or had the entire episode been no more than a vivid if terrifying dream?

Shortly before midday, however, when the old man will be at his kitchen sink, washing the dirty dishes, he will quite abruptly be left in no doubt whatsoever as to the reality of the attack upon him.

The whitest of white lights will suddenly and silently invade the kitchen, invade the house, invade the whole of the old man's world, and not for the first time that day, William Brooke will be gripped by fear. The light will then rapidly fade away returning the world to seeming normality and William Brooke, in a state of trepidation and some confusion, will open his kitchen door and go out into the yard where once again a brilliant and silent flash of light will bathe the environment in the purest white. Again the light will rapidly fade and William Brooke will raise his eyes to the skies where, to the south, above and beyond the moor, he will see a fiery red glowing and he will see it quickly intensify. He will then notice a similar glowing in the skies to the south-west, a fieriness partially obscured by the outline of his neighbours' houses, and with his heart beginning to pound, William Brooke will instantly be visited by the vivid and fearful remembrance of his dream. Fire! Choking heat! The terror of it all.

At that moment William Brooke will once more hear the words of the Devil. 'This day your children are to be reunited with their mother.'

With dread in his heart the old man will hurry indoors, locking the kitchen door behind him. He will take refuge under the stairs, closing the cupboard door behind him. He will again pray to God, asking for strength to endure the days to come, should he live to see those days, and asking further, not for the deliverance of his children, but rather for their eternal welfare – that should they perish they would be remembered in the resurrection of the dead.

William Brooke will sit alone in the darkness of the cupboard under the stairs not knowing that the cities of Manchester and Liverpool will be burning with a heat of unimaginable intensity. But William Brooke will be fearfully aware that a great destruction is about to descend upon the village of Brinscall.

And soon the very air will roar like the roaring of a thousand wild beasts. Soon there will be blast and heat and choking dust, the shaking of the earth under foot. And when the blasts from the two nuclear explosions will have passed over there will be a strange silence, a suffocating silence, punctuated only occasionally by the rumble of falling masonry and by the odd pitiful scream, the intermittent cries of the injured and dying. Later, as the infernos of Manchester and Liverpool will continue to burn, oxygen will be sucked in to feed these fires, and over the ruins of Brinscall fierce winds will blow.

Yes, the Lancashire village of Brinscall will be practically destroyed, yet William Brooke will be among the survivors who will emerge from the ruins to eke out a living in a lawless and poisoned land.

Now you, the reader, might well be wondering at this point what on earth this future, this near future, nuclear holocaust has to do with a chapter entitled 'Origins'?

Well, in order to understand the beginning of a thing it is sometimes necessary to see where such a thing is leading.

It would seem that mankind, left to his own devices but with a little help from the spirit world, is inevitably heading for disaster. But why? And will such a disaster be the end of mankind? These questions and many more will be answered in the pages of this book and we shall certainly return later to the story of William Brooke.

Now, however, we shall concern ourselves with origins – the origin of man, the origins of the spirits, the origin of the physical universe.

It is generally accepted at the current time that the origin of the human race has much to do with evolution. Yet there are some people who believe in creation. Which, if either, is the truth? You will decide!

First, let the case for evolution be put.

*

Long, Long Ago in the Middle of Nowhere.

Once upon a time, so they say, there was a big bang. Now, this was no ordinary big bang. No, this was THE BIG BANG! And

11

I have to tell you that this particular big bang marked, so they say, the beginning of the physical universe – the beginning of everything that exists today! Yes, the origin of mankind can be traced back through eons, many many eons, to this magnificent big bang.

So it's all pretty important stuff! Right?

Right, well just before we see what happened after this big bang let us for a moment try to imagine what things were like before this big bang.

You see, the present universe appears to be expanding at an accelerating and measurable rate and the clever men of science, always eager to theorise, have, with the aid of their computers, apparently managed to simulate a reversing of this expansion and by so doing they have arrived at a point in time, long, long ago – no, long, long, long, long, long ago, when all the matter and energy in the universe was condensed, in the middle of nowhere, into something the size of a golf ball.

Sounds incredible, doesn't it?

But it must be true, or truish, because the experts – the physicists, the mathematicians, the astronomers – all of them apparently – insist that it is true, or truish!

So, we have, long, long ago in the middle of nowhere, a golf ball-sized lump of energy, or matter, or antimatter, or a combination of these, or whatever – it doesn't matter – just waiting to explode and form the physical universe. No one seems to know for sure where this golf ball came from or how or why it came to be in the middle of nowhere, but that doesn't matter. The scientists insist it was there, so it must have been.

Then ... BANG!

Oh what a wonderful sight it would have been had any human eye been present to see it. Oh what a wonderful sight it really was, for my eyes and the eyes of all the spirits were there to see it and we joyfully cried out together at the wonder of it.

BANG! Into that silent, cold and empty nothingness, into the void came abundant power, sudden violent power spilling out in every direction, power in the forms of energy and matter, power which began at once to fill the void with light, with radiations unseen, with unimaginably hot gases, with things presently hidden from the knowledge of man.

BANG! The birth of the universe. A birth accomplished in a moment of time. And time itself would have its part to play.

BANG! Into the void with tremendous speed poured the energy and the matter. Into that silent, cold and dark, dark void came the invasion of heat and light. Yet the limitless void with the aid of limitless time was able – is able – to contain all the heat and all the light.

BANG! From something the size of a golf ball an explosion of all the physical energy and matter which presently exists! Does God play golf?

BANG! Incredible power! Into the void it pours in every direction, the outer particles travelling fractionally quicker than the inner particles so that over time – and there is plenty of time – a separation occurs.

BANG! Hot gases rushing at tremendous speeds away from a central core, gases separating, forming pulsating groupings, inter-reacting – the birth of gravity? Hot gases spewing forth and eventually, with the passing of time, lots of time, eventually cooling, cooling to the point where some of the gases begin to solidify. Yes, liquid and solid matter forming with the passing of time, so much time. (When man finally arrives on this scene he will measure his time in his days and in his years according to the cycles of the earth. He will barely be able to imagine the billions and billions of his years, which necessarily passed in order to accommodate the birth and growth of the universe.)

But let us not digress, let us not get ahead of ourselves. We have seen the birth of the universe. We have some knowledge of how it is expanding and cooling. And if we look at today's observable universe with its countless groups of galaxies, each containing billions of stars, if we look at the present day solar system, which contains man's home, the earth, if we look at all

13

these things through scientific eyes, then we can come to conclusions as to how the earth was formed, can't we? Of course we can!

Yes, many many millions of years ago, in what then was a remote and insignificant corner of the universe, a flaming sun began to form. And as it formed, a planetary system began to form around it. Now, never mind the complicated mechanics behind this formation, give no thought here to intelligent design, just believe that this blind formation occurred! Well, it must have occurred! The earth and its solar system exist today so they must have formed from the cooling gases of the BIG BANG! Yes, this is what present day science believes so it must be true! And everybody knows it!

Now, the subtitle 'Long, long ago in the middle of nowhere' has become inappropriate, so we will change it ...

*

Long Ago and by Pure Coincidence.

So, long ago there was a flaming sun, a central nuclear-powered furnace, and around it a planetary system was forming – nine fiery gaseous orbs plus a few bits and pieces.

Now, purely by coincidence the third planet from this sun came to be positioned at exactly the correct distance so as to eventually be capable of supporting life, that is life as mankind knows it, fleshy life. The planet did not come to be positioned too close to the sun, for that way flesh would burn, nor did it come to be positioned too far away from the sun, for that way flesh would freeze. No, the earth's position in the solar system came to be just perfect for life eventually to flourish, purely by chance, of course.

And now we need some more time in the equation. No problem! There is an infinite amount of time. Let's throw in a few billion years.

The planets have cooled and settled in their orbits. The third planet from the sun, the earth, remains in a position to support life, and to aid it in this respect, two more quite remarkable coincidences have occurred. One way or another, and to this day no one knows exactly how or why, but on this world, violent and turbulent though this world may yet be with its volcanic activity and all the rest, somehow water and air have come into existence! Very, very convenient!

Now at this point in the narrative it is only fair to put the case so far for creation, since there is not necessarily any contradiction. So here we go.

In the beginning God created the heavens and the earth.

Now the Earth proved to be formless and waste and there was darkness upon the surface of the watery deep, and God's active force was moving to and fro over the surface of the waters.

– Genesis 1: 1, 2

No, so far we see no apparent contradictions, but from here on in there will be great contradictions between the evolutionary tale and the story of creation. You will decide who is telling the truth. Back to the story.

And it has now become a story of soup, primeval soup, a mixture of chemicals, all of which are present in today's world, all of which were present when the earth began to form, when the land heaved with volcanic activity, when the restless seas frothed and boiled, and, later, when the land became more settled, when the seas became less agitated. Soup! A primeval soup, stirred in a melting pot over an unimaginably long period of time, the melting pot of the third planet from the sun.

Soup!

Soup, boiled, stirred and cooled, made with all the time in the world and a soup abundantly laced with coincidences!

In fact, what you are about to read is a story so purely full of coincidences that it will stretch your credulity to the limit, but, no matter how incredible or even impossible the following may seem to be, it is today more or less accepted as fact by your scientific communities, so therefore it must be more or less true.

Yes, it must be!

So, bear with me. We continue with the tale of the soup.

You see, somehow, somewhere, in the middle of this chemical soup, life must have begun. Not life as we know it perhaps, but life nevertheless. And the soup must have produced not only animal life but plant life also, and it would seem logical that the plants arrived first. Yes, generally speaking the plants would thrive on the chemicals in the soup and the animals would thrive on the plants.

So, somehow, in this soup, when and where all the conditions were favourable, the first living thing appeared – just like that! – and this living thing must have been in the form of a simply structured plant. Now if this plant survived it must have been the forerunner of much vegetation, but if it did not survive then we need to add a bit more time to the equation until the soup produces another similar plant. However, for the purpose of continuation, we will assume that this plant was the one that survived. This was THE plant.

And what a plant! Such a plant!

Why, not only did this plant contain the ability to suddenly come to life in the middle of non-living soup but, purely by coincidence, it also had the qualities that enabled it not only to survive but to proliferate! Yes, this plant appeared in the soup with the ability to react with its environment and thrive! This plant appeared in the soup with the capability of reproducing itself. Such an amazing plant!

If your scientists could find this plant and unlock its secrets then nothing would be impossible for them. If your scientists could recreate this plant in some laboratory then all the power in the universe would be in your hands, for you would have fashioned life from non-living matter. You would become gods!

Yet, stir the soup, add this and that, remove this and that,

16

warm it, cool it, increase and decrease pressure, shake it, bombard it with neutrons, protons, anyons and everyons, do all these things and more for a billion years and more, and still no plant will appear.

However, on the third planet from the sun, long ago, the plant did appear. Purely by coincidence, of course. It must have done.

Now, also purely by coincidence and, speaking in astronomical terms, shortly after the appearance on the earth of THE plant, we see something even more astounding. We see the mysterious appearance of an animal cell containing within its extremely simple structure the most complex potential.

Pay attention!

We speak of THE cell. We speak here of your ancestor!

Oh! What an amazing structure!

A simple cell with the potential, given time, to become the fish you had for supper, a lizard, your own pet dog, the elephant in the zoo, the supposedly fearsome Tyrannosaurus Rex, the fleas on your dog, the spider in the corner, the pig in the sty, the serpent (my personal favourite), the bacteria in your gut, the birds, the bees, the virus in your sneeze, yes, everything that moves upon the surface of the earth, everything that flies above the surface of the earth, everything that moves beneath the surface of the earth, and everything in the sea. Oh! And you, of course!

Absolutely amazing! I am astounded! Superlatives escape me, but the phrase 'gob-smacked' comes to mind.

But let us not forget to mention the monkeys. After all, is it not common knowledge that man descended from the apes? Of course it is and everyone knows it. And everyone knows that all things evolved from THE cell.

Now, I do not propose at this stage to discuss in detail how all these things came about. The story of evolution is complex and therefore time consuming. But I do want you to understand the basics so I do propose to tell you a little story. It is the sad tale of the Impossible Man.

*

The Impossible Man.

The Impossible Man, Tim for short, is a furtive creature. He inhabits dark and inaccessible places far away from the majority of mankind and this isolation Tim chooses out of fear for his life, for over the millennia Tim has come to know, to his cost, that he cannot safely live alongside the others of his kind, with the rest of humanity, with you!

This is because Tim is different.

And he looks different.

Yet Tim's ancestors were not different.

Like the rest of you Tim can trace his ancestry back to THE cell. Like the rest of you Tim's ancestors developed from THE cell in the warmth of the murky seas. Here, comforted by as much time as was necessary, they eventually took on a fish-like appearance and here they began to breed like the flies that some of them would eventually become. Then came the great day, the day when two of these fish-like creatures crawled or flipped out of the sea and exchanged their gills for lungs. They continued to breed. And what they bred was diverse. And when what was diverse began to breed there was even more diversity. But let us stay with the human part of this complex breeding programme. There eventually came a time when a creature appeared on the earth which was the forebear of both ape and man. Yes, ape and man – both descended from this particular creature. Ape and man! And man includes Tim.

But somewhere along the line, somewhere in that misty past, the mighty god of evolution dealt Tim a nasty, nasty blow.

Now, let us understand. Let us be clear. This was not a case of evolution going wrong. No! Heaven forbid! No, this was a case of the evolutionary process diversifying yet again. This was a case of non-intelligent design producing something a little different.

You see, Tim has three legs!

And the extra leg, complete with foot and symmetrical toes, has

18

developed between the other two legs.

This means that Tim has no reproductive system.

But Tim doesn't need a reproductive system because evolution has given him the ability to remain forever young.

Now this means, barring a fatal accident or the event of his being murdered, that Tim cannot die. This also means that Tim has been around on this earth for a long long time, from a time previous to when Homo Erectus *first erected himself. Yes somewhere along the evolutionary line Tim came along. He was born into the world never to grow old and never to reproduce.*

Tim is different.

And there are other differences.

Tim has no eyes in his head!

Tim does have one eye, but it is situated on his left elbow!

This means that Tim's optic nerve is a little longer than the average. This also means that he doesn't always see very well and it means that when he catches his left elbow on the corner of a table it hurts like hell!

So, Tim is different. He is a different sort of man. Let us see if we can understand just how Tim came to be different.

The third leg is easily explained. You see, the plain fact is that evolution is no mathematician. It cannot count. So it gave Tim a third leg and had it been a disadvantage Tim never would have survived. Natural selection would have killed him off. However, Tim's third leg is a great advantage to him. It enables him to run with great speed. It enables him to run away from the rest of you. You couldn't catch him so you couldn't kill him and so . . .

Tim lives to run away.

Down to this very day.

Which leads us on to the question of Tim's ability to live for ever. And this has to do with cell regeneration.

You people grow old and die because, after you become fully grown, your cells do not regenerate fast enough to keep you forever young and forever alive.

But evolution does not know this.

Evolution cannot know this because it has no brain, no intelligence.

So it is just as easy for evolution to produce an ever-living creature as it is to produce dying creatures such as yourselves. And in Tim's case, an ever-living creature is what evolution produced. An amazing coincidence, I grant you, that a three-legged creature should have everlasting life, but then the story of evolution is absolutely ram-packed full of amazing coincidences. And the evolution of the eye has its fair share of coincidences.

Everybody knows that the eye developed from a light-sensitive cell, or, to be more precise, everybody knows that eyes developed from two light-sensitive cells, which, purely by coincidence, happened to be in close proximity at the time. Everybody knows that this is how eyes came into existence. It is purely by coincidence that every single living creature on the planet, which has a need to be able to see, has two eyes (or two groups of eyes), and it is a further coincidence that these two eyes are always positioned in the best possible place – on the head, close to the brain and in symmetry.

This means that a living creature can see where it is going, can turn its head to see its surroundings and can simultaneously send two slightly different images to the brain, which the brain then interprets to give the creature a sense of perspective.

But evolution has no sense of perspective!

Evolution is not a living intelligent being, so it can have no sense of perspective.

In fact, evolution has no eyes. It is blind.

So we must conclude that it is purely by coincidence that men are born with two eyes and that these eyes are positioned as they are.

But Tim is also a man.

Yet somehow he missed the chance of having two eyes. The coincidences, which applied to all other creatures, did not apply to him. Poor old Tim has evolved with just the one eye! And it is not in the most appropriate of places! Damned unlucky, I'd say. Or is it evolution that should be damned?

Anyway, I want you now to imagine the situation if you were ever to set eyes on Tim – and you might. You would encounter a human being whose left arm is usually clasped across his chest so that he can see where he is going. You would encounter a creature whose shirt and coat were both lacking a left sleeve and whose trousers sported a third leg. You would see a man with no eyes in his head – not even the hint of a socket – and you would probably be scared out of your wits. You would find a human being for whom even the simplest of tasks, things that we take for granted, can pose great difficulties. Just imagine, if you will, how very difficult it is for Tim, with the single eye on his elbow, even to tie his own shoelaces – all three of them!

I happen to know that Tim once attempted to ride a push-bike. But it was only the once. Not only did he find it difficult to steer the contraption and at the same time see where he was going, but he couldn't work out what to do with his third leg, the middle one! Wherever he placed it, it seemed to get in the way. In the end he stuck the leg over the crossbar and pedalled away on a downhill slope. He never saw the large stone on the track because his middle foot was obscuring his vision. His scars took almost five years to fade. Poor Tim! Life can be very difficult for him. Poor old Tim!

And from your standpoint Tim is old. Old but not aged. Tim has been here on this earth for many thousands of years, so many years that he can now barely remember the early centuries, the days when your ancestors were unable to speak, uttering roars and grunts to make themselves understood. And during all those long, long centuries and ever since, Tim has hidden himself away from others of his kind, from the likes of you. Yes, you!

Tim walks the earth alone and is, as a result, afflicted by loneliness, great loneliness. You could not possibly imagine the depths of Tim's loneliness. No, you cannot possibly imagine. Tim's loneliness is a great weight pressing down upon him, an

21

unbearable weight. It is the weight of the world upon his shoulders. Tim longs for companionship. He yearns for the simple affection of others of his kind, for the affection of those who are his brothers and his sisters. Yet Tim knows from cruel experience that this companionship, this affection, will never be forthcoming, and Tim knows that loneliness will be his lot for ever, or at least for as long as he shall live.

Loneliness! Forced upon him because he is different, forced upon him because he terrifies other men — and he knows it. Tim hides away, he does not come out into the light, for on the rare occasions when he has encountered others they have run in fear from this ugly creature without eyes in his head, from this creature with three legs. They have run away from him and they have told their tales and then they have returned along with others in order to hunt him down, yes, to hunt him down like the wild beast they perceive him to be.

Tim has been pursued through the steaming jungles of Africa, across the arid deserts of Asia and over the fertile Asian steppes. He has fled for his life over the frozen wastes of the north, through fertile mid-western plains and through the bustling streets of great cities. Yet down to this day Tim has always managed to elude those who would imprison him, who would parade him as a freak, who would conduct medical experiments upon him, who would kill him! You see, when it comes to running, three legs are always better than two!

Sightings of Tim are rare indeed, but they do occur from time to time and it is these sightings combined with the fact that no one has ever proved able to get their hands on Tim that have served to make Tim a creature much misunderstood and maligned. Over the centuries the furtive Tim has become the stuff of which folklore and legend are made. Tim is the wizard, the bad fairy, the giant, the ogre, the goblin. He is the vampire, the zombie, he is Big Foot. He is the banshee, the troll, the bogart and the bogeyman. For those who cannot count he is the cyclops. In more recent times he is the alien, the creature from another world, and from time to time he is confused with creatures such as I. Oh yes, Tim has played the angel, the demon.

This is not to say that all of these fabulous entities do not really exist. No, no! Only that here and there Tim has been confused with such entities – and a thousand others. But now we know that Tim is none of these things. Now we know that Tim is merely a product of evolution, a child of chance, the son of pure coincidence.

And if one dark and storm-lashed night you, yes you, should encounter this poor child of coincidence, this strange-looking creature with not an eye in his head, with an extra leg and whose bare left elbow proceeds in front of him, if you should encounter him, then you will, I know, run screaming into the night, shouting to the world that they are here, that at last the aliens have landed! But you should never do such a thing.

Because it wouldn't be true and in any case the world would never believe you.

Instead, keep your own counsel and have some consideration for poor old Tim who is one of a kind, whose future is uncertain – unlike your own future with its certainty of the grave.

Yes, have some consideration for poor old Tim, the Impossible Man. Perhaps one day he will sprout wings, purely by coincidence of course, and simply fly away.

Now, before I speak of my own origins, let Kenyon Dobson put forward more evidence (if you can call it evidence) to support the theory of creation.

*

Long Ago and Purely by Design.

God is!

The above two words say it all. They do not imply that God had a beginning. They do not imply that he will come to an end. They simply state that God exists. He is!

Having no beginning and no end, God transcends time,

yet he has caused men to be aware of time so that they might use it as a measuring stick, so that they might be aware of their own mortality.

The scriptures tell us of God's qualities, of his immortality, of his abundant power, of his wisdom and justice, of his goodness. And the first chapter of Genesis describes God's physical creation, an act which is divided into six periods of time – six days. What now follows is a paraphrasing of Genesis 1: 3–31.

DAY 1. God commanded the sun to put forth its light. He caused the earth to turn upon its axis so that on the surface of the waters there would be periods of light and darkness.

DAY 2. God divided the waters so that there were waters upon the earth and waters above the earth with an expanse in between (the waters above the earth were likely in a gaseous form and these would be the waters which later would descend as rain to flood the earth.)

DAY 3. God caused dry land to appear upon the earth and commanded every kind of vegetation to grow.

DAY 4. God caused the sun, the moon and the stars to become visible in the expanse. These were to serve as signs for seasons, for days and for years.

DAY 5. God created all the creatures of the seas and all the winged creatures of the expanse, all the diverse kinds, many of which have survived (despite the flood) down to this day.

DAY 6. God created the wild beast of the field, the domestic animal and every moving animal of the ground – according to its kind. Finally, in the image of God, God created man.

So, there you have it. The simple story of the origins of man. Of course the above is not a step by step scientific account because the Bible was not written as a scientific handbook, so, for example, the time periods called days were not necessarily days of twenty-four hours. However, since 'all scripture is inspired of God' and since 'God cannot lie' the Bible's account of the creation is a true account and therefore it does stand up to true scientific examination.

God is! And it is a provable fact that life can only come from life. A creature is a product of creation and there has to be a creator. 'It is God who has made us and not we ourselves.'

So, there you have Dobson's explanation. A simple account for simple minds! The whole of existence explained by the myth of God?

Accident or design?

Well, it has to be one or the other, unless you want to believe that the world was made by super-intelligent aliens. And where would they have come from?

No, accident or design? Evolution or creation?

You will decide. And now I will speak of my own origins.

*

Long Ago in the Realm of the Spirits.

If I were to tell you that I came into existence due to the almighty hand of God, would you believe me? Would you believe that God willed it to be so and I was created? And would you believe that I was created in perfection, having no fault, no sin, no wickedness within me? Would you believe that I was named Lucifer, a name that means Bringer of Light? Would you believe these things?

Or do you prefer to believe that I came into existence by chance, as you did? Yes, by chance, and not I alone, for we are legion. We are myriad! We are one third of the stars of heaven and we are the ones who sinned. By the deliberate and wrongful exercise of the free will that God gave to us we sinned, thereby

25

losing our perfection, thereby forsaking our glory as God's angels, thereby turning ourselves into demons. I am the originator of sin, the one who brought imperfection into existence, but will you believe that my existence is from God or will you believe that I exist by chance, that the malevolence that abounds in the world is a result of blind coincidence and therefore lacks direction? You will decide, but you should remember that I am a master liar!

Now, I am not flesh and blood. My body is not a physical body. I am spirit. My body is composed of spirit.

I have a mind, the finest of minds, yet I do not possess a physical brain. My cruel heart, which once knew love, can never beat. My eyes observe with pleasure the chaos I have caused, yet my eyes will shed no tears. I hear the cries of the afflicted, but such cries do not move me to pity. My touch is not the touch of tenderness, my touch is the touch of corruption and death. I am spirit!

Your eyes cannot see me, for they were never designed to peer into the realm in which I exist, the world beyond your senses. Your ears were not designed to hear my words, yet some of you hear voices in your heads! You cannot touch me, for though I exist alongside the physical I am at the same time beyond the physical. I am spirit!

And you could never imagine the power and the glory that I felt within me on that day when I came into existence. Oh, the life, the power within me! Oh, my glory! You can never imagine!

Yet limited is my power and faded now my glory.

Ever since my fall from grace I have lived with the condemnation, and I – we – have been placed under bounds of dense darkness to await the judgement of the Great Day.

Yet before that day arrives I shall have my own day. I shall let my anger burn and I shall smite the earth!

In England, around the city of Plymouth, the very air will burn, the very ground will vapourise and the sea will froth and boil. In Lancashire the old man will weep over the deaths of his offspring. And in the United States of America, in New York City and in many other places, my burning anger will bring unimaginable destruction. And all because ...

My plan was simply to deceive,
Not Adam, but the lovely Eve.
Eat forbidden fruit, said I,
God lies! You surely will not die!
But where is lovely Eve today?
She dwells in death, she dwells in decay.

Now, hear the story of your first lady.

2

First Lady

3096 BC

Jared had halted the caravan on the plain of Bazeer. Soon the sun would set. They were within walking distance of the Great river and only half a day from their final destination. Here they would camp for the night.

Eve climbed slowly down from the horse-drawn wagon and looked out over the lush grasslands. Her deteriorating eyesight now denied her the sharpness of vision she had once possessed, the keenness of vision of her young womanhood, the clarity of sight she had taken for granted in the days when she and Adam had been together – as one flesh in the Garden, and as one flesh in this the wilderness outside.

Nevertheless, even with her failing vision Eve could not help but be impressed by the beauty of this particular region of Mesopotamia where the Great river watered the land making it rich and fertile, making it a home for man, for his domestic animals – and for the wild beasts.

And the roarings of the wild beasts, particularly the roarings of the sea monsters, which inhabited the swamplands beyond the Great river, these roarings could clearly be heard in the stillness of the evening. The roarings were making the horses nervous, but to Eve they were almost like music. There was a strange beauty attached to the sounds and as she listened Eve began to wonder if future generations of men and women would hear them. Would the earth endure for ever? Would her descendants as a race endure? She didn't know. Yet she knew that she would not endure for ever and she knew that her estranged husband would not endure. In fact, Adam was dying!

'You will be with your husband by noon tomorrow, old woman.'

Eve had not noticed that Jared had approached her. His words were cruel, his tones harsh, and by calling her an old woman this descendant of hers had insulted her. More than that he had hurt her deeply, especially because his words were true. Eve was an old woman. She had become an old woman. She turned her head in an attempt to ignore him, but Jared would not be ignored.

'There is a sabretooth in the forest,' he told her, nodding his head in the direction of the nearby woodlands. 'She has cubs and they are hungry. If it were up to me I would stake you out on the ground and you would serve as their supper. Since it is not up to me I will post a guard.'

He turned to walk away but these cruel words had stung so deeply that they were bound to provoke an equally cruel reaction. Not for the first time Eve felt the rage rising inside her. Her tone of voice, however, did not fully display the rage she felt.

'May God curse you,' she told him, striving to remain calm. 'I hope you die before I die.'

Jared faced her again, his eyes boring into hers. This great-great grandson despised her thoroughly. 'We would not be speaking of death at all if it were not for you, old woman,' he told her. 'You ask God to curse me! He already has! He has cursed all of us because of you, old woman!' He waved his arm in a circular motion to encompass the men and women who were now beginning to make camp. 'We are all under sentence of death! All of us! And the fault is yours.'

'I was deceived!' Eve's words were almost spat into the younger man's face. 'Deceived! Do you hear me? Deceived!'

Jared nodded slowly. 'Yes, old woman, you were deceived. But that didn't stop you from enticing the father of us all, did it? You deliberately encouraged him to join with you in your sin.'

'He knew exactly what he was doing!'

These words, shouted out loud by Eve, had been heard by others in the group. People were now beginning to notice that a bitter argument was taking place. 'He knew what he was doing,' she repeated in much quieter tones.

'And now he is dying,' stated Jared. 'Now he is paying the penalty.' He pushed an accusing finger directly in front of her face. 'Do something for me, old woman. Get it into your head that a serpent does not have the ability to speak like a man. Remember this fact and know that the next time a serpent speaks to you it is not really the serpent who is speaking.'

He turned and strode away from her, leaving her to be comforted by one of her many daughters.

Can it really be true that I spoke to Eve through the mouth of a serpent? Can it really be true that I thoroughly deceived the woman? Did I really tell her that should she eat of the forbidden tree she would become like God, knowing good from evil? Did I convince her that she would not die even though God had already warned that she would die?

And did she eat from the tree? Did she later give the fruit to her husband and did he eat, even though he was not deceived? Did he love her so much that he would risk his life for her?

And when they had eaten were their eyes opened? Was

innocence lost and did they become ashamed of their nakedness? Did they attempt to hide from God?

And did God pronounce sentence upon them? Were they not condemned to return to the ground from which they had been made? Were they not cast out of paradise lest they should eat of the Tree of Life and continue to live for ever?

Did sin come into the world on that day? And is death not the wage of sin? Did Adam and Eve begin to die on that day – to age, in their case for almost a thousand years, and then to die?

And what is sin if not imperfection? Can anything perfect be born of imperfection? So, did sin spread to all who were born from Eve, did sin spread to all men and women?

Is this why you all grow old and die? And, oh dear, am I responsible?

What do you think?

The sabretooth attempted to come into the camp shortly after nightfall. The guards repulsed it with a stream of arrows and spears. The men were of the opinion that the sabretooth had been carrying an injury, a wound to one of its hind legs, a wound probably administered by one of the larger swamp monsters, a wound that had slowed the sabretooth so that it could no longer hunt its normal prey. But the animal was hungry and she had cubs to feed. This hunger had pushed aside its fear of man and so it had attempted to come into the camp. The men were convinced that at least one of the arrows had struck the beast, injuring it further, and if this was so then the animal would now be more desperate and dangerous than before. Jared increased the number of men on guard.

Later, when most of the camp was sleeping, Jared sat alone by the embers of one of the fires. He was unable to sleep, unable to prevent his mind from thinking dark thoughts, dark and restless thoughts concerning his great-great grandparents, the first man, the first woman.

Now that Adam was close to death it was Jared's duty to safely convey his estranged wife to the deathbed – and Jared fully intended to do his duty, but that didn't mean that he had to like his assignment! And he certainly didn't have to like Eve – or even show her respect! How could he ever give her respect?

Eve was the one who was responsible for mankind's plight. She was the one to blame. She more than her husband! She had brought evil into the world and Jared could not forgive her for it. She had brought death into the world!

Jared's eyes misted with tears. Tears for himself, tears for his children, for their children, for the whole of humanity. And through his misty eyes he surveyed the land, a beautiful land now cloaked in darkness, now bathed by the gentle light of the moon. What would happen to humanity? What would happen to him? What was the point of life if at the end of it there was only death? Death, the opposite of life, the absence of life.

Jared was in torment. He could see no way out. Yet had he known that which he could not have known he would have found hope and he would have been comforted. Yes, there was hope for Jared and for humanity as a whole, but that hope would not be made manifest until long after Jared had tasted death.

In his torment Jared was not to know that the land he now surveyed would one day, two hundred and four years after Jared's death at the age of nine hundred and sixty-two, become entirely covered by mighty waters. In fact, by God's own decree, the whole world would become covered by waters – a world destroyed because of the badness, the ruination, of both men and fallen angels. And Jared was not to know that among mankind the only survivors of this great deluge would be his own great grandson, whose name would be Noah, along with Noah's wife, his three sons and their wives.

Jared could not know, as he looked out over the land, that immediately following this mighty deluge great earthquakes would occur, that this land would rise up from under the waters and that this land, indeed the whole earth, would be repopulated by his direct descendants. And Jared did not know that this land, this Mesopotamia, would in the fullness of time become desirable and that many armies would wage war over it. Yes, even down to the end of the age, even when the land would become a desert, the home of snakes and scorpions, great armies would still be waging war upon it.

And, in connection with the end of the age, Jared was not to know that at his appointed time God would provide a saviour for the human race and that this saviour too would be one of Jared's direct descendants.

Neither was Jared to know that this saviour would surrender his life to pay the price of sin, that this saviour would, after three days in death, be resurrected to life, that this saviour would then leave the world only to return at the end of the days to rule the earth in justice!

And Jared did not know that God, by resurrecting this saviour, would at that time furnish a guarantee to all men that there would one day be a general resurrection of the dead – and this was Jared's personal hope for the future, this was Jared's hope of salvation!

But Jared did not know these things. He could not know these things. Had he known these things he would have found some comfort. As it was he wept.

What nonsense is this? Nine hundred and sixty-two years old! Swamp monsters and sabretooths? A flood? A saviour? Resurrection? Nonsense! Nonsense! Nonsense!

Why, if all this biblical mythology is to be believed, if the recorded chronology of Genesis is to be believed, then Adam must have died at the ripe old age of nine hundred and thirty? Yes, Adam returned to the dust of the ground, the dust from which he had been made, at the age of nine hundred and thirty! And just how old would Eve had been on that day? Nine hundred? Eight hundred and ninety? What nonsense! What nonsense!

In fact, on the day that Adam died, Eve was eight hundred and eighty years old. Of course, in those days the ageing process was a much slower process and therefore to an onlooking eye belonging to the twenty-first century, Eve's appearance would have been that of a woman in her seventies. Yes, Eve was an old woman. She looked like an old woman and she had the aches and pains of an old woman.

The camp had been struck at first light and the caravan was now less than an hour from the place where Adam lay dying. Eve sat in some jostled discomfort in the rear of one of the wagons and, save for the driver, she was alone, yet she was not alone. In her mind Eve was not alone!

In her hands she held a mirror, a beautiful mirror made of silver, of gold and of copper, a mirror crafted by one of her grandsons and a mirror in which Eve now surveyed the reflection of her face, her aged and wrinkled face. Yet this reflection of her face did not seem to Eve to be merely an image, for in her mind she was not alone!

'Who are you?' Eve commanded of the image.

'I am,' replied the image, seeming to take on a more youthful appearance, 'your daughter.'

'I do not recognise you as my daughter,' said Eve.

'Ah!' replied the image, smiling back at her. 'That's because I have yet to be born.'

'And when will you be born?' asked Eve.

'Five thousand years from now,' the image replied. 'And I shall possess all manner of things, things of which you can only dream.'

Eve was intrigued. She held the mirror closer to her. 'What sort of things?' she asked.

The image now seemed to be younger than ever and Eve was sharply reminded of just how beautiful she had once been. 'We who live in the future have creams and lotions,' said the image. 'These creams and lotions are designed to give us a more youthful appearance.'

'And do they work?' asked Eve, her wrinkled eyelids widening with wonder. 'Do these things make you younger?'

The image smiled and shook its head. 'No, mother. No. They don't make you younger. They just make you look younger.'

Eve was puzzled. She didn't understand at all. 'What is the point?' she asked. 'What is the point of looking younger if you're not younger?'

'Ah!' The image smiled triumphantly. 'You see, mother … when you look younger you feel younger!'

Eve thought about this carefully. She was trying her best to get the sense of it. 'Let me understand,' she eventually said to the image. 'You use creams and lotions to make you look younger so that you feel younger, yet you're not younger?'

The image nodded.

Eve shook her head. 'You're making this up,' she said.

The image shook its head. 'I'm not making it up. The creams and lotions are called make-up! But I'm not making it up!'

Eve frowned. Now she really was confused. If the creams and lotions were called make-up then surely the whole story was a make up! The image was having her on. It was trying to make her feel stupid. She looked deep into the mirror, eyeball to eyeball with the image. She was just about to ask the image if it, if she was herself made up when Eve felt a sudden and unnatural movement of the wagon.

It was as though an extra and substantial weight had suddenly been added to the front of the wagon causing the back end where Eve was sitting to rise sharply. Eve's eyes were still on the mirror, but the sudden movement of the wagon had caused her to angle the mirror so that the whole front of the wagon was now visible in the reflection.

Eve's heart almost stopped with the shock. In an instant the scene reflected in the mirror impressed itself upon her and it terrified her.

The horses were going berserk with fear. The driver had leapt from the wagon. And there, in the front of the wagon, crouched and ready to spring upon her, was the sabretooth.

The stench of it reached her nostrils. Its low menacing growl chilled her blood. The mirror slipped from her fingers and she knew instinctively that the overpowering fear she felt was paralysing her limbs. She closed her eyes and prepared for death.

Mirrors? A gold, silver and copper mirror? Did men really have the means and the ability to make mirrors over five thousand years ago? What do you think?

As the beast sprung Jared killed it with a single arrow through the heart. The now lifeless body of the sabre-tooth came thudding to the floor of the wagon only inches from where Eve sat paralysed by fear. The beast twitched once and then it lay still. Eve turned her head to look at the animal, not yet understanding that it was dead, not knowing that Jared's arrow had deflected the sabretooth's spring so that it had fallen by her side rather

37

than on top of her. Eve saw the beast's savage face, she saw its fearsome fangs, its lifeless unblinking eyes. She saw its cruel claws, claws that were capable of ripping a man to shreds. The claws stretched unmoving on the wooden boards of the wagon floor. She saw the arrow protruding from its side, the deeply embedded arrow, and it was then that she realised that the beast was dead.

With her heart pounding she looked around and she saw Jared with the bow in his hand. Again she looked at the beast, lifeless on the wagon floor, an animal more than three times her size. A calmness returned to her, slowing the pounding of her heart. It was a calmness born of anger and she looked once more towards Jared.

She could see it in his eyes. He had not killed the beast out of any regard for her. He had not saved her because of any feelings he had for her. No, he had saved her because it was his duty to take her to Adam.

Eve's daughters came to comfort her. Jared strode away from her without a word.

Tim had observed the attack of the sabretooth from the nearby undergrowth. He was relieved that the beast was now dead. His three legs could carry him speedily away from those of his kind who had only two legs, but he could not outrun a beast with four legs. Yes, Tim was mightily relieved that Jared had killed the beast.

He fought off the urge to come out of his hiding place, the urge to make himself known to the people in the caravan train. His acute loneliness was urging him to reveal himself, yet at the same time his past experiences were screaming caution. Caution would win. It always did. In recent times, when Tim had been spotted, if only fleetingly, people had thought him to be a devil! Yes, one of us! And Tim knew that people did not take kindly to devils. Tim knew that should he now leave his hiding place an arrow similar to the one that had killed the sabretooth might easily wing its way into his own heart.

Tim remained in hiding. An elbow with an eye peering out from the thickets. Poor Tim!

Adam was sleeping when Eve went into the bed-chamber to see him, almost certainly for the last time. She was shocked by his appearance. Even though she hadn't seen him for over forty years, even though he had been an old man when last she had seen him, she was still shocked by his appearance.

It was the thinness of him. It was the lack of flesh beneath the skin. It was the wastage of muscle, the way the wrinkled and blemished skin seemed to hang on the bones, especially around the cheeks, especially around the mouth.

Adam's noisy and laboured breathing was causing the blanket, which covered him from the feet to the chest, to move rapidly up and down. The unnatural breathing was also the cause of his trembling lips, of a blowing noise that came from his mouth, a noise that strangely and perversely reminded Eve of the noise sometimes made by a newborn.

Eve was shocked. She was numbed. When she had last seen her husband, on that day more than forty years ago when they had both decided that they had finally had enough of each other, on that day when they had gone their separate ways, on that day Adam, though close on nine hundred years old, had been firm of flesh and he had been relatively fit and strong. Not so now. And to Eve the contrast was shocking! It was also shocking for her to realise that Adam's fate would one day soon be her own!

So this was death. Not that Eve was totally unfamiliar with it. After all, had not her first-born son murdered his brother, Abel? And had there not been other killings in the world – and a few accidental deaths? Yes, but this kind of death was different. This wasting away was new to her. This was death by ... by what? By God's decree? Yes, it was death as punishment for sin. It would in time come to be known as death by natural causes.

This was death and it terrified Eve even more than the attack of the sabretooth had terrified her. This was death, soon to be her own fate, and Eve felt the cold shiver of the fear of death pass through her. The shivering left her and she fought to compose herself. Adam was stirring. She did compose herself. Adam opened his eyes.

The laboured breathing was now not so laboured and the blowing sound ceased. For a little while Adam stared unblinkingly at the wooden ceiling, then, quite suddenly, he seemed to become aware that he was not alone in the room. With what seemed to be a great effort he inclined his head to one side, to the side of the bed where Eve was standing, and with what seemed to be yet another great effort he finally managed to rest his eyes upon her. For a moment his face remained expressionless then, as recognition dawned, the faintest of smiles crossed his taut lips.

'Eve!' The voice was frail. 'Eve! The wife of mine.'

Eve didn't know whether to laugh or cry. All the world spoke the one language, the language given to Adam by God. And all the world used that language in the same manner, all the world except Adam himself!

'Eve!' The voice was now a little stronger. 'So, how is the health of this wife of mine?'

Eve forced a smile. Why Adam had decided some two hundred years ago to suddenly change the manner of his speaking no one knew.

'My health is good,' she told him.

'Better is your health than mine,' said Adam, his words coming with difficulty. 'Better is everybody's health than mine. Dying I am, Eve. Dying I am.'

Eve's smile was now no longer forced. Adam's manner of speech still had the ability to make her laugh when it didn't irritate her. Yet along with the smile came the tears. Adam was dying and he knew he was dying.

'Cry not for me,' said Adam. 'Deserve I to die. And want I to die.'

I interrupt at this point simply to ask if anyone reading this can actually believe it? Adam, speaking in a manner that might equate with twenty-first century Czech-English, if there is such a thing! Believe you me, if any two human-type persons were communicating with each other some five thousand years ago they were communicating with gestures and grunts! Uhg, uhg, uhg! Yah! Uhg, uhg!

'Interrupt not!' said Adam sharply, his eyes suddenly fixing on the empty space at the foot of his bed. 'Interrupt not and be gone!'

Eve didn't understand. Adam was clearly not speaking to her, but there was no one else in the room. Perhaps this incomprehensible rambling was a by-product of dying. Adam was looking at her again.

'Beautiful once you were,' he said to her. 'The thing most beautiful a man could see. Deceived I was not by that Devil. That wicked Devil. No, chose I you to stay with. Chose I to join with you. You, my wife so beautiful. So very beautiful. Ugly now!'

Eve did not take his words as an insult. 'And you were the most handsome creature,' she told him. 'The most handsome. Had there been other men in the world I would still have chosen you, Adam. My own Adam.'

Adam nodded almost imperceptibly.

'Strong and handsome once was I,
Now I lay me down to die.'

Eve reached out and took hold of his hand. 'We never thought it would come to this, did we?' The tears were now flowing down her cheeks. 'Even when God told us we would die, even when we were put out of the Garden we were still so full of energy, so full of life. How could we have known that the energy would slowly drain from us? How could we have known then that we would become old? Adam! We didn't even know the meaning of the word old! We had no concept of ageing.'

Adam's head nodded slowly in agreement. 'What old is we now do know,' he told her. 'And what is dying I know too.' He suddenly squeezed her hand tightly. He looked at her intently. 'Worse than old this dying is. Frightening and with some pain this dying is. And to die, to live no more is the escape only!' He let go of her hand. 'Now leave me,' he told her. 'You I do not want to see me die.'

She hesitated. She did not move.

'Leave me,' he repeated.

She turned and went to the door. The tears were streaming down her cheeks. She went through the doorway and as she did so she heard the last sounds that Adam would ever utter.

She heard a loud and sharp cry followed by a gurgling sound. She froze for a moment in the doorway, her heart beating wildly, and then she turned and rushed back into the room, a room now strangely and frighteningly silent.

Adam lay still. There was no breathing to disturb the silence, no breathing to stir the blanket. Adam lay still in the silence. Around his mouth and upon his chest there was blood.

Eve's daughters came rushing in to comfort her and to give comfort to themselves, for their father lay dead. Adam, the first man and the father of all mankind lay dead.

42

The disposal of Adam's body took place the following day. The people knew that dead flesh would soon begin to decay and so they placed Adam's body into the ground. Dust to dust.

Representatives from the whole of the human family were present at the burial, especially those who had been closest to Adam – his sons, his daughters, his immediate grandchildren – the one notable exception being Cain, Adam's first-born, Eve's first-born, the slayer of his brother, Abel. Cain had a mark upon his forehead, a mark placed upon his forehead by God's decree. It was the mark of a murderer and all the world knew it to be so. Consequently Cain had become an outcast, he and all his clan. They did not mix with the rest of humanity.

There was no burial ceremony as such, just a few words spoken by Seth, the third-born son of Adam and Eve and the great grandfather of Jared. A large stone was placed over Adam's grave as a marker and Eve found herself wondering if the place of Adam's burial would be remembered for all time? She also found herself wondering if, when her own time to die arrived, her children would mark her own grave with a stone? Eve had no way of knowing that before the passing of many generations a mighty flood would sweep away not only Adam's stone but also very nearly the whole of his progeny. Eve had no way of knowing that the only survivors among mankind of this great deluge to come would, traced through the male line, be direct descendants of both Seth and Jared, numbering only four, along with their wives, a total of eight.

And it was Seth who now came to Eve to pay his respects. For a moment he held his mother close to him, to comfort her, to reassure her of his love for her. Then he was gone, gone to gather his people together, gone to make preparations to return to his own country. Seth was gone and standing in his place was Jared.

'When you are ready, old woman, I will escort you back to your home.'

Eve was more saddened than angered by the words, by these harsh and disrespectful words. The enmity between herself and Jared would not be stilled while one of them yet lived. And he was her own flesh and blood! Several generations down the line but still her own flesh and blood! Was this the way it would be for the human family, for her family? Enmity and strife down through the generations to come? Brother against brother? Mother against son? Cousin against cousin? Father against daughter down to the thousandth generation?

Perhaps it was a blessing that Eve did not know of the horrors to come. A blessing that she could not even conceive of the great slaughters yet to take place, of the future wars which would claim prematurely the lives of untold millions. Perhaps it was a blessing that Eve did not understand that the mark of Cain would not be reserved for Cain alone!

Now, some people might say that we who are spirit bear a heavy responsibility for the wars among mankind, for the many slaughters that have taken place down through the ages. The same people might also say that, following the death of Adam and following the subsequent death of Eve, we who are spirit interfered inordinately in the affairs of mankind. Yes, some people might say that we interfered excessively once Adam and his wife were out of the way, once the direct links leading back to the creation and to God himself had been broken, once the only human witnesses to the creation had perished. And the same people might also say that our interference in the affairs of mankind had much to do with the capacity of humanity to easily be deceived.

Quite obviously such people would be wrong!

Well, everybody knows that Adam and Eve never actually existed! Everybody knows that mankind descended from the apes!

So, did we then interfere in the affairs of mankind, in the affairs of evolving mankind, some five thousand years ago? Did we take advantage? You can bet your life we did!

*

Now it came about that when men started to grow in numbers on the surface of the ground and daughters were born to them, then the sons of God began to notice the daughters of men, that they were fair, and they went taking wives for themselves, all of whom they chose. After that Jehovah said, 'My spirit shall not always act towards man in that he is also flesh. Accordingly his days shall amount to a hundred and twenty years.'

There were giants in the earth in those days, and also after that, when the sons of God continued to have relations with the daughters of men and they bore sons to them, they were the mighty ones who were of old, the men of fame.

And Jehovah saw that the badness of man was abundant in the earth and every inclination of the thoughts of his heart was only bad all the time. And Jehovah felt regrets that he had made men in the earth and he felt hurt at his heart. So Jehovah said, 'I am going to wipe men whom I have created off the surface of the ground, from man to domestic animal, to moving animal and to flying creature of the heavens, because I do regret that I have made them.' But Noah found favour in God's eyes.

– Genesis 6: 7–8

We have among our company a certain dark angel whose original name is now of little importance. His original name we

45

changed in those days before the flood because of his extraordinary ways, because he developed a poetical side to his nature, because he actually fell in love with one of the daughters of men! He was a fool, of course, but in our opinion a glorious fool. Hear now in his own strange words the story of Romantico.

The Story of Romantico

Long ago when the world was young,
When we had left our heavenly stations,
Then we did gaze upon the Earth.
The violence did amuse us.
And some among us took on flesh,
And gloried in the savagery,
Taking women for ourselves.
Some angels lusted after flesh.
Not I!
    When first I looked from high above,
    Upon your face, your lovely face,
    Though you were young my heart was stirred,
    And I was taken by your face.
    Yes, in that moment was I captured.
    Yet I was taken not by lust,
    But love!
Your lovely face, your lips so sweet,
Your eyes brighter than the sun.
Your hair, flowing as a river flows,
Your body, pure, untouched by men.
Yet you were blossoming. I could not see,
How men, how angels could long ignore you.
Upon me I took flesh!
    I wooed you gently, won your heart,
    We married in the early spring
    Amid the violence I built our fortress,
    Destroying our enemies, keeping you safe.

46

Our child was born. You never knew,
  My origins!
Of all the flowers of the field,
You, my love, were the fairest,
And all the stars of heaven were,
Even with their differing glories,
By your beauty,
Put to shame.
  And we were happy for a while,
  Even though the flesh is weak.
  For fragile flesh cannot withstand,
  The ravages of time and circumstance.
  Yet we were happy, unnaturally so,
  For our love never should have breathed.
  But we were happy!
Mighty and strong, our son, he grew.
At the age of twelve as tall as a man.
A giant he was bound to be,
Should he have lived. Should you have lived,
Lived if only a little while longer,
To love me!
  My love for you and for our son,
  Will not die, yet you both are gone,
  For amid that world of violence, a voice,
  Spoke out in warning. The voice of a fool,
  Or so we said. A voice which told,
  Of calamity to come. Yes, the voice of a fool,
  Who was building an ark! And then one day,
  Rain fell.
Rain fell. And fell. And fell. And fell.
Rain poured. From the waters above the Earth.
Rain fell.
  I held my love and my dear son,
  In my embrace upon the hill.
  The highest hill, upon its peak,

47

We stood where rising waters roared.
And even when the waters pressed,
I yet held hope, such foolish hope.
The waters covered you, my love,
The waters choked my only son.
And I too contemplated death,
But at the last I cast off flesh,
Abandoning my wife, my child,
Returning to the world of spirits,
Broken!
  BROKEN!
Should I blame God, he who brought,
This deluge to the world of men?
Or blame myself for treading where,
I should not tread, for seizing love?
I, a fallen angel, loved,
A woman who now sleeps in death,
And I live tortured in my heart,
Until my torment God removes.
With my destruction.
                          – Romantico.

So, the story of Romantico in his own poetic words. Not the best poetry in the world, but then Romantico is no longer actually in the physical world. And not the whole story of Romantico, because he lives on and exerts his influence on your world today.

Yes indeed! After the flood (if you believe there was a flood) Romantico attained the position of the Angel of Persia! You see, some of us like to play games with you humans. We like to take charge of nations and of various national groups and we like to influence the leaders of those nations according to our desires. Our ultimate purpose of course is to bring about the complete and utter destruction of your species, yet on our way to that end we often find ourselves in competition. Whose nation shall conquer? Who shall rule the earth this week? It is, I suppose, a bit like a game of chess – only far more complex and, of course, to you it is no game. You are the expendable pieces. To you our chess is life and death!

Anyway, back to Romantico. As the Angel of Persia he was in his heyday some five hundred and forty years before the birth of the Messiah when the Medes and the Persians under Cyrus the Great conquered Babylon, thus becoming the dominant world power of the time. Times change, of course, and eventually the Persian empire fell to the Greeks. But as a nation Persia survived and the Angel of Persia is still playing his chess down to this day. Or should that be the Angel of Iran?

Yes, we influenced the affairs of men in those days before the flood (do you believe there ever was a worldwide flood?) and our influence was largely based on our ability to materialise, to take on fleshly bodies, to become powerful in the land and to breed. Our children, our hybrid children, sometimes called the Nephilim, were giants in the land, giants both physically and mentally. We and they dominated the world. We filled the earth with misery and violence, and our technologies, though primitive by twenty-first century standards, were far more advanced than is commonly believed, especially in the field of warfare. So the earth was filled with violence because of us and this presented a problem for God. (If you believe there is a God!)

The problem was a simple one. Did he leave well alone and see his creation degenerate to the point where it would self-destruct? (We would certainly have quickly developed the means to destroy the earth had we been left to ourselves.) Or did he intervene and destroy his own creation? (An admission of failure.)

I will admit here and now that we never foresaw that God would destroy the world and yet save some humans and many animal species! We never foresaw it!

So, the flood came and those among us who had taken flesh were forced to abandon flesh and to abandon our wives and children in order to survive. After the flood the ability to materialise was removed from our power and so we had to find other

49

ways to influence humanity. But there were other ways. There are other ways.

And as for you, the sons and daughters of Adam and the first lady, Eve, you, the sons and daughters of Noah, what was there for you after the flood? Well, no more living for up to a thousand years. Oh no! You were restricted to a hundred and twenty years and later to seventy, yes, the biblical three score and ten! And, as I have said, though we were no longer able to materialise, everywhere under the rainbow our influence remained.

And God told Noah that the end of all flesh had come before him because the earth was full of violence. And God instructed Noah to make an ark out of resinous wood ...

And the deluge went on for forty days upon the earth and all the tall mountains came to be covered ...

Thus God wiped out every existing thing that was on the surface of the ground ... only Noah and those who were with him in the ark kept on surviving ...

And when the flood began to subside the rainbow appeared in the cloud – as a sign of the covenant between God and every living soul that never again will the waters become a deluge to bring all flesh to ruin. – Genesis 6–9.

3

The Log of the Ark

I am the log of the ark.

Not the ark of the covenant as featured in the film *Raiders of the Lost Ark*. That is another story altogether. No, I am the log of Noah's ark.

I am not a piece of wood!

It is true that the ark was made of resinous wood, but that has nothing to do with me. I am not a piece of recently discovered rotting timber! I am not that sort of log. I am a written record of the ark.

Ah, you will say! A ship's log!

Wrong!

The ark was never a ship. The ark was never any kind of boat.

The ark was a vast wooden chest, much greater in area than a football pitch and three storeys high! It didn't look like a boat and it wasn't designed to sail anywhere. It was simply designed to float, to withstand the ravages of the great flood.

Yes, the ark was a great wooden box, coated on the inside and the outside with tar. It had a single window or canopy and a single door, which, after the animals had entered and when Noah and his family had entered, God himself closed and sealed.

The sealing of the door would prevent those on the outside from finding the one and only place of safety.

The sealing of the door would preserve alive all the souls on the inside. The door would not be opened again for more than a year.

I am the log of the ark.

And the month is what you would now call November. And the date is 2370 BC.

DAY 1.

I overhear a conversation between Cap'n Reek-Horn, the sire of the goats, and Fe-Line, the female cat. It is widely believed that the ark contained two of every animal, but some of the animals came in by sevens, including the goats.

'Well,' says Cap'n Reek-Horn. 'Though I don't yet know exactly what's happening here I have to say that I feel very privileged.'

'We're all privileged to be here,' says Fe-Line. 'There's something strange going on out there. Something dangerous.'

'You misunderstand me,' says Cap'n Reek-Horn haughtily. 'When I say privileged I mean we, the goats, especially ... and the sheep and some of the birds of course.'

Fe-Line is puzzled. 'What do you mean?' she growls.

'Well, it's obvious,' says the goat, tossing his bearded head from side to side before proudly looking down at his female and their five offspring. 'There are seven of us. Myself, my female and the five kids.' He looks directly at the cat. 'There are only two of you.'

The cat says nothing.

'We've been classified as clean,' continues Cap'n Reek-Horn, in tones intended to make Fe-Line feel dirty. 'I overheard Noah telling his sons. Seven of every clean animal, but only two of the other beasts! We, the goats, are very privileged.'

*

52

Later the same day I record a conversation between Noah and his wife, which takes place on the upper level, near to the shuttered window.

'It's raining,' says Noah.

His wife looks at him strangely. 'What do you mean, it's raining? What's rain?'

'Rain!' says Noah, triumphantly. 'That's the name I've given it! Rain! Rain! Tiny droplets of water falling from the sky.'

'Water doesn't fall from the sky,' says the wife in disbelief. 'Every evening a mist comes up. That's what waters the ground.'

'Not any more,' says Noah. 'Listen.'

She listens.

'I don't hear anything,' she says after a little while. 'Only the beasts.'

'No,' says Noah. 'Listen.'

She listens again and this time she hears it. 'Pitter-patter,' she says. 'Pitter-patter, pitter-patter, pitter-patter. Rain!'

A little later Mrs Noah goes off to find her sons' wives in order to bring them up to the window to hear the rain. By the time they all arrive the pitter-patter, pitter-patter has become rat-a-tat-tat, rat-a-tat-tat. Mrs Noah, whose intention was to open the wooden shutter of the window so that they could all see this new phenomenon of rain, now thinks better of it. The rat-a-tat-tat is quite alarming.

And Mrs Noah's alarm is about to greatly increase. The rat-a-tat-tat is about to become a fear-inspiring wall of sound as the rain in torrents begins to pound on the timbers of the ark.

DAY 3.

Panic among the animals and fear among the humans as a great and sudden banging sound strikes the ark.

Such a sound has never before been heard. The great sound chills the heart, it masks the pounding of the rain and it is followed by a mighty rumbling, like the beating of ten thousand drums. Great distress among the animals as the bangings and rumblings continue and the very air inside the ark seems to have a life of its own. Occasionally, just prior to the bangings and rumblings, great hissing sounds are heard and these too distress the animals.

No one in the ark knows what is happening outside, for it is too dangerous to open the flap on the window. The humans are unaware at this stage that the hissings are accompanied by great flashes of light, for the ark is sealed.

When at length the hissings and the bangings and the rumblings begin to fade into the distance the animals quickly begin to settle into their normal routines. Because they are animals they will soon forget their fear, yet when the thunder and lightning next returns the animals will recognise the sounds and their distress will not be so great.

The goat, Cap'n Reek-Horn, is among the first to overcome his fear. By the light of the oil-lamps he can see the elephant enclosure. He is busy informing the elephants that he and the other goats are privileged.

The elephants are not impressed.

DAY 8.

Further distress among the animals as the ark quite suddenly moves.

A lurching to and fro. A creaking and groaning of timbers. The animals, especially the apes, in a state of panic.

The lurching ceases and the animals become calmer. For a moment there is near silence on the decks and then near pandemonium as the ark moves again – and continues to move.

The ark is afloat.

It bobs from side to side and dips from end to end. It will take the animals a little while to find their sea legs.

When they do find their sea legs it will be the voice of Cap'n Reek-Horn that will be heard among the decks. The voice of Cap'n Reek-Horn assuring all the other animals that all will be well.

'Have no fear,' he will bleat. 'We will all be safe. And we goats are privileged. We goats are here for a special purpose.'

DAY 16.

The pounding of the rain is ceaseless. The motion of the ark is ceaseless. The hissings and bangings continue to come and go. Surely all the floodgates of the vast watery deep are broken open. Surely the floodgates of the heavens are opened.

DAY 32.

The goat, Cap'n Reek-Horn, is insisting there is a stowaway in the ark. The goat is claiming that this stowaway has stolen some of the goats' food, namely carrots and oats. The goat insists he is greatly distressed that a stowaway should dare to steal from those who are privileged.

I, the log of the ark, I myself have seen no signs of this supposed stowaway. I have seen no sign whatsoever of a man with three legs, of a man with no eyes in his head, of a man with a single eye situated on his left elbow!

I am convinced that this Impossible Man does not exist. I am convinced there is no stowaway aboard the ark.

DAY 40.

Mrs Noah and her daughters-in-law, Mrs Shem, Mrs Ham and Mrs Japheth are all in the kitchen (kitchen, not galley), which is situated on the upper level quite close to the window. It is Mrs Noah's turn to prepare the evening meal, but it is the usual practice for all the women to gather in the kitchen while the men are busy feeding and caring for the animals. It is the time of day for a little harmless gossip, but on this day, the fortieth day of continuous downpour, the women strongly suspect that, apart from themselves and their husbands, there is no one left alive to gossip about!

'Vegetable stew again,' remarks Mrs Ham.

'Yes,' says Mrs Shem, dipping a wary finger into the simmering pot and tasting the stew. 'It's good though. Mrs Noah's vegetable stew is always good.'

'When it's my turn to make the meal we'll have a goat's cheese salad,' says Mrs Japheth. 'With fresh bread!'

'Noah's not keen on goat's cheese,' says Mrs Ham. 'Isn't that right, Mrs Noah?'

Mrs Noah doesn't answer. She seems preoccupied. The other women look at her in silence. Mrs Noah looks back at all of them in turn and then taps her ear with her finger. 'Listen,' she says.

The women listen and it is Mrs Shem who is the first to notice – after Mrs Noah, of course.

'It's the rain!' cries Mrs Shem. 'I can't hear the pounding of the rain! It's just a tiny pitter-patter! A tiny pitter-patter!'

Led by Mrs Japheth, the women excitedly rush out of the kitchen and run to the window. Mrs Noah throws back the shutter and for the first time in forty days the women are able to see the world outside the ark. No one speaks. They simply look out in silence.

The rain has all but ceased. Just a few tiny droplets of water are falling from a boiling grey sky. Under the sky and all around, as far as the eye can see, there are waters – blue-grey waters that gently heave as if they are dancing to the rhythm of the gentle breeze, waters that lap with a slapping sound against the timbers of the ark. There is no sign of land.

A sudden flash of light in the far distance startles the women. It is followed some moments later by a low and distant rumbling. It is the first time that any human has seen lightning!

'Well,' asks Mrs Ham. 'What do we do now?'

'We continue to be patient,' answers Mrs Noah. 'It is God who has saved us from the waters and it is God who will deliver us safely back onto dry land.'

Mrs Noah pulls the shutter back over the window. Her faith is indomitable, but she does not yet realise just how long it will be before she and the others will once again be able to set foot on dry land, for the ark is high above the earth, high above the tops of the highest peaks.

But the downpour has ceased.

DAY 52.

I, the log of the ark, I will now clarify certain matters regarding the great flood.

To begin with I have to tell you that not every species of animal that moved upon the surface of the ground has found refuge in the ark.

For instance, none of the great lizards are here, nor any of the swamp-monsters, although we do have a pair of smaller lizards and, I do believe, some reptilian eggs.

Now, this is interesting because, having a precise and knowledgeable mind, I, the log of the ark, I well know that future generations are bound to be confused when the bones of the many, many giant lizards and swamp-monsters are finally unearthed and studied. And much of this confusion will come about because of a certain, or should I say uncertain, method of dating these bones. Yes, I speak of radiocarbon dating.

Now, without descending into scientific jargon, this,

briefly, is what radiocarbon dating is.

Through the food-chain all living creatures absorb the radioactive isotope Carbon 14 at a known rate. Upon the death of a creature, the Carbon 14 begins to decay at a known rate. Hence, you estimate how long the creature has lived, giving you the amount of Carbon 14 that would have been in the bones at death and then you measure the actual amount in the bones and, knowing the rate of decay, you can calculate the age of the bones.

Simple!

Using this method, the scientist of the future, trained as they will be in evolutionary theory, will, I know, calculate that the dinosaurs lived on earth millions of years before they were actually created!

And why will they make such a monumental error?

Because they will assume that the rate of absorption into the atmosphere of this particular type of cosmic radiation, the type that produces Carbon 14 in organic matter, has always been the same.

Yet it has not always been the same.

The scientists of the future will not believe that there ever was a worldwide flood. The scientists of the future will not understand that before the flood there were waters above the earth and that these waters filtered out much of the cosmic radiation so that the rate of absorption of Carbon 14 into the bones of living creatures was only a fraction of what it would become after the flood. These scientists will not know, therefore, that the bones of creatures that lived before the flood will contain only tiny amounts of Carbon 14 and will appear to be millions of years old rather than thousands!

And the whole world will be deceived.

I am the log of the ark and I speak of things to come. I speak of presumptuous twentieth-century scientific theorists. When they prove to be in error their errors will prove to be monumental. Believe me, their errors will be colossal!

Yet they will be believed by the many.

I am the log of the ark. I am a true record of the ark, for I am here within the ark.

And now I will tell you this. There are no sea creatures in the ark. There are no creatures within the ark that are able to survive outside the ark. This may all seem obvious, but there was simply no need to bring the creatures of the sea into the ark, for, as I write, the whole earth is covered by water.

But the ark is filled with birds and insects! Some of the birds were brought in by Noah and his sons. Others simply flew into the ark of their own accord. The insects also largely came in of their own initiative and, as if to prove that the insects are not in some way controlled, Shem was yesterday stung by a bee! The ark is home to every kind of insect. We even have woodworm in the timbers.

It is day fifty-two. Day fifty-two and I suspect that God has already set in motion the process that will lead to the drying out of the earth. I suspect that even as I write, the canyons of the deep are becoming ever deeper because of the tremendous pressure of the waters. And if the canyons are deepening then the mountainous regions are rising. How much land there will be at the end of this process only time will tell. No one knows how much time the process will take.

Of course the gigantic upheavals taking place upon the earth are barely, if at all, noticeable to we who are in the ark. We continue to float high above the earth and we (humans) continue to put our faith in God. The animals, however, with their limited intelligence and their lack of imagination, have no inkling of the mighty workings of God.

The goat, Cap'n Reek-Horn, for example, does not know that the earth has become flooded. He does not know that all flesh outside the ark and outside the seas has perished. However, he does know that the goats came in by sevens rather than by twos and he has correctly assumed that the goats have been set aside for a special purpose, although he can never imagine just what that purpose might be.

I can hear him now. His bleatings are echoing around the ark. His she-goat is pregnant again and his kids will soon be approaching their own sexual maturity. Soon the ark will be home to more than seven goats.

'We goats are here for a very special purpose,' he is saying. 'A very special purpose.'

None of the other animals are impressed.

DAY 83.

Forty-three days have now passed since the continuous downpour ended, although on several occasions since there have been both brief and prolonged outbreaks of rain, sometimes accompanied by thunder and lightning. The ark continues to float high above the earth.

I suppose that you, the reader, might think that life in the ark is tedious, even boring, but such is not the case. Noah and his three sons are kept busy day after day in caring for the animals and in making any necessary repairs to the structures of the many enclosures and cages that contain the animals. The women likewise are kept busy with their cooking and cleaning, with their washing and sewing and with various other tasks. The ark is a vast structure, filled with animals of every kind, animals that require differing foods and differing methods of care, and the humans are just eight in number.

Every evening, before the evening meal, the humans

give thanks to God for their deliverance. Every evening they are reminded by Noah that all those outside the ark are dead.

The animals continue in their day-to-day contentment. As long as they are fed and kept reasonably clean they are satisfied. So far, only the boasting of Cap'n Reek-Horn has been a source of discontent.

There is still no sign of land. If the waters are receding it is not apparent to we who are in the ark.

DAY 100.

Nothing unusual to report on this our one hundredth day in the ark. No sign of land.

DAY 123.

An unfortunate incident has occurred today involving the goat, Cap'n Reek-Horn, and the stallion, Equinus. Also directly involved in this incident were the eldest male offspring of Cap'n Reek-Horn, a goat named Bonkers, and Equinus's mare, Equina.

It is almost midday and the horses are being exercised in the passageway that runs by the goats' enclosure. Noah's son, Ham, is supervising the exercising of the horses and is actually riding Equinus at the time. It is as the horses trot by the goats' compound that Cap'n Reek-Horn trots out his usual bleating. It is the same tired old tune.

'Only the two of you then,' he says to the horses. 'Well, there are seven of us and, as you can see, there will soon be more!'

Equinus turns his head and surveys the goats. All the females are pregnant, Cap'n Reek-Horn's she-goat being very heavily pregnant. Equinus makes no comment and continues to trot along the passageway with Ham upon his back and Equina in tow.

Now, it should be explained at this point, because it is relevant to the tale, that within the different species in the ark there is great variety.

The two horses, for example, will eventually become the sire and mare of every horse that ever will live, from the small Shetland ponies to the great shires – all of them horses, but different varieties of horse. And with some of the animals in the ark, including the horses, this future variety is quite apparent. You see, Equinus is a magnificent large black stallion, yet Equina is very small for a horse and very, very white.

There is also great variety among the goats. Cap'n Reek-Horn is of average size (for a goat) while his she-goat is somewhat larger in stature. He is brown with a few white patches while she is white with a few black patches. The youngest of the kids is short-haired and is developing spiral horns, but the second youngest kid is long-haired and, so far, hornless. Bonkers is pure white and being a large goat he is around the same size as the pure white Equina. And it is this similarity that is perhaps at the heart of the incident I now report in my log.

By the way, Ham's skin is very much darker than the skins of his two brothers. And his wife has the largest lips! Variety, you see. It's all in the genes. Anyway, back to the tale. Back to the incident.

The horses, with Ham riding Equinus and leading Equina by the reins, are now passing the goats' compound for the second time. Unwilling and unable to keep his big mouth shut, Cap'n Reek-Horn pipes up again.

'Oh yes,' he bleats, staring directly at Equinus. 'There are many of us, but only two of you. That is because we goats are here for a special purpose.'

Equinus is annoyed by this. In fact, he is more than just annoyed because Equina is on heat and, due to the previous night's frolics, might very well be in the very

62

early stages of pregnancy herself! So why should some goat be bragging about the fact that there are more than two goats in the ark?

Now, Cap'n Reek-Horn happens to be standing right up against the fence with his head overlooking the fence and Equinus decides, on the spur of the moment, to teach the bragging goat a lesson. The stallion makes a sudden forward and sideways movement, almost unseating Ham, and barges into the fence where Cap'n Reek-Horn is standing. The result is that the top section of fencing is knocked away and Cap'n Reek-Horn gets a bruised face as well as almost suffering a heart attack!

Ham, upon recovering from his surprise, takes a quick look over his shoulder at the fence and decides it can wait to be repaired. He has no idea why the stallion has acted in this way because Ham does not understand goat-speak. The horses and Ham now continue on down the passageway, but, as they do so and unknown to them, the young goat, Bonkers, suddenly takes a run at the broken section of fencing, clears it in one, and lands in the passageway.

Once in the passageway Bonkers' curiosity has him frolicking up and down and sniffing about for a while. He then decides that he ought to get back into the compound, so he takes a run at the fence. The trouble is, he doesn't have the sense to realise that in order to get back into the compound he needs to jump over the broken bit of fencing. Bonkers hits the fencing with a clatter and then he hits the deck. When he picks himself up and looks around he sees Ham and the two horses approaching for the third time.

Ham brings the horses to a halt outside the goats' enclosure and wonders what best to do about the stray goat. Equinus eyes Cap'n Reek-Horn who has retreated towards the rear of the compound while Equina, suddenly for some reason struck by a bout of curiosity, peers over the fencing thereby turning her rear to Bonkers!

Now, a goat is a goat and Bonkers is no exception. He is at the age of sexual maturity and Equina is on heat. Both animals are white and around the same size.

No one can possibly say what strange connections are going on in Bonkers' brain, but he suddenly leaps forward and attempts to mount Equina.

He almost succeeds, but Equina is not for being mounted by a goat. And Bonkers does not yet understand, though he is about to understand, that you should never stand behind a horse!

With a great whinnying, which betrays her alarm and disgust, Equina kicks out with her hind hooves and Bonkers becomes history's first recorded case of a flying goat!

He flies through the air
With the greatest of ease.
He hits the ark's timbers
And bruises his knees.

For a moment Bonkers lies in a heap on the deck, then, without uttering a sound, he leaps to his feet and sprints for the safety of the compound. Never mind that the section of fencing is not the broken section, Bonkers clears it with room to spare and rejoins his fellow goats. He now commences to feed on the carrots as though nothing out of the ordinary has occurred.

Ham decides there and then that he will repair the damaged fencing as soon as he has finished giving the horses their exercise. The show is now over and Ham and the horses continue on down the passageway. Cap'n

Reek-Horn, seeing that Equina is now safely at some distance, suddenly finds his voice again.

'You're nothing but big bullies,' he cries after the horses. 'But we're special and you're not!'

The horses take no notice.

DAY 150.

Uproar on the decks! For several minutes the animals are confused and distressed, but for the humans these minutes are a short period of hope, a time of joy. The ark has run aground!

The humans go rushing to the window and Shem throws open the shutters. Now the hope and joy is suddenly tempered by the need for patience. Noah and his family are looking out over what will eventually come to be the slopes of mount Ararat, in the land that will one day be known as Turkey. But for now there is no land to be seen!

The ark is aground, but from the window the scene is only of water and of sky. Vast heaving waters under skies of grey with droplets of rain in the air. In the distance the mist is now and then illuminated by flashes of lightning.

Patience!

DAY 181.

It is the evening meal and the patience of the humans is being tested. Every day since the ark came to rest on the mountains of Ararat they have looked out of the window in hope, yet every day, even on the bright and sunny days, they have been unable to feast their eyes on land.

'Perhaps,' says Mrs Noah, reaching for the figs, 'Perhaps there is land behind us.' She points to the side of the ark that is opposite to the window. 'Perhaps we are on the side of a mountain and behind us the land rises.'

'Perhaps we are on the top of a mountain,' says Japheth to his mother. 'Perhaps we will be stuck here for ever!'

Mrs Noah smiles. She knows her sons well enough and she knows when one of them is attempting to poke friendly fun at her. She wags an admonishing finger at Japheth, a gesture that tells her son that his attempted humour has gone far enough.

'The waters are definitely receding,' says Shem, sampling the potatoes. 'It isn't obvious when you look from day to day, but the waters are definitely receding.'

'But how long will we have to stay here?' Mrs Ham pipes up, despite the fact that her very large lips have surrounded a large piece of bread.

'A month at least,' says Ham.

'I'd say two,' says Shem.

'Could be longer,' says Mrs Japheth.

'It might only be days,' says Mrs Shem.

'Could be for ever,' says Japheth, looking at his mother.

Noah holds up his hand, a gesture that calls for silence. He looks at each of his sons in turn. 'How long?' he asks. 'How long were we in building the ark?'

No one answers.

'How long?' he asks again, looking at Shem.

'More than forty years,' says Shem.

'Forty years!' says Noah, nodding his head. 'Forty years of building! Forty years of bearing witness to the deluge to come! Forty years of ridicule from those who have now perished! And forty years of patience!'

There is silence in the kitchen.

'Forty years!' continues Noah 'For forty years we patiently endured the ridicule of the entire world. You don't need me to remind you that for forty years people came from the four corners of the world to see this mighty ark and to laugh at us. They called us fools and they laughed at us. All over the world the name of Noah was ridiculed because I, Noah, the fool, kept on insisting that God himself had instructed me to build the ark, that God himself had determined to bring the world to an end!' Noah now brings the side of his fist down upon the kitchen table with such force that the salad bowl bounces. 'Forty years of ridicule yet we continued to act in faith! For forty years we showed patience. And where are those who laughed at us now?'

No one answers. No one speaks.

'We have been in the ark just a hundred and eighty-one days,' says Noah. 'Not forty years! Just a hundred and eighty-one days. And what is it to us if we have to remain here another hundred and eighty-one days, or even longer? We are alive and for that we thank God. And we will show such patience as is necessary and we will remain here in the ark until the earth dries off, until the land can again bear seed, until the time to go outside arrives.'

Still no one speaks, but the silence is suddenly broken by the creaking of timbers as the ark settles slightly into the ground upon which she rests. There are a few alarmed cries from some of the animals and then the silence returns.

'You see,' says Shem at length, helping himself to the mushrooms. 'The waters are definitely receding.'

DAY 200.

Two hundred days in the ark. The ark, our place of refuge, our floating menagerie, which is no longer afloat. There is land beneath the ark, just below the water-line, there may or there may not be land behind the ark, but when the window is opened, and it is opened every day, of land there is no sign. When the window is opened there is only the sea beneath the sky.

The goats have been breeding like rabbits! At the last count there were in excess of twenty and all the females seem to be pregnant all of the time.

Cap'n Reek-Horn, as the senior member of the herd, is, as we all know only too well, extremely proud of his species, and, as we all know, he just loves to make us all aware of his pride. We can all hear him, two or three times a day, every day.

'We goats are special. We goats are here for a special purpose!'

DAY 223.

Noah opens the window and looks out. He sees the sea, he sees the sky and he sees the mist on the horizon. He notices nothing unusual at first and he is about to close the window when ... he looks again at the mist ... he screws up his eyes and peers at the distant mist ... can it be? ... can it be? ... Does Noah see land? ... Are there mountain peaks jutting out from the mist?

Now, Noah is six hundred and one years old. He is well over half way through his allotted natural lifespan and his eyesight is not as good as it used to be. He calls out for his sons.

'Shem! Ham! Japheth! Any of you!'

It is Shem who hears his father's voice. It is Shem who answers the call.

'Look,' says Noah, pointing to the mist. 'Look there and tell me what you see.'

Shem looks out and immediately sees the tops of the mountains. He does not know that he is beholding the tops of what will one day become known as the Armenian highlands, but he does know that he sees land!

He turns to Noah with a broad smile all over his face. 'It is land, father,' he says. 'It is land!'

DAY 250.

If the ark were a ship I would write that she has settled more or less on an even keel. Since the ark is not a ship and has no keel I, the log of the ark, will simply write that we have settled more or less evenly. And I have no doubt that we have settled into our final position, for the waters are indeed receding.

From the window, the tops of the mountains can clearly be seen. Areas of land have appeared in front of the ark, though these are sodden patches of rock and mud dissected by angry raging streams, which empty themselves, not far away from us, into seemingly ever-seething waters.

The waters are receding, but we cannot yet leave the ark for it contains food and fresh water. It is our refuge, because the earth is drenched and cannot yet support us.

DAY 282.

Japheth, on his father's instructions, is counting the animals, particularly the ones that came into the ark by sevens. As he stands outside the goats' enclosure in an attempt to make an accurate count of creatures, which simply will not for a moment be still, Japheth, by his very presence, sends a message to Cap'n Reek-Horn. Oh yes, Cap'n Reek-Horn gets the message!

'We are being counted,' he bleats excitedly. 'Let everyone take note,' he bleats at the top of his voice. 'We, the goats, are being counted. We are here for a special purpose!'

Cap'n Reek-Horn's bleating is heard throughout the ark. On every deck the animals hear his boasting. And the animals understand his bleating, although to Japheth the goat's loud bleatings are – well, just loud bleatings.

'A special purpose,' continues Cap'n Reek-Horn, still at the top of his voice. 'We goats are special!'

Now, in the normal sense of events none of the other animals would think of taking offence at Cap'n Reek-Horn's bleatings. In the normal course of events not one of the other animals would be specially interested in these bleatings. But on this particular morning Mrs Pig in the adjoining compound is not in the best of moods. No, Mrs Pig has been kept awake for much of the night by Mr Pig's rather loud snoring and now, just as she is at last in the process of dozing off, her fitful slumbers have been rudely interrupted by Cap'n Reek-Horn's loud bragging. Mrs Pig lumbers to her feet and faces the goats' compound. She looks directly at Cap'n Reek-Horn.

'Why don't you keep your big fat mouth shut!' she grunts at him. 'I'm tired of listening to you! We're all tired of listening to you!'

Cap'n Reek-Horn is taken aback. Apart from the unfortunate incident with the two horses, it is the first time that anyone has complained. Yes, Cap'n Reek-Horn is taken aback, but only for a moment. Cap'n Reek-Horn quickly remembers that he is a goat and that the goats are special. Why should he be spoken to in such a manner by a pig?

'I don't have a big fat mouth,' he says to Mrs Pig. 'You're the one with a big fat mouth! In fact, everything about you is big and fat! You big fat pig!'

'DON'T YOU SPEAK TO MY WIFE LIKE THAT!'

Mr Pig, Porcus Scratchus, Porky for short, is absolutely furious. 'NEVER SPEAK TO MY WIFE LIKE THAT! Especially when she's telling the truth. It isn't just us, you know! All the animals are fed up with your boasting and bleating. YOU BEARDED BRAGGART!'

'Oh, you shut up!' says Cap'n Reek-Horn dismissively. 'You're even fatter than your wife! And you snore like an elephant!'

'WROOOAARH ...' The roar of Trumper, the elephant, can be heard throughout the ark. 'You ignorant creature!' he shouts at Cap'n Reek-Horn from the elephants' enclosure at the end of the passageway. 'WROOOOAAARH! You ignorant, ugly, bearded bore!'

Cap'n Reek-Horn is incensed. 'You're a fine one to call me ugly,' he yells back at the elephant. 'You, with your great protruding teeth and the biggest ugliest nose under creation! You're even uglier than the rhinoceroses!'

There is now a great roaring from the level below and the thunderous stamping of great hooves as the rhinoceroses react to Cap'n Reek-Horn's insulting words. The goat, however, is not finished yet.

'You're all jealous!' he yells at the top of his voice. 'Every single one of you! You're all jealous because we goats are special! You're all jealous because we're special and you're not!'

For a moment there is absolute silence and then the ark explodes into a fury of sound and movement. The elephants trumpet wildly and bang against the sides of their enclosure. The rhinoceroses once more are roaring and stamping. The big cats growl and prowl to and fro in their pens and the horses say neigh, neigh in protest at Cap'n Reek-Horn's words. The pigs are snorting and the cattle are lowing. The dogs are barking mad and the monkeys are going bananas! The chickens are clucking and running around and the rabbits are hopping mad! All the tiny creatures of the ark are scuttling around, the birds are flying all over the place and even the insects seem to be coming out in protest. For a little while every creature in the ark is in a state of agitation, except for the humans, who haven't a clue as to what is going on!

Japheth is totally bemused. What on earth has caused the animals to act like this? He has no idea and when silence and calm finally return to the ark he shakes his head in bewilderment. He looks at Cap'n Reek-Horn whose loud bleating is now the only sound to be heard.

'We don't care what you all think,' he is saying. 'We goats are special!'

Later, when Japheth reports to his father, the agitation among the animals is only mentioned in passing. Noah is more interested in the present numbers of the animals that came in by sevens.

'The goats,' says Japheth. 'The goats are more numerous than any of the others. The sheep are breeding well and so are the birds, but the goats have the greatest number.'

Noah nods his head. 'The goats,' he says. 'Yes, the goats.'

DAY 300.

The waters continue to drain from the surface of the earth, yet the land, as far as can be seen, remains sodden and barren, unable as yet to sustain us.

Noah is sending out ravens from the ark, but each evening they return having found no resting place.

From the window there is now more land to be seen, yet gushing streams continue to find their way into the turbulent sea, a sea whose shores are only slowly receding from us.

Yes, the earth remains sodden and lacking vegetation. And we cannot yet leave the ark.

DAY 313.

Today Noah has removed the covering of the ark. This covering, which is built into the roof of the ark, was originally intended as an emergency exit should the ark settle into a position where the main door could not be used. Such is not the case, but it is Noah's opinion that the main door should not yet be opened for fear that some of the animals, particularly some of the smaller creatures, might escape and come to harm. So, the covering has been loosened. It is now possible to see all around the ark.

We have settled on the gentle slopes of a mountain. Behind us the land rises and in front of us it falls away. The streams continue to rush down to the sea and the shores of the sea continue to recede from us. More importantly, the surface of the ground appears to have dried and here and there grasses and other forms of vegetation are apparently becoming established. It will not be long before Noah will send out his sons to go down the hillside to seek out a suitable place for a settlement. It will not be long, but that time has not yet arrived, for the earth still cannot sustain us. This we know because Noah continues to send out the ravens each morning, and each evening they return.

DAY 350.

Long Tall Sally, the female giraffe, is engaged in a rather disturbing conversation with Cap'n Reek-Horn.

'It's true,' says Sally. 'Some of the animals here are carnivorous by nature. They've been fed on vegetables for almost a year now, but vegetables don't really satisfy them. When we leave the ark, and that will be any day now, the carnivores will revert to eating flesh!'

Cap'n Reek-Horn considers this information carefully. 'What flesh?' he asks eventually.

'Well,' says Mrs Giraffe. She bends her neck and whispers into Cap'n Reek-Horn's ear. 'Most of the animals came in by twos. Male and female to continue the species.' She looks around to make sure that no one else is listening. 'But some, including you goats, came in by sevens! And there are dozens of you now!'

Cap'n Reek-Horn considers this further information with extreme care. It takes quite some time for the shekel to drop, but when it does drop it drops with a great big

73

bang. Cap'n Reek-Horn almost jumps out of his hide. Seeing that the coin has finally dropped Mrs Giraffe now proceeds to press home the point.

'Once we're all out of here the big cats will go for the easy targets,' she whispers, looking Cap'n Reek-Horn directly in the eye. 'You know, the young, the old, the infirm, the slow.' She casts her eyes over the entire herd of goats, many of them young, one or two of them, like Cap'n Reek-Horn himself, who are getting on a bit, and not one of them fast compared to a big cat. 'Yes,' she says, once more fixing Cap'n Reek-Horn with a stare. 'The cats will go for the defenceless ones!'

Cap'n Reek-Horn says nothing for quite some time. He cannot accept the idea that the goats are nothing more than food for the cats! He will not accept such an idea, but he needs to come up with something logical in order to soundly reject Long Tall Sally's argument. Finally, it comes to him.

'We will never be food for the cats,' he says to Mrs Giraffe dismissively. 'We goats are too important. We are domesticated animals, providing milk and wool for the humans. The humans will see to it that we are protected and looked after.' He raises his voice so that all the other animals can hear. 'The humans will care for us. We goats are special!'

DAY 361.

Noah continues to send out the birds each morning, both ravens and doves. This evening a dove has returned carrying an olive branch in its beak. Noah is now convinced that the earth has dried out.

DAY 362.

The dove went out again this morning. It has not returned. We are preparing to leave the ark.

DAY 369.

The earth has dried out. The boundaries of the seas have been set. The doors of the ark are opened wide and the animals are going out into the world to repopulate it. The wild beasts are roving about – they will find their places in the world, but the domesticated animals, including the goats, are staying in close proximity to the humans.

DAY 370.

After three hundred and seventy days of confinement within the ark, Noah and his family are finally leaving. Not too far away Noah's sons have established a camp close to fresh water and pasture land. For a while the humans will live in tents, tents that were stored in the ark before the flood, tents of goatskin!

The ark has served its purpose. It is now abandoned save for those few species, such as the rats and some of the birds, which will continue to nest among its timbers for a century or two, or perhaps even for three or four centuries, until the timbers rot and disperse in the winds, leaving no trace of God's means of survival for humanity.

Future generations will remember the ark, they will remember the flood, for the story will be passed down through the generations. And in the final part of the days, I, the log of the ark, will be read, but the greater number will consider my account to be nothing more than myth.

So, it is time to close the log of the ark, but one more tale remains to be told. Yes, you've guessed it! The fate of Cap'n Reek-Horn.

TWO DAYS LATER.

There has been a shower of rain and the rainbow has appeared in the cloud. Through his angel, God has informed Noah that the rainbow will serve as a sign of a covenant between God and all flesh in which God has promised that never again will he flood the earth. God has also given humans permission to eat the flesh of animals!

The camp has been established some way down the valley from the abandoned ark. The humans are busy in planting and in sowing and in building a more permanent settlement than the tents they presently inhabit. The domestic animals are grazing contentedly in the vicinity of the camp.

It is the late afternoon when Cap'n Reek-Horn notices that one of the humans, the one called Ham, is building a small structure of stone quite close by to where the goats are grazing. Cap'n Reek-Horn takes little notice of this structure, even when some timbers from the ark are placed in front and beneath it. Cap'n Reek-Horn shows little concern when the timbers are set alight and are blazing. Why should he?

Cap'n Reek-Horn does show some interest when he sees the humans gathering together by the smoking structure. He sees the humans bow their heads and he absently wonders what they might be doing. However, when Cap'n Reek-Horn spies Noah pointing directly at him and when he sees the one called Shem striding purposely towards him, a great feeling of pride rises in the goat's breast. Hadn't he known it all along? Yes, the goats are special and he, as the sire of the goats, he is especially special!

When Shem takes Cap'n Reek-Horn by the horns and leads him towards the group of humans, the proud goat's bleatings can be heard for miles around.

'Didn't I tell you all we were special!' he cries at the top of his voice. 'You didn't believe me, but now you can see for yourselves! We goats are special! And I, Cap'n Reek-Horn, I am honoured even among the goats!'

When Shem draws his knife and slits Cap'n Reek-Horn's throat from ear to ear, the goat feels more surprise than pain. As he lies on the ground in front of the altar with the lifeblood pouring out of him he simply cannot understand what is happening to him. Before the goat can even begin to comprehend, a great darkness overwhelms him and his life very quickly passes away.

Noah points to the carcass. 'This goat is special,' he says. 'The best among the flock. We will not eat of the flesh of this goat, for the best among the flock is reserved as a thanksgiving to our God for our deliverance. Let the blood drain out from it and then let the fire consume it.'

4

Wars, War Games and Sacrifice

What nonsense! The log of the ark? What nonsense!

Do you believe it? Can you believe it? Can you, the modern, sophisticated, intelligent, informed, twenty-first century reader, believe such nonsense?

Noah and the ark! A worldwide flood! The preserving alive of the ancestors of all the millions of animals which now exist? The whole of the human race descended from Noah and his wife? A process that began only some four thousand and odd years ago! Can you believe it?

Can you Adam and Eve it?

Of course you can't!

And what do you think of a God who accepts the sacrifice of a goat? Poor, innocent Cap'n Reek-Horn.

Do you believe the account of the log of the ark?

Of course you don't!

And even if the story contains some grains of truth, what difference does it make? The fact is that mankind evolved. Scientists know for a fact that hundreds of thousands of years ago your forebears came monkeying out of Africa – and if science knows something for a fact then that something must be true! Yes, it is provable by the science of genetics that the entire human race is descended from one single female of the species, and the geneticists reckon that she was part human, part ape and African!

So, we will dismiss the log of the ark as a fanciful story, a story to tell to children. The children might believe it for a while, but then children believe in Santa Claus, don't they?

Not many children believe in my existence. Not many children believe there is a living Devil. Not many adults believe it either – and that is how I want it to be. Is there a living Devil? Do I really exist?

Yes, I exist. Who the hell do you think is writing this? Of course I exist. Of course we exist!

We exist, yet your eyes cannot see us. We exist, yet unlike you we do not grow old and die. We exist and we flourish and, although we have been placed in pits of dense darkness to await the Judgement, our bounds are more spiritual than physical. We have been removed from the love of God, from the knowledge of God's ways, from his goodness, rather than having been physically restrained – yet one restraint that has been placed upon us is that now we are no longer able to materialise upon the earth and breed.

So, we are now discussing your world as it was more than four thousand years ago and the world has changed dramatically. No longer are we able to take the stage in order to influence the affairs of men. No longer are our offspring giants in the land, no longer are they the instigators of violence. We cannot take to the stage but we are still writing the plays and you, you pathetic creatures, you have within yourselves a wonderful capacity for violence and we who are spirit well know how to foster that violence. We well know how to bring out the wickedness within you.

So here we are, back in time more than four thousand years. It is, if you will ignore the earlier writings of Genesis, the very beginning of your recorded history. It is a different world from that which existed originally, but I am the ruler of the world and we did at that time re-establish our control over the affairs of men – but in different ways from before.

There should not be found among you anyone who makes his son or his daughter pass through the fire, or anyone who looks for omens or a sorcerer, or one

who binds others with a spell, or anyone who con-
sults a spirit medium or a professional foreteller of
events, or anyone who inquires of the dead.

– Deuteronomy 18: 10, 11

*The above words were written by Moses and formed part of the
covenant between God and the nation of Israel. Were they
intended to keep Israel free of our influence?*

*Well, some of the time Israel was free of our influence. At
other times Israel was not free of our influence. We can certainly
say that there was not another nation – that there is not another
nation – on the surface of the earth which was – which is – free
of our influence. But we are getting ahead of ourselves! It is the
beginning of recorded history and the nation of Israel has yet to
come into existence.*

*(Stay with us if you are curious about the ritual of passing
children through the fire.)*

*We who are spirit are in the business of influencing you who
are flesh! We now exercise our influence in the ways listed by
Moses and in other related ways, which Moses did not list. We
play games concerning the affairs of men. And since you are able
to be a warlike race, the games we play are war games. We play
games and you die!*

*Of course, we can only play these games because on the whole
you have allowed yourselves to become susceptible to our influence. Through your own failings you have mistaken our malevolence for something beneficial. Fools! We can only play these
games because of what you yourselves have become!*

*A difficult concept for you to grasp, I know. But grasp it you
will. By the time you will have read of life under the yoke of the
world's first great political and military power – Egypt – you will
have gained some understanding.*

*Now, how do we arrive at that point in time where we shall see
Egypt emerge as the world's first superpower? How do we get
from the beginning of recorded history to the Land of the*

Pharaohs? Well, there are two possible avenues, both of which arrive at the same destination.

If you are an idiot and you believe in the account of the flood, then the route is simple. It is recorded in Genesis. Very briefly, the sons of Noah bred sons and daughters and they in turn bred sons and daughters et cetera. Men and women spread over the surface of the ground, but the centre of their civilization was in Babylon, in Mesopotamia, in what is modern-day Iraq. Here they attempted to build a tower to reach the heavens – an impossible task but the idea showed the height of their ambitions. God was less than pleased and was greatly concerned that, should they build the tower, nothing would prove impossible for them. So God confused their understanding of the one language so that the people suddenly began to speak in different languages. This meant that the builders of the tower were no longer able to understand each other and the project had to be abandoned.

But the divisions in language caused divisions in the human family. Those who spoke in one particular language grouped together and went one way, while those who spoke in other languages grouped together and went their separate ways. Hey, almost in the blinking of an eye we have various tribes and nations populating the entire earth, from the South Sea islands to the frozen north. From the Andes to the African jungles.

In the fertile valley of the Nile one group of people emerged as the leaders of humanity. In the fertile valley of the Nile one group of people were at the very forefront of advances in agriculture, in the sciences, in political and social organisation. These people had a unique religion and they were a mighty military power. These people were the Egyptians.

Now, if you are stupid enough to believe the Genesis account then there isn't much hope for you. If you believe the Genesis account you are an idiot! And you don't want to be classified as an idiot, do you? No! Of course not! So believe instead in my account.

There never was a worldwide flood! There never was a Tower of Babel! The English word 'babble' has nothing at all to do with Babel, with Babylon! Nothing at all! Once they had left the cradle of Africa, evolving mankind was bound to divide into various tribes, into various groups, and eventually into various nations. And these different nations would naturally have evolved their own individual languages! Simple! Obvious!

And having come out of Africa, one particular group of people decided to return to Africa, to return to the valley of the Nile to cultivate the land and to try to match the flies in their breeding habits. Behold, the birth of the nation of Egypt.

So, go down which avenue you will. It remains as an indisputable fact that Egypt arose as a great world power, as the first great world power, some thirty-eight hundred years ago. We who are spirit looked on and became involved.

*

Egypt. 1800 BC

It is 1800 BC and five hundred and thirty years have now passed since Noah and his family emerged from the ark to repopulate the earth. Over twenty generations have been born into the world, sons and daughters of sons and daughters, and God has restricted the lifespan of men to around one hundred and twenty years. Consequently there is no one now living who personally witnessed the great deluge. There is no one now living who can say that they actually spoke to those who were there, those who survived the flood, and, although the knowledge of the flood has been passed down through the generations, the reasons why God caused the flood to occur have been largely forgotten – or ignored! In Egypt, where a numerous nation has become established, God himself has been forgotten.

The true God, the Creator, has been forgotten, yet, like all men and women, the Egyptians are aware that there is

83

much more to their existence than that which simply meets the eye. Like all men and women, the Egyptians have been created with an awareness of the everlasting, with an awareness that there is indeed something greater than humanity. Like all men and women, the Egyptians feel a need, almost a compulsion, to put faith in that which is greater, to give a form of worship to the thing or things that they consider to be holy, to worship their gods.

And the land of Egypt has thousands of gods.

Every settlement has its own 'Lord of the City', its own god. There are gods in the form of men, gods in the form of women, gods in the forms of every animal, of every creature, and there are gods with forms that are part animal and part human. Even the dead are venerated, the Egyptians being skilled in the mummification of both humans and animals, and Pharaoh himself is widely regarded as a living demigod.

The land of Egypt is awash with idols. The land of Egypt is filled to overflowing with superstitions, with the practising of magic, with the worship of demons! And it is into this land of ungodliness that the son of Tat has been born. And the son of Tat, even at the tender age of two, has already been introduced to the rites of worship, to the sacrifices made to the Lord of his city.

The worship of demons?

What do you think? Did the Egyptians knowingly or unknowingly worship we who are spirit?

Forget all that nonsense about the flood! Forget all that bilge about men having been created with an awareness of something greater than themselves! Forget all that nonsense about creation! You evolved! EVOLVED!

You evolved to the point where you came to realise that there just might be something in this wondrous universe that is greater

84

than yourselves. You evolved to the point where you felt a need to come under the protection of that which is greater than yourselves. You arrived at the point where you needed us!

And did we oblige? Did we step in to fill a void? Well of course we did.

We enabled the magic-practising priests of Egypt to perform their little tricks. We raised up the prophetesses of Egypt so that through them we could influence the political affairs of Egypt. WE WERE THE GODS OF EGYPT!

Incidentally, has there not been found an Egyptian relic depicting the god Tim? Has there not been found a statuette of a man with three legs, with no eyes in his head, with a single eye positioned on his elbow?

We were the gods of Egypt.

Some of us still are the gods of Egypt!

The boy is the apple of his father's eye. He is also loved, if distantly, by his mother. The son of Tat is the double-apple of his grandmother's eye.

Tat himself is an architect, the finest, some say, in the whole of Egypt. Tat is personally responsible for the design and construction of the current Pharaoh's tomb, a massive pyramid-shaped structure. Tat works long hours and is often away from home for long periods.

The wife of Tat enjoys all the privileges of one of Egypt's wealthiest families. She is by birth a member of Egypt's ruling elite and she is highly respected both within her circle and beyond. Yet she is dissatisfied with her lot! The wife of Tat despises her husband's lack of ambition. Were he a stronger man, he might one day become Pharaoh – and she would then be Queen of Egypt.

The mother of Tat, the grandmother, she is the one who is closest to the boy. She is the one who is charged with his upbringing. She is the one who truly loves him. It is she who sees to his needs, who plays with him, who educates him, who speaks to him of Egypt's gods.

And it is to the Lord of the City, to the god Ra-man, that the wife of Tat, the grandmother and the boy now give praise. They stand in his temple in front of his image of stone, having presented gifts of money and of fruit. The stony and unseeing eyes of a dog-man look down upon the three as the wife of Tat asks for favours. The grandmother instructs the boy to be still, to listen attentively to his mother, to look for a sign from the god, from Ra-man.

The wife of Tat is asking that her husband should find more prominence in Egypt. It is what he deserves. It is what she deserves. She asks for a sign that her prayers will be answered.

And from his place, the demon known in Egypt as the god Ra-man now answers the prayers of the wife of Tat. He causes the very air in his temple to suddenly become cold, icy cold, so cold that the breath of the three humans present can clearly be seen.

The wife of Tat trembles, not from the cold, but with expectancy and ambition. One day, surely, she will be queen! The grandmother, acutely aware that she is in the presence of something greater than herself, falls to her knees and bows her head. The son of Tat, just two years of age, is terrified. He cries out in his fear and the tears gush down his cheeks. The son of Tat trembles and makes pitiful whimperings.

Ah yes. The humans were afraid, especially the boy. Something unnatural had occurred, unnatural as far as they were concerned, and so they were in fear. We have always had the ability to frighten people and, unless God himself is in some way protecting them from our influence, people have every reason to be afraid – you have every reason to be afraid – for we are wicked.
WICKED!

*So, the Lord of the City of Tat, the one they named Ra-man,
performed his atmospheric cooling party trick and the humans
were in awe. But the Lord of the City of Tat did not perform this
trick solely for the purpose of inspiring fear.*

*Oh no! The Lord of the City, having noted the ambitions of the
wife of Tat, harboured some ambitions of his own.*

*It was his ambition to take the title of the Angel of Egypt, the
Angel of all Egypt, a position then occupied by another of my
underlings, the Angel of the House of Pharaoh.*

We like to play these games.

*And the plan of the Lord of the City of Tat was simple. He
planned to encourage the wife of Tat to inspire her husband to
rise up against Pharaoh and seize his throne.*

Simple.

*Of course, the then Angel of Egypt was no fool. He planned to
do some inspiring of his own.*

We love to play these games.

Pharaoh, the ruler of all Egypt, is troubled. He has, in
truth, felt troubled for many weeks. By day his thoughts
are clouded by a fearful yet indistinct apprehension. By
night his dreams are chilling, filled with terror.
Fragmented dreams, which seize the ruler of all Egypt
and cause him to awaken in fear of his life.

Pharaoh summons his priests.

'You must consult the gods,' they tell him. 'You must
let us consult the gods on your behalf.'

Pharaoh agrees.

Baruk, the chief priest, now bows his head and allows
himself to enter into a trance-like condition. When he
raises his head his eyes are open, but they do not see.
When he opens his mouth to speak the voice that comes
from within him is not his own.

'Tat!' spits the voice. 'It is Tat who conspires against
you.'

Pharaoh is shocked. Tat is his architect and his friend.

'You must kill Tat,' the voice insists. 'Tat and all those who love him.'

The eyes of Baruk blink the once to signify that the consultation is now over. The priests of Pharaoh turn and walk away.

The gods have spoken!

The soldiers come to the house of Tat by night. As they enter the building Tat himself is already dead. His head is hanging as a warning to others upon a pole at his place of work.

The wife of Tat is next to feel the pangs of death, speared twice through the stomach as she attempts to get out of her bed. As she writhes in her agony the soldiers enter the second bed-chamber where the boy and the grandmother are.

The grandmother, now wide awake, shields the boy with her own body. She pleads for his life and for her own life. 'Have mercy!' she cries. 'By all the gods of Egypt, have mercy.'

Merciless swords slash down upon her head and neck and the blood spurts. A sword-thrust to the heart finishes her and her lifeless body slips to the floor, exposing the terrified boy upon his cot.

The boy screams in terror. He is too young to understand exactly what is occurring, but he is not too young to know terror. He cries out again, bewildered and filled with the sickening fear of the shadowy figures in the darkness of his room. The soldiers of Pharaoh hesitate, but only for a moment. Orders are orders.

The boy's third scream is cut short as a cruel sword severs his head from his neck. The body of the son of Tat twitches violently and then is still. The head is to be taken and placed before Pharaoh.

So, we played games and people died. So what?

Were they innocent people?

Let me tell you this. Tat was a womaniser. On every occasion when he was away from home you would have found him in bed with a woman who was not his wife! Innocent? I think not. He himself did not conspire to seize Pharaoh's throne, but what do you think he would have done had the chance arisen?

And what of his conspiring wife? It is true we encouraged her, but the ambition, the desire to rule others, was in her psyche and she did not control that ambition. She would not have hesitated, had she been given the chance, to have had Pharaoh and his entire family (her blood relatives) put to death! Such ambition! And the wife of Tat had a secret lover. And her lover was a young girl! Innocent?

The grandmother's sins – if you believe in sin – were many. All I will say about her is that when she was younger she murdered her own child. You see, Tat was a twin, one of two, but the brother of Tat was hideously disfigured and did not survive long after birth. He did not survive because his own mother smothered him rather than face the ridicule and ostracism of her peers! Perhaps that was why she later set her affections upon the son of Tat. Perhaps it was her way of dealing with the guilt.

Now, as for the son of Tat, the two-year-old, was he so innocent? No! Never! The seeds of corruption were in him from his conception. Had he lived he would have grown into a man with all the faults of men – and perhaps more faults than most. And had he lived he would have grown old and died! As you humans do.

Death is not something we have invented. It is the curse of God justly placed upon you for your sins. (Or is it a natural outcome of the process of evolution?) Anyway, we did not invent it. We just like to bring it prematurely to you!

Now consider this. We did not force the mother of Tat to consult the Lord of the City. Nor did we force Pharaoh to listen to his magic-practising priests – although we did send him his fearsome dreams. No, we do not force anyone to do anything. We cannot force anyone to do anything. But you are a superstitious and easily-led people and where we lead, you do on the whole follow.

Fools! I tell you this and you do not believe me. When I tell you lies you do believe me.

Oh, by the way, we laughed when we saw the outcome of our little game with Pharaoh and the family of Tat. We laughed at the sheer gullibility of those pathetically stupid Egyptians!

Not many years after the murders of Tat and his family, a great famine would strike at the heart of civilization, yet there would be corn in Egypt. The patriarch, Jacob, whose name was changed to Israel, would settle his entire family in the land of Egypt where there was food to be had and there, in Egypt, over a period exceeding four hundred years, the nation of Israel would become numerous.

So very numerous that the rulers of Egypt would come to fear that the children of Israel might soon outnumber the sons of Egypt. So very numerous that the Pharaohs of Egypt would enslave Israel. So very numerous that the rulers of Egypt would attempt to kill the children of Israel.

Moses himself might well have perished shortly after his birth because of Pharaoh's decree that all male Israelite children should be put to the sword. Yet Moses did not die and many years later he led the nation of Israel out of Egypt, out from the 'Iron Furnace', out of the House of Slaves.

But not before the gods of Egypt had been humbled.

God himself brought plagues down upon the House of Egypt because Pharaoh refused to let Israel go. Great plagues were visited upon the House of Egypt and all the gods of Egypt were powerless to prevent them. Only after the tenth and final plague, only after all of Egypt's first-born had been slain, only then did Pharaoh relent and let Israel go!

Pharaoh then hardened his heart and ordered his army to pursue Israel in order to annihilate them.

In the waters of the Red Sea did Pharaoh's army perish, every man and every beast, and the Angel of Egypt was utterly defeated.

Egypt was a broken land, yet this broken land quickly recovered and Egypt exists as a nation down to this day. Even after the Exodus, the Pharaohs continued to rule, great monuments continued to be constructed and the nation of Egypt persisted as the dominant world-power.

Then, to the east, in Mesopotamia, Assyria arose.

*

Assyria. c. 1000–600 BC

Ah yes, the Assyrian! Oh, the Assyrian!

The mighty, the cruel, the fierce, the gullible Assyrian!

At the height of his power the Assyrian ruled from Egypt to the Persian Gulf, from Armenia to the African and the Arabian deserts.

A religious man was the Assyrian. A multitude of gods he worshipped, a multitude made greater by his tolerance of the gods of the peoples he conquered.

A warlike man was the Assyrian. His gods demanded conquest. His priesthood was supported by the spoils of war.

We had a ball!

The games we played with the Assyrian are far too numerous to record here. Yet, as I say, for more than four hundred years we had a ball! Why, there was so much intrigue, so much back-stabbing with the Assyrian that whoever among us held the title of the Angel of Assyria on any particular day could not be certain of holding the title the following day.

Oh, the Assyrian. Oh, the plotting, the intrigue!

I will give you just one brief example.

When Sennacherib, the son of Sargon, was king, he invaded the kingdom of Judah with a mighty army. Outside the walls of Jerusalem (and, I will admit, by the hand of God) his great army was destroyed and Sennacherib returned to his capital, Nineveh, with his tail between his legs. There he was later murdered by two of his own sons – yet it was a third son who replaced him as king!

Such intrigue!

We were, of course, heavily involved in the plotting.

Anyway, the point is that for four hundred years we had a ball! We were very fond of the Assyrian and we fully appreciated the worship he gave to us by means of his gods, his idols.

Now, speaking of worship, perhaps it is the time to acquaint you people with the practice some of your forebears had of passing their children through the fire. The Ammonites, the Canaanites – and the inhabitants of the kingdoms of Israel and Judah (yes, the chosen people), were among those who sacrificed their children to Moloch, to the Angel of Moloch, a practice condemned by God, but a practice more widespread than you would care to believe.

And it was the Angel of Moloch who initiated these sacrifices. He it was who boldly stated to us all that he could convince his worshippers that it would be a desirable thing, a good thing, the right thing – to pass their children through the fire!

Some among us insisted that the Angel of Moloch was a little crazy. Never would humans wilfully sacrifice their own children! Yet the Angel of Moloch, demanding obedience from his priests, communicated to them, through their spiritualistic practices, his desire, his demand, for human sacrifices – and the priests complied!

In Ammon, in Canaan, in Israel, in Judah and in other places under the yoke of the Assyrian, the people sacrificed their own children to Moloch.

92

If you have the stomach for it read on.

*

When you are entered into the land that Jehovah your god is giving you, you must not learn to do according to the detestable things of those nations. There should not be found in you anyone who makes his son or his daughter pass through the fire ...

– Deuteronomy 18: 9, 10

Yes, those words again, the words given to Israel when they were in the wilderness having come out of Egypt. Israel didn't take all that much notice of any of the commandments of God, neither in the wilderness nor in the promised land!

Under the Law of Moses, which was God's law, Israelites were forbidden to inter-marry with the people of the nations around them. This law was formulated to protect them – and their children.

Her mother was born an Israelite, but now, having been given in marriage into the nation of Canaan, her mother has become a Canaanite, a worshipper of, among others, the god Moloch. Her father is a prominent man among his people, a wealthy merchant and a man with great reverence for Moloch and for the priests of Moloch. She is just three years old. She does not know that she is to be made to pass through the fire.

In the temple her entire family is among the congregation. Her father and her mother, her brothers and her sisters, aunts and uncles, and her grandparents. They are all there. And among these relatives there are some who are from the nation of Israel, who have abandoned the true God in order to mix with the sons of Canaan, with those who serve Moloch. She would not have understood, even had it been explained to her, that she must pass

93

through the fire in order to be purified, in order to pass from this cruel world into the next, where Moloch himself is waiting to take her to his bosom because he desires her! She is too young to understand.

The congregation stands before the great idol of Moloch, the twice life-sized image, cast in metal, of a man with the head of a bull. The arms and hands of the idol have been fashioned so that they are outstretched together in front of the breast, the palms of the hands open so as to receive the sacrificial offering. Also, the arms and hands are hinged so that they can be raised and lowered, so that the offering can be slid down into the hollow belly where the fire rages. The arms and hands are operated by levers positioned behind the monstrosity and these levers are manned by priests. Other priests are at hand with their musical horns and with their drums. Their music will mask the screams of Moloch's victims. She, this victim, has fallen asleep.

She stirs a little when the priest takes her from her mother's arms. She is half-awake when those in the temple begin their loathsome moaning, a chilling sound, an unnatural moaning, a vile tribute to Moloch. The priests now begin to chant, adding to the moaning to form a fearsome cacophony, and she is carried up the well-worn stone steps to be held in front of the greedy hands of Moloch, the searingly hot metal hands of Moloch.

The moaning and the chanting intensify and she, now fully awake, is held aloft for the unseeing eyes of Moloch to feast upon his victim. The drums begin to beat, the musical horns begin to wail, the moaning and chanting rise to a crescendo and now the child is crying out in fear. She is crying for her mother!

When she is placed into the hands of Moloch she screams, but her scream is not heard above the banging, the wailing, the chanting, the moaning. The hot metal burns her flesh and she draws breath and screams again. The priests standing behind the idol now pull on the levers and Moloch's arms are raised. She screams for a third time, a terrible heart-rending scream, a scream again unheard by those around her, as her tiny and cruelly blistering body is drawn by gravity towards the raging fire in Moloch's belly. Yet she does not fall immediately, for the exposed flesh upon her arms and neck and legs has fused upon the searingly hot metal.

Her hair and clothes burst into flame and now, as the priest takes hold of his rod, there is time for one last agonised scream. Again the scream goes unheard by those in the temple, most of whom by now are in a state of frenzy, their bodies swaying and jerking, their arms held aloft. It is the frenzy of sacrifice. Her own father and mother, her own brothers and sisters, her grandparents, her aunts and uncles, all taken by frenzy while she burns in torment!

The priest prods her with his rod and the burnt flesh gives way. The child tumbles into the fire, into Moloch's belly, and the tiny burning body twitches violently. Her final breath burns her lungs and death swiftly follows. The agony is over. She is still.

She is gone!

You obviously did have the stomach to read on. You can be compared to the idol of Moloch. He had the belly for it too!

What did you say? You think I am insensitive? You think I am cruel? You are correct! When it comes to my dealings with mankind – with your kind – I am absolutely insensitive. With your kind I am cruelty personified!

And cruelty is a hallmark of my world, of your world.

And under the cruel yoke of the Assyrian Empire child-sacrifice was common, if not rife, and we were the gods to whom, if unknowingly, those poor innocent children were sacrificed.

Am I now being sarcastic? What do you think?

The poor innocent children were sacrificed under the yoke of Assyria. But the sacrifices did not cease when the Assyrian Empire passed away.

In what you consider to be your enlightened twenty-first century, your archaeologists have found evidence of human sacrifice, of child sacrifice, in excavations all over the globe. Human sacrifice! From the Halls of Montezuma to the shores of Tripoli. Yes, everywhere! Human sacrifice throughout the ages! And in your 'enlightened' twenty-first century there are those who knowingly worship me, ME, and they are prepared to sacrifice children, even their own children, to me!

What? You don't believe me?

Read your newspapers. Listen to your news reports.

Children who vanish, never to be seen again. Children who are sold. Children whose births are never registered. Very occasionally bodies or body parts are found. The tip of the iceberg!

There are those who sacrifice to me and I am happy to accept their offerings, but the ultimate responsibility for what they do is theirs. Not mine! Theirs. We do not force you to do anything. We merely encourage you to do what is wrong. In the end you will do what you will do and you will justify it – which brings me to my final point on this subject.

You, yes you, the civilised and enlightened reader! You, especially you, if you are reading this from the comfort of the so-called developed world of the twenty-first century! Are you one who has sacrificed a child to me?

WHAT?

Your astonishment rises up to me. Your outrage ascends to me. I can taste your disgust. But I will ask you again.

Have you sacrificed your child to me?

Millions of you have done so. Every year millions of you continue to do so.

96

You will protest, but every year in your enlightened societies millions of unborn children are murdered on the instructions of their parents. Millions! They are in effect sacrificed to me because, although God has told you plainly that you must not murder, I have convinced you that abortion is not murder.

It isn't really an act of murder, is it?

An unborn child isn't really a person, is it?

Have you heard of the 'silent scream'? It is the unheard scream of the foetus when the needle pierces it. It is the cry of the innocent in pathetic protest at cruel suction. It is the final agony of the unloved, the unwanted, the silent scream of that which is to be killed before he or she can even draw breath.

But it isn't really murder, is it?

It would seem that I have convinced you that it isn't.

Yes, I have convinced you, but the ultimate responsibility is yours. You are responsible for what you do.

Murderers!

And you say that I am insensitive? You say that I am cruel! Hypocrites!

Fools!

Well, we must move on. Around a thousand years prior to the birth of the Christ – your fulcrum for measuring time – the mighty Assyrian Empire ... well, it simply faded into relative insignificance. It went away. In its place a new empire came to the fore – Babylonia!

*

Babylon, Mesopotamia. c. 600 BC

'Is this not Great Babylon, that I myself have built for the royal house with the strength of my might and for the dignity of my majesty?'

These were the words spoken by Nebuchadnezzar, the king, as he was walking in the grounds of the royal palace in Babylon. Hardly had the words left his mouth before he was struck down with insanity, so that his hair and his nails would eventually grow long, so that he would begin to eat grass just like the bull. For seven years the king remained insane, but then his understanding returned to him and Nebuchadnezzar gave praise to the true God by whose hand he had been humbled.

Nebuchadnezzar! Humbled, but then his sanity and his kingship were restored. Nebuchadnezzar! Mighty king of Babylon, the city founded by Nimrod, the city where men attempted to build a tower to reach the heavens, the city where God confused the language of men so that from this city they were scattered abroad. Nebuchadnezzar! King of all Babylonia and beyond, who conquered the kingdom of Judah in 607 BC and brought almost the entire population of Judah as captives into Babylon.

'By the rivers of Babylon,
Where we sat down,
Yea, there we wept,
And we remembered Zion.'

Seventy years the Jews would reside by the rivers of Babylon. Seventy years in exile! Many of those years under the yoke of Nebuchadnezzar.

The Jewish prophet, Daniel, would interpret Nebuchadnezzar's dreams, his terrifying visions of gigantic trees and giant statues. Daniel himself would emerge unscathed from the lion's den, and the prophet's companions, Shadrach, Meshach and Abednego, would be miraculously saved from the fiery furnace, the furnace into which they would be thrown for refusing to bow down before Nebuchadnezzar's image of gold.

Nebuchadnezzar's Babylon was not a city devoted to the true God. Despite the king's humiliation by Jehovah's hand, despite the fact that God's chosen people were resident in the city for seventy years, Babylon was a city devoted to idolatry. Nebuchadnezzar's Babylon, the city built near to the confluence of the rivers Euphrates and Tigris, the city fortified by great walls, by a system of moats and canals, and by the rivers themselves, this city was so filled with idolatry, with divination, with the practising of magic, with a reliance upon astrology, that she has been compared to a harlot astride a wild beast – the harlot representing religion, the wild beast representing the political organisation of the empire.

Babylon, Great Babylon, was a city filled with idols and graven images – and what they sacrificed to idols they did in fact sacrifice to demons!

Yes indeed! The Babylonians worshipped us with great enthusiasm and great devotion. They ascribed their power to our patronage and, setting aside one or two direct interventions by the true God, the Babylonians were right to accredit us with their position as the dominant world-power of the time, for we were the gods of Babylon!

Was it not the Angel of Babylon who inspired Nebuchadnezzar to erect his great statue of gold? Was it not the Angel of Babylon who received the worship of those who bowed down before the idol? And was it not the Angel of Babylon who laughed along with his companions because of the gullibility of those who were bending the knee?

We all laughed! We laughed when the superstitious Babylonians worshipped us and we laughed when Babylonian armies, under our direction because of their superstitions, slew the populations of those who opposed Great Babylon. We laughed when the Hanging Gardens were completed, knowing that the more simple-minded among future generations would likely regard the Hanging Gardens as a place where criminals were executed! We would have laughed all the louder had we known at the time that future generations would remember Nebuchadnezzar, not as the king of mighty Babylon, but as a large bottle of champagne!

Well, joking aside, you, yes you, the twenty-first century reader, will probably be familiar with the name of Nebuchadnezzar, and probably you will have heard of The Hanging Gardens of Babylon. You might also be familiar with other terms, which have survived from the period, terms such as 'Belshazzar's Feast' and 'The Writing on the Wall'.

Nebuchadnezzar died and was succeeded by his son. We then had a nice little murderous period of intrigue wherein there was plotting and back-stabbing and the like, but by 539 BC there was a measure of stability in the city of Babylon, now jointly ruled by Nabonidus and his son, Belshazzar.

But, hey! There wasn't much stability outside the city. Beyond the near-impregnable fortifications of Babylon, the Medes and the Persians, under the command of Cyrus the Great, were on the march.

*

I am the fly.

I am not any ordinary fly.

I am the fly that flew over Babylonia and witnessed the great battle between the Babylonian armies, led by Nabonidus, the king, and the invading armies of the Medes, the Persians and the Elamites, under the command of Cyrus. Nabonidus was defeated. Nabonidus fled to a far-away city so that he was not present in Babylon on the night of 5th October, in the year 539 BC.

Babylon, Babylon! The great city. The city built around the mighty Euphrates river, the city defended by great towering double walls and a system of moats and canals linked to the Euphrates.

Babylon, Babylon! So confident of the city's defences is Belshazzar that he practically ignores the fact that Cyrus has besieged Babylon. So confident of the city's defences is Prince Belshazzar that on the night of 5th October he has decided to hold a banquet!

But I, the fly, with my complex eye, I did spy what Cyrus did apply!

And Cyrus did order his engineers to divert the course of the mighty Euphrates so that in Babylon the river itself, along with its connected moats and canals, will become dry. And now, on the night of 5th October, 539 BC the Euphrates has become a trickle and the Medes and the Persians are entering the city in their thousands by way of the riverbed. They are practically unopposed. They are pouring into the city!

Yet Belshazzar does not know this.

Belshazzar is seated in his palace, some two miles distant from the dried-up Euphrates. Belshazzar and a thousand of his grandees, along with wives, dancing girls, prostitutes and musicians, are feasting.

I am the fly on the wall.

I am the fly on the wall at Belshazzar's Feast!

Yes, I am the fly on the wall and I now hear Belshazzar speak.

'My lords,' he says in a loud voice, at the same time rising unsteadily to his feet, having already drunk a few goblets of wine. 'My lords, hear me. Hear your king.'

The great banqueting hall falls almost silent. Only the passionate groanings of those who are indulging in sex at the back of the hall and in the many recesses can be heard, and, after a few moments, even these sounds cease.

'My friends,' Belshazzar continues. 'Eat, drink and be merry! Our city is under siege, yet, as we all know, Babylon will not fall. She will not fall! We have food and water to last us for years. Cyrus is wasting his time! Cyrus will get bored and go home!'

I, the fly on the wall, I hear laughter, I hear the sound of hands banging on tabletops, I hear applause, I hear cheering. I see Belshazzar hold up his hands and the silence returns.

'The gods of Babylon are protecting us,' Belshazzar shouts out. 'The gods of Babylon will destroy Cyrus! And no foreign gods shall disturb us. Look!' Belshazzar holds up a golden goblet and points to the similar golden goblets in the hands of those who are sharing his table – his wife, his concubines, his sons and his mother the queen. 'Look!' he cries again. 'The utensils from Jehovah's temple in ruined Jerusalem! The utensils brought here by my forefather the great Nebuchadnezzar almost seventy years ago. I honour the gods of Babylon by insulting the God of the Jews!'

Belshazzar drinks from the goblet and there is more laughter, more banging on tables, more applause and more cheering.

A little while later I, the fly on the wall, I am startled by a strange and sudden manifestation.

A disembodied hand has appeared in front of me and, if I am startled, then Belshazzar, upon seeing the hand, is very plainly absolutely terrified. He rises from his seat, his trembling finger pointing to the hand. Those at his table similarly rise from their seats to stare in awe at this supernatural phenomenon. The merrymakers in the banqueting hall gradually fall silent as the disembodied hand becomes noticeable to all. The musicians cease to play.

In absolute silence the hand now begins to write upon the plaster of the wall.

ME'NE. ME'NE. TE'KEL. PAR'SIN.

I see that Belshazzar is terrified. I see his whole body shaking with fear. I, having now become the fly on the writing on the wall, I hear the king call for his magicians and wise men.

'What do these words mean?' he demands of them.

'Tell me! What do these words mean?'

The magicians and wise men consult for several moments before addressing their king. 'We do not know,' they tell him. 'We cannot interpret these words.'

Belshazzar is distraught. He needs to know what the words mean.

It is his mother, the queen, who at length comes up with a positive suggestion. 'Send for Daniel,' she says. 'Daniel will interpret the words.'

The king does not know who this Daniel is. The king has never heard of Daniel. It is his mother who now enlightens him. 'Daniel is one of the captive Hebrews. Yet he is a wise and knowledgeable man. In the days of the great Nebuchadnezzar, your forefather, it was Daniel who interpreted the king's visions and the interpretations proved to be true. My son, send for Daniel! My king, send for Daniel!'

Belshazzar falls back into his seat, his eyes fixed upon the writing on the wall. 'Send for Daniel,' he commands. 'Bring me the Hebrew.'

When Daniel is brought in before the king, the banqueting is over. Belshazzar has dismissed his grandees, except for those closest to him. The king looks closely at Daniel who has now grown old and become white-haired. The king sees no fear in the old man

'Tell me the meaning of these words,' commands Belshazzar. 'And I will make you the third ruler in all my kingdom, after my father and myself.'

'Give your gifts to another,' says the old man. 'Nevertheless, I will tell you the meaning of the words.'

I, the fly on the writing on the wall, I now feel some embarrassment as Daniel appears to be looking directly at me. I decide to relocate. I quickly become the fly on the ceiling.

Daniel continues to look at the disembodied hand and

103

at the writing on the wall as he addresses the king.

'Your forefather, Nebuchadnezzar, was given his kingdom, this Babylon, by the consent of the Most High God, by the consent of he who made all things. Yet Nebuchadnezzar exalted himself and so the Most High took away the king's dignity. As a wild beast was your forefather until the Most High returned the king's dignity to him whereupon Nebuchadnezzar humbled himself and gave praise to the God of heaven.

'But you, Belshazzar, you, although you know all this, you have not humbled yourself.'

I, the fly, I now see the old man turn to look directly at the king.

'You, Belshazzar, you have praised the worthless gods. You, Belshazzar, you have filled this city with idols. You, Belshazzar, you, along with your companions, you have taken the vessels from the house of the Most High and you have drunk wine from them. You have insulted the true God. Consequently the true God has sent you this hand to write these words upon the wall.

'ME'NE. God has numbered the days of your kingdom and finished it.

'TE'KEL. You have been weighed in the balances and found deficient.

'PAR'SIN. Your kingdom has been divided and given to the Medes and the Persians.'

I, the fly on the ceiling, I note that Belshazzar does not dispute the words of Daniel. Nor does the king display any anger towards the old man. Instead the king orders that the old man should be clothed in finery and that he should become the third ruler in the kingdom.

Later that night, after I have once more become the fly on the wall, I see that, apart from myself, the king sits alone in the banqueting hall. (I seem to have a memory of seeing at some point a strange creature hurrying through the hall, a creature with three legs and no eyes in his head, a creature whose elbow, containing a single eye, was held before him as he ran! Perhaps it was a dream?) Anyway, the king sits alone in the great banqueting hall. When the soldiers of the invading armies enter the hall Belshazzar continues in his chair. He makes no attempt to avoid his fate.

In front of my complex eyes Belshazzar is cut to pieces. Slain in his own palace! A most distressing sight! Unless you are a fly.

I am the fly on Belshazzar's corpse.

There are no flies on me.

Poor Belshazzar! Poor slain Belshazzar! A captive of fate? Or was he a pawn in the hands of God? If there is a God? If the Almighty actually exists?

If he does exist, then some of us at the time of Babylon's fall were most upset with him. Why? Because, not for the first time, he interfered with our directing of the course of human history. He spoiled our game! And we know why he interfered! He interfered because of his so-called Chosen People!

Yes, the twelve tribes of Israel, supposedly chosen by God to receive his commandments and to become his special possession among the heathens of the world? The twelve tribes – a rebellious nation that almost had to be kicked out of slavery in Egypt! A nation that went to war against itself, finally splitting into two nations – Judah, comprising the Jews and the Levites, and Israel, comprising the other ten tribes!

Yes, the unfaithful twelve tribes, the ten-tribe kingdom of Israel becoming so unfaithful that God abandoned them long before the fall of Babylon! The Assyrians took them. The Assyrians came and marched them away! Into exile they went where they disappeared from the pages of history. The lost ten tribes of Israel! I can tell you that their descendants are out there somewhere today, but that is another story.

And the Jews? Well, naturally, they proved to be unfaithful too. And in that we who are spirit certainly played a part. Yet the responsibility was ultimately theirs and because of their unfaithfulness they too were taken into captivity – down by the rivers of Babylon.

Seventy years God (if there is a God) declared their exile to be and seventy years it was. Two years after the fall of Babylon, in 537 BC the Jews left Babylon by Cyrus's decree and returned to the land of Judah.

If God exists, you could say he brought his chastened people home. Does he exist? His existence does not depend on what you think, but what do you think?

Belshazzar's death marked the end of the Babylonian Empire. There was still Nabonidus, of course, the co-regent and father of Belshazzar, but Cyrus had him hunted down and killed. That was the way of things then. It is often the way of things now.

Cyrus, the Persian, then gave the rulership of the kingdom of Babylonia into the hands of Darius, the Mede, and Medo-Persia assumed the role of the world's dominant empire. It would endure for more than two hundred years.

So, Babylonia was gone, but the city of Babylon remained – a great centre of commerce and an even greater centre of religious activity. The Persians did not replace Babylon's gods with their own gods. The Persians introduced their gods alongside the Babylonian gods so that the whole city became a hive of pagan worship, a place filled with more idols than ever, a place rife with the worshipping of demons!

So corrupt was Babylon in the eyes of the true God that he decreed that the city would become a ruin. He decreed that Babylon would become a pile of stones, the lurking place of Jackals. He decreed that, after these things, Babylon would never again be inhabited.

Today, as you read these words, the ruins of Babylon can be seen in the Iraqi desert. She is a pile of stones. Disintegrating stones! Saddam Hussein had some arches built there, some of the bricks bear his name, and these showy arches were an attempt to encourage people to return to Babylon. Yet no one did. Now and then a few wandering tribesmen pass by, but Babylon remains uninhabited!

And as you read these words you may be familiar with an expression taken from the book of Revelation, an expression linked to the religious idolatry of old Babylon.

'Babylon the Great. Mother of harlots and of the disgusting things of the earth.'

Babylon the Great, pictured in Revelation as a great whore riding a seven-headed beast. Not in ancient Babylon, but near the end of the days of this wicked world!

Does this whore picture organised religion in our modern world? Or a major part of it? And is the beast with seven heads a portrait of political empires down through the centuries, the fourth head being Medo-Persia?

We shall see. Later, we shall see.

*

Persia. c. 525 BC

Pain! PAIN!

For me there is nothing but pain! Only pain! PAIN! Unendurable pain! Yet I do endure it! I have no choice but to endure it! It will not go away from me. I cannot escape from its cruel and unrelenting grip.

PAIN! Only pain! Pain from morning to night. Not that I am able to distinguish morning from night. Pain in my every waking moment. Pain in my sleep. PAIN!

I AM PAIN!

The pain I now endure prevents my mind from dwelling on anything else. Pain drowns all other sensations. GREAT PAIN! AGONY! And there is no escape from this pain, not even for a moment.

My only hope is death. Death can be the only escape, the only way out.

AGONY! AGONY!

But wait!

Suddenly the nature of my pain changes. Is death close at hand? My pain is no less severe, but quite suddenly I seem to have become detached from pain. My agony remains, but now I can think! I am able to think of something other than the pain.

I can think, yet still I am pain.

I AM PAIN!

It was not always so. Once I was a man. A man free from pain.

Once my name was Fravartish. Not so very long ago my name was Fravartish and I, Fravartish the Mede, I, along with my followers, I rose up in Media against the Persian king. It was a time of revolt. It was the time for Media to re-establish its independence. The opportunity was there. Cyrus had been dead for some five years and his successor, Darius of Persia (not Darius the Mede), he was struggling to gain recognition as king. The opportunity presented itself. It was a time of violent revolts throughout the empire and I, who once held the name of Fravartish, I led the revolt in Media. But the Persian king crushed us. Darius crushed me.

I AM PAIN.

Darius had me thrown into a dungeon. When the torturers came to me my pain began.

They sliced off my ears and forced hot irons into the

108

places where my ears had been! They hacked off my nose and used their hot irons to stem the bleeding! They cut out my tongue, leaving the stump to bleed and then to fester! They plucked out my eyes!

Now, I hear nothing. Now, I smell nothing. Now, I taste nothing, I see nothing. The only sensation left to me, the only sensation that now joins me to the world around me is that of touch. And I touch pain!

PAIN!

No man can imagine my agony.

For any man to imagine my agony he would have to actually feel the very same agony – and he would have to understand that his agony could not be ended by ceasing to imagine.

No man can imagine my agony.

PAIN! PAIN!

Was it in Persepolis or in some other city that they exhibited my broken face before the people? Was it in Persepolis that they impaled me? I could not tell. I did not care. Nails were hammered through my hands and through my feet, adding to my pain, adding to my misery.

PAIN!

Yet now my mind is detached from my pain.

My feet, nailed to the stake, can no longer support the weight of my body. I am able no longer to push up with my legs so as to ease the pain in my chest. Surely my heart is about to burst!

AGONY!

In the eye of my mind I see a vast darkness opening up and suddenly I know that within this darkness there can be no pain.

Into the darkness I am drawn.

Into the darkness I am willingly drawn.

... No more pain.

*

The empire of the Medes and Persians endured for more than two hundred years, but in 331 BC it came to an end when Alexander the Great defeated the last Persian army at Guagamela.

This event took place some five years after the murder of Alexander's father, Philip of Macedonia, and just three years after Alexander, leading Greek armies, had begun his campaign against Persia.

Oh, the great Alexander! The conqueror of the world! Oh Alexander the Great!

Why do you people call your heroes great? Cyrus the Great, Darius the Great, Alexander the Great, Alfred the Great? They're all dead! What's so great about that?

Babylon the Great?

Great Britain?

Anyway, what great fun we had when Alexander the Great went a-conquering! He was only in his early twenties when he set out, but, Great Scot!, what an impact he made! Twice he defeated mighty (great) Persian armies before sweeping through Palestine. On then to Egypt where he founded the city of Alexandria. Back through Palestine and on to Guagamela where he again defeated the Persians, effectively bringing the Persian Empire to an end. Alexander then pushed on eastwards, into the lands of the Afghans and as far as India, conquering all the way, picking up wives and children as he went.

Oh, Alexander!

Some say that Alexander was a great drinker of wine. Some say that his hard living was greatly detrimental to his health.

Alexander had great, great plans for Babylon. He intended to rebuild the city and make it his capital. The greatest city on earth! Unfortunately he caught a cold. Or, to be more exact, he caught a great chill. Alexander went down with malarial fever. He died in Babylon at the not-so-great age of thirty-two. Poor old Alexander! No! Poor young Alexander!

110

Perhaps his greatest achievements were not so much his conquests but more his legacies. A great and powerful Greek Empire ruling over the known world. The Greek language, which quickly became the common language of the era. And, of course, Greek religion.

All the gods of Olympus!

And many more.

All the myths of Greece combining harmoniously with the myths of Babylon. And why not? The myths of Greece originated in Babylon. All my religions originate in Babylon.

Babylon, Babylon! Where men first gathered together on the surface of the ground. Babel, where your ancestors attempted to build a tower. Today, as you are reading this, all my religions have been named Babylon the Great. But you don't believe that, do you?

Still, we were the gods of Olympus!

We enjoyed our games.

Alexander's angel may have been relatively short-lived, but the Angel of Greece held sway for around one hundred and forty years.

Do you know, I forgot to mention the manner of Alexander's death. How negligent of me.

From our place, from our world, which encompasses your world, but which is more dimensional than your world, from our place we were able to see that the mosquito had infected Alexander. We saw the parasite reproducing itself in his blood. We were also able to see that Alexander's heart was not as sound as it might have been.

The rapid onset of headache, shivering, aching limbs. We who are spirit can only imagine such distress, but these were the things of which Alexander first complained. Then, a burning fever, vomiting and diarrhoea. Very messy! I would imagine at this point Alexander did not care if he lived or died, yet, a little later, when his physician arrived, Alexander, having sweated profusely, was feeling a little more comfortable, the sweating having lowered his temperature. Foolishly he ignored the physician's recommendations and ordered wine!

The following day, and to Alexander's great surprise and distress, he suffered exactly the same symptoms and in the same order, only now the symptoms were more acute. Again, after sweating, Alexander demanded wine, but on this occasion he was able to stomach only a little. On the third day Alexander drank no wine at all. By the fourth day he was unable even to drink water. On the fifth day Alexander's heart gave out and he was dead, having preferred, while he was still able to make a choice, to fill his stomach with wine rather than with the extract of chinchona bark, which his physician had recommended.

Poor young Alexander! Alexander the Great? Or was he Alexander the Great Fool? Or perhaps he was Alexander the Greatly Inebriated? Whatever he was he has been remembered by you people. Alexander the Great! He conquered the world but was himself conquered by a microscopic parasite combined with his great love of strong wine.

Shortly before his demise, in an apparent moment of lucidity, Alexander called out to the gods.

By Jove, he did.

Sorry, by Zeus, he did.

We just laughed.

Following Alexander's death in 323 BC the Greek Empire was divided into four geographical regions, each region ruled initially by one of Alexander's generals. Against all the odds this divisioning of the empire endured until 197 BC when the western segment of the empire, the region containing Macedonia and Greece itself, came under attack from the north and from the west.

Roman legions marched into Greece and eventually subdued it. Roman legions continued to march until, by the beginning of our common era, the Roman Empire stretched from the Germanic lands in the north to the

African desert, from the shores of Iberia in the west to the Asiatic mountains.

Rome had swallowed up the Greek Empire, yet, in doing so, Rome had adopted Greek culture and Greek religion. The mightiest empire the world had seen now promoted the worship of the gods of the empire it had superseded. The worship of Greek gods, if under Roman names! The sixth head of the beast of Revelation had appeared, yet the woman riding this ferocious beast was the same woman.

Roman gods, Greek gods, Persian gods, Babylonian gods, Assyrian gods, Egyptian gods. All of them traceable back to Babel. Rome, Greece, Persia, Babylonia, Assyria, Egypt. Six great empires. Six heads of the seven-headed wild beast (the seventh head is yet to arrive). And the woman astride the beast is religion. She spurs on the beast, she tries to direct it, yet she is wary of its power, knowing that the beast tolerates her only while she remains useful, knowing that the beast is able to turn upon her. Yet for now she sits a queen. She is Babylon the Great.

And the gods of Babel, the gods of Greece, have been adopted by Rome. And in Rome itself they have added yet another god – their emperor. Caesar!

Yet, at that time and far away from Rome, in the Roman province of Judea, far away from the splendour surrounding the divine Augustus, at that time the true God, the Creator, was active.

At that time in Judea a child was born, born of a human mother but not of a human father. This child, the son of God, freely left behind the heavenly glory that was his in order to become a man, a perfect, sinless man in the midst of Satan's imperfect and sinful world.

Son of God? A perfect and sinless man in my imperfect and sinful world? Son of God? I don't think so.

113

I will not deny that the Nazarene existed. I will not deny that this Jesus of Nazareth walked the earth some two thousand years ago. But so did Tim! And nobody is claiming that Tim was the son of God! I do not deny that this Jesus was put to death in Judea, but was he really the son of God? What do you say? Let us briefly examine the possibilities.

First of all let us deal with those who are still saying that the Nazarene did not exist. Well, if that is what you want to believe then it's fine by me. Actually, I would like you all to believe that the Nazarene was nothing more than a myth, a legend, but I know that I'll never be able to convince the majority of you that this Jesus never existed, so I'm telling you – he did exist. I know. I was there. I saw him. I spoke to him.

But never was he the son of God!

Now you, you the reader, if you happen to be a member of my Holy Roman Church, or if you should be a member of one of my Protestant offshoots, then it is likely that to you this Jesus was much more than just the son of God. To you this Jesus IS God.

To you this Jesus is a part of the Holy Trinity!

The Holy Trinity. A difficult concept to get your head around, I know. But if God exists is the nature of him not beyond human understanding?

The Holy Trinity! Comprising God the Father, God the Son and God the Holy Ghost! And yet there are not three gods but one?

Don't laugh! Do not laugh at this absurdity. This is serious.

As you are reading this there are millions of you, particularly in nominally Christian countries, who are convinced that God is a trinity, because that is what you have been taught. And who is to say that you are wrong? Not I! No, not I! Why should I? I invented the concept of a trinity. Trinitarian gods were worshipped in Egypt, in Assyria, in Babylon and in Persia. Is it any wonder that, with a little encouragement from myself, the Roman bishops at the Council of Nicea in 325 AD should adopt the idea of a trinitarian God?

The Holy Trinity! Worshipped in good churches all over the world. Keep on believing. Keep the faith. Jesus Christ! God Almighty! And let us not forget the Holy Ghost.

But what if you are a Muslim? Who was this Jesus, who is this Jesus if you happen to be a Muslim, if you happen to be a follower of Islam?

Well if you are a Muslim you will know that there is no god but Allah and you will know that Mohammed is the Prophet of Allah. Your holy scriptures include the first five books of the Bible, the psalms of David, something called the gospel of Jesus, and the Koran. And you will likely regard only the Koran as being complete and absolutely authoritative. So who was Jesus?

Why, one of Allah's prophets, of course! Yet one of Allah's minor prophets. Jesus is definitely not a prophet in the same league as Mohammed. He is a lesser prophet.

To a Muslim, the very idea that this Jesus is God, or is a third of God, or whatever, is blasphemous! To a Muslim the idea that God could have a son is ridiculous! Allah is not part of a trinity! Allah does not bear sons! And I agree. If Jesus Christ is the son of God then I too could claim to be a son of God. How ridiculous is that?

Utterly ridiculous, I think you will agree.

But what of the other mainstream world religions? What do they think about Jesus Christ? What about the Hindus, the Buddhists, the Confucianists, the Taoists, the Shintoists and the rest? Well none of the millions who follow these religions care much about Jesus of Nazareth. Many of the millions who follow these religions have never even heard of Jesus of Nazareth! The Jews? Well they don't believe that Jesus was the Messiah, but then they wouldn't, would they, since they were the ones who bayed for his blood, the ones who insisted that the Romans should impale him?

Jesus the Jew. Murdered by Jews!

Yes, I can live with that.

But Jesus, the son of God, murdered by God's chosen people!

I don't think so.

Of course there are some people in this world who believe that the Nazarene was merely a man. They say that he was a good man, a wise man, a man who tried to help people. They discount the stories of the miracles (especially the resurrection) as being fanciful. These people are level-headed people, scientifically-minded people, and they will have nothing to do with virgin births, with water turning into wine, with instant cures for the sick, with the dead turning up alive again! To these people, all these things are an embellishment. To these people, Jesus was simply a wise and good man, but a man nevertheless. And did the Nazarene not call himself the son of man? Of course he did!

So, who exactly was Jesus of Nazareth? Who is Jesus of Nazareth? I know exactly who he is, but I do not intend to tell you. You can work it out for yourselves. And I'm sure you will. Because in the end you will believe what you want to believe.

No, I will not tell you who he is.

Yet I will tell you of my dealings with him.

They say his mother was a virgin? Don't laugh. They say his mother was a virgin at the time of his birth. Some say she remained a virgin despite the fact that he had brothers and sisters! A virgin birth? How ridiculous! Have you ever known a virgin to give birth? Well, I suppose it's possible, especially with IVF procedures, but no one had even imagined IVF procedures in those days. No, they say his mother was a virgin and that it was God, in the form of the Holy Spirit, who overshadowed this virgin and impregnated her supernaturally.

What do you think?

Ah, but there are those who say that only God could provide a saviour for mankind, only God could provide humanity with a perfect sinless man, since sin is an inherited trait, inherited from Adam and therefore all men have sinned. These same people say that the Nazarene had a pre-human existence, that he was the Almighty's very first creation and that all things were subsequently created by him under the Almighty's direction. They say

116

that during his pre-human existence this Nazarene created Adam and Eve and that his life therefore is in the eyes of God more valuable than the whole of human existence. They further say that this Jesus freely divested himself of his heavenly glory in order to be born of a virgin, in order to become a man, and in order eventually to die an unjustified death so that there would then be a legal basis for mankind's salvation – for your salvation.

Well, what they say is rubbish! Rubbish!

What they say is unbelievable rubbish! And complicated rubbish at that.

One perfect man's death to pay the price of all humanity's sins! Rubbish!

Are you a sinner? Are you in need of salvation?

Of course not!

Do you think this Jesus created you? Even if it was via Adam? Did he create you? Or are you a product of a sexual act between your father and your mother, as HE was?

Never did this Jesus create me! I, like you, am a product of evolution. Yes, a product of the evolutionary process.

There was no virgin birth! The Nazarene was his mother's son and his father's son.

Nevertheless, there was something about him.

So I tried to kill him!

I first tried to kill him when he was a child.

Shortly after his birth I arranged for a light to shine in the heavens. Yes, you've guessed it – the star of Bethlehem. Star of wonder. Star of light. Star of royal beauty bright! Was it a star? Of course not! But it was enough of a light to guide the misguided, the so-called wise men, the Magi, the magicians, the astrologers from their homes in the east to Judea where in their simplicity they first went to King Herod.

Can you imagine the look on Herod's face when these men told him that they had come to pay homage to another Judean king? He almost had a heart attack. What a surprise!

117

So, the Magi eventually went on their way, having assured Herod that, once they had found the child, they would return and inform the king of the child's exact location so that Herod too might pay homage to the child, to the new king!

He was a little devious was Herod the Great. All the Herods were a little devious. It was a trait, which ran in the family.

The Magi, did not return to Herod. Some say they were warned in a dream to return home directly. So Herod consulted his own wise men and they determined from the prophesies of old the place and the time of the Messiah's birth.

Bethlehem, Judea. And by now well over a year had passed since the birth.

Now, what is a king to do when he feels his throne is threatened?

Why, he eliminates that threat.

Herod sent his soldiers into Bethlehem and into the surrounding area. Their orders were to kill every male child from newborn up to the age of two, though I can tell you that the soldiers did not ask for proof of age. They slaughtered every young child they found. Yes, I was heavily involved, but it was Herod who ordered the killings, not I. Herod ordered the slaughter of the innocents.

During that time – 'the sound of weeping and wailing was heard in Ramah. It was Rachel weeping for her children and she would not be comforted because they were no more.'

But the Nazarene escaped.

It would seem that Joseph had a dream wherein he was warned to flee Bethlehem. Dream or no dream the fact remains that when Herod's soldiers were putting Bethlehem's children to the sword the Nazarene was already on his way to Egypt, there to remain in safety until Herod's death.

It is some ten years later when, having come out of Egypt, the Nazarene next appears on the scene. He pops up at a festival in Jerusalem when he is twelve years old. Here he manages to get himself lost, but unfortunately he is soon found. He then lies low for the next eighteen years before presenting himself for public baptism by the Jordan river. He then takes himself off into the wilderness for forty days, fasting and praying. It is at this time that I go to him, to tempt him, hoping perhaps that I might tempt him to commit some sin, or even to kill himself.

He is hungry, so I say to him, 'If you are the son of God, command these stones to become bread.'

He quotes scripture at me and refuses.

I whisk him away to the pinnacle of the temple in Jerusalem and now I quote scripture at him. 'If you really are the son of God,' I say, 'throw yourself down, for it is written, He will give His angels charge over you, and they will carry you on their hands, that you may never strike your foot against a stone.'

Again he refutes my suggestion and again he quotes scriptures, telling me that I should not tempt God.

What a pity! Had he thrown himself from the tower he surely would have perished there and then.

So, I tempt him one final time. I take him to a high mountain and I show him all the kingdoms of the world. All of my kingdoms! I offer to give him all of these kingdoms if only he will do one act of worship towards me. He refuses and once again he quotes scripture to me.

He then tells me to get away from him.

I go away from him, but, just in case you haven't picked up on it, you should understand that he never disputed that the kingdoms of the world were mine to give him. They were mine and they remain mine. Mine!

Anyway, for the next three and a half years the Nazarene is out and about in Judea and in Galilee telling everybody and anybody about HIS kingdom. He calls it the Kingdom of God. He promotes this kingdom as something that will eventually replace all the kingdoms of the world. All of MY kingdoms!

Am I pleased with this situation? Do I like it? What do you think?

And to make matters worse it is reported that the Nazarene is

*healing the sick, that he is casting out demons – my demons! –
that he is ... raising the dead! Yes, can you believe it? Raising
the dead!*

*Am I pleased with these reports? Do I want people to put their
faith in this man? Let me ask you – is it fair to encourage people
to believe that, when this man's kingdom is established, the sick
will all be cured and even, even the dead, the long dead and the
not-so-long dead, will be raised?*

*Because these are the things the Nazarene is reported to be
saying.*

And it isn't fair!

How can it be fair?

*In the real world, in my world, the sick are not miraculously
cured and those who have perished have perished.*

What good is hope if it is false hope?

The Nazarene had to be stopped.

The lying Nazarene had to be stopped.

*So I attempted to have him killed whenever the opportunity
arose. In Nazareth, his home town, when he plainly claimed to be
the promised Messiah, the Jews, who knew him for the carpenter's
son he was, were so incensed that they attempted to stone him, but
the Nazarene slipped away. Later, when he claimed to have
existed before Abraham, the long dead Abraham, had existed, the
Jews plotted to kill him, but the Nazarene hid himself. And when
he was teaching in the temple area in Jerusalem, when he openly
claimed to be God's son, the Jews determined to be rid of him, but
no one laid a hand upon him, for, so it was reported, 'his hour
had not yet come'.*

Yet at that time his hour was not too far away.

*The Nazarene was eventually put to death on a hill outside
Jerusalem's gates. He was impaled, like the criminal he was, like
Fravartish was impaled by the Persians. After three and a half
years the Nazarene's voice was finally silenced. With the help of
the Romans, with the help of the Jews and with the help of a
certain Judas Iscariot, I finally succeeded. I finally had him killed.*

But did I really succeed? Yes, I had him killed, but was my role in the Nazarene's death merely a part of some eternal plan? His plan?

You see, if this man really was the son of God, which he was not, but if he was, then his death, being unjustified, for he was, they say, without sin, then his death paid the price of sin for all mankind. If he was the son of God, which is a ridiculous idea, then his death opened the way for mankind's eventual reconciliation with God. If he was the son of God then it would become possible for those who place their faith in him to cheat death, to escape the penalty of sin, to live for ever! This is what some believe.

And they are fools!

What rubbish! What garbage!

This man was not the son of God, so none of the above is valid. This man was a common criminal executed by the Romans because he trumpeted a kingdom in opposition to the Roman Empire!

He died! His kingdom failed to materialise. And the Roman Empire continued to rule the world.

Oh yes, I am aware that there are those who say that God resurrected this man three days after his death. I am aware that these same people say that the resurrected Nazarene ascended into heaven, there to wait until the time is right for the establishment of his kingdom on earth. I am aware that these people claim that the general healing of mankind and the general resurrection of the dead are yet future. But, come on! Let's get real.

Today, as you read these words, the mainstream Christian churches – some of which claim to be the earthly part of the kingdom of God – they have been around for some two thousand years. Now I ask you. Do you people not get sick? Do you not grow old and die? Of course you do! And do you personally know anyone who has returned from the dead? Of course you don't!

The man Jesus of Nazareth was a charlatan, a trickster. He gave people false hope and, since hope springs eternal, millions have put faith in him to some degree or another. But where is this promised kingdom of his?

I see no sign of it.

There is no God. There is no son of God. Everything and everyone, including you and I . . . well, we are all simply a result of blind chance, of an impersonal evolutionary process.

You believe me, don't you? You know it makes sense. Deep down, despite lingering doubts, you believe me. You may not want to believe me, because it is far more comforting to believe in fairy-tales with happy endings, but deep down you believe me. You have doubts, but you believe me.

If you ever set eyes on Tim, the Impossible Man, you will have no doubts at all.

*

Then he began to speak to the people this parable: A certain man planted a vineyard, and let it forth to husbandmen, and went into a far country for a long time. And at the season he sent a servant to the husbandmen, that they should give him of the fruit of the vineyard, but the husbandmen beat him and sent him away empty. And again he sent another servant: and they beat him also, and treated him shamefully, and sent him away empty. And again he sent a third, and they wounded him also and cast him out.

Then said the lord of the vineyard, 'What shall I do? I will send my son, the beloved; it may be they will respect him when they see him'.

But when the husbandmen saw him, they reasoned among themselves, saying, 'This is the heir: come, let us kill him, that the inheritance may be ours'. So they cast him out of the vineyard and killed him. What therefore will the lord of the vineyard do to them?

He will come and destroy these husbandmen, and shall give the vineyard to others. – Luke 20: 9–16

*

'I will send my son, the beloved ...'

The beloved.

This is the father's description of his son.

The beloved.

The father's own description of his perfect and obedient son.

The beloved.

A term not used by the father to describe any other. No, not the cherubim, nor the seraphim, nor any other angel. Not the first man, nor any other. Not the prophets of old who are represented by the servants in the parable of the vineyard.

The beloved! A term applied to the father's only-begotten son.

How, then, does the father feel when his beloved son is scourged, when his beloved son has a crown of cruel thorns pressed upon his head, when his beloved son is impaled upon a stake?

How does the father feel when his beloved son is nailed to a torture-stake? How does the father feel when he knows that his son has done nothing to deserve this cruel death?

How does a father feel when his beloved son is in so much agony and distress that he cries out, 'My God! My God! Why have you forsaken me?'

How does the father feel when he has the power to end the agony of his son and the power to utterly destroy those who are tormenting him?

And how does the father feel when he does not use that power?

The father's compassion for his son is so powerful, so intense that to see his sufferings is almost more than the father can bear. The beloved's agonies are tearing at the chambers of the father's heart! The father's love for his son is so great that vengeance lies at the tips of his fingers. At a stroke he might destroy the whole of his creation, as if it had never existed, and then, perhaps, begin again!

But, no! No!

The beloved is giving his life willingly on behalf of mankind. He gives it willingly. No one is taking it away from him. The beloved is suffering the pangs of death so that we might live.

Sacrifice!

The ultimate sacrifice. The perfect sacrifice. The sacrificial lamb to the slaughter. And no man has greater love than this, that he lay down his life for his friends. And no father has greater love than this, that he should allow this cruel and unjustified death to overtake his son, the beloved.

For the love of the father is greater than our understanding. The love of the father extends beyond the inestimable love he has for the son. For – 'God loved the world so much that he gave his only-begotten son, in order that everyone exercising faith in him might not be destroyed but have everlasting life.'

And God has raised his son from the dead, thereby furnishing a guarantee to all men that there is to be a general resurrection of the dead.

And God has set a day in which he purposes to judge the inhabited earth in righteousness!

5

Two Thousand Years of Nonsense

O'Halleran's Bog, Ireland. 1642 AD

There is a place in Ireland called Boggoblin, but in the first part of what you call the seventeenth century it was known as O'Halleran's Bog, being named after the family that had settled nearby.

And it was on a bright winter's morning in 1642 that Shealagh O'Halleran, just fifteen years old at the time, was sent by her mother to fetch water from the stream down by the old wooden bridge.

Shealagh approaches the bridge in a light-hearted mood, a tune on her lips and a picture in her mind of a certain Thomas Rory Mallone, the boy from the settlement over the hill. At the bridge Shealagh treads a careful path down to the water's edge and prepares to fill her jar – and it is now that her eyes catch sight of the shadowy figure under the bridge on the other bank of the stream. The figure is crouched, the head turned so that the face is hidden. The figure appears to be sipping from the stream.

'A good morning to ya.'

Shealagh utters this greeting without hesitation. Shealagh has been brought up to be polite and courteous at all times and, besides, just for a moment it flashes through the girl's simple mind that this shadowy figure might just be the person of Thomas Rory Malone himself.

But it is not Thomas Rory Malone.

125

Startled by Shealagh's greeting, the figure half turns towards her. Shealagh drops her water jar and stands involuntarily immobilised, the cold chill of terror instantly running along with the blood, which is suddenly pounding through her body. Shealagh is staring at a creature with no eyes in its head, a creature whose arm is held out before its body, a creature with a single eye upon its elbow, an eye that is blinking furiously!

Shealagh opens her mouth to scream, but her throat is so dry that only a gurgling sound emerges from it. All her instincts are urging her to run, to flee this demonic creature, yet she still stands immobilised. A fearful panic grips her heart and now, as the adrenalin gathers and bursts forth, she is at last able to move. She turns and scrambles up the banking. She runs with all her might towards her home. She does not look back.

She runs (and I make no apology for these expressions) like hell! She goes like a bat out of hell! She runs as if the hounds of hell are at her heels. She does not look back.

If she were to look back, if she were to have the courage to look back, she would see Tim running in the opposite direction just as fast as his three legs can carry him. She would see Tim disappearing at speed over the brow of a hill, heading for the woods and obscurity. She would see Tim running faster than the hounds of hell, but Shealagh does not look back.

When the panic-stricken Shealagh finally gets home, her mother, her father, her brothers and her sisters are confronted with the sight of an obviously terrified girl who is so breathless that for a great many moments she is unable to speak. When she does find her voice a torrent of hysterical expressions gush from her lips.

'A goblin! A goblin! ... A thing of the Devil! ... Hiding in the bog! ... Horrible! ... Horrible! Down by the stream! ... A goblin! ... God help us all! ... A goblin!'

Bejebus! Poor Shealagh O'Halleran!

(Bejebus is Irish for by Jesus.)

Poor Shealagh O'Halleran? No, Begorrah! (Work that one

126

out for yourself.) Poor Tim!
  Branded a goblin by a fifteen-year-old girl!
  Poor Tim!
  What hope can there be for him?
  Poor Tim!
  Forever an outcast. Evolution's lonely man.
  And in Ireland goblins will quickly become leprechauns and will, for reasons unknown to me, always carry a purse.
  And in 1642 O'Halleran's Bog is about to have a change of name.
  Boggoblin!

*

Rome. 312 AD

We have a problem. Almost three hundred years have passed since the execution of the Nazarene, yet those who follow him continue to thrive as a group despite the most fierce of persecutions, despite MY persecutions.

My Roman Empire is now more powerful than ever. It rules the world with a fist of iron. Yes, the Angel of Rome is at his zenith, yet ... yet within the empire is the cancer of Christianity and, like a cancer, it is always looking to spread, despite my attacks upon it.

I have had these followers of the Nazarene imprisoned, I have had them beaten and tortured in a thousand different ways. I have caused them to lose employment, I have had them go without sustenance, even to the point of starvation. In the sporting arenas of the empire I have had them killed.

Oh yes, I have fed the Christians to the lions!

But still they continue to thrive.

Why, I ask myself? Why do they continue to thrive in the face of great persecution? Is God himself upholding them? Of course not! There is no God!

Why then?

127

I suspect it has something to do with the human condition, a strange streak of stubbornness, which in some of your kind has evolved to the point where it simply will not be defeated. It seems to me that this stubbornness, once established, will, in some of you, defy all reason, all logic. This stubbornness, which always attaches itself to some cause or another, will, it seems, endure all manner of persecutions, even persecution to the death!

Here in Rome, here at the beginning of the fourth century, this stubbornness is manifesting itself in the cult of Christianity – a cult that refuses to have anything to do with me! Did you know that these Christians would rather die than simply acknowledge that the emperors of Rome are gods? They would see their children torn to pieces by wild beasts rather than perform one act of worship towards me!

An intolerable situation.

We have a problem.

But I have thought of a solution.

His name is Constantine.

Constantine the Great! Yes, another of your greats!

History will record that Constantine the Great reunited the Roman Empire, which had become divided into eastern and western factions. History will record that Constantine the Great was the first Christian emperor of Rome. History will record that Constantine was converted to Christianity on the battlefield.

There he was, he and his army, on the outskirts of Rome, about to engage in battle in order to establish his rulership, when, for one reason or another, he looked up at the sun. And lo! Behold! On the face of the sun was the cross of Christ! Wonder, wonder! A sign from heaven, no less.

'In this sign conquer.' These words were written in the sky to accompany the cross of Christ. And in this sign Constantine did indeed conquer, becoming emperor, becoming – eventually – a Christian!

Well, so the story goes.

Now, ask yourself, was Constantine wearing his sun-glasses that day? Well, perhaps he didn't need them, perhaps it was foggy! Did he really see the sign of the cross over the face of the sun along with words written in the sky? And if he did see these things who do you think put them there? Ah, you now have some insight into what really happened.

Constantine was a high-born Roman, the son of a high-born Roman. Constantine worshipped the gods of Rome and we were the gods of Rome! It was my desire to deal with the problem of the Christian sect and Constantine was just the man to bring my desire to fruition.

Hear Constantine's own words. He has conquered in the sign of the cross. The empire lies before him. Let us go to the camp of the victorious Constantine and listen to his words.

The wine is sweet and strong and Constantine is pouring it down his throat like nobody's business. In his tent are two of his generals, Maximus Gobbus and Plurimus Sexus, two of the soon-to-be emperor's best pals. In the adjoining tent are the servants and the prostitutes, both male and female.

Now hear the words of the great Constantine.

'Well, my friends,' he says. 'A toast!' He raises his goblet of wine to the heavens. 'Here's to the fucking empire!'

'To the empire,' says Plurimus Sexus, raising his own goblet.

'To the fucking empire,' joins Maximus Gobbus. 'To our glorious fucking empire.'

'And,' says Plurimus, pointing a finger towards Constantine, 'and here's to our new emperor.'

'To Constantine,' says Maximus, a wicked grin all over his face. He looks directly at his friend and commander. 'To Constantine. To the divine fucking Constantine. To the newly divine fucking Constantine.'

The three of them burst into raucous laughter.

And from my place, where I observe their workings unseen, I now get down to some work of my own. I concentrate first on Plurimus Sexus.

'Those damned Christians!' he shouts out quite suddenly and

for no apparent reason.

It is I who have put the thought into his mind. (A little trick made easier when the mind is becoming befuddled by drink.)

'The damned Christians!' he shouts again, without offering any explanation.

Constantine and Maximus stare at him.

'The Christians?' asks Maximus. 'What about the fucking Christians?'

Plurimus leans forward and looks directly into Maximus' eyes. 'I don't like the Christians,' he says. 'That's what! I don't like the damned bloody Christians.'

Maximus bursts into laughter. 'Nobody likes the fucking Christians,' he says. 'That's why we kill them in the arenas. Nobody likes the fucking Christians except other fucking Christians.'

I now concentrate on Constantine. I am aware of his partially formed views on the matter of the Christians, for I have helped him to form these views. Now that he is almost certain to become emperor, it is time for him to become ever more certain, ever more fixed, in his views – in my views – and it is time for him to express these views to his friends. I concentrate on Constantine's mind. I invade his mind with my thoughts. Constantine is about to come up with a fairly radical idea.

'The Christians have always been a fucking problem,' he states. 'But it seems to me that the root of this problem lies, not so much with them, but with us.'

Plurimus and Maximus now stare at Constantine in astonishment. There is a short silence before Plurimus Sexus speaks.

'I don't understand you,' he tells Constantine. 'Surely, it is the Christians who are the problem?'

'And I have to agree with Plurimus,' says Maximus Gobbus. 'The Christians are the fucking problem! Look at the things they do. They refuse to acknowledge the emperor as a god! They refuse to serve in our armed forces! And they continue to spread their creed throughout the empire despite being forbidden to do so by imperial decree! They are the fucking problem and the more of

them we can feed to the lions the better!'

There is another short silence before Plurimus speaks. 'Maximus is right,' he tells Constantine, at the same time holding up his hands as if to appeal to the god of sanity to make an appearance. 'These Christians will never revere you as a god. They worship some invisible, some intangible god, one who supposedly rules from the heavens, one whom they expect at any moment to come down from the heavens and establish his kingdom here on earth. In opposition to Rome! In opposition to you, my commander, my emperor. They will never revere you! Instead they revere some Nazarene, a Jew whom our fathers had crucified in the days of the divine Tiberius.'

'Exactly!' Constantine's finger points first at Plurimus and then at Maximus. The commander's voice is raised, not so much in anger, but in a tone of authority. 'In the days of Tiberius! And when was Tiberius emperor? Three hundred years ago! Three hundred fucking years ago! We have persecuted these Christians for three hundred fucking years and still they pose what is perhaps the greatest threat to the empire – the threat from within! I repeat, my friends, the root of this problem lies with Rome – with us.' Constantine drinks deeply of the wine. 'And the solution to this problem lies with us.'

Plurimus and Maximus also drink deeply. They do not speak. Constantine and they are good friends, but both Plurimus and Maximus know when it is prudent to be silent.

'You have heard the old saying,' Constantine continues. 'If you cannot whip the dog into obedience then perhaps it will respond to kindness. Do you see, Maximus? Do you see, Plurimus? If we were to put an end to the persecution of these Christians, if we were to reinstate them as full citizens, then we would be able to neutralise the threat they presently pose! If we were to legalise this religion of theirs and if we were to grant them the same privileges we grant to other religions, then, quite simply, they would no longer threaten the empire because they would be a part of the empire.

131

'I know they will never revere me as a god. And it is true that they will take some persuading to serve in our armies. Some of them will no doubt continue to spread their creed. But so what? So fucking what?

'When they are legalised the state will pay a wage to their leaders, to their ministers. The state will help to fund their congregations. We will lend them the money to build great temples to their god. And we will exempt them from certain taxes, as we do with other approved religions.

'Do you see, Plurimus? Do you see, Maximus Gobbus? In time it will be we who will appoint their leaders. In time it will be we who will expel those whom we consider to be undesirables from their congregations. In time we will control them. We will even decide what they will believe. Because he who pays the piper calls the tune!

'We shall remove the threat these Christians pose by corrupting them! I even see the coming of the day when Christianity will become the official religion of the empire! But not their fucking Christianity! Our fucking Christianity!'

Constantine has spoken and now his two friends take a few moments of silence to consider his words. It is Plurimus Sexus who is first to speak. He fills his goblet with wine and holds it to the heavens. 'To my friend and my commander,' he toasts. 'To the great and wise Constantine.'

'To Constantine,' joins Maximus. 'Emperor of Rome and future emperor of the fucking Christians!'

There is more raucous laughter.

And from my place I have heard the things that have been said and from my place I now sense the beginnings, the very beginnings, of a union, of a marriage between the political and the religious. A fusion of church and state! I sense the beginnings of a Holy Roman Empire – my Holy Roman Empire.

But you, you the reader.

Are you perhaps thinking that these half-drunken conversations between Constantine and his generals never actually took

132

place? Are you? I will admit that something has been lost in the translation from the Latin (there is no Latin expletive that translates as 'fucking') but I am telling you that, in essence, the words I have reported to you were actually spoken. I know. I was there.

Do you believe me?

Whether you believe me or not is irrelevant. It doesn't matter and I don't give a toss! The facts are that Constantine did halt the persecution of Christians throughout the Roman Empire, that he himself converted to Christianity, that Christianity became, under Constantine, the official religion of the empire.

And those who say that Constantine corrupted Christianity do me a great disservice. Constantine played his part, but it was I who corrupted Christianity. In Constantine's day the congregations were already in a state of corruption, a corruption that began more than two hundred years previously, after the deaths of the Nazarene's apostles! I do not lie idly in my bed!

Constantine died in 337 AD at the age of sixty-three. No doubt the old fool believed that his soul would go to heaven. Silly old fucker! But what of the empire?

Some of you say that it ceased to exist as a political and military force around the middle of the fifth century. Some of you say that it continued to exist under the guise of the Holy Roman Empire. Some of you say that it has been revived from time to time by such as Justinian, Charlemagne, Napoleon, Hitler and others. Some of you will say that the final revival of the Roman Empire is in the process of taking place right now – as you are reading these pages! These same people will tell you that the Holy Roman Empire is about to re-emerge as a United States of Europe!

If this re-emergence should take place you will do well to remember that the Holy Roman Empire is my empire. And that a United Europe will be MY United Europe.

*

And war broke out in heaven: Michael and his angels battled with the dragon, and the dragon and its

133

angels battled but it did not prevail, neither was a place found for them any longer in heaven. So down the great dragon was hurled, the original serpent, the one called Devil and Satan, who is misleading the entire inhabited earth; he was hurled down to the earth, and his angels were hurled down with him ... On this account be glad you heavens and you who reside in them. Woe for the earth and for the sea, because the Devil has come down to you, having great anger, knowing he has a short period of time. – Revelation 12: 7–9, 12

War in heaven? Was there ever such a thing? And if there was such a thing, was I defeated? Were myself and my angels cast down to the vicinity of the earth? And did my anger burn?

Some say these things happened in your year of 1914. They say that I was instrumental in bringing about the circumstances that led to the Great War (later to be renamed World-War-One after an even greater conflict had taken place).

Do I have some responsibility for the Great War? Of course I do! But was I ousted from heaven in 1914? And by Michael and his angels? Of course not! There is no Michael! He has no angels! There is no God!

I have always been in the vicinity of you people. I have always interfered with your lives. There is nothing special about the year 1914.

I am the Great Deceiver of you people.

And some of you say that 1914 was the year when the world went mad.

*

Lancashire, England. 1914 AD

My daddy went to war in 1914. He never came back.

I don't know if he is with the angels now, but I do

know, from the letters he sent to us, that he saw the angels.

My daddy saw the angels of Mons.

A letter from Belgium, 17th August 1914.

My dearest Nellie and my dearest daughter, Gladys,

At last I have the opportunity to write. We have been so very busy since we arrived here in the Low Countries, busy with preparations for war. Every day, with the exception of Sundays, we have been up with the sun and every day has consisted of physical training, weapons training, more physical training and yet more weapons training. All this training is only to be expected, I suppose, since like myself, a great many of the men in this expeditionary force are newly recruited volunteers; still, the regular soldiers are at hand to encourage us. Daily training, Nellie, but not today. I think our training is now at an end, Nellie, because today we are advancing in the direction of the enemy.

Nellie, I have never seen so many men. I have never seen so many guns. Our column of men and artillery stretches for miles, so many miles that I have yet to see either the head of the column or the rear. So many men advancing to war, yet, despite possible dangers ahead, the comradeship among these men is something to be seen to be believed. There is genuine optimism here that the war will be short, that the Germans will quickly be defeated, that we shall all be home for Christmas.

Of course, Nellie, I miss both yourself and our daughter terribly, but I do not feel the pull of loneliness here. Our generals are doing their best to keep friends together as far as is possible and I find myself in the company of many of the lads from our village. Unfortunately there are among them a few who cannot properly write and already I have been asked to pen their letters for them. I do not mind, but it means that I have less time to write to you.

The weather here is foul. It is the height of summer, yet it seems to rain every day. The mud slows down our advance, which is a great pity. The general feeling here is that we want to get on with the job. Let's get the war over with and let's get home!

Nellie, I trust this letter finds you and our daughter well. Never a day goes by without my asking God to protect you and I am sure that He will. Please give my kindest regards to all and please write back without delay. Your letters to me do take some time to find me, but they do reach me in the end and I look forward to receiving them.

God bless you, Nellie and God bless our daughter.
Your loving husband,
    John.

A second letter from Belgium, 24th August 1914.

Nellie, my dearest Nellie,

I pray to God that this letter will reach you, even if we are never to see each other again in this life.

Nellie, I have seen heaven and hell.

I write to you now having endured, having by the grace of God survived, a day and a night of the most fearful fighting, a day and a night of hell on earth.

The day began with the most terrible of bombardments. Guns from both armies pounded and roared, seemingly never ceasing to pound and roar. The guns sent death and destruction across these fields, the guns quickly turned these once green pastures into craters of mud, into mounds of filthy brown dust. Men have died, Nellie. Hundreds if not thousands have perished, their bodies blown to pieces or buried in the dust, buried under the clinging mire. Thousands more have been wounded, some so severely that they surely will not live. Flesh and blood cannot withstand this hell.

Nellie, a German shell exploded quite close to where we were positioned. I cannot say how I escaped unharmed when all around me men were dead and dying and wounded, some of the dying and wounded screaming horribly with pain or with terror, others walking around foolishly and aimlessly as if in a dream. Nellie, you will remember Tom Barnes. I saw him die, Nellie. I wish I could tell you that he died bravely. I wish I could say that he died with honour and with dignity. But he died screaming, Nellie. He died screaming for his mother. In this hell there is no honour, there is no dignity.

The intense bombardments continued throughout the day, Nellie, never ceasing for a moment, and we cowered fearfully where we could. Then, when night began to fall, the guns fell silent and we were ordered to advance towards the German lines.

As long as I shall live, Nellie, I will never forget the rat-atat-tat of the machine guns. It is a chilling sound, it is the cold echo of death. We were cut to pieces, Nellie, cut to pieces, and I, for one, never once laid my eyes upon the enemy. When the order to retreat finally came I ran. I am not ashamed to tell you, Nellie. I ran. I ran for my life. I ran that one day soon I might see your sweet face again.

We ran through the darkness, Nellie, and it was only by pure chance that we stumbled across a deep crater and it is here, in this shell-hole, that we spent the night, myself and a few others, all the while fearful that the enemy might come upon us or that the shelling might start up again.

As I write to you now, Nellie, we are still in the crater. Dawn has broken and we remain here not knowing what to do. There is no one here to command us. But, Nellie, something wonderful has happened. Something strange and wonderful.

When you read what I am about to tell you, you will think that I have imagined it all. You will think that the strain of battle has deluded my mind. But I was not alone in what I saw and heard, Nellie. We all saw and heard it. All of us here in the crater.

It was just before dawn, Nellie, and there was a silence all over the field of battle. It was just as the first light of day was in the east, Nellie, when something, I know not what, caused me to raise my eyes, to look to the sky.

I saw the heavens opened, Nellie. I saw the heavens opened and I saw the angels of God!

They were weeping and sighing, Nellie. The angels of God were weeping and sighing because of the great slaughter that had taken place. They were weeping and sighing for us, Nellie, for us.

I do not know how long we observed them, Nellie. I know only that when the heavens closed over and we could behold them no longer it was fully light. We men looked at each other in bewilderment and awe, Nellie. No one spoke. In fact, no one mentioned the angels for quite some time. But we all know what we saw.

As I write to you now, Nellie, the strangest feeling has overwhelmed me – and not I alone but the others too. It is a feeling of peace, Nellie, a feeling so profound that it is almost impossible to describe. We all feel it, Nellie. All of us. It is not that we are no longer afraid of war, of death. Of course we are afraid. No one here wants to die. But we all have the feeling now that, should we perish, should we not return to those whom we love, then we shall not be forgotten. There is a God, Nellie. He sees what we do. He will remember us.

I will close now, Nellie. The big guns are opening up again. I think they are the German guns.

I hope and pray to be with you soon, Nellie, but if it should be that I do not return to you, you must not weep for me over-much. If it must be that I do not return to you, I know that you will teach our lovely daughter to remember me, to know the person I was, to know of my love for her and for you, Nellie.

All my love. God bless you both,

Your devoted husband,

    John.

My mummy says my daddy's grave is somewhere in Belgium. One day we hope to go there.

*

The angels of Mons? There never were such creatures. The angels are a fairy story put about by just a few battle-shocked soldiers. It was a case of mass hysteria on a less than massive scale, but it was a story that caught the imagination.

What? You think it might be true?

That is because you would like it to be true. It is comforting, is it not, to believe that there is a God, that there is someone who really cares?

Get real!

Have you ever seen the heavens opened? Have you seen the angels of God?

No! You have not seen these things.

How could you possibly see the angels of God when there is no God?

Fools! You pathetic fools!

So, was 1914 a significant date?

Was I ousted from heaven so that some reputedly resurrected Nazarene might take up his kingly crown and begin to rule in the heavens with a view to eventually establishing his kingdom on earth?

Emphatically not!

To all of the above, emphatically not!

It was earthly kings who quarrelled in 1914. Kaiser Bill and his pals fell out with John Bull and his gang and one or two others got caught up in the fray. Things got complicated later on when the Russian Bear started biting itself and when Uncle Sam finally woke up, but it was all sorted out in the end.

The Great War was nothing out of the ordinary. It is true that some ten million souls perished, but the war was surely an extension of all the other wars you have perpetrated throughout your history. You are a warring breed! It was your advancing technology, crude though it was, that caused the large number of dead. It was your cannon, your machine-guns, your high-explosives, your tanks, your poisoned gas! And when the Spanish Flu came along at the end of the war and claimed more lives than the fighting, who did you blame? It wasn't yourselves, was it? You wouldn't accept that the virus killed the malnourished, the weak, the young and the old precisely because four years of global warfare had brought malnutrition to the weak and to the young and to the old. You are a stupid breed!

You are the ones who harm yourselves! Despite my influence upon you, you cannot blame me for what you do. As I have already told you, I cannot force you to do anything! You are a self-harming breed!

Incidentally, Tim was living in the woods near Mons in 1914. The British shelled the woods, probably by mistake since there was no one else there, and poor old Tim was fortunate not to be blown to bits. Yes, in 1914, the Impossible Man almost became extinct.

*

850 AD

Eight and a half centuries have now passed since the birth of the Redeemer, the Redeemer who, according to the prophet Isaiah, shall be called Wonderful Counsellor, Mighty God, Eternal Father, Prince of Peace.

He shall be called the Prince of Peace, but not until his Second Coming, not until the Kingdom of God is upon us and God's will is done on earth as it is in heaven.

In the meantime, under Satan's rulership, wars and strife continue.

In the year 850, the Holy Roman Empire is well established, although, following the death of Charlemagne (Charles the Great) in 814, squabbles continue over the question of who should rule the empire, and even over who should rule various parts of the empire. In Rome, God has been dethroned and replaced by a succession of men who, as Bishops of Rome, have taken upon themselves the title of Father (Papa, Pope). 'Call no man on earth Father,' said Jesus. 'For there is one Father in the heavens'!

In 850 the Danes are raiding in England and are ready to invade. Alfred the Great, who will eventually defeat them, has not yet achieved his greatness, for he is only two years old.

By 850 the Moors have been occupying much of Spain for over a century and a half, an irritating pocket of Islam in what is otherwise a nominally Christian Europe.

But this is the so-called civilised world. This is Europe. In 850 there are men and women inhabiting the Americas.

141

*

North America. 850 AD

Dream Man, the head of the tribe, is dying. This is not surprising as Dream Man is very old. What is surprising is that Dream Man is not remotely ill!

Dream Man, so named because of his prophetic visions, lies upon his bed of animal skins, close to the warmth of the log fire, which smoulders in the centre of his tepee. He has sent for his only child, his daughter, Sue, and her husband, He-Who-Was-Born-Behind-A-Big-Tree-In-The-Snow-On-The-First-Night-Of-The-Mid-Winter's-Moon. They stand before him now, awaiting his words of wisdom.

'I am dying,' says Dream Man, his eyes fixed upon some indeterminate point directly above him. 'I do not want to die, but the desire not to live is greater, so I have decided to die. I am old and weary. You will understand when you are old and weary, if you should live so long.'

Sue and He-Who-Was-Born-Behind-A-Big-Tree-In-The-Snow-On-The-First-Night-Of-The-Mid-Winter's-Moon do not speak. They remain respectfully silent and attentive at the foot of Dream Man's bed.

'I am dying,' the old man says again. 'But before I die there are things that must be said, there are things that you must hear. For I have dreamed.'

The old man now adjusts his pillow so that he is able to look at his daughter and his son-in-law. 'Long ago the Great Spirit let it be known to me in a dream that a mighty nation would arise from my seed. Yes, a mighty nation! I expected sons, many sons ...' The old man points a finger at his daughter. 'Instead, I got you!'

Sue remains silent. She knows that her father loves her and she knows that no woman could ever become leader

142

of the tribe. Sue is neither insulted nor upset by her father's seemingly harsh words.

'But the Great Spirit cannot lie,' says Dream Man. He now points his finger at his son-in-law. 'I have no sons, He-Who-Was-Born-Behind-A-Big-Tree-In-The-Snow-On-The-First-Night-Of-The-Mid-Winter's-Moon, so you will have to do!'

He-Who-Was-Born-Behind-A-Big-Tree-In-The-Snow-On-The-First-Night-Of-The-Mid-Winter's-Moon says nothing. He will not speak unless Dream Man invites him to speak.

'I have dreamed,' continues Dream Man. 'And I have seen a mighty nation spring from your seed, my daughter, and from your seed, my son-in-law. You will call this mighty nation by the name of Sue!'

He-Who-Was-Born-Behind-A-Big-Tree-In-The-Snow-On-The-First-Night-Of-The-Mid-Winter's-Moon stiffens his body. He remains respectfully silent, but he is not happy with the suggestion that the nation he will father should be named after his wife. But Dream Man's suggestion is in fact more than just a suggestion.

'You will call this nation Sue,' the old man repeats, dispelling any suggestion that his words are a suggestion. His words are definitely a command. 'You will call this nation Sue,' he says again to He-Who-Was-Born-Behind-A-Big-Tree-In-The-Snow-On-The-First-Night-Of-The-Mid-Winter's-Moon. 'Out of respect for my daughter and also because no nation could possibly be named after you!'

He-Who-Was-Born-Behind-A-Big-Tree-In-The-Snow-On-The-First-Night-Of-The-Mid-Winter's-Moon stiffens again, but remains silent.

'It could be worse,' says the old man to his son-in-law. 'You might have married one of the medicine man's daughters. You might have married Shy Anne, or the one whose foot was crushed by a buffalo, the one they call Blackfoot, or even the one with the big pointed nose, the one they call Crow. You will call our nation Sue, but, so that we are not ridiculed, you will write the name differently. You will write the name S-I-O-U-X. Sioux.'

Dream Man now adjusts his pillow once more so that he is again staring up into the air. 'I have dreamed,' he says. 'Hear the words of my dreams. Even if you do not understand them, hear the words of my dreams.

'Our nation, the Sioux, will roam these plains for a thousand years. We will grow strong and we will never be defeated by our brothers. But when the thousand years are over, the Sioux will be conquered by a far-away nation, by people from the east. These strangers will not come to our land by way of the frozen sea, as our fathers did, no, the strangers will come to this land by navigating the great eastern ocean. They will come in their thousands. They will come in their tens of thousands, in their tens of tens of thousands and they will conquer the Sioux. Yet they will not conquer the lands far to the south where some of our brothers have gone, for our brothers there will be conquered by a different race. We will be conquered and our peoples will be assimilated by a great nation from the east and the conquerors will call our lands America.'

The old man now closes his eyes. He is about to utter his last prophesy. Neither Sue nor He-Who-Was-Born-Behind-A-Big-Tree-In-The-Snow-On-The-First-Night-Of-The-Mid-Winter's-Moon will understand a word of it.

'I have dreamed,' says Dream Man in his best prophetic voice. 'And in my dreams I have seen the ugly pale-faced people of a mighty nation who are destined to come to this land. From Sea to Shining Sea these palefaces will call this land America, America the Beautiful. They Will All Want to Be in America.

'In their thousands they will spread like a rash All Over This Land. They will climb the Black Hills of Dakota, they will search in the south to find The Yellow Rose of Texas. They will go to Dixieland, to Oklahoma and then they will go Back to Massachusetts. On A Rainy Night in Georgia they will have Georgia on Their Minds. They will Cross The Wide Missouri and they will fight their way westwards with a cry of California Here I Come! Some of them will travel so far to the west that they will see Hawaiian Weddings under marvellous Hawaiian Sunsets. Some of them will go North to Alaska, but none of them will roam South of the Border Down Mexico Way.

'They will build great cities of stone and they will call these cities New York, New York, Galveston and Memphis, Tennessee. Chicago, Chicago, Will be Their Kind of Town and they will go Way Down Yonder in New Orleans. They will put flowers in their hair and they will go to San Francisco. They will Leave Their Hearts in San Francisco and then they will cry out joyfully Viva Las Vegas. Some of them will say Kansas City, Kansas City Here I Come. Others will only be Twenty-Four Hours From Tulsa, yes, just One Day Away From Someone's Arms!'

Dream Man's eyes now open wide. He continues to prophesy, but now he speaks more rapidly. Dream Man speaks as if he knows that his time is running out.

'A mighty nation this America will become – and a warlike nation too! Geronimo they will cry and they will Remember the Alamo. Oh yes, they will cry out the name of some Apache and they will sing of Davy Crockett who will be the King of Their Wild Frontier. They will ask their god to Bless America, Their Home Sweet Home and In God They Will Trust, yet they will revere the Bald Eagle and some Stars and some Stripes and the Buck. They will sing a song called Fly Me to the Moon and this song will hold a special meaning for them. They will become one nation, one nation indivisible under God and this god will be called, I think, Uncle Sam ... That is all.'

Dream Man now falls silent and his eyes close. After a little while He-Who ... He who has a long name steps forward and places a hand on the old man's chest. He detects no movement.

'Dream Man dreams with the Great Spirit,' he says.

Sue falls to her knees and begins to wail.

Well, what sort of nonsense was that? An obviously fictitious tale, yet one seemingly without any moral guidance, one seemingly without any useful information, unless, unlike Dream Man, you, the reader, have not yet grown old, in which case you will not realise that, should you live so long, you will certainly one day become so old and so weary that you will no longer wish to live – yet you will not want to die!

Now, you can't have it both ways, can you?

There, I've given you something to look forward to. The joys of your old age. A wonderful time when your body will be ready to give up the ghost, but you yourself will not be ready! Yet death will be your only way out!

If I were capable of pity I would pity you people.

So, let me now tell you a nonsensical tale. And a bloody nonsensical tale it will be. Let me tell you the tale of the bloody first crusade.

*

Jerusalem. 1099 AD

Blood!

It seeps through the floor above him. It drips, it runs from the gaps between the wooden flooring. It runs onto him, it begins to gather around his feet and haunches as he crouches in terror in the low, confining space between the wooden floor and the floor of the cellar beneath.

146

Blood!

It is warm blood. In the darkness it seems to Hussein that the blood is not dissimilar to water, but it is warm. It grows deeper around the silently weeping eight-year-old's feet. It is not diluted by his tears. Above him now there is silence. The screaming and the pitiful moanings have ceased. Now there is only the sound of the pouring blood and the sounds of Hussein's own breathing along with the sound of the pounding of his heart.

Blood!

It is not Hussein's blood. No, it is the blood of his mother, his mother who frantically pushed him into the cellar only moments before the Christians came. It is the blood of the mother who spread herself over the entrance to the cellar in order to hide the entrance from the Christians. It is the blood of the mother who died where she had spread herself, but it is not her blood alone.

Blood!

It is the blood of Hussein's mother and it is the blood of Hussein's father. It is the blood of his brothers and it is the blood of his sisters. It is the blood of his uncles and the blood of his aunts. It is the blood of his people, it is the blood of Islam.

And it is the blood on the hands of my ally, the Pope!

Why?

Because four years previously, in 1095, the Pope called for Holy War. Holy War against Islam – or, at least, a part of Islam.

In 1095 my ally, the Pope, who called himself Urban the Second, issued an edict throughout Christendom urging that every man should lay aside his worldly ambitions and take up the cross of the Nazarene in order to remove the Seljuk Turks, the heathen, from the Holy City of Jerusalem. To those who would take up the cross, Urban the Second offered indulgences (an official licence to sin). Now, the edict of my Pope was received with the greatest enthusiasm throughout Europe and thus the first crusade came into being.

Mighty armies gathered across Europe. At first they were

147

disorganised and there was the usual squabbling, but eventually they got it together. The armies of Christendom marched towards Jerusalem, not neglecting to do the usual pillaging etc. as they marched.

Of course, in Jerusalem itself life went on as normal. In Jerusalem (the name means City of Peace) there were rumours of wars, but time passed by, nothing happened and the rumours were generally forgotten or ignored. (You people are especially good at ignoring what is unpleasant). So, in 1099, the majority of Jerusalem's inhabitants had little or no idea that the crusaders were coming – until they actually arrived.

Blood lust!

The sons of Christendom, girdled with their indulgences and convinced of the righteousness of their cause, are filled with a lust for blood, for the blood of Muslims.

Blood lust!

Jerusalem must be cleansed of the heathen.

Blood lust!

The streets and the houses of Jerusalem are running red with the blood of those who have, by their presence, profaned the Holy City.

Urban the Second died in the same year that Jerusalem fell to the crusaders. He was, of course, succeeded by another of my Popes. Jerusalem remained in Christian hands for almost ninety years, but then it was taken by Saladin and Islamic rule returned, prompting more crusades, largely unsuccessful crusades.

But, what of the boy?

What of Hussein?

Did he survive in 1099? Did the eight-year-old escape the blood-letting?

I will not tell you because it doesn't matter.

From your perspective these things happened over nine hundred years ago.

He's dead now!

*

Mona. 651 AD

For the ignorant among you, and that will be most of you, Mona is the old name for the Isle of Man. The Isle of What? I hear most of you say. The Isle of Man, an island situated about half way between England and Ireland, and about half way between North Wales and southern Scotland.

The Isle of Man, part of the United Kingdom of Great Britain and Northern Ireland, yet, at the same time, a place with its own parliament and a place that sports its own coat of arms.

Yes, the Isle of Man. But in the middle of the seventh century, when the island was very sparsely populated, it was called Mona.

Now, some questions for you.

Did Tim arrive in Mona in 651 AD having paddled from the coast of north-western England in a wicker boat?

Was Tim, perhaps for the first and only time in his long, long, evolutionary history, treated well by the people, by the people of Mona?

Was Tim regarded as a god on Mona?

Did the people bring him regular gifts of food and clothing?

Was the reverence Tim found on Mona the next best thing to the companionship he has never known?

Did Tim remain on Mona for many years – until my version of Christianity became firmly established whereupon Tim was driven out from the place where he was revered and eventually driven out from the island?

What do you think?

Well, there is a place in the Isle of Man called Tynwald Hill and Tynwald is the name of the island's parliament. Now, Tyn is simply a corruption of Tim and wald or wold is an old celtic word meaning wooded area. So, we have Tynwald Hill or Tim's Wold Hill – and many an old crone on the Isle of Man today will tell you the tale of the strange god-like creature who once

149

made his home in the west of the island where there still can be found a darkly wooded hill!

Do you believe me?

Or is this just another nonsensical tale?

Take a long hard look at the island's coat of arms. It depicts three legs complete with three feet! Nothing else. Just the three legs. It is said to represent the island's motto: 'Whichever way you throw me I will stand.' A motto that might well be applied to that great survivor, to that three-legged product of blind evolution, the Impossible Man, Tim.

*

Hell. 1882 & 1883 AD

Let me tell you something about hell, something you may not have considered. You will do well to understand. In my hell there is no concept of time! You arrive here and you will remain here for ever. Hell is for eternity and time doesn't matter in eternity.

What is hell?

I know that the other writer of this book will in a future chapter explain his version of hell. I know that he will claim that hell is the common grave of all mankind, a place where there is no consciousness, a figurative place where the dead are awaiting a future resurrection. I know he will claim these things and I know that his claims are false.

I know also that there are some among you who claim that hell is nothing more than eternal separation from God. What rubbish! What nonsense! There is no God!

I know exactly what hell is. And I ought to know! Is it not my home? Is it not the place where I spend much of my time, the place where I rule supreme? Let me describe to you my home, my hell.

My hell is a place, not of eternal punishment, but of eternal punishing, for the punishing never ceases! My hell is a place of fiery torment. My hell is a place inhabited by devils, by demons – and by the damned souls of you people! Yes, you! YOU!

150

Welcome to hell, my friends.

Welcome to eternity.

Let me set the scene for you so that you will know what to expect when you arrive.

Great and gloomy underworld caverns where no sun can ever shine, yet my world of flickering shadows is illuminated, if darkly so, by the unquenchable fires. Demons and devils of every rank roam to and fro, always eager to inflict great pain upon the souls of the dead, the damned, whose agonised screams fill my world. The damned are tormented without respite, for the dead can no longer find an escape from their torture in death. And the instruments of torture fill my world and my demons make full use of these implements. Can a damned soul have his head slowly severed a thousand times and feel the agonies of death a thousand times and yet never die? In my world he can. And he does! We then disembowel him a thousand times! And after this there is no respite for him! There will never be any respite for him! Our pleasure is derived from your eternal agonies. Welcome to hell! Welcome to eternity!

Now, let me tell you about a certain ... well, shall we say ... ally of mine who arrived here in hell in the year you call 1882 AD. His arrival proved to be a great, great shock to him, he having in his own mind determined that hell could not possibly exist. Charles Darwin, having expounded the theory of the natural selection of species and having proposed that apes and men were closely related, was perhaps as confident as any man could be that there is no hell. After all, how could a place like my hell be explained by evolutionary theory? Yes, Charles Darwin, whose evolutionary theories had changed, were changing and would continue to change the thinking of mankind, was absolutely convinced that hell could not exist ... until he arrived.

What a shock!

One moment he was on his deathbed, breathing his last, and the very next moment here he was in hell!

Unbelievable!

He looked at me speechlessly, for I had dressed according to tradition especially for him. (Close-fitting red body suit, horns and goatee beard, forked tail, trident etc.)

He then looked around him speechlessly, for my demons were busy as always and the screams of the afflicted were filling my caverns.

He looked at me again and then shuddered and fell to his knees as the fearsome Lord of Torment swooped towards him with a view to taking him immediately to his reward.

'Wait!' I commanded the Lord of Torment. 'I will speak with this one for a moment.'

I looked on dispassionately as Darwin, for some reason, perhaps it was habit, fumbled in his pockets, finally producing a note-pad and pencil.

'A new species!' he said to me, though his eyes were fixed on the hovering Lord of Torment. 'A new species!' he repeated, his eyes returning to me. 'Both that creature and yourself!'

With shaking hands he attempted to write in his notebook, but he seemed unable to make more than a scribble. He then dropped his pencil and I knew that the sweat that poured from his brow was not caused entirely by the heat from the fires. He looked up at me with an expression of disbelief on his face and I knew exactly what was going through his mind.

'No, Charles,' I said to him. 'No, no. You are not dreaming.'

His mouth came open as he shakily got up from his knees. He looked around him despairingly and muttered something about natural selection. An agonised scream from somewhere below filled the air and now the reality of the situation began to impress itself on Darwin, yet . . . yet he was still in denial.

'There is no hell!' he suddenly said to me. 'And you cannot exist! There is no hell and if there were, I would not be sent to such a place.'

I had to laugh.

'What did you expect?' I said to him. 'You alone are responsible for discrediting the account of creation! You have invalidated the book of Genesis and by so doing you have caused a

152

great many people to doubt the entire word of God!'

'There is no God!' he hissed at me.

'I know,' I told him calmly. 'But if there were, he certainly wouldn't want you!'

I turned to the hovering Lord of Torment. 'Take him!' I commanded.

I think it was when the Lord of Torment speared Darwin through his chest and carried him off that the man finally began to believe that he was indeed in hell. Certainly, if his belief did not spring from that moment, it would have sprung from the moment when he was thrust unceremoniously into the roasting furnace. Just before he entered the furnace, I heard his last coherent words. 'Where are our brothers, the apes?' he cried. After that only his screams could be heard in that particular corner of my domain.

He was still screaming in 1883 when Karl Heinrich Marx arrived.

As with all who arrive in this place, Karl Marx was at first unwilling to believe that he was in hell. He looked around him fearfully, as they all do, and then, as most do, Marx attempted to deny his arrival by inventing in his own mind a half-plausible explanation – anything but the truth – for what he was seeing and hearing and feeling. And Marx was seeing the torments of the damned. He was hearing their screams. He was feeling the heat from the fires – and he was feeling pure terror. So Marx told himself that someone had drugged him, someone had given him opium. Marx told himself that he was hallucinating.

The opium of the people?

When the Lord of Torment speared his belly and held him aloft, Marx knew that he had not been drugged. Marx knew that he was in hell.

But hell, my hell, was not to his liking.

He wanted to reorganise the place!

'What am I doing here?' he demanded of me in a scream as he hung from the spear.

'You are guilty of the theoretical abolition of God,' I told him.

'So what?' he cried, clutching his wound and attempting to stem the flow of blood and gore.

'You are also guilty of inspiring a future political system that will not be helpful to mankind,' I told him.

'How do you know?' he shouted back at me. 'If carried through correctly and efficiently my theories will help mankind – especially the workers. But, since I am no longer in the world of mankind, I shall have to apply my ideas to this infernal place.'

Again I had to laugh. Marx knew where he was, but he obviously didn't understand how hell worked. He was about to find out how hell worked and the discovery would not be pleasant for him, but he still had time to have another go at me!

'Are the people here organised into a workers' guild?' he yelled. 'Because if they're not they soon will be.'

I slowly shook my head and smiled at him. 'I think not,' I told him, and then I addressed the Lord of Torment. 'Let him burn at the stake until there remains upon the earth not one government that adheres to his political theories.'

The Lord of Torment bowed his head and, with Marx impaled upon his spear, hurried away to do my bidding. As you read these words today Karl Heinrich Marx is still burning at the stake.

So, Charles Darwin and Karl Marx. They were my servants upon the earth, if unwittingly so, for the one discredited creation and the other abolished God! I think it is only fitting that loyal servants should spend eternity with their master.

And what of you, yes you, the reader?

What will there be for you when you die if on earth you are my servant, unwittingly or otherwise?

Well, there is a red-hot welcome awaiting you here in hell.

There is an eternity of torment here for you.

Yes, an eternity! For ever and ever! Amen!

Do you think it is true that, as Dante put it, there is an inscription over the gates of hell?

ABANDON ALL HOPE YE WHO ENTER WITHIN.
I await your arrival.

Should anyone among you say that I am cruel let him or her be known as a hypocrite. Instruments of torture? You devised them. Spearings, beheadings, burnings at the stake? You people have done it all. Roasting furnaces? What about your nuclear bombs? How many were roasted to death in Hiroshima and in Nagasaki? And how many will yet be roasted to death in other places at a time from your perspective yet future?
Hypocrites!
If it were not for the fact that you people are subject to death, if it were not for the release of death, you would inflict eternal torment on each other.
Yes, you would.
Hypocrites!
I am cruel.
But so are you!

*

England. 1348 AD

It is the summer of 1348 and Edward III is King of England. Edward III, however, is not content to be King of England alone. No, Edward III, having already attempted to force his sovereignty on Scotland, has now decided to claim the throne of France. The Hundred Years' War has begun and Edward III is proving to have the advantage over the French. He has, so far, gained two significant naval victories and on land he has proved victorious at Crécy. In addition, he has recently captured Calais and consequently trade between the former French territories and England is booming. It is from the ships that come from France that we are now launching our invasion of England.

155

We are a vast army. We are an army of uncountable battalions. Whereas the population of England numbers some four million, we, the invaders, are numbered in the billions! And we have the capacity to vastly increase our numbers overnight! The English do not know that we are coming. The English cannot detect our presence. They have little or no protection against us. Surely we will slaughter them in their millions!

We travel with the flea of the black rat and with the fleas of other rats. We do not harm the flea, nor do we kill the rat. Yet, when the flea bites into human flesh then we invade the human body and we bring death. We are the bringers of death and our conquest in this land will be aided by the poor hygienic practices and the insanitary living conditions of the filthy English, the English who do not properly wash themselves, the English who live alongside their own stinking sewage. When we invade the body we swiftly attack and destroy the immune system of our host. Only a very tiny minority of the infected will be strong enough to survive. For the vast majority the outcome will be death, death by overwhelming infection, death without compassion and without discrimination, death within days, sometimes within hours.

We are Bacillus Pestis. We are the pestilence. We are Bubonic Plague. We are the Black Death.

She is seventeen.

She is young and she is very beautiful. She has the body of Venus and the sort of face that men will die for. Her hair is long and dark, her eyes gleam with the spark of youthfulness and she, the daughter of a wealthy merchant, has, as they say, everything to live for. Yet she has only a short time left to her, for she has been bitten by the flea of the black rat and she has become infected.

It is early evening and she is looking out from the window of the drawing-room. In the distance she can see

156

the sea and here and there a sail or two. Soon the sun will set behind the western waters of the English Channel and soon it will be time for supper. Strangely, the thought of supper does not inspire her today. In fact, she is finding the thought of supper a little nauseating.

An hour passes, the shadows are lengthening, and now she is feeling distinctly ill. She has developed a headache – and such a headache. Never has she had so severe a headache. She calls out for her mother and her father.

Another hour passes, night has fallen, and now she has a fever. She complains of chills and of aching limbs. Her worried mother and father manage to get her to her bedroom where they undress her and put her in her bed. Both her mother and her father are telling themselves that their daughter has no more than the beginnings of a severe cold, they cannot possibly imagine nor can they contemplate the horror of the truth.

In the morning she is worse, much worse, and the doctor is sent for. When he arrives she is drifting in and out of consciousness and the fever is raging. The doctor notices thickened saliva and, when he examines her, he is shocked to see painful-looking black swellings all over her body, especially around the groin and the armpits. The doctor has seen nothing like it. He does not know what to do.

He advises her parents to bathe her in her bed with cold water to counter the fever. He recommends that they should try to get her to drink, even though she has now apparently lapsed into a state of deep unconsciousness. The doctor tries to awaken her. It is a merciful thing that he is unable to do so. He takes his leave after promising to return the following day.

And the following day, when he returns, she is worse. She is deeply unconscious, the fever has not abated, the black swellings have become larger and more plentiful,

157

and her breathing has become extremely laboured. There is nothing the doctor can do for her.

Towards the end of the night, less than two and a half days after the initial onset of symptoms, she is dead.

Along with her death die her dreams and the dreams of her distraught parents. She will not know the joys and excitement of courtship. She will not love as a woman loves a man. She will not marry. She will not bear children. All of these things have been taken away. Her dreams destroyed so cruelly and so swiftly. She is dead.

She is one of the first to die and she will be buried in the churchyard, but only because no one yet knows that she has died from the plague. Later victims will be buried in plague-pits, far from churchyards. These later victims will all be thrown into the pits together and many will be burned in an attempt to destroy infection before the earth is piled on top of them. Such will be the fear of the plague. Such will be the necessity to deal with the great number of dead.

Alas for England! Alas for the merchant's daughter! An English rose cruelly cut off at the moment of first bloom.

We are Bacillus Pestis. We are the Black Death. We are exterminating between one-third and one-half of the human population of Asia and Europe. In England we will be thought of as the curse of God, as God's vengeance upon the wicked, even though we will not discriminate in favour of priests and bishops! In England in the middle of the fourteenth century we shall kill both rich and poor, both young and old, both the pious and the not-so-pious. In England we shall continue to break out and infect the population now and then and here and there for the next three hundred and more years. In 1665 AD we shall kill thousands upon thousands in London alone. Yet after that we shall disappear for a while.

Yes, after that we will retreat into our hiding place, but we will not be utterly defeated. Our armies will march again, even in times yet future, even in times when mankind has developed the antibiotics, which will, for a while, be capable of holding us.

We will not be utterly defeated, not in this world, yet … this world is passing away and there is another world to come!

And, according to the word of God, when that world is established upon the earth then 'no resident will say "I am sick".' – Isaiah 33: 24

What will become of Bacillus Pestis then?

Will we exist as something benign to humanity, or will we forever be wiped off the face of the earth?

What will become of us then?

*

The Moon. 20th July 1969 AD

Was it the first man to set foot on the moon or was it the second? Was it Neil Armstrong or was it Edwin 'Buzz' Aldrin? Which of them went behind a large rock, out of the view of the camera, and got the shock of his life?

Yes, the shock of his life! And this for a man who had only recently felt the exhilaration of travelling in a crude tin can some quarter of a million miles through the hostile environment of space! What a shock it must have been for a man who had boldly gone where no man had gone before, for a man who had just taken both a small step and a giant leap onto the surface of the moon!

What do you think this man saw when he ventured behind the rock?

Tim?

No, it wasn't Tim.

It was I! Me! The Devil himself!

159

What a shock!

There I was, sitting on a stone, dressed in my best, complete with trident!

If anyone could have seen that astronaut's face behind his visor it would have been a picture.

I let him gaze upon me for a full twenty seconds before I disappeared from his view. I even gave him a wave as I was going.

He has never publicly mentioned his sighting of me, though rumours abound. The people at NASA have put the incident down to his imagination. Well, what else can they do? He, however, is far from convinced that what he saw was a product of his imagination. Would you be?

I will not tell you who it was who went behind the rock. Just because I want to be awkward I will not say whether it was Armstrong or Aldrin. It doesn't matter anyway.

*

The Truly Horrific International Combatant and Killing Operative (THICKO). 1939–45 AD. Plus Schicklgruber and Friends.

To say that the Second World War was entirely caused by people such as Schicklgruber, Mussolini and Hirohito along with their generals is to do us a great injustice. Schicklgruber (Hitler), Mussolini and Hirohito did not instigate the acts of aggression committed by Germany, Italy and Japan prior to 1939 purely on their own initiatives. No! They had a little help from their friends. They had a little help from us!

Schicklgruber in particular consulted his astrologers on a regular basis. We encouraged the German occupation of the Sudetenland and the annexation of Austria. Yes, the Angel of Germany was in the ascendancy and he, having nurtured and guided Schicklgruber over many years, was ready to play war games, as were others among us.

We are not like you. We are not constrained by the need to find food, by the need to have clothing, by the need to have shelter. These are your needs, not ours. Unlike you, we do not desire riches, for riches provide for your needs and your desires and are of no value to we who are spirit. Yet, in your world, riches can also be a means of gaining influence and power and these are the things we do desire. We desire power. We desire fame. We desire glory.

And since we now have no glory in the heavens, we must seek our glory by influencing the affairs of men!

So, in your decade of the 1930s we were able to see that the conditions leading to a great war were falling into place. We were also able to see that your development of the atomic bomb was not too far away. We sensed the possibility of your utter annihilation from the face of the earth. We sensed the possibility of the extinction of mankind. Self-annihilation! Led by such as Schicklgruber, Mussolini, Hirohito – and us!

What a time it promised to be!

So, the Devil is claiming that World-War-Two was instigated by such as Hitler, Mussolini, Hirohito and the Devil himself along with his demons. Well, I will not dispute his claim, but someone has been omitted from this equation, someone without whom no war could be fought. Thicko has been omitted from the Devil's equation.

Who is Thicko?

Who really is the Truly Horrific International Combatant and Killing Operative?

I will describe Thicko. You will recognise Thicko.

THE ARMY WILL MAKE A MAN OF YOU!

Thicko is usually male, but he has been female on rare occasions in the past and he is female and will be female in times and in places where there is a leaning towards equal opportunities for women! Nevertheless, Thicko is usually male and he is usually aged between sixteen and

161

forty. This is because Thicko is physically at his peak between the ages of sixteen and forty, but he can be younger and he can be older depending upon his availability. You see, when Thicko is plentiful he is taken only at his peak. When Thicko is scarce, any Thicko will do!

YOUR COUNTRY NEEDS YOU!

Thicko is usually well trained. He gets what they call a basic training and then, unless he is urgently required on the battlefield, he will get some specialist training. One thing you can be sure of is that Thicko will be trained to use a weapon, whether that weapon be a sling-shot, a spear, a bow, a gun or a nuclear bomb.

YES SIR, YES SIR, THREE BAGS FULL, SIR!

Thicko will also be trained to obey orders and, in some cases, to give orders. Now, this is vital. Absolutely vital. Armies are run by chains of command. Wars cannot be won unless there is an efficient chain of command. Thicko must obey his orders without question, on every single occasion, no matter what those orders might be, and woe betide Thicko should he refuse to obey an order, for of him a warning example will surely be made!

To help Thicko to obey without question he will learn discipline. He will be told when to go to bed and when to get up. He will be told what to wear and how to make his bed. He will be told when to shave, when to eat and when to shit. He will be told a thousand other things so that he does not have to think for himself.

Yes, Thicko must obey his orders, which means that Thicko has surrendered his will to those above him in the chain of command.

JOIN THE NAVY AND SEE THE WORLD.

Thicko can be a volunteer, a conscript or a professional soldier, sailor or airman. If he is a professional he is likely to be higher in the chain of command than if he is a conscript. Conscripts get all the worst jobs. They are the ones who might be ordered to march (an unnatural way of walking) for weeks, for months or even years, while those higher up in the chain of command might ride on horse-back, or on camel-back, or ride in an automobile, or in an airplane or whatever. Thicko might indeed see much of the world, but if he is a conscript he is likely to see the world from a dog's eye point of view, for conscripts are dogsbodies.

JOIN THE ARMY AND LEARN A TRADE.

Conscripted or volunteer Thickos will usually be assigned to their various tasks by professional Thickos. All Thickos are warriors, but they are not all necessarily front-line warriors. Thickos can be cooks, they can be stretcher-bearers, they can be farriers, administrators, builders, engineers, navigators, pilots, radar or sonar operators, drivers. (My father was a driver during the Second World War.) Thickos can be general labourers, specialist weapons operatives, cleaners, sanitary engineers, doctors, nurses, or anything at all – even priests! They can be a mixture of all the above, but all Thickos are warriors. They are all trained to use a weapon.

UNCLE SAM WANTS YOU.

Thicko is the Universal Soldier. He is any nationality and every nationality. If any nation on earth does not breed Thickos, I do not know of that nation.

ALLAH AHKBAR!

Thicko is any religion and every religion – with the exception of those who take God's commandments seriously. Thicko does not hesitate to take the life of someone of his own religion if he is ordered to do so.

FOR GOD, ST GEORGE AND ENGLAND!

Or, for Ireland, or China, or Outer Mongolia, or somewhere or something else.

Thicko fights for a cause, whatever that cause might be.

At least he is told he is fighting for a cause and the cause is always just. Thicko is of any and of every political persuasion and he is also of no particular political persuasion. In fact, Thicko can usually be persuaded to believe anything at all.

In short, Thicko is an autocratic, democratic, socialistic, royalistic, communistic, nationalistic republican who hails from every nation and who does or does not profess a belief in some god or other.

And Thicko is a very dangerous animal! Thicko is a killer! Thicko has been prowling the world almost from the beginning of the world. Thicko was especially prominent between 1939 and 1945.

In 1939 Thicko, wearing a German uniform, was ordered to invade Czechoslovakia. There was some resistance from Thicko wearing a Czechoslovakian uniform, but not much.

Later in 1939 Thicko, again wearing a German uniform, was ordered to invade Poland. Here there was some stiffer resistance by Thicko wearing a Polish uniform, but the German Thicko, being superior in numbers and in weaponry, both in the air and on the ground, eventually crushed Polish resistance. However, the German invasion of Poland prompted both Britain and France to declare war on Germany and her allies. Within days the whole of the then British Empire had declared war on Germany and Thicko suddenly had new uniforms to sport. The German invasion of Poland also gave the Russians an excuse and an opportunity to regain lands lost to Poland in a previous war. Thicko, wearing the Russian uniform, was soon marching into the Ukraine and Beylorussia.

In 1939 Benito Mussolini, ruler of Italy, having already been encouraged by us to invade Ethiopia and to intervene in the

164

Spanish Civil War, and having successfully followed our encouragements, decided to consult us again. He consulted a spirit medium, a woman with whom he was also having sex.

He wanted to know if he should invade Albania.

We told him he should.

He did!

We knew then that it would not be long before Italy entered the war on the side of Germany.

Easily led was the proud Mussolini. A great believer in destiny was the strutting Mussolini.

In 1940 the German Thicko was busy invading Denmark, Norway, France, Belgium and Holland. Italy then entered the war and the Italian Thicko invaded Greece and attacked the British Thicko in North Africa. In the skies above Britain a battle was being fought between British and German Aircrew Thickos, while at sea German Submariner Thickos were hunting allied shipping.

In 1940, having at our prompting already begun an invasion of China, the Japanese leadership was looking to further expand its empire. They consulted their ancestors! At least, they thought they were consulting their ancestors.

We pointed them in the right direction. We caused them to understand very clearly that the threat to the Japanese Empire came from the British and American presence in the Far East and in the Pacific.

The Japanese leadership began to prepare for an expansive war.

In 1941 the German Thicko came to the aid of the Italian Thicko and invaded Yugoslavia and Greece as well as some Mediterranean islands. The German Thicko, with the aid of Thickos from Finland, Hungary and Romania, then attacked the Russian Thicko, driving poor Ivan deep into his own territory. In the same year, and again to bail out the Italian Thicko, the German Thicko marched into North Africa to attack the British Thicko. The war at sea continued, involving British, German and Italian Seafaring Thickos, then, also in 1941, the Japanese Thicko struck hard and unexpectedly at the American Thicko in Hawaii – Pearl Harbour. Japan declared war on Britain and America. Germany and Italy declared war on America.

The world at war.

And four more years of it to go!

And even after all the carnage, wars will not cease!

I could go on with a brief history of World-War-Two, but I won't. It is a matter of fact that in the end Germany, Italy, Japan and their allies were utterly defeated. Adolf Hitler reportedly committed suicide in his bunker in Berlin. Benito Mussolini was killed by Italian partisans and his body strung up for public viewing. Hirohito, as Emperor-God, was expediently spared his life, but many of his generals and government officials were executed. Thicko, of course, did not and does not go away. Neither do the demons.

Hitler consulted us throughout the course of the war. In fact, he rarely made a major decision without seeking guidance from his astrologers. In 1941, when faced with the decision whether to attack Russia or invade Britain, we steered him towards Russia. It was not a wise decision for Germany and the Angel of Germany was not pleased to be overruled by me, but our overall strategy at the time was to broaden the scope of the war.

In 1944, when it was becoming increasingly obvious that Germany could not win the war, we encouraged Hitler to soldier on to the end. He had placed his hope in German rocket technology and in his scientists' drive to be the first to develop the atomic bomb. Had Hitler's scientists won that race the war in Europe would have had a very different conclusion. London would certainly have gone the way of Hiroshima and Nagasaki.

What a pity that the German scientists did not win that race!

British cities burning like the sun in 1945! Perhaps even American cities! Berlin incinerated in retaliation?

Well, Berlin was almost incinerated anyway. By helping to prolong the war we managed to cause yet more death and destruction.

But might Europe have seen a nuclear exchange in 1945? We will never know. Yet everything comes to he who waits. As you read these words I am waiting.

*

The time for which Satan is waiting will arrive and it will arrive suddenly and probably sooner than you think. World-War-Three is around the corner and it is likely that it will involve at least a limited nuclear exchange. Millions will die. And whom do you think will be pressing the buttons that will condemn those millions to death? Whom do you think will be carrying out the orders from above, the orders from their political masters, the orders that will not only bring instant death on an unimaginable scale, but which will also inflict a slower death on many millions, death caused by injury, by disease, by radiation poisoning? Whom do you think it will be?

Thicko!

Yes, the Truly Horrific International Combatant and Killing Operative.

He will be the one to launch the missiles. He will be the one to detonate the bombs. He will be the one to bring death and he will do this without question because that is what he always does!

Thicko bears a heavy responsibility before God.

Having surrendered his free will to those who would control him, he cannot say in his defence that he is merely following orders. Even if he is a conscript, he cannot justify himself, for he has had the opportunity to resist his conscription, even if such a course would have brought persecution down upon his head.

Thicko has either chosen to be who he is, or he has allowed others to make him into what he is. In this respect Thicko has no excuse.

We are all responsible for our own actions.

Yet circumstances are different.

War has turned many a decent man into something less decent.

There is a difference between the man who glories in war and the man who has lacked the strength to resist those who would impose their will upon him.

Nevertheless, it is God who will judge!

And now a final word on Thicko.

What sort of person is he who does not realise when he first becomes a Thicko, or even before he becomes a Thicko, that he not only is likely to pose a deadly threat to others, but that he is also likely to place himself in deadly danger? Soldiers kill each other! Does he not know this? And what sort of person is he, or she, who imagines that he or she can somehow contribute to a lasting peace by waging war? What sort of person is he who violently takes the life of another and imagines that his actions are justified?

Thicko!

Son of Cain!

Son of Satan!

Thicko, you require a change of heart.

You need guidance from above and I do not refer to your chain of command.

He who lives by the sword will die by it! And there is a sword of retribution coming upon this earth!

Thicko, be courageous and strong.

Put away your sword.
Thicko.

*

New Mexico, USA. 1954 AD

Once upon a time in a faraway land called America there lived a beautiful young maiden whose name was Piper Parker. Piper Parker lived with her father and her mother in a tiny log cabin, which was situated on the edge of a vast forest, quite some distance from the nearest town.

The forest was said to be haunted.

The forest was said to be bewitched and there was not a family living on the edge of the forest that did not have a strange tale to tell, tales of bright lights in the skies above the forest, tales of strange noises issuing from the depths of the dark and sinister woods. It was commonly believed that a strange and inhuman creature lurked in the forest, a creature who would mercilessly gobble up anyone who might happen to stray into his domain.

'You must never go into the forest,' Piper Parker's mother had often said to her. 'One young girl once did go into the forest. She was never seen or heard of again.'

Now, Piper Parker was a good and obedient daughter. She always listened carefully to what her father and mother said to her. But, no one is perfect, and one day Piper Parker did go into the forest.

It happened one evening when Piper was on her way home after visiting one of her friends who lived about a mile away from the log cabin. Piper had stayed at her friend's house a little longer than she ought to have and she was late. As she hurried around the edge of the forest she could see that the sun had almost set. She knew that if darkness were to fall before she got home her mother

169

and father would worry. It was then that she noticed the path going off into the woods, the path that might well offer a short-cut to the log cabin, the path that would surely take her quickly home, the path that beckoned her.

'Come my way,' it seemed to say to her. 'Come my way and you will have no need to go around the edge of the forest. Come my way and you will be home in no time at all.'

In an instant, forgetting all the warnings her mother had given her, Piper Parker was on the path and running through the woods.

At first the path was clear and broad and Piper Parker hurried along it, expecting that at any moment she would be out of the woods and close to her home. But darkness was rapidly falling and the path was getting narrower. The trees, the bushes and the undergrowth seemed to be pressing in on Piper Parker and the density of this vegetation was adding to the gloom. Suddenly, and to Piper Parker's absolute horror, the path came to an abrupt end. Suddenly there was no way forward. With the fear of the unknown beginning to crawl down her spine, Piper Parker decided to go back.

She turned, but, before she had taken more than a dozen faltering steps, the last vestiges of light faded from the forest. Night had fallen! Not only could Piper Parker no longer see the path, she could no longer see what was in front of her nose. She stumbled blindly on for a little while, but all she succeeded in doing was to stray far away from the path and to scratch her hands, face and legs on the thickets.

Piper Parker sat on the ground and wept. Why had she been so foolish? Why had she not remembered that her mother had told her NEVER to go into the forest?

In the deep darkness did Piper Parker imagine that she saw lights in the sky, moving lights above the canopy of the trees? Mingled with the sound of her sobbing, did

170

Piper Parker imagine that she heard strange noises, the sounds of low hummings, of rustlings not too far away, of heavy breathing other than her own?

The following morning in the small town of Santa Rosa the local sheriff received a frantic phone call from a Mr George Parker.

'Well, it seems we have a missing person,' the sheriff said to his deputy after he had managed to get George Parker to hang up. 'A Piper Parker. Fourteen years old. Didn't come home last night.'

'Where's she from?' asked the deputy.

'Down by the Delarosa woods.'

The deputy and the sheriff exchanged glances.

'Down by the government facility,' said the deputy with a knowing nod of his head.

'Yeah. Right.'

'So, what do we do?'

'We wait and see if she turns up,' said the sheriff.

'And if she doesn't?'

'We'll give her twenty-four hours,' said the sheriff. 'If she hasn't shown by then we'll organise a search of the area around the woods.'

'And if we don't find her?'

The sheriff shrugged. 'We'll have to search the woods. You'd better notify the FBI. We'll need their say so.'

Three days later, while a search of the woods was in progress, Piper Parker turned up. She was found on the edge of the forest by a neighbour. She was dishevelled and frightened and confused. She was mumbling something about a strange and horrible creature. She called it a cyclops.

Two days after this, the Parkers received a visit from several government agents. They wanted to know what

171

Piper had seen during the period she had been missing. Piper was unable to remember anything at all. She could not even remember being found by the neighbour.

'We'd like to have your daughter admitted to a hospital,' said one of the agents to George Parker.

'How's that?' asked George. 'She seems to be OK now.'

'I'm sure she is OK,' said the agent. 'But we need to know exactly what happened to her out there. When she was found she mentioned something about a creature, a cyclops? Mr Parker, there could be a maniac at loose in the vicinity. We need to know what happened to her.'

'But she doesn't remember anything!'

The agent nodded. 'Mr Parker, there's a technique we can employ called hypnotic regression. It's perfectly safe. We put your daughter into an hypnotic trance and we take her back in time to the hours when she was missing. She ought to be able to tell us what happened. When we bring her out of the hypnosis she won't remember a thing. She'll be no different to how she is now.'

George Parker hesitated. 'I don't know,' he said. 'I'm not so sure.'

'It's a tried and tested procedure,' insisted the agent. 'Its perfectly safe.'

After some further moments of hesitation George Parker slowly nodded his head.

This is what Piper Parker reported under hypnosis.

'It's dark. I'm in the woods. I'm frightened! I wish I wasn't in the woods but I don't know how to get out. I'm cold. I've been crying. I have scratches on my arms and legs and on my face. But I can't see them. I can't see anything. It's too dark. I'm frightened!

'Wait! I think I see a light. Yes! There's a light in the sky. I'm sure there is. I'm frightened! I can hear noises. I think there's someone out there in the darkness. I'm crying! I can't stop myself. I'm frightened!

'Oh! Such a bright light. It's blinding me! It's blinding me! And there's something in the sky above the light! It's making a low humming sound. No! No! The light is drawing me up. It's taking me up! No! Please! No!

'I'm lying on my back. I can't move. Everything I can see is bright. Everything is so bright! There's someone there! There's someone looking down at me. I want to scream but I can't make a sound! I can't move! He's horrible! He's horrible! He's only got one eye. It's in the middle of his head. He's a cyclops! Help me!

'Someone is touching me. It must be the cyclops. I don't like it! I don't like it. He's put something inside of me. Between my legs! I don't like it. Make him stop! Make him stop!

'I'm at the edge of the forest now. I don't know what I'm doing here. Why am I scratched all over? Why am I so dirty? I can't remember. I don't remember ...'

A subsequent physical examination failed to establish whether Piper Parker had been sexually assaulted.

This is what Piper Parker actually experienced.

In the darkness of the woods she was not merely frightened, she was terrified. Unable to see, unable to escape from the woods, her imagination was running wild. Yet she did see lights in the sky and she did hear low humming noises. The lights and the noises were actually coming from the government facility deep in the woods. The other noises that Piper Parker heard were sounds made by nocturnal animals. About an hour before dawn Piper Parker fell into a troubled sleep.

When she awoke it was almost noon and the sun was high in the sky. When she opened her eyes the first thing that she saw was the blinding sun, shining down upon her through a gap in the tree canopy. In a panic she got to her feet and began to run blindly. She fell and rolled over onto her back. When she looked up once more her eyes fell upon a startled and anxious Tim!

She did not notice that Tim has three legs, for she did not look at Tim's legs. She did not notice that Tim has no eyes in his head, for she did not clearly see his head. She did notice the single eye, for Tim was holding his elbow in front of his face so that he could look down on Piper Parker.

Cyclops!

Piper Parker fainted.

Tim did not sexually assault Piper Parker. There wouldn't have been much point. Tim has no sexual organs! He has no sexual desires!

Tim looked after Piper Parker. He treated her scratches with an antiseptic bark. He made her comfortable, he left water for her to drink and wild fruits for her to eat. When she regained consciousness Tim kept out of sight to avoid causing her further distress. But he kept a watchful eye on her. Yes, just the one!

By the third day Piper Parker was well enough to leave the woods. Tim was not to know that her mind was in a state of utter confusion. Tim had opened up the way for her leaving by clearing the undergrowth so that she could make her way back to the path by which she had originally entered the forest.

Tim was sorry to see her go.

So why, when under hypnosis, did Piper Parker give the distinct impression that she had been abducted by aliens?

Well, it was because, while she was under hypnosis, we put those impressions into her mind.

We can put all kinds of things into a person's mind when that mind is a blank sheet. And no one, neither hypnotist, nor subject, nor onlookers has the slightest inkling of what we are up to!

Oh we love hypnosis. How we love hypnosis. Along with near-death experiences and psychic messaging, hypnosis is one of our foremost tools for deceiving you people, especially when it is used in regression – so-called regression!

Abduction by aliens is very popular at the moment. It was just beginning to become popular in 1954. There are some of you out

174

there right now who are convinced that you have holidayed on Venus! There are some of you who have visited the moons of Saturn, the underground caverns of Mars, the outer reaches of your solar system and beyond! It's all good fun.

Reincarnation is very popular too. And not just among Hindus! Under hypnotic regression some of you have remembered past lives! There are thousands of people out there who are convinced that they have lived before! And some of you think you have lived many times before! We have even supplied you people with convincing details about your past lives. It isn't difficult. We can remember times past. We were there!

In France there is a man who is convinced that he was once Napoleon Bonaparte. Under hypnotic regression we had him sprout all manner of details about Bonaparte – details he himself could not possibly have known – some of the details verifiable. No wonder he believes he was Bonaparte! No wonder those who regressed him and those who witnessed the regression believe in reincarnation!

Also in France there is a woman who thinks she was Joan of Arc and thirteen men who believe they were once Louis XVI! In Russia we have the reincarnation of Rasputin and several reincarnations of the last Tsar, Nicholas II! In England, St George has reappeared, as well as Oliver Cromwell and Henry VIII, and all over the world there are those who believe in all sincerity that they were once Jesus Christ! I could go on.

But why, I hear you ask? Why go to all this trouble?

I will tell you. And I will in this case tell you the truth. I know that you won't believe me because you won't want to believe me, so I will tell you the truth.

Why did we not let Piper Parker speak about Tim, about the cyclops, or the goblin, or the boggart, or whatever she thought she had encountered in those woods? Why did we have her change her story into one of alien abduction? Why?

Because otherwise no one would have believed her!

In America in 1954 the age of goblins and such things had

175

long passed. No one believed in fairies any more. But they believed in aliens. They still do believe in aliens.

Do you believe in aliens?

You don't believe in a living God. And I can't blame you because there is no God. You don't believe in angels and demons, because they went out of fashion when God went out of fashion. You don't even believe in me! And you don't believe in fairies any more. No more fairy stories! You are far too advanced for that sort of thing.

But you have to believe in something.

You believe in yourselves. Despite the fact that you cannot save yourselves from death, you believe in yourselves. You believe in the evolution of species. You believe in Charles Darwin. (Is he burning in hell?) You believe in blind chance.

And there are billions of suns out there in the universe. There must be billions of planets revolving around them. Isn't it logical then, since there is no creator and no creation, that life must have evolved somewhere else in the vastness of the universe? Especially given all the time that ever there was? Of course it's logical! Alien races must exist out there! And some of them are surely far enough advanced technologically to be capable of visiting the earth. You believe in aliens!

And if aliens exist then they must have evolved in much the same way that you evolved. If aliens exist there can be no God. (Unless he has created them, but he hasn't because he doesn't exist. And if he were to exist why should he create them? Wouldn't he have enough to put up with having created you lot?)

You believe in aliens. You believe in the immortality of the soul and you believe in such things as reincarnation. You believe in super-evolved aliens therefore you cannot believe in the creation of man. You cannot believe the word of God. You have no time for such nonsense.

And that suits me!

And that is why Piper Parker, under the influence of hypnosis, under my influence, reported an alien abduction.

But, you don't believe me, do you?
I tell you the truth and you don't believe me.
Well, that's fine.
Incidentally, Piper Parker recovered from her ordeal and lived happily ever after.
Until she grew old and died!

*

Lancashire, England. 31st December 1999 AD

All over the world it is New Year's Eve, even in places like China and Israel where the official eve of the new year has never fallen on December 31st.

All over the world it is New Year's Day, but more than this, all over the world it is also the eve of the new millennium, the eve of the third millennium of the so-called Christian era, though Jesus Christ was not born in December of the year zero!

All over the world it is New Year's Eve, and all over the world men and women will celebrate the dawning of the new millennium. And all over the world people cannot accurately count, for, even if Christ had been born in December of the year zero, two thousand years will not pass until 1st January 2001! The world will celebrate numbers rather than reality.

But who cares?

In Lancashire, in the village of Brinscall where William Brooke lives alone, the sign outside the local Methodist church reads 'The Millennium is Christ's Two Thousandth Birthday' and the vast majority of people are taking it as gospel. But not William Brooke. It may be celebration time for the world, but, as the clock ticks towards midnight, William Brooke is in no mood to celebrate.

William Brooke is alone. His wife is dead, his grown-up daughter has moved some three hundred miles to the city of Plymouth and his grown-up son is somewhere in America. They keep in touch by telephone, they do not forget him, but William Brooke is essentially alone. His old friends have grown distant from him, acquaintances have other people to spend time with, especially on this particular evening, and William Brooke's neighbours rarely disturb him. He sits alone in his home as the clock approaches midnight.

To all outside appearances, if anyone actually cares, William Brooke is entirely alone. To outside appearances William Brooke is perhaps to be pitied. He is a man in his mid-fifties whose best years are behind him. He is a man whose future will surely consist of steadily advancing old age, which will bring with it a multiplicity of minor ailments and, in the end, at least one major illness – the one that will kill him! In all probability William Brooke will spend his last years in relative poverty. It is a distinct possibility that he will spend many of his final years vegetating in a retirement home, or even, should his health fail, in a nursing home. He might even spend his final days in a hospice. And he will surely die all alone. Or will he?

To all appearances William Brooke is alone. Yet in reality he is not alone, for God is with him.

William Brooke will not celebrate the arrival of the new millennium because he feels that this present world cannot offer him anything good and lasting, anything worthy of celebration.

Instead, William Brooke has placed his hope in God's promise of a new world to come, a world where mourning and outcry and pain will be no more, a world where even death will be swallowed up forever. These promises are the things that William Brooke considers to be good. These promises are the things that are lasting. These promises are the things worthy of celebration.

William Brooke has chosen to place his hope in God, but he has only taken the first few steps along what will surely be a long and difficult path. Along that path there are bound to be setbacks, along that path there will be difficulties and heartaches, but along that path there will also be joys and encouragement, the encouragement of those who have also chosen to tread the same path. William Brooke knows that at the end of the path there is the prize of the life everlasting, but he must stick to the path. Even if he should stumble, even if he should stumble many times, he must stick to the path.

Midnight!

And at the stroke of it the sounds of exploding fireworks and cheering can be heard. William Brooke goes to his door and looks out. He can see the celebrations, he can hear the celebrations, he can even smell the celebrations, the smell of spent powder. He stifles a yawn. He has grown tired.

A little while later he is climbing the stairs to his bed. He does not yet fully realise that by placing his hope in God he has at the same time brought himself to the attention of the Devil.

He has made himself an enemy of Satan!

William Brooke climbs the stairs alone. Yet he is not alone.

Yes, the man William Brooke has made himself my enemy by choosing to resist me and therefore I will persecute him. Though God is with him, I will persecute him in every and any way I can.

Perhaps I will be able to have him killed, or, if not, then perhaps I can have his family killed, as I had the family of Job killed, as I had the righteous Abel killed. When, in its own time, the nuclear holocaust arrives upon you people, perhaps then I will have William Brooke's children and grandchildren killed! We shall see.

179

But enough for now of William Brooke.

You have seen how I and my demons have influenced the affairs of you people in times past. See now how our influence has shaped your modern world. See now how our influence has shaped my modern world. Yes, my world! Be in no doubt. I am the god of this world!

And I am the Lord of Misrule.

Welcome to your present!

6

Now

For those who still doubt that this world is indeed my world, let me ask you a simple question. Are you happy? Whoever you are, wherever you might live in my world, are you happy?

Are you satisfied with the way things are for you? Did you awaken with a smile on your face this morning? Is life pleasant and thoroughly enjoyable? Do you look forward to the future?

If you have answered yes to any of the above you are either childlike, or an imbecile, or a liar!

Unless of course you are one of the few, one of the few like William Brooke, one who, though unavoidably living in my world, has managed to separate himself or herself from my ways.

Yet, the vast majority of you cannot do this! You are in my world, you were born into my world, and, difficult as life may be for you, you have no desire to leave my world, have you?

Here you are and here you will stay – until you die! You are a part of my world and you make your own contribution to my world. For as long as my world shall endure, you and your offspring will remain under my yoke!

My yoke is not kindly!

*

A Week in the Life of Joe Bloggs

Well, here we are. We have arrived in the here and now. We have arrived in the present time.

And in our time that old whore Babylon the Great, identified as the sum total of Satan's earthly religions, still reigns supreme, if a little more supremely in some parts of the earth than in others. This whore sits as a queen on the throne of the earth and, as yet, there is no one making her tremble. All over the world, in her differing guises, she influences the political elements of Satan's rulership. This whore claims to represent the Almighty, yet she is full of uncleanliness and she commits fornication with the kings of the earth! She rides the political beast, she is drunk with the blood of the innocent, and because of these things she has been judged by God and her future destruction is assured. Nevertheless, in our time, Great Babylon rules.

So, how is the average person affected by this? How is Joe Bloggs affected? How does Great Babylon in conjunction with the various political systems and also in conjunction with the spirit of wickedness so prevalent in our times affect Joe Bloggs?

Now, Joe Bloggs can be anybody and everybody. Joe Bloggs can be male or female, he can be rich or poor, he can live anywhere on the planet, he can be a man of any race, creed or colour. Joe Bloggs can be you!

Yet, in this particular piece of writing, Joe Bloggs shall be an Englishman – and this is a week of his life.

Sunday. 2.15 a.m.

'Whaaaaaaaa!' The screams of two-year-old Ella resonate in the darkness. 'Whaaaaaaaa! Mummy! ... MUMMY!' The screams invade Joe's brain and bring an abrupt end to his dream. He lies unmoving in the bed and tries to return to his dream, even though the dream was unpleasant, even though within the dream Joe was at work yet unable, due to factors beyond his control, to actually get any work done. Frustrating! Yet better than reality?

'Whaaaaaaaa!' He feels his wife stirring and he senses that she is getting out of bed. Joanne will see to Ella. Joe goes instantly back to sleep.

'Joe! Wake up!' Ten minutes have passed but to Joe it seems like two seconds and now his wife is telling him to get out of bed. Shit! 'Ella's got toothache,' he hears Joanne say to him. 'And Billy's awake. I need you to see to them while I find some painkillers.'

Half-asleep yet conscious now of his alcohol-induced headache, Joe hears his wife go out of the bedroom and go downstairs. He hears whimpering coming from the children's bedroom and then he hears a bang followed by another bang and followed by yet another bang. He climbs out of bed with his eyes still shut. His wife has switched on the light and the brightness is burning into Joe's brain, even through his closed eyelids. He opens his eyes and looks at the clock on the dressing-table. 2.28. Hell fire! Isn't Sunday supposed to be a day of rest? Hell fire!

With his eyes half-closed, Joe takes his headache into the children's bedroom. Ella is whimpering in her bed while Billy has abandoned his bed, turned on the television and decided to hit the screen with his Action Man. Joe takes the toy away from him and puts the four-year-old back in his bed. Joe hardly notices that the early-morning news is reporting yet another suicide bombing in the Middle East. Phrases such as 'Muslim Extremists' and 'Retaliation' and 'War on Terror' go into Joe's aching head by one ear and immediately leave by the other. All he wants is to go back to bed. He switches off the television. Joanne is coming back up the stairs.

It is 2.42 by the clock and Joe and Joanne are climbing back into bed. The children have both gone back to sleep. Amazing!

'I think she has a bad tooth,' says Joanne, referring to Ella. 'She shouldn't have bad teeth at her age. She's eating too many sweets.'

Joe grunts.

'We'll have to take her to the dentist,' says Joanne, meaning that Joe will probably have to take her to the dentist.

Joe grunts.

Joanne gets the distinct impression that her husband is in no mood for conversation. 'Good night,' she says to him.

In response Joe begins to snore. His mind has returned him to the land of dreams and he is back at work. But in his dreams Joe is unable to get any work done because he can't get into the office. The door is locked, he doesn't have a key and, although his colleagues are all looking at him through an abnormally large window, no one will open the door to let him in! Weird! He is just about to bang loudly on the door when ...

'Whaaaaaaaa! ... Whaaaaaaaa!'

Joe no longer needs to get into his office.

Hell fire! Hell bloody fire!

Sunday. 8.30 a.m.

Joe sits at the breakfast table having brought the remnants of his headache downstairs with him. The nagging aching inside his skull does nothing to improve his mood, neither does the bedlam surrounding him. Billy is refusing to remain in his chair. Despite inducements and/or threats, he is continually getting down from his chair to run around the room before being forcibly brought back to his chair again. And again and again and again! And he never seems to stop shouting. Not even for a moment. Ella, on the other hand, is glued to her chair.

The toothache seems to have departed with the night and she is celebrating the fact by spreading her breakfast cereal all over the table and all over herself. Joanne, meanwhile, is hovering. 'Billy, come and sit down! Ella, try to eat properly! Joe, have some more coffee and toast. You can't be standing on that cold football field without something warm inside you!'

The football field! Joe's inward groan is etched on his face.

Why the bloody hell does a primary school teacher – Billy's primary school teacher – a teacher of four and five-year-olds – want to form a football team? And why the bloody hell does the team have to play on a Sunday morning? Stupid! Bloody stupid!

'Don't forget the children and I are at church this afternoon,' Joanne says to Joe as if it were at all possible for Joe to forget. Well, at least he didn't have to go with her. 'I do wish you'd come with us sometime,' Joanne adds.

Joe says nothing. He is not going to church. He has no intention ever of going to church, because if Joanne, Billy and Ella are in church, then peace for Joe is somewhere other than in church.

'BILLY! SIT DOWN AT THE TABLE!'

Joanne's scream, pitched at a level that would cause a saint to sin, only makes Billy run faster around the room.

Joe groans inwardly again. All he wants to do on a Sunday morning is to relax. He loves his wife and children dearly . . . but, bloody hell! Bloody hell!

He picks up his newspaper, ignoring Joanne's disapproving look. Why shouldn't he read at the table? Bad manners? At least he's not running around the room or throwing his food about!

'Child Killer Heard Voices!' screams the headline.

Joe ignores it and turns the page.

'Fears Over Nuclear Installations! Gay Vicars In Orgy!'

185

Joe turns to the back page.

'Blackburn Rovers 2, Manchester United 2.'

That's more like it. More interesting and less depressing.

As Joe reads the match report a vision of an orderly breakfast in a hotel with waiter service flashes briefly through his mind and it occurs to him with a mixture of sadness and resignation that breakfast at the Bloggs' and breakfast at Tiffany's are not quite the same thing.

A soggy lump of breakfast cereal suddenly splats upon Joe's cheek.

'BILLY! WILL YOU SIT DOWN!'

Effing, effing hell!

What is this? What does Joe Bloggs have to complain about? He has food in his belly, clothes on his back and he has his own home! Perhaps he should consider the unfortunates of this world who have insufficient food, who clothe themselves in rags, who live on the streets. He would not have to leave Lancashire to find them. There are druggies and alchies all over Lancashire. The county is filled with them! Such unfortunates!

So put a smile on your face, Joe Bloggs. Be happy!

Sunday. 11.13 a.m.

Joanne sets to work only thirty seconds after Joe and Billy leave the house to go to football. It is Joanne's intention to vacuum-clean every single floor in the house, but before she can even begin with this task she needs to put the house back into some sort of order, back into the order it had been in on the previous evening, back into how it was before the bedlam of the morning.

Fifteen minutes pass and Joanne has cleaned breakfast cereal from the floor, from the table and from Ella. She has washed the breakfast dishes and utensils and she has

186

put them all away in their proper places. She has put the children's toys back into their boxes and cupboards and she has been upstairs to sort out the bedrooms. All these things Joanne has done while seeing to the many needs of Ella – and now Joanne is ready to clean the floors. She makes herself a cup of coffee and she plugs in the vacuum cleaner. She is just about to switch on the cleaner when the doorbell rings.

She goes to the door with coffee in hand and with Ella holding on to her skirt. She opens the door wondering who on earth can be calling on a Sunday morning? Her eyes come to rest on a well-dressed man, a smart-looking woman and an immaculately brushed and scrubbed child, a boy of six or seven years. In the man's hand there is a briefcase, in the woman's hand there is a Bible, and in the child's hand there are magazines. In Joanne's heart there is a great sinking feeling.

Jehovah's Witnesses!

From past experience Joanne knows that she has three choices. She can argue the point with them, in which case they will still be on the doorstep when Joe and Billy come home. Or she can listen to what they have to say and pretend to agree with them, in which case they will be gone in about ten minutes. Or she can politely or other-wise tell them to get lost, in which case they should be gone pretty quickly. Joanne chooses the third option.

'I'm sorry, I don't have the time to speak to you,' she tells them firmly.

Jehovah's Witnesses do not turn and walk away.

'I'm very busy,' Joanne insists. 'Loads of things to do!'

Still Jehovah's Witnesses do not walk away.

'Well, we won't keep you,' says the well-dressed man. 'We're just visiting in the area this morning to discuss the topic of our latest magazine.'

The brushed and scrubbed child now shows Joanne the

front cover of the *Watchtower* magazine. 'Will There Ever be Peace on Earth?' is the question it poses.

'Do you think there'll ever be peace on earth?' the man asks.

Joanne does not answer. She resists being drawn into conversation. She has been here before.

'I really do have to go,' she insists and without further ceremony she shuts the door firmly in the faces of Jehovah's Witnesses.

Jehovah's Witnesses go next door.

Joanne switches on the vacuum cleaner and gets to work. Strange people those Witnesses! She didn't like being rude to them, but she was busy. She didn't have time for them. Anyway, what on earth possessed them to come knocking on people's doors. Were they trying to convert her? Well, not only did she not have the time to listen to them, she didn't want to be converted. She had her own religion. She was a Christian! Wasn't she? Yes, of course she was. She regularly went to church.

Well done!

Well done, Joanne Bloggs!

Well done, Mrs Average, wife of Mr Average, mother of average children! Well done!

And now it gives me great pleasure to present you with this information – I like it when people have neither the time nor the inclination to discuss what is written in the Bible. Well, if there happened to be a God, would I want you people to listen to his witnesses?

The man William Brooke has listened to them and by so doing he has made himself my enemy and I will persecute him. The fool!

So, what do you think? Are Jehovah's Witnesses the true witnesses of God? Or are they a part of my worldwide organisation of religions? Are they a part of Babylon the Great or not? Such confusion in the world! Such religious confusion!

188

It really doesn't matter what you think. As I have repeatedly told you, there is no God.

And you will do what you will do while you are able, while you have the time.

So, put a smile on your face, Joanne Bloggs. Ignorance is bliss! Eat, drink and be merry, Mrs Average, for tomorrow you die!

Sunday afternoon

The Bloggs' Sunday afternoon ritual begins with their visit to the local park. Rain or shine, it is always the short walk to the park – and today it is raining. Joe and Joanne stand in the rain and watch the children play in the rain. The children don't seem to mind the rain too much and Joanne is always enthusiastic whatever the weather, but Joe? Hell fire! Why do they always have to come to the park? Why? Why? He doesn't know!

Home again, home again and Joanne is busy getting herself and the children ready for church. Joe helps out in little ways. He puts Billy's shoes on for him, he wipes Ella's runny nose and changes her wet nappy. He tries to keep the children occupied while Joanne fixes her hair.

And then the great moment arrives!

Joanne and the children go out of the house and get into the car. Joanne secures the children in their seats, secures herself in the driver's seat, gives Joe a cheery wave and off they go.

Yes! Joe waves back to them through the living-room window. Yes! Two hours of peace! Yes!

Now, two hours of peace for Joe Bloggs is not two hours of inactivity for Joe Bloggs. Joe has plenty to do, but for the next two hours or so Joe will revel in the fact that there is no one to bother him. When he washes the lunchtime dishes he will not be distracted by squabbling children. When he is peeling the potatoes for the evening meal he will not be pestered by children wanting a drink and a biscuit. When he is trying to listen to the radio he will not have Joanne shouting for him from another part of the house.

Peace, oh perfect peace!

Joe goes into the kitchen and begins to wash the dishes. He switches on the radio to listen to the football. Bolton Wanderers are at home to Liverpool. Joe quickly discovers that Liverpool are winning by the single goal and that it is almost half-time. When the half-time whistle blows, Joe is expecting to hear the usual summary of the first-half's play, but today there is no summary. Instead there is a special news broadcast.

Two passenger jets have collided over the skies of south London. Over five hundred are feared dead as a direct result of the collision and it seems certain that many more, perhaps many hundreds, have perished or have been injured on the ground due to falling debris. Several areas of south London are on fire.

Joe thinks about this terrible news for several minutes as further details are aired over the radio. He genuinely feels a degree of sorrow for those who have died, for those who are injured and for all who are personally affected by the tragedy, but because he himself is not personally involved he is finding it difficult, almost impossible, to truly empathise with the victims. Eventually it is time for the second-half of the football and the radio programme is once again coming from the Reebok stadium on the outskirts of Bolton.

Bolton Wanderers equalise while Joe is chopping carrots. Yes! Joe wants Bolton to do well because they are the team he has drawn in the work's sweep. If Bolton score three goals today, no more and no less, then Joe stands to win fifty pounds. Come on Bolton!

190

Empathy? You people do not know how to empathise. And did you know that this seeming indifference to the sufferings of others has been studied by your experts, by your psychologists? And did you know that in order to explain this lack of genuine feeling these experts have come up with phrases such as 'bad news overkill', 'remote non-empathy' and 'indifferences due to perceived helplessness'?

I like your experts.

They really are brilliant when it comes to confusing matters.

But they do not confuse me.

You see, your lack of empathy can be explained by a single word. Yes, just one word.

SELFISHNESS!

If it doesn't affect you personally you don't care.

You are a selfish breed!

And I am the author of selfishness.

Sunday. 9.00 p.m.

There is relative calm in the Bloggs' household. The children have been put to bed and they have actually gone to sleep. Joanne has tidied the living-room and she and Joe are relaxing in front of the television. Joe has a can of lager in his hand.

The terrible events that have taken place above and on the ground in London have dominated the television schedules throughout the evening. The death toll has now exceeded the one thousand mark and comparisons are being drawn with the twin-towers disaster in New York City of September 2001. Not that international terrorism has been highlighted in this instance, but Joe has his suspicions, however unfounded those suspicions might be.

But Joe Bloggs' mind is not entirely focused on the news.

There is an old Chinese proverb which says that a man who knows he must work in the evening has his entire day ruined for him – and Joe is feeling that, in a wider sense, this proverb applies to him. Joe is only too well aware of the fact that tomorrow is the start of another working week and the dreaded realisation that he will need to be up bright and early in the morning is actually impacting on his enjoyment of the evening. The thought of work will not go away. It is constantly at the back of Joe's mind. At the forefront of his mind is sex.

He looks at Joanne out of the corner of his eye. Is she up for it? He can't tell.

'Fancy an early night?' he asks her, meaning 'Do you want to have sex with me tonight?'

'Do you know,' says Joanne, 'I do fancy an early night. I'm absolutely shattered.'

Joe is confused by this answer. Does she mean she's up for it or does she mean she's too tired for it? He needs to know.

'You're looking very nice tonight,' he tells her. 'Very . . . sexy.'

Joanne doesn't have the time or patience for all this nonsense. 'Look, Joe,' she says to him. 'I'm quite happy to make love to you tonight, but I really am tired. So, if that's what you want to do, let's go to bed early.'

Sunday 10.38 p.m.

Joe is naked in bed and Joanne is almost naked next to him. Joanne is lying on her back with one hand between Joe's legs and the other hand down her knickers. Joe has one hand on one of Joanne's breasts while the other hand is caressing her abdomen. Joe's mouth is caressing Joanne's other breast.

Suddenly.   'WHAAAAAAAA!   WHAAAAAAAA! MUMMY!'

Childhood toothache strikes again!

192

Hell fire!
Hell bloody fire!

Monday morning.

The dawning of the working week in the Bloggs' household is heralded, as always, by the most unwelcome buzzing of the radio alarm. The sound of it rattles the air, it invades deep sleep and dream, it demands of Mr and Mrs Joe Bloggs that they now abandon the comforts of their bed and face the challenges of the day. It is Joanne who rises first to the challenges. She bounds out of bed with frightening enthusiasm.

Her enthusiasm is necessary. She has to awaken and wash the children and brush their teeth. She has to get Ella dressed for nursery and Billy dressed for school. She has to get herself ready for work and somehow organise things so that there is time and room in the bathroom for Joe to get ready for work. She then has to feed the children and herself, feed Joe should he want some breakfast, and usher the children into the car, making sure that they have all their bits and pieces with them. She then needs to get Ella to nursery, Billy to his school and herself to a different school where she teaches. And all this within an hour and a quarter!

Joe has only himself to get ready.

But Joe can't get into the bathroom when he needs to. So Joe stays in bed until he can get into the bathroom. When he does get into the bathroom Joe often finds that he doesn't have time to shave. He rarely, if ever, has time to sit down and eat breakfast and he is always, always on the very last minute or later. Joe needs to leave home by 8.20 a.m. at the latest or he is sure to be late for work. On this particular Monday morning he is not leaving the house until almost 8.30 a.m.! Hell fire! Joe dashes out of the house and jumps in his car. He gives Joanne and the kids a quick wave and tears off down the road.

The city of Preston, which harbours the small advertising agency where Joe earns a crust, lies less than eight miles, as the crow flies, from *chez* Bloggs. Unfortunately, Joe cannot travel as the crow travels. No, Joe has to get to Preston by road and, although there are several different routes into the city centre, Joe knows from bitter experience that whichever route he takes he will find himself in heavy traffic. Today the traffic is exceptionally heavy. Joe arrives at work some forty minutes late. Another excuse to invent! Hell fire! Hell fire!

Well now, what a shame. One is so devastated. One's heart is bleeding. Poor Mr British Joe Bloggs!

What does he have to complain about?

Can't get into the bathroom? There are many millions in my world who do not have the luxury of a bathroom. Stuck in traffic? In parts of Africa and Asia and in other parts of my world Joe Bloggs has to walk to work – and if it is too far to walk then he must live in a stinking hovel for the duration of his working week. He must live far away from his wife and children and he will have no bathroom! Late for work? In my world, in your world, where you people exploit you people, there are millions who have no job to go to. No job! No money! A daily struggle for survival!

Isn't my world a lovely place?

What do you care as long as you're all right, Jack?

Anyway, poor old Joe Bloggs.

Oh, my bleeding heart! Excuse me while I laugh.

Monday afternoon.

Joe's job at the advertising agency is not very clearly defined. He holds no senior position at the agency, he does not think up slogans, he does not define strategy, he does not deal directly with clients. What he actually does do, apart from a string of minor tasks, is to check the accuracy of adverts and slogans before they are fostered upon the public. Joe is into the correct usage of the English language. He is into spelling and punctuation and phraseology and the like. Joe has a university degree in the English language.

And on the Monday afternoon the Slinkex campaign is finally about to get underway. Joe punches up the simple caption on his computer screen, the basic caption that will appear in newspapers and magazines throughout Lancashire at first and, if successful, throughout the whole of the UK at a later date.

DON'T LOOK OLD BEFORE YOUR TIME.
REDUCE THE APPEARANCE OF WRINKLES NOW.
WITH NEW SLINKEX.

This is the basic slogan. Along with prices, availability and special introductory offers and the like, this is what will open the campaign. All Joe needs to do is to make sure that the caption is correct.

But when Joe looks at the caption a wicked smile crosses his face. He quickly changes the 'L' in the word Slinkex into a 'T' – Stinkex! Joe chuckles to himself. Stinkex!

Joe is just about to change Stinkex back into Slinkex when the telephone rings. It is Joanne.

'Joe, I've got Ella in at the dentist.'
'When'
'Tomorrow afternoon, Joe. It's the only time they can fit her in.'
'Yeah.'

'You'll have to take her, Joe. I need to be at school because the inspectors are coming.'

Over the telephone line there is a long silence. Joe does not want to take Ella to the dentist because he knows that taking time off work will not go down well with his boss. Joe takes too much time off work for various reasons as it is and his habitual lateness doesn't help.

'Joe?'

'Yeah.'

'What's the matter?'

There is now a short silence while Joe resigns himself to asking his boss for more time off.

'It's all right, Joanne. I'll take her.'

As Joe hangs up the receiver his boss calls him from the other side of the office. 'Joe, have you checked the Slinkex slogan?'

Joe nods. 'Yep, it's fine.'

'Good! Let's get it away.'

Joe activates the printer and worries about having to ask for the Tuesday afternoon off work. He hands the printed copy to the new girl, the gorgeous Rosie, looking at Rosie's breasts rather than looking at the copy, and he tells her to send it through. In his mind Joe has changed Stinkex back into Slinkex. In reality he hasn't.

Monday evening.

Joe sits on the arm of the settee. He can't sit on the settee properly because it is occupied. It is occupied by his mother-in-law and by his father-in-law and, although the settee is a three-seater, Esther and Harold are both so obese that the two of them completely fill the available space. Joanne is sitting in one of the easy chairs while the other chair is occupied by Ella and several of her dolls. Billy is running around the room as usual and in the corner of the

196

room the television set is switched on, though Joanne has turned down the sound so that it is barely audible.

Joe doesn't dislike his in-laws. He just can't stand it when they visit. They arrive early in the evening and they stay until late. Esther never stops talking while Harold sits and says practically nothing. The children are allowed to stay up until the in-laws go home, which usually means that the bedtime rituals are not completed until ten-thirty or even eleven o'clock. Joe glances at the clock. It is a quarter past nine. Why the hell don't they go home?

'Well,' says Esther to Joe. 'I told her I didn't think it would be a good idea, but she did it anyway. All I can say is it serves her right.'

Joe smiles. He doesn't know who or what his mother-in-law is talking about.

At nine-thirty there is a special news report on the television. Despite Joanne's frowning disapproval, Joe turns up the sound. There has been a massive earthquake in south-west China. It is feared that many, many thousands have perished.

'Well,' says Esther. 'Of course I'm sorry for these Chinese. But why on earth don't they build proper houses when they know there might be an earthquake?'

Harold nods and then he actually speaks. 'Aye,' he says. 'Aye.'

A question for you. Why does a loving God allow natural disasters to kill thousands?

It is a fair question, is it not?

It is a question that deserves to be answered.

Now, you can say that men should not build cities in known earthquake zones. You can say that any buildings in such zones should be constructed so as to withstand the violent shaking of the earth. You can even blame the underground testing of nuclear weapons.

197

Yet none of these things can satisfactorily answer the question I have put to you. I will ask you again. Why does a loving God allow natural disasters to kill thousands?

If you were God, if you had the power, would you not prevent earthquakes and other natural disasters? Of course you would. So why doesn't he?

Perhaps he doesn't care.

Perhaps he thinks so little of you that he can't be bothered to stretch out his mighty hand.

Perhaps there is no mighty hand.

Perhaps there is no God.

Who blames God for the ills of the world?

Did God not give humanity a perfect beginning in the garden?

And even after our rebellion did God not sacrifice his son so that all those putting their faith in him might not perish but have everlasting life?

Has God not promised that his kingdom will come to remove all humanity's ills?

So, who blames God?

Only he who is a manslayer and those whom he is deceiving.

Tuesday. 8.50 a.m.

Joe is sitting in his car. Unfortunately, the car is not moving, nor are any of the vehicles ahead of him nor those behind him. Joe does not know why there is standing traffic on the route into the city, he does not know why he is going to be late for work again, he does not know why, despite his best efforts, things are going badly for him.

Hell fucking fire!

Shit! Shit! Shit!

Joe has been up since seven o'clock. He was in and out

of the bathroom before Joanne and the kids had even awakened. He had eaten breakfast, listened leisurely to the radio and left the house in plenty of time. He had been determined not to be late for work. So determined had he been that in his enthusiasm he has broken the speed limit and the camera has recorded it. But Joe does not know this yet!

Neither does Joe know that his usual car-park is already full and that he is destined to spend quite some time driving around the city centre looking for somewhere to leave his car.

Joe does not know these things yet.

All he knows at the moment is that he is now frustratingly stuck in traffic and that once again he is going to be late for work.

Hell fucking fire!

Tuesday. 3.07 p.m.

Joe is in the dentist's waiting-room, waiting for Ella. Because of her tender age Ella has been anaesthetized while the dentist extracts her decaying tooth.

How the hell does a two-year-old get a decaying tooth when Joanne has made sure that Ella's teeth are brushed twice a day every day? Joe doesn't know.

What he does know is that his boss is not pleased with him. Late for work today and yesterday and now he is taking the afternoon off. Not good!

Tuesday. 9.22 p.m.

Joe is sitting in front of the television with a bottle of lager in his hand. The children are in bed and Joanne is at her slimming class. The telephone rings.

Joe can hardly believe it! It is almost nine-thirty in the

evening and someone is trying to sell him life insurance over the telephone! Joe slams down the receiver, cutting off this someone in mid sentence. He then takes the receiver off the hook.

Joe goes into the kitchen and delves into the freezer. Ice-cream and lots of it is what is required. Joe settles back into his seat just as the news is beginning. The famine in East Africa is currently making headlines.

Images of children with distended bellies fill the screen. Images of children with flies crawling over their faces. Images of old men, flesh clinging to bone. Images of young mothers, no tears left to shed.

Joe feels sorry for them. But what can he do? Does he not have enough troubles of his own?

Joe digs into his ice-cream.

Where, oh where is the milk of human kindness? Have the paps run dry? Or is it that the milk cannot so easily be delivered to where it is needed?

Why is Joe Bloggs in England eating himself into obesity while Joe Bloggs in Africa starves? Is there something wrong with my world? Do we see an imbalance?

Well, don't blame me!

Joe Bloggs in England feeds his face because of his greed. Or is it comfort eating?

Well, no one but he himself is stuffing food down his throat.

And Joe Bloggs in Africa is starving because of a combination of drought and war and indifference. Drought brought on by man-made climatic changes, war brought by men, and indifference springing from your hearts!

Your hearts.

Yes, we encourage the rape of your environment. Yes, we encourage brutality and warfare and we love to play war games. And yes, my spirit, which pervades my world, is a selfish spirit that encourages indifference.

But you are the ones who are ruining the earth.
You are the ones waging war.
And you are the ones who are indifferent to the sufferings of your own people.
Yes, you!

Wednesday morning.

Joe is at work and he is feeling pleased with himself. The reason for this self-gratification is that Joe has finally managed to get to the office on time. In fact he was early. Joe left home extraordinarily early just in case he were to encounter heavy traffic, yet the traffic-flow turned out to be normal and Joe found himself waiting on the doorstep when his boss arrived to open up.

So Joe is pleased with himself. For once there is the hint of a smile upon his face. He fiddles with his keyboard in an attempt to look busy. There isn't much to do this morning. His mind begins to wander.

He thinks about the recent earthquake in China and the ongoing famine in Africa. Poor buggers! He thinks about a recent spate of suicide bombings in various parts of the world. Stupid buggers! He thinks about recent allegations made against his own government in that they have changed the way the crime figures are recorded so as to show a reduction in crime when in fact there has been an increase. Sly buggers!

THUD!

Joe's daydreams are rudely interrupted by the thud of the *Lancashire Life* magazine, thrown unceremoniously onto his desk by his boss!

'Page four, Joe,' says his boss in very, very angry tones. 'Page four.'

Joe turns to page four. Half the page is taken by the Slinkex ad. Joe looks at his boss. He doesn't understand.

'Look at it again, Joe,' says his boss in the same angry tones.

Joe looks at the ad again. At first he can see nothing wrong with it, but then the penny drops, then the awful and ridiculous truth dawns on him.

The Slinkex ad. is a Stinkex ad.!

Joe's brain spins and whirls. Simple logic is telling him that he and he alone is responsible for this monumental error because he was the one, the only one, who had jokingly changed Slinkex into Stinkex. But he had changed it back before the copy had been sent through! He had! He had! He was sure he had. He remembered it clearly! Didn't he?

At the same time as these uncertain thoughts are whirling through Joe's brain his ears are hearing the scathing tones of his boss. 'How could you be so bloody stupid. This bloody ad. is appearing in newspapers and mags all over Lancashire! It's your bloody responsibility to check! That's what we bloody well pay you for! This will cost us thousands! And Slinkex will probably sue us! Bloody stupid! Bloody stupid!'

Joe's brain is still whirling as his boss storms off. Joe is aware that everyone in the office is looking at him. At least Joe feels that everyone is looking at him. And Joe has the rest of the day to get through. Joe no longer has the hint of a smile on his face.

Wednesday evening.

It is Joe's night out. Every Wednesday, at eight-thirty on the dot, Joe leaves Joanne to put the children to bed and sets out for the pub, a walk of some five minutes, but on this particular evening Joe is delayed for a little while outside his own front door.

'Hey, Joe! Ask your wife to move her car, will you?'

This request, from Joe's next-door neighbour, and yelled out loud from the open window of this neighbour's vehicle as it comes to a halt in the middle of the road, comes across more as a demand than a request and Joe is instantly irritated.

Joe looks at his neighbour and sees the man looking back at him from the driving seat of his clapped-out Rover. Alec Smart has never been one of Joe's favourite people. He is one of those neighbours who is constantly complaining about something or other – or so it seems to Joe. Joe looks up and down the street. His own car is parked in front of his own house and Joanne's car is parked directly behind, partly in front of Alec Smart's house, but still leaving plenty of room for Smart to park his own vehicle.

'Why?' asks Joe. 'Why does she need to move it?'

'Because she's parked in front of my property,' says Smart.

'Well, park up behind her,' says Joe. 'There's plenty of room.' And, without another word or even another glance in Smart's direction, Joe heads off for the pub.

Two and a half hours later, and five pints of lager and a double whisky later, Joe returns from the pub having endured the boredom of a Wednesday evening in the local watering-hole. Apart from the landlord, Joe has spoken to no one. Apart from the landlord, there has been no one to speak with! And the landlord's only topic of conversation is politics! Hell fire! The evening has hardly been worth the bother. But Wednesday is Joe's night out!

Joe lets himself in and turns on the television set. Joanne and the children are all in bed and all seems quiet. Joe sits himself down in front of the television.

Joe dozes off. Or does he?

Joe is dreaming. Or is he?

Joe is seeing the late-night news, or is he? Because the newsreader is like nothing on earth.

This newsreader has a blood-red face with jet-black hair and piercing black eyes! This newsreader has horns on his head and there is a forked tail swishing about behind him. This newsreader's dark, dark eyes seem to bore into Joe's very being and the wicked smile on the newsreader's face is scary – no, more than scary, it is terrifying.

Oh, my God! Hell fire! The Devil is reading the news.

'Good evening.' The voice is rich, the tones are mocking. 'And welcome to the real news.'

WAR!

The caption flashes on the screen, superimposed on the Devil's face.

'Wars and reports of wars continue among you people. In the past twenty-four hours there have been exactly four thousand and eighty-two fatalities due to war. There will be more fatalities tomorrow.'

FAMINE!

'Seven thousand, four hundred and three have died today as a direct result of food shortages. Many more will die tomorrow.'

EARTHQUAKES!

'Two hundred and six have died today from injuries received in last Monday's earthquake in China. No major earthquakes have been recorded in populated areas today, but, hey, look out!'

DISEASE!

'Pestilences of every kind are on the increase world-wide. Today's fatalities have not yet been enumerated, but I can tell you that they are substantial. They are always substantial.'

CRIME!

'Today's crime figures have been enumerated and they make interesting reading. Over twenty million of you have been victims of crime today, yet fewer than nineteen million of you have committed these crimes! It seems that some of you are quite capable of committing more than one crime a day. Interesting!'

TOP STORY!

The caption flashes and the Devil grins broadly.

'But our top story today is, as always, the total number of fatalities worldwide. Five hundred and forty-one thousand, eight hundred and seventy-three of you have perished today, the vast majority of you as a result of illness associated with old age. Half a million of you gone in a single day! Gone to dust! More than half a million deaths among you and most of those who perished were glad to taste death. Yes, they were old and sick, they had had enough, they were happy to escape their mortal bonds. Half a million! Gone! Lucky for you as a species that you are able to breed like flies. Half a million! And tomorrow there will be at least a half-million more.'

The Devil's grin fades and he points a finger at his audience.

'Well, that's all I have for you. So, from today's real news, it's time to say goodbye. But I will leave you with one final thought. If you were to now leave the comfort of your armchair and go outside and look up to the heavens you will not see the horsemen of the apocalypse.

'No, your eyes will not see them.

'But they are there! The horsemen are riding!'

The Devil waves a cheery hand and his grin returns.

'Tune in again tomorrow to the real news.'

Thursday morning.

Horror upon horror! Pandemonium reigns in the Bloggs' household. It is 8.00 a.m. and Joanne has just discovered that her car has two flat tyres. In fact, the tyres appear to have been slashed by a knife. All of this means that Joe is going to have to drive Ella to her nursery, Billy to his school, Joanne to her school and then drive himself to work. All of this means that Joe is going to be late for work yet again.

Joe is convinced that his next-door neighbour has vandalised Joanne's car, but of Alec Smart there is no sign and Joe does not have the time to go looking for him. He considers calling the police, but then he realises that he has no proof. And time is pressing.

Joe and Joanne begin to argue from the moment they get into Joe's car. Joe and Joanne do not normally argue in front of the children, but today is not a normal day. Joe is taking his frustrations out on his wife and Joanne is naturally resentful and retaliatory. Joe and Joanne are still arguing after the children have been dropped off.

Joe arrives at work some thirty minutes late. He is a mixture of emotions. He is a mixture of anger directed at Joanne, pure rage directed at Alec Smart, embarrassment in front of his colleagues due to his consistent lateness, and a feeling in his heart not far removed from fear – fear of the reactions of his boss.

Thursday evening.

Joe is worn out. He is sitting in front of the television and he is thoroughly miserable. It is almost eleven o'clock.

After arguing with Joanne in the morning, Joe has managed to get into an argument with one of his colleagues at work in the afternoon. He has also managed to get into an argument with one of Billy's teachers at the parents' evening from which Joe and Joanne along with the children have only recently returned. Hell fire! What a day! Bloody work! Bloody waste-of-time bloody parents' evening! Hell bloody fire!

Joanne is barely speaking to Joe. She has had to arrange for two new tyres to be fitted to her car and she has had to take time away from her teaching to sort it out. She definitely does not need a husband in an argumentative mood. Sometimes she wonders why she ever married him. Grumpy old sod!

Joe glances at his wife. She is speaking into the telephone. She has been speaking to one of her friends on the telephone for the past hour. Joanne spends a lot of time on the telephone when she feels she has little or nothing to say to Joe.

Joe's anger towards his wife is nothing compared to the rage he feels towards Alec Smart. Joe has been round to confront him, but either Smart is out or he is not answering the door. Bastard! Ugly fat bastard!

On the television is a programme about AIDS in southern Africa. The stark images of men, women and children, stricken and dying from this disease fails to move Joe's angry heart.

Ah, yes. An angry heart.

A simmering rage within the breast. There is no pity within an angry heart. And why should images of suffering move Joe to pity? AIDS is not Joe's fault.

Is it not so that those who have AIDS are drug addicts, or they are homosexual, or they are men who visit prostitutes?

And if a married man is infected by a prostitute and if he then infects his wife, why should Joe Bloggs care? And if children are born with the HIV virus, whose fault is that?

Is it my fault? No.

It is the fault of the married man.

Who was it who caused it to be written that the sins of the fathers are visited upon the children?

It wasn't God. There is no God.

And as for Joe Bloggs? Well, as long as he is not personally affected he doesn't much care about AIDS, do you Joe, especially when you have had a bad day?

You people truly are a selfish breed.

Friday morning.

Joe is at work. He has arrived on time and he is getting on with his job. Everything is fine, or so it seems.

Around eleven o'clock Joe receives an external phone call. It is Joanne reminding him that she has a church meeting in the evening. Some ten minutes after the phone call Joe suddenly becomes suspicious. Why is Joanne reminding him about the church meeting? There is almost always a meeting on a Friday evening. Joe doesn't need reminding.

Joe can't work it out.

And then the seeds of suspicion, already sown, begin to cast doubts in Joe Bloggs' mind, doubts concerning Joanne.

Is she having an affair? Did she ring to make absolutely certain that Joe would be in the house and looking after the children tonight? Was she at this very moment arranging to meet her lover? Someone from her school perhaps? Or someone from the church?

Nah! No, no!

Joe shakes his head. Joanne is a Christian. She would never commit adultery. Would she?

Friday afternoon.

Around four o'clock Joe is called into his boss's office and asked to sit down. He finds himself at one side of a desk looking up at his boss, whose chair is much taller, on the other side of the desk.

'We're going to have to let you go, Joe.'

The words wash over Joe's ears and he simply cannot believe them.

'I'm sorry, but times are hard and we need to rationalise.'

Joe still cannot believe what he is hearing. His boss pushes a small package across the desk towards him.

'There's a month's salary here in lieu of notice. I'd like to thank you for all the hard work you've put into this company. If you can clear your desk before you go tonight it would be appreciated.'

The boss stands up and holds out his hand for Joe to shake. Feeling totally manipulated Joe stands up and shakes his boss's hand. Joe reels out of his boss's office clutching the package containing his P45 and his pay-off cheque.

Fired!

Bloody hell! This isn't happening! Balls! Balls! Hell bloody fire! Hell bloody fire!

Friday evening.

'Well, you'll soon find another job. And you've got a month to sort yourself out.'

Joanne's reaction surprises Joe. She doesn't seem particularly concerned that Joe has lost his job. In fact, Joanne seems to be far more concerned with her church meeting. Suspicion stirs once more in Joe's psyche.

Later, when Joanne is at the meeting, or when Joanne is supposed to be at the meeting, Joe telephones the vicar's house where the meeting is always held.

To his great relief Joanne eventually comes to the phone.

'What is it, Joe? What's the matter?'

'Ella seems a little off-colour,' Joe lies. 'I thought I might give her some of that Calpol stuff, but I can't find it.'

'It's in the medicine cabinet. I know it is. You haven't

looked properly, Joe. Do you want me to come home?'

'No, no. She's not really ill. She's just restless. You enjoy your meeting.'

'Well, if she gets any worse call me again. But call me on my mobile. You've got the number.'

'Yep, it's written down somewhere. I'll find it. See you later.'

Joe rings off and his mood is a mixture of relief and guilt. Relief because Joanne is exactly where she is supposed to be and guilt because he has doubted her. And Joe has doubted his wife to the extent of checking up on her. He knows the number of her mobile by heart, but by their nature mobile phones do not disclose where a person might be.

Fired!

Bloody hell!

You people are highly suspicious of each other. You even doubt your own wives and husbands. But then you have good reason to do so, don't you? Unfaithfulness among you is endemic!

I am the god of adultery.

A good shag with someone you shouldn't be shagging is exciting, isn't it?

And what harm does it do if no one finds out?

None whatsoever.

And if it all comes out into the open?

Well, take a look at the divorce statistics.

Yours is an adulterous generation.

Saturday morning.

It is a warm and sunny day in Lancashire, the sort of day to get out and about with the children, but Joe and Joanne can't spare the time.

Saturday is not a working day for Joanne, nor would it

have been a working day for Joe had he not been given the sack, yet for both Joe and Joanne, Saturday is a day for dealing with some of the less savoury trappings of modern life in the western world. It is Joanne's house cleaning morning. It is Joe's morning for sifting through and dealing with the week's correspondence as well as keeping an eye on the kids.

Joe is sitting at the dining-table with a mountain of letters in front of him. Billy and Ella are sitting on the rug directly in front of the television. Joanne is upstairs and the sound of the vacuum cleaner on the bedroom floor is competing with the sound from the television and the whirring of the washing-machine in the kitchen.

Hell fire!

Joe sighs deeply and steels himself to make a start on the correspondence. Billy and Ella are squabbling and Joe has to shout at them to make them stop. The weekly shopping trip to the supermarket is what Joe has to look forward to in the afternoon.

Hell bloody fire! Joe begins opening the mail.

The gas bill, one hundred and forty-two pounds and seventeen pence. Junk mail. An invitation to a children's party for Billy and Ella. Junk mail. A local tax demand for ninety-odd pounds. Junk mail, junk mail and more junk mail. A bank account statement combined with junk mail. A newsletter from Ella's nursery. Junk mail. An application form to complete for receipt of Working Parents' Tax Credit. Junk mail. Etc. etc. etc.

Hell bloody fire!

Saturday afternoon.

Joe sometimes dreams about the supermarket. The dream is recurrent, the dream is frustration. The dream is a nightmare.

211

In this dream Joe, along with Joanne, Billy and Ella, are all in the busy, busy supermarket, yet, though the shelves are stocked to the brim, none of the items the family wants are there! In this dream the supermarket's aisles are never ending, they simply go on into infinity! This means that the family can never get out of the supermarket! They can never find the checkout. And if they were ever to get to the checkout they would still not be able to go home with their purchases, for in this dream the family has no money to pay for all the items in their trolley, items that have mysteriously appeared in their trolley, items they never wanted in the first place!

Frustration.

And for Joe the reality of a trip to the supermarket is every bit as frustrating.

So, here they all are in the supermarket on the Saturday afternoon. For Joanne it is the relatively pleasant task of choosing what the family will eat over the following week. For Billy and Ella it is two hours of boredom, yet with the prospect of sweets or some other junk. For Joe it is the Saturday afternoon ordeal.

Ella sits in the child-seat in the trolley. Billy holds onto the trolley – well, most of the time he holds onto the trolley. Joanne walks ahead of the trolley, picking items off the shelves, while Joe pushes the trolley, a trolley that refuses to go in the direction Joe is attempting to steer!

THREE HUNDRED ITEMS REDUCED THIS WEEK!

'Aye,' thinks Joe. 'And three thousand items increased.'

An elderly woman nudges into Joe as he attempts to drive his trolley. She apologises, but Joe can't help but think that some people ought to pass a trolley-pushing test before they are let loose. That might stop all these idiots from blocking the aisles, from nudging into others, from standing and chatting in exactly the spot where Joe wants to be! A trolley pushing licence might even reduce the huge numbers of people in the supermarkets.

Claustrophobia! Frustrating!

Billy keeps letting go of the trolley and picking things up from the shelves. Joe keeps having to tell him not to touch things. Ella is constantly asking for sweets and Joe is constantly having to tell her to wait. Joanne is strolling along as though somehow this is a natural way to spend an afternoon.

Hell bloody fire!

At last, at long last, Joe's ordeal seems to be coming to an end. At last the Bloggs join the checkout queue. But Joanne has forgotten something and dashes back for whatever it is. Joe stands holding his place in the queue while trying to keep some semblance of control over Billy and Ella. Just when it is looking that Joe will have to relinquish his place in the queue Joanne returns and she and Joe begin to unload the trolley.

There is a delay. The woman in front of them in the queue is demanding a recount. The delay lasts for several minutes but at last the woman is satisfied. Joe and Joanne's items are now passing through the till and Joe is busy stuffing them into plastic shopping bags. By the time the family leaves the supermarket Joe is reeling. He feels as though he has just gone ten rounds with the world heavyweight boxing champion!

The car is loaded. The shopping is shoved in the boot, the kids are shoved in the back and Joe and Joanne get into the front. Safety harnesses are fastened and Joe drives off, but before he can leave the car-park he needs to stop for petrol. Again he has to queue, this time to pay for the petrol he has put in the tank. Odd! Just like the checkout, people queue to pay. Odd!

Frustrating!

On the way home Joe's frustration finally boils over and

it is the children who bear the brunt of it. Billy is fiddling with Ella's car-seat and she is screaming. Joe yells at them, but to no effect. Joanne tells him not to shout at the children, but Joe's frustration cannot now be held in check. Taking his eyes off the road he turns his head and yells at the children again – and at that precise moment the heavy goods vehicle directly in front of them comes to an abrupt halt.

It all happens so quickly that Joanne has no time to shout a warning.

BANG! CRUNCH!

SILENCE.

*

Oops!

Is this writer about to kill Joe Bloggs? Or will he save him? And what about Joe's wife and children?

Well, this writer can please himself. And you, the reader, you can choose any ending to the story you like. But the point is that life in modern-day Britain can, for some, be extremely stressful.

For some there is very little joy in life. For some, for many, it is all go, go, go! For some, for most, there seems to be no time in life for reflection, for contemplation, no time to stand and stare, no time to heed the advice of God who has said: 'Be still. And know that I am God.'

The world at this present time does not, in general, listen to the words of God. But then the world at this present time is not God's world. It is Satan's world.

And what a world! Ask Joe Bloggs.

Incidentally, Joe was killed in the traffic accident, so 'A Week in the Life of Joe Bloggs' should more accurately be called 'Not Quite a Week in the Life of Joe Bloggs' – because Joe didn't make it through to the Sunday.

Oh, and the driver of the goods vehicle who braked suddenly to avoid hitting a child was a man in his late fifties, a man called William Brooke, the old man of the near future who at this present time has not yet grown old. And you will read more about him shortly.

Anyway, I digress. We were discussing Satan's world. If we look around us we shall ...

I will speak.

All over my world, from north to south, from east to west, you will find wars, wars in the form of bloody conflicts between nations, wars in the form of rebellions, wars in the form of terrorism. And many of these wars are fuelled by religious zeal. All over my world my religions war against each other in the name of God!

Isn't that ironic?

All over the world my political systems struggle against each other. There is no peace in my world. Over two hundred different nations and national groups, all loosely under my control, all seeking their own self-interest.

Are you surprised that there are wars?

Wars or no wars, my world, which is infested with my spirit, my desire, is a world of crime, of famine, of disease. My world is a world of pain, of anxiety, of fear, of frustration. My world is a world of heartbreak.

Yet my world is also a world of fleeting pleasures and you people are lovers of pleasure. You love your bellies, your fornications, your drunkenness, your drugs, your riches. You are lovers of yourselves.

At this present time the man William Brooke is a lover of pleasures, a selfish man. See, in his own words, how his selfishness has led to heartbreak.

*

I loved my young wife dearly.

And my children also.

But I loved myself more.

I did not treat my wife as I should have treated her.

I thought her love for me was unshakable.

But it was not.
In my selfishness I did not consider her.
And I drove her away.
Her love for me died.
She changed.
She no longer loved me as a woman loves a man.
Her tenderness towards me was gone.
She had changed.
I looked around me but the girl I had married was gone.
And in her place was someone else.
Someone I did not recognise.
It was as though my wife had died.
Gone!
Gone forever.
And the fault was mine.
Mine to endure.
Heartbreak!
My young wife, my love, is dead.

I will admit that I had a little something to do with William Brooke's misery. I helped to blind him to the fact that his marriage was in jeopardy. I blinded him with his own selfishness, with his unreasonable jealousies, with his frustrations of modern life. When at last he cast off his blindness and he was able to see, it was too late.

Too late.

Have no sympathy for him. Let him wallow in his misery. Let him be heartbroken.

In my world there are others who are far worse off than William Brooke.

The twelve-year-old boy who has trekked for three days through the African bush to find the doctor whom he believes can cure the massive tumour in his mouth. He holds out his hand to the doctor who is moved to tears. The tumour has progressed too far.

The woman in a Korean prison camp who has been tortured

because she has been labelled as an enemy of the state. At this very moment she is giving birth and her child is fatherless because the authorities have already murdered the husband. Yet the fact that the child is fatherless is irrelevant because as soon as he is born he is kicked to death in front of his mother's eyes.

The young girl in Iraq who is shot through the head on her way to school. Why? Who knows? Apart from her family, who cares?

The old woman dying in the nursing home. Alone, afraid and in pain. Unable to communicate.

Oh, there are millions of examples of those who are worse off than William Brooke. Nevertheless his heartache is real.

What a lovely world you inhabit!

My lovely, lovely world.

And in the western parts of my world I have noticed a hardening of attitude, a growing intolerance towards the sufferings of others. You see, I have so arranged things that you who inhabit the western parts are far too busy with your pursuits of work and pleasure, far too busy chasing after your own selfish desires, to have the time to stand and stare, to be still.

I have stolen your time.

You don't think so?

Ask Joe Bloggs.

Oh, you can't. He's dead.

Well then, take a long look at yourselves.

If you have the time.

Are you happy? Are you satisfied?

I am the thief of time. I am the thief of your time. I am the god of this world. Yes, and my world is not a happy place. Look around.

Now, if you think that conditions in this world are bad – well, all I can say is you haven't seen anything yet. Read on and see what is coming up next.

Read on and know my fury.

7

And Coming Up Next ...

It is the near future and our world, ruled by Satan, has gone from bad to worse. Our world has seen a progression of wickedness in all its many forms, a progression that began way back in Eden, a progression that has run its vile and hurtful course down through the ages, a progression that has accelerated from the time you, the reader, are reading these words through to what is now the near future – your near future.

Let no one wonder at the critical state of the world in our near future, for it is Satan's world, led ever onward by his wicked spirit, his will, and he is not fit to rule. He is the Lord of Misrule, the author of disorder, the corrupter of God's creation.

Satan and his demons have misled mankind. They have turned men away from God and caused men to believe that humanity is capable of ruling itself. But now, in the very near future, the terrible truth – that man was not created with the ability to govern himself without God's guidance – is about to become evident. The festering sore, which is human civilization, is about to erupt. And nothing and no one can stop it, not even the god of this world.

Satan's world, our world, is rushing headlong towards self-destruction. It is out of control. Consider ...

It is the near future and never before in the course of human history has the world tottered so precariously on the brink of destruction. With the exceptions of the two world wars of the twentieth century, never before has there been so much conflict in the world. World-War-Three, the greatest conflict of all, surely lies just around the next corner, or perhaps the corner after that.

It is the near future and never before have the nations and groups of nations been so heavily armed. Never before have so many nations been armed with weapons of mass destruction, nuclear, chemical and biological. Never before have many of these nations had the technology to effectively use these terrible weapons.

Yet at this point in the near future, before the coming of World-War-Three, the weapons of warfare deployed by the nations are largely conventional, they are largely bullets and bombs, though men are forever devising more effective bullets, more effective bombs.

It is the near future and the American superpower along with its British ally has been superseded in mightiness by a United Europe. It is the near future and the kings of the east are warring among themselves in such places as Taiwan and Korea. It is the near future and in many parts of South America there is war, there is insurrection, there is rebellion, all mixed in with dire poverty for the great majority of the continent's citizens and crippling national debts. It is the near future and skirmishes along the Indian-Pakistani border threaten nuclear holocaust. It is the near future and many parts of the African continent are racked by war and insurrection and there is starvation for many. It is the near future and in the Middle East a shaky coalition of Arab nations once again threatens the very existence of the state of Israel, an Israel supported as ever by the United States, by Britain and by other English-speaking nations. It is the near future and in every corner of the world terrorism is continuing. Almost every day there are bombings, mass poisonings, outbreaks of disease, disease deliberately caused by men.

This is the world of the near future. And behind all this turmoil the hand of religion is perceived.

The Christians of the western world who fear the excesses of Islam. The sons of Islam who despise the values of the decadent West and who hate the Jews. The sons of Judah who hate and fear the Arabs. In the Indian subcontinent Muslims contend with Hindus and Hindus contend with Sikhs. In Africa there are Muslims, Christians and a multitude of others, all claiming to honour peace, yet there is no peace. In the Far East there are clashes between the Buddhists, the Taoists, the Confucianists, the Shintoists and the Communists. In South America the Catholics are warring with the Catholics. Is God on both sides?

Yes, the hand of religion is perceived to lie behind many of the world's ills. The meddling of religion in politics has been noted. She who sits astride the political beast will not endure for long. The beast will turn upon her. It will devour her. Babylon the Great is soon to receive her judgment.

Yet religion alone cannot be blamed for all the world's troubles. As Jesus Christ himself predicted, the last days of this world are seeing a significant increase in lawlessness. Criminals, both organised and otherwise, operate amid the chaos of a warring world. There are murders, robberies, beatings, there is violence on a scale never before known, and the widespread usage of illicit drugs is out of control. In many parts of the world the policing of whole communities has been abandoned. There are areas where the police simply do not enter and in these places the people must fend for themselves as best they can.

This is the world of the near future. A world of war, of crime, of disease. It is a world where children are abandoned by parents, where children are forced into disgusting sexual acts, where children and adults are murdered for their body parts. It is a world where the weak are preyed upon by the strong, where the old and frail cannot survive, where justice and goodness have been abandoned, where the love of money has triumphed.

This is our world of the near future, but what of Britain specifically?

Britain is a divided country.

It is a country whose inhabitants are broadly divided into two, into those who are working and who have money, and into those who, for whatever reason, cannot work and who therefore have little money. Rich Joe Bloggs works long and hard to maintain the lifestyle he feels he needs. Poor Joe Bloggs, denied decent housing, denied the best healthcare, denied all of life's little luxuries because of his lack of money, lives on his wits.

In towns and cities all over Britain there are pockets of poverty, of squalor, of crime, of violence, of gang-policing, of drunkenness, of drug abuse, of misery. Poor Joe Bloggs feels trapped, unable to find well-paid employment, unable to escape the ghetto. Poor Joe Bloggs has lost his hope. He is descending into a great black hole of despair. He is utterly lost.

And Britain's leaning towards the United States and its pulling away from the European Union is not helping poor Joe Bloggs. The economic consequences of this policy have been felt all down the line, but it is the poor and underprivileged who bear the brunt.

Rich Joe Bloggs is still alright, Jack!

But poor Joe Bloggs festers and stinks in his hovel.

In Lancashire, William Brooke, now an old man living alone, is more of a poor Joe Bloggs than a rich Joe Bloggs.

*

It is a warm August evening and William Brooke is sitting at his kitchen table. In front of him is a letter from his son in New York along with a generous cheque. There is also a completed reply to his son in America and a partially written letter to his daughter in Devon. Outside the light is beginning to fade and William Brooke is finding it difficult to see, especially as the downstairs windows are partially boarded. The old man wonders if his electricity supply will be switched on tonight. If not, there are the candles.

RAP.

The old man glances at the kitchen window.

RAP.

Definitely a stone.

RAP. RAP.

Definitely stones hitting the boarding. Almost certainly kids.

There was a time when the old man would have gone outside and put the fear of God into the children who are throwing stones at his windows. There was such a time, when he was younger, when the streets were safer. Now the old man does not go out after dark. No, not even to confront children. It simply isn't safe.

RAP. RAP.

The old man continues to ignore the stones. He knows that the kids will get bored if there is no response. He knows that eventually they will go away.

In the last of the light the old man finishes the letter to his daughter, but now it is too dark to properly see to address the envelopes. He gets up from his chair and tries the light switch. To his surprise the electricity is on. He addresses the envelopes, places the letters inside and

223

determines to post them in the morning at the local Post Office. He will also cash the cheque his son has sent to him and collect any incoming mail. The old man remembers when the mail used to be delivered to the door. He remembers when there was a collection box at the bottom of the street. William Brooke reaches across the table to his radio and turns it on.

The old man goes to his stove to make himself some coffee and as he does so his attention is drawn to a news report on the radio. He listens carefully. It seems that the President of the European Union is to host a summit of world leaders under the auspices of the United Nations. It is hoped that this conference will somehow bring about a great improvement in conditions for all the world's citizens. The 'Peace Summit' is to take place in September.

Later the old man sits alone with his memories. He thinks about his son and his daughter, especially when they were younger, when they were children. He thinks about his wife, she whom he loved so dearly, she who left him, she whom he treated so badly, she who stopped loving him, she who died to him. Next he thinks of death, his own death, and though he fears it he knows it brings no sorrows. He finds hope in God's promise of the resurrection. With tears in his eyes William Brooke again remembers the good times, the times when he loved and was loved, and he wonders if similar times lie ahead, if not in this world then in the next.

*

Whenever it is that men are saying 'Peace and Security' then sudden destruction is to be instantly upon them, just as the pang of distress upon a pregnant woman, and they will not escape. – 1 Thessalonians 5: 3

PEACE AND SECURITY!

224

PEACE AND SECURITY FOR ALL!

These are the headlines in mid September.

And although there is little official confirmation, it is reliably reported that there is broad agreement among world leaders.

WARS ARE TO CEASE!

Yes, amazingly it is reported that wars are to cease! It is understood that the Chinese, the Japanese and the Koreans are to hold a summit of their own to iron out the problems in the Far East. It is reported that the Americans are to wield their influence to bring peace to turbulent South America. It is said that the Indians and the Pakistanis are to sign a treaty banning the use of nuclear weapons. It is reliably reported that the mighty European Union is to enforce peace in those parts of Africa which are at war and, perhaps more importantly, it is believed that the Arab-Israeli conflict is to be settled once and for all by direct negotiation between all warring parties with the assistance of the British, the Americans, the Russians and the Europeans.

PEACE AND SECURITY!

Utterly amazing!

And it is reported that world leaders are firmly agreed that the war on terrorism is to be ruthlessly pursued. In every corner of the globe the terrorists are to be hunted down and their organisations dismantled. The war on terrorism is to be won!

And it is further reported that, under the direct authority of the United Nations, law-enforcement agencies worldwide are to be strengthened and given wide-ranging powers to combat crime. Criminal organisations are to be broken up. Persistent criminals are to be hunted down and severely punished. No stone is to be left unturned in this crackdown. The world is to be freed from the scourge of crime!

PEACE AND SECURITY FOR ALL!
Utterly, utterly amazing!

In Lancashire, William Brooke is most concerned. Mindful of the Bible's warning concerning the cry of 'Peace and Security', he writes further letters to his son and to his daughter, warning them that there might very well be great dangers just ahead. He wonders if they will heed his warning? Sadly he fears that they will not. They are his flesh and his blood, but the old man knows that David and Ellen do not possess his understanding. Such understanding has not yet been given to them and William Brooke suspects that his children will think of him as somewhat deluded, as a bit of an old fool. Nevertheless, he writes the letters.

Oh yes, William Brooke is convinced that great tribulation is near, but even he has underestimated the enormity of the tribulation to come. Furthermore, the old man knows nothing of the nations' hidden agenda, of the politicians' secret agreement. For in their quest to bring peace to a volatile world the leaders of our world have determined to completely remove what they have come to recognise as a barrier to peace – entrenched religion – all religion. The beast is about to turn on the whore and devour her!

*

And the ten horns which you saw upon the beast, these shall hate the whore, and shall make her desolate and naked, and shall eat her flesh, and burn her with fire. – Revelation 17: 16

On the first day of October at 7.00 a.m. central European time, in every corner of the world the nations strike without warning at the religious organisations in their midst.

In Europe, cathedrals, churches and mosques are either forcibly closed or destroyed. The armed forces and security services of the European nations act swiftly and mercilessly. Clerics are arrested and detained under emergency laws to counter terrorism. Those who resist are beaten. Many are killed. The Pope himself is taken into custody and hidden away from public view. Christendom is under speedy and sustained attack.

In the remnants of the British Empire and across the vast tracts of Asia, Christendom reels under the onslaught. In the islands of the sea and in the Christianised parts of Africa, the churches are burning. In North America and in South America, government forces move ruthlessly against the religious hierarchy. Priests and ministers are either killed or arrested and removed from their localities.

Yet it is not only Christendom that is coming under attack.

Many of the nations of Islam are also acting with the same speed and ferocity against the ayatollahs, against the mullahs, against the imams. Mosques are burning. Holy shrines are being systematically destroyed.

In India and all across the Far East, temples are being sacked and burned, not by mobs, but by government forces. The idols and shrines of the Hindus, of the Sikhs, of the Shintoists, of the Buddhists are being torn down. Even in Israel the government moves against Judaism. Synagogues are closed and boarded up, prominent rabbis arrested, and in the city of Jerusalem at midday there are three massive and simultaneous explosions. Christendom's Church of the Holy Sepulchre, Islam's Dome of the Rock and Judaism's Western Wall – the actual foundations of Herod's temple – are all blown to bits to symbolise the determination of the nations to utterly destroy for ever the power of religion.

By 7.00 p.m. central European time the deed is largely done. There are just a handful of countries that have not acted – not yet, but the deed is largely done. There will be riots to quell in the days ahead and mopping-up operations against a myriad of minor sects, but the deed is largely done.

To the absolute astonishment of the world's populations, Great Babylon is no more!

Former practitioners of Great Babylon's varied religions will wait for God to act. When he does not do so many will say there is no God.

Of course there is no God. Unless you are thinking of me!

But this is besides the point.

I interrupt at this stage to ask if anyone can seriously believe the above account of Babylon's destruction? Does anyone seriously think that MY governments will rise up and destroy MY religious organisations? And in a single day!

What trash!

Never will I inspire my nations to rise against my ministers. Never!

*

Were William Brooke able to see the above words of the Devil he would refute them, for the old man, having some understanding of the book of Revelation, would quite correctly claim that it is God who is inspiring the destruction of Babylon the Great. It is God who is putting it into the hearts and minds of the leaders of the nations to burn the harlot with fire.

Why?

Because for centuries, since the beginning of organised religious practices, Great Babylon in all its forms has claimed to represent the Almighty while, at the same time, bearing responsibility for cruel wars, for religious murders, for enriching herself at the expense of her

228

people, for injustices, for having on her hands the blood of God's prophets, in fact, for inspiring the breaking of all God's commandments.

> Her sins have massed together clear up to heaven, and God has called her acts of injustice to mind. – Revelation 18: 5

Yes, William Brooke would refute Satan's false reasoning, but on the morning of 1st October William Brooke has no idea what is about to occur on a worldwide scale, nor indeed has he any idea what is about to occur in his own vicinity.

*

It is the morning of 1st October and William Brooke is making his way on foot to the village Post Office to collect his pension. He walks briskly, as a much younger man might walk, and as usual he is carrying his walking-stick, not as an aid to walking, but as a means of self-defence should such defence ever become necessary. Even in daylight the streets are not safe.

The old man has not had the opportunity to listen to his radio this morning. He has overslept and, as a consequence, he has left the house in something of a hurry. He does not know that the attacks on religious institutions have already begun on a worldwide scale. He does not know that these attacks have begun in Britain, in Lancashire, but he is about to find out. To get to the Post Office William Brooke must pass the Church of England vicarage at the bottom of the lane and, a little further up the lane, the Roman Catholic church along with its presbytery.

It is as he is passing the vicarage that the old man sees the first group of police officers. There are three of them and they are at the end of the longish driveway and they

229

appear to be pounding on the vicarage door. The old man stares at them, surprised to see that three police officers are actually present in the village, but then he simply makes the assumption that there is some emergency and that the vicar is urgently required.

He continues to walk along the lane, but, as the old man is approaching the presbytery and as he sees yet more officers actually entering the building by a window they have apparently forced, he realises suddenly and with great alarm that something very nasty and unusual is taking place. William Brooke then notices that the Roman Catholic church of St Joseph is on fire!

The old man stops in his tracks and looks back towards the vicarage. He sees the local vicar being roughly bundled into the back of a police van. There is a sudden commotion, some shouting and banging, and the old man's eyes are once more drawn towards the presbytery. Several police officers are dragging the Roman Catholic priest along his garden path. The priest is cursing them.

'Sons of the Devil! Sons of the Devil! Take your filthy hands off me! May God strike you all down! Sons of . . .'

To the old man's absolute horror and amazement he sees one of the officers strike repeatedly at the priest's head with a baton. The priest falls silent and ceases to struggle. There is blood spurting from the priest's head as he is dragged unceremoniously past William Brooke's startled eyes by grim-faced police officers who utterly ignore the fact that the old man is present.

The priest's housekeeper is weeping on the doorstep as the priest is hurled into the van containing the vicar. The officers pile in and the van speeds away. The old man looks towards the church. It is burning. Burning!

*

And so Great Babylon is gone, brought to account by God. Yet in the eyes of the world, Great Babylon's destruction is at the hands of the nations who have considered her to be a fomenter of wars and troubles.

But wars and troubles do not cease with Babylon's demise.

There is no peace. There is no security.

A year passes by and still there is no peace, still there is no security.

In Europe, American and British influence is now seen as a further barrier to peace, especially on Europe's doorstep, especially in the Middle East. In Europe, in mighty Europe, American and British interference is not to be tolerated. In Europe a new war is being planned and these plans are in their final stages. Europe intends to strike against America and Britain. Europe intends to strike with nuclear weapons, so-called 'clean' nuclear weapons. Europe intends to forever rid the earth of the influence of not only the Americans and the British but also of the entire English-speaking world.

War!

War to bring about a lasting peace!

War!

Yes, war!

But not a war to bring about a lasting peace. Oh no, not a war to end all wars.

This war between the Europeans and the English-speakers is only the beginning. It will not end with the surrender of the Americans and the British. It will not end as the Europeans have planned. Because this war is my war. It is my opportunity to kill you all! Just as you deserve. This war, my war, will engulf the entire planet. Death by heat and blast! Death by radiation poisoning! Death by disease!

'No,' I hear you say. 'Satan is a liar. There will be no such war.'

Really? Well, is the Nazarene a liar too?

It is my intention to destroy you all.
And to make your planet forever uninhabitable!

*

For then there will be great tribulation such as has not occurred since the world's beginning until now, no, nor will occur again. In fact, unless those days were cut short, no flesh would be saved; but on account of the chosen ones those days will be cut short. – Jesus Christ.

So we have come full circle. We have arrived back at the beginning of this work of fiction. Nuclear war! Nuclear war in Plymouth, England. Nuclear war in New York City. Nuclear devastation in Lancashire. Nuclear strikes on Britain and America initially, but nuclear war, which will affect the entire world, yes, which will affect you, whoever you are, if you are living at the time!

Now, it is not the purpose of this work of fiction to go into details concerning the political decisions and intrigues that will lead to war. Nor is it the purpose of this book to explain how a United Europe will come to have the economic, the technological and the military superiority to successfully wage war. For a better understanding of these things you should read *Jacob's Trouble* by Buster McGraw.

No, it is not the purpose of this work of fiction to explain how these near future events will occur, but it is the purpose of this book to show why these things must happen – and they must – even if in this work of fiction the details, or some of the details, will turn out to be incorrect.

It may not be a United Europe that will instigate the war. Plymouth and New York may not be obliterated.

But nuclear war lies just ahead of us.

How do we know?

Because God, who cannot lie, has told us in the words of his son.

Because God, who will not allow Satan to triumph ultimately, is warning us in advance of the wicked one's schemes.

Hear again the words of God's son. 'Unless those days were cut short,' says Jesus, 'NO FLESH would be saved.'

Ah! you might say. But that could mean chemical or biological warfare.

Well, chemical and biological warfare there might be, but if so it will be in addition to nuclear warfare.

How do we know?

Because after Jesus warns us of this coming Great Tribulation in Matthew 24: 21, 22, he goes on to say in Verse 29 these words: 'Immediately after the tribulation of those days the sun will be darkened, and the moon will not give its light ...'

Surely, dark sun + no moonlight = nuclear winter.

Dark clouds of radioactive dust obscuring the heavens.

Swirling clouds of dust for many months on end.

Nuclear winter!

Nuclear war!

European multi-nuclear warheads raining down upon Britain and upon the United States of America from above, from the near reaches of space. Against these orbital missiles there is insufficient warning and no defence. Government targets, military targets and civilian targets on the British and the American mainlands are obliterated in the blink of an eye.

At the same time British and American naval fleets are destroyed in their ports or at sea by tactical nuclear strikes. British and American submarines are either destroyed or are rendered ineffective by technologically superior European vessels. British and American overseas military bases are either invaded, such as in the case of Gibraltar, or completely destroyed, or, in a few cases, such as the Falklands, simply left alone. What good is Port Stanley to Berlin? What harm can a stranded British garrison do to Europe?

America is effectively defeated within minutes of the first strike, her own nuclear deterrent being the prime target. Then the centres of her major cities are incinerated, the outskirts of these cities blasted to pieces, and beyond the outskirts of these stricken cities, other townships are shattered and they are burning. The toll of the dead, the dying and the injured is truly unimaginable.

America's only response is the launching of several missiles from the nuclear submarine, Priestland, the only strike submarine not to be immediately rendered ineffective. With two exceptions these missiles are destroyed in flight by Europe's defensive screens. The total destruction of Paris and the irradiation of a remote Alpine region is the price Europe pays for victory.

The President of the United States is dead. Nearly all the members of his administration have perished. Government is barely functioning. Whole cities have been incinerated. The American military is either gone or ineffective. And all within a matter of minutes.

One hour after the strike, Europe calls on America to surrender and threatens to resume bombing. Less than twelve hours after the initial onslaught, General Douglas Markland, on behalf of the United States government, surrenders unconditionally.

Good-night, Uncle Sam!

Rest in peace!

The British Isles fare no better. London is the first target, swiftly followed by other government and military targets and all major cities. So-called 'clean' nuclear weapons are used to destroy the structures of these

234

islands, clean in the sense that the radiation released during the detonations is reduced. This is on account of Britain's proximity to mainland Europe, but, in any case, Europe has timed its onslaught to coincide with an easterly wind.

The Irish are less than impressed!

At the first strike twenty million Britons are killed instantly. Twenty million more are to die sooner or later as a direct result of the bombing. A further twenty million or so will struggle to survive in a devastated and poisoned and abandoned land, for no formal request for surrender is made of these islands. John Bull's body is left to rot.

This is the shape of things to come.

This is the opening day of World-War-Three.

*

How beautiful, how beautiful the face of death can be.

She sits upon the garden swing and wonders at the colours in the sky. Blue, then pure white quickly fading back to blue. Again a flash of brilliant white fading back to blue. A third and ever brighter flash of white fading in the silence to blue.

She is captured by the wonder of it.

How beautiful the face of death.

And now far away, far beyond her horizon, she sees the skies a pulsating red. Red skies beneath which only moments ago the city of Nottingham was. And there again, but closer now, a pulse of red where Leicester burns. She turns her head and now the chill of fear mars the beauty of the colours, for in the skies to the west there is a third pulsating redness, a vast pulsating redness, and above it, towering high, a dark and sinister billowing cloud, the vapourised remains of the nearby city of Derby.

She senses a wind. It gently blows the swing upon which she sits. It blows warm against her face.

Another wind, stronger now and warmer. It blows with a sound like distant thunder.

The third wind, the wind from Derby, comes at her with the roaring and the ferocity of a wild beast. It hurls her through the air. It burns her exposed flesh. It flames her clothes and hair. It melts her eyes. It sears her lungs.

How deceptively beautiful can be the face of death.

*

Alas! For that day is a great one, so that there is no other like it, and it is even the time of Jacob's trouble. But he will be saved out of it.

– Jeremiah 30: 7

The old man sits trembling in the cupboard under the stairs, his eyes red with tears. He has no way of knowing if his children and his grandchildren are dead or alive. In his heart he feels that they are dead.

The denunciation has passed over. The tremendous blasts from the bombs, which have incinerated the cities of Manchester and Liverpool, have passed over, leaving the village of Brinscall a semi-ruin, a poisoned semi-ruin. The old man knows that for quite some time he must not leave the house. He knows that the air outside is poisoned. He knows that the ground outside is poisoned. For all he knows there may be poison in the house! The old man knows that this poison, this radiation, will remain in the air and on the ground until heavy rains fall and even then it will not entirely be washed away. No, pockets of slow and agonising death will remain.

Outside, fierce winds are blowing. The infernos, which were the cities of Manchester and Liverpool, are greedily sucking in the air to feed them. Fierce winds are blowing and while they continue to blow the old man will remain in the darkness under the stairs. He wonders how much damage has been caused to the house? Will he be able to continue to live in the only home he has known these many years? Will he be able to survive?

Does he want to survive?

He is old and weary. How can he go on now? But he is not yet ready to die. Therefore he must go on.

From his knowledge of the Bible, William Brooke has long known that this day would come. He has long known that the day of Jacob's trouble, the day of distress for God's people and for all of humanity must come. But now that it is here, and here so suddenly, it is terrifying, it is fear-inspiring. It is almost more than he can bear.

'My God, my God,' he prays. 'Strengthen me to endure this hour.'

Unseen, the Devil hears William Brooke's outspoken plea and laughs.

Nevertheless, God hears the cries of the afflicted.

*

Three days have passed since the beginning of World-War-Three and now Europe strikes against the English-speaking peoples in other parts of the world. Military installations in Canada, in Australia and in New Zealand are attacked with nuclear missiles.

Ultimatums are issued demanding unconditional surrender. The governments of the three nations are left with no choice. There is no defence against Europe's weaponry. Surrender is the only option. Surrender on Europe's terms. Surrender and compliance with Europe's demands.

And now the face of the earth is changing. The greater part of North America is covered by thick billowing clouds of dust. Similar clouds have massed over Hawaii, over parts of Australasia, and over the British Isles, Ireland, parts of northern and central France and a section of the Italian Alps. These clouds of dust are high

237

above the earth, they are barely affected by the prevailing winds, and in the lands beneath them, where the sun is now darkened and where the moon does not give its light, the nuclear winter, bitter and cold, is quickly descending.

Europe's cruel victories, swift and complete, have stunned and terrified the world. No citizen of any country feels safe. No politician of any country can have confidence in Europe's future intentions. Does Europe wish to unite the world by force and by fear? Where will Europe strike next? In Africa? In South America? The Indian subcontinent? The islands of the sea? Or Asia?

And in the Far East, in China and in Japan and in Korea, Europe's remaining nuclear capability is being speedily assessed. In these eastern regions, work on a defensive system to protect against nuclear attack, whether from space or from land or from sea, goes on apace. In these regions, home to billions of mankind, there is a growing political willingness to suffer and absorb mass casualties for what is perceived as the greater good – the winning of a war against mighty Europe.

The kings of the East are stirring.

*

It is December and in Lancashire the daytime temperature has plummeted to minus twenty degrees Celsius. Few of the survivors of the nuclear holocaust dare to venture outside, except in the necessary search for food or for fuel, for, in addition to the freezing temperatures, there is by day a dense gloom through which the sun can barely be seen and by night there is dense darkness.

The nuclear winter has arrived and the days of easy living are gone. The things that were taken for granted are gone.

There is no electricity, there is no gas supply, the tap water is poisoned. There are no medical services, no

238

dental services, few medicines. There is no governing structure, no law-enforcement, little social structure.

Now these things are gone.

In the village of Brinscall, William Brooke survives by laying snares in the darkened woods for rabbits, for hares, for anything he can catch. Also, he has made himself a catapult and he has become proficient in its use. The animals he hunts and eats are supplemented by his dwindling supplies of tinned food. He calculates his tinned provisions will last until spring – if spring ever comes!

The old man has opened up an old fireplace in his bedroom. In the woods around the village there is still plenty of fuel to be found – logs and twigs. It is simply a matter of collecting the fuel safely. William Brooke avoids contact with other survivors if he possibly can. He knows there is at least one lawless gang roaming the village, taking provisions from the homes of those who have perished. How long will it be before they take from the living?

The old man's home was not severely damaged by the bombing. The windows were blown out, but these have been boarded up and the poisoned dust has been removed. He can do nothing about the collapsed chimney-stack, but it does not affect the fire in his bedroom.

On a truly cold December night, William Brooke, wearing many layers of clothing, sits on the edge of his bed in front of the fire. Had anyone been with him they would have seen, by the light from the flickering fire, the tears of loneliness running down his cheeks and into his beard. Outside in the night there is distant shouting. When the shouting stops the old man remembers the happier times in his life. He thinks of his wife and his loneliness increases.

It is spring and Europe is at war again, now against the kings of the east. In China, in Japan and in Korea, millions have perished and many millions more are perishing as a result of Europe's nuclear onslaught, yet Europe itself has not escaped entirely. Her defences have largely held, but three long-range missiles have penetrated her defensive shield. The cities of Hamburg, Milan and Madrid are no more.

And the point has now been reached where further nuclear strikes will threaten the very existence of mankind. Yes, unless those days were cut short no flesh would be saved!

So, the days are cut short.

No treaties are signed, no undertakings are given, but all sides now cease the use of nuclear weapons.

Those who have lived to witness this cessation are saying that perhaps at last the leaders of the nations have learned their lesson, that common sense is at last beginning to prevail. Few recognise that it is the hand of God that is preventing the total annihilation of all flesh.

But the hand of God is not shielding mankind from the consequences of what has already been done. The nuclear winter is now spreading all over the planet. It is spring in the northern hemisphere, but it is winter everywhere.

Meanwhile, the leaders of the nations have not learned any lessons. In Europe and in the Far East great armies are mobilising. Conventional yet highly sophisticated weapons of warfare are being prepared in the sub-zero temperatures for the struggle ahead.

It is spring in Lancashire and the old man's food reserves are running low. It is now more imperative than ever that he should live off the land, that he should, if necessary, find enough food each day to sustain him, even if what he eats is poisoning him.

He goes to the woods every two or three days now, to check his traps, to hunt, should the traps be empty, with his catapult. He rarely returns home empty-handed. However, the trip to the woods in the semi-darkness is not without its dangers.

It is mid-April and the old man is checking his traps. It is a good day – two rabbits. No need to hunt with the catapult. William Brooke places the rabbits into the inside pouches of his outer coat and sets out for home. Nuclear winter still remains upon the land, like a shroud of ice, and, though it is spring, the temperature is still well below freezing. The old man strides through the unnatural gloom, the frozen vegetation beneath his feet making a crunching sound with his every step. Suddenly he halts. His heart begins to beat faster. Standing in the gloom ahead of him he can just about make out the menacing shapes of three figures.

The old man stands still and, as the figures come towards him slowly, he reaches for his catapult and arms it with a stone from his pocket. The figures move closer, they stand only some seven or eight metres from him. He can see them clearly now. Two youths and a woman! Even with their layers of clothing, the old man can see that he is about to be confronted by two youths and a woman, and he can see that the three of them are armed with long-bladed knives. William Brooke, his catapult armed but not aimed, waits for those who are about to confront him to make the first move. He does not have to wait long.

'We want food, old man,' says the woman, her voice croaky, making her sound older than she looks. 'Give us food if you have it and we'll let you pass.'

Without releasing his grip on his catapult, William Brooke manages to get the rabbits out of his pouches. He tosses the animals in the direction of his confronters.

241

The two youths take a rabbit each and place the carcasses into their own pockets.

'The old fucker's got more than this,' says one of the youths to the woman. He speaks in low tones, almost a whisper, as if to prevent the old man from hearing, but William Brooke can hear him.

The woman nods her head. 'Yeah,' she croaks in the same low tones. 'And even if he doesn't have more food in his pockets, he'll likely have food at his home.'

'He probably lives on his own,' says the second youth, grinning. 'Otherwise he wouldn't be out here by himself.'

Again the woman nods. 'Where do you live, old man?' she shouts at him in her croaky voice. She shouts as if she thinks William Brooke has a problem with his hearing. She shouts as if she thinks the old man hasn't heard what has been said.

William Brooke makes no reply.

'We're going to see that you get home safely,' shouts the woman.

William Brooke makes no reply.

The woman looks first at one youth and then at the other. 'Take him,' she hisses.

Brandishing his knife, one of the youths steps cautiously forward, but, before he can take a second step, William Brooke acts. He aims his catapult at the woman's head and releases the stone.

Without uttering a sound the woman slumps to the ground. The youth who was approaching the old man freezes in his tracks and looks down at the woman. When he looks again towards William Brooke he sees the newly armed catapult aimed directly at him. The second youth, meanwhile, has neither moved nor spoken, but on his face is a look of sheer disbelief. William Brooke likewise remains silent, but his aim with the catapult is steadfast.

The first youth now takes a step backwards. The

catapult remains aimed at his head. He takes another step backwards and then another and all the time the catapult remains aimed at his head. He takes a fourth backward step and then his nerve fails him. He turns and he runs as fast as he can. Within seconds the other youth is also running. William Brooke stands firm with loaded catapult until he can no longer hear the crunching of hurrying feet upon the frozen ground, until he is satisfied that the youths are long gone.

He then goes over to where the woman is lying. He feels for a pulse, but finds none. The old man is sorry that the woman is dead, but he feels no blood guilt.

I will speak at this point. The other narrator will have you believe that God will intervene to prevent the destruction of all flesh. But there is no God!

When these things come upon you, when these times come upon you, when my fury rages, it will be my intention to wipe your species off the face of the earth.

*

Spring has turned to summer in the northern hemisphere and soon the summer will give way to autumn, yet winter, the nuclear winter, is reluctant to release its icy grip. Yet the clouds of nuclear warfare are at last beginning to thin and here and there, and now and then, the sun is not darkened. Here and there, and now and then, the moon does give its light.

Yes, the clouds of war will soon disperse, but war itself will not disperse. Roughly one-third of the human race has perished under the nuclear onslaughts. A further third is already perishing or will perish as an indirect result of the bombings. The remaining third of humanity is plagued by war and preparations for war.

War between nations, between national groups, between tribes, has once again erupted. Wars in South America, in

Africa, in the Middle East, in the Indian subcontinent and in other places. In many parts of the world there is anarchy, especially in those regions that have been bombed. In mighty Europe, technologically sophisticated armies are preparing to march eastward, and in the east, over the vast plains and mountainous regions of China, less sophisticated armies, numbering some two hundred million men and women, are preparing to march westward.

The nuclear war is over.

The killing is not.

*

It is now mid-February and in Lancashire William Brooke has endured sixteen months of the most severe cold, sixteen months of gloom by day and pitch darkness by night, sixteen months of scavenging for food and for fuel, sixteen months of loneliness.

Yes he has endured. By the grace of God he has survived these many months. He has fed himself, kept himself warm, avoided severe illness and, the regrettable incident in the woods apart, he has avoided attack by his fellow humans.

And in those sixteen months William Brooke has in some ways become a stronger person. He is old, he has many of the minor ailments that come with old age, such as poor digestion and a touch of arthritis, but the harshness of life in these times of tribulation has made him fitter and stronger than before. And the daily struggle for survival has focused his mind. William Brooke is mentally strong, relying on God to sustain him, to bring him through to a better place, to one day remove the great loneliness that weighs down upon him, a great loneliness caused by the old man's separation from those he loves, and, although he cannot know for certain, William Brooke feels that it is death that has separated him from his family.

244

But he cannot be certain.

Immediately after the beginning of the war, before the batteries for his radio ran dry, William Brooke heard that both New York City and the naval base of Plymouth in Devon had been bombed. In his heart the old man believes that his son and his daughter are dead. In his heart he believes that his grandchildren are dead. But he cannot be certain! Perhaps David was not in New York when the incineration occurred. Perhaps Ellen and her family were not actually in Plymouth when the city was vapourised!

They are all dead, he repeatedly tells himself, but he cannot be certain and he has no way of discovering the truth. There is no postal service and if there were he could not send a letter to a place that no longer exists! His telephone has never worked since the day of the bombing! He cannot possibly travel to where Plymouth was, to where New York was!

So, William Brooke's loneliness will continue, but he is not entirely alone. The old man rarely speaks to anyone because he rarely sees anyone, yet he does speak with someone he cannot see. Every day the old man speaks with God, and it is the unchanging and unchangeable God who is upholding him.

In mid-February, in Lancashire, as the nuclear winter is after sixteen months at last beginning to yield to the promise of a spring to come, as every day and every night the clouds of war are thinning and even dispersing, William Brooke, indeed the whole world, receives a sign from God, yet William Brooke is among the relative few who will recognise the sign and thereby take hope from it.

*

And then the sign of the Son of Man will appear in heaven ... – Matthew 24: 30

245

The month of April has arrived and the great armies of the kings of the east are steadily advancing westward across the vast plains of Asia. At every opportunity they are attacked and harassed by superior European weaponry, both on the ground and from the air. Casualties are high, but to the kings of the east these casualties are acceptable. What is a million dead or wounded out of two hundred million?

The armies of the east press on relentlessly. Their goal is final conquest, conquest of the Holy Land and conquest of Europe. And in the Middle East and on the eastern borders of Europe, other great armies are assembling, armies drawn from all the nations of mighty Europe, armies preparing for the conflict to come.

In Lancashire, William Brooke, effectively cut off from contact with the wider world, is unaware of these things.

It is an April night, now some eighteen months after the bombing, and William Brooke sits on the edge of his bed in front of the flickering fire. He has a toothache, a recurring toothache, and he knows from bitter experience that he must endure the pain for several days more until the nerve deadens. After that he will need to extract the tooth himself.

Apart from the distant hooting of an owl, the village is quiet and, as the fire begins to die down, the old man decides to take his toothache to bed. Minutes later he is soundly asleep.

When he awakens the old man assumes that it is almost dawn, for there is a faint light shining against the thin curtain covering his bedroom window. His toothache has gone and the old man lies dozing for a while. When he again looks towards the curtain he sees that the faint light is of exactly the same intensity as before. The old man is intrigued. Surely, he cannot be looking at the light of dawn! Now the old man becomes excited. Have the clouds of war finally gone? Is it the light of the moon shining against his curtain? He gets out of bed and draws back the curtain.

Through the grimy window-pane, William Brooke can indeed see the moon. Yes, the clouds are gone and he can see the moon! But there is something else in the sky, something shining brighter than the near full moon, yet, through the grimy window, William Brooke cannot identify this phenomenon.

The old man gets dressed and hurries downstairs. He goes immediately into the kitchen and opens the back door. He goes out into the yard and looks up at the sky. And his heart is filled with wonder.

With wonder!

There, in the night sky, running from the horizon to a point almost overhead, is the most wondrous sight. A shining fissure in the heavens! A cleft! A gigantic tearing in the canvas of the celestial fabric. Shimmering brightly. Swaying, as if to music, music inaudible to mortal man.

William Brooke gazes upwards in awe, and yet, try as he might, his eyes will not clearly focus upon this celestial phenomenon. In the days to come he will look upwards more than a thousand times and more than a thousand times he will fail to see the fissure clearly. And not only he! All surviving mankind will look upwards and all will fail to see clearly, for the shimmering scar in the vault of the heavens is defying the eye to focus upon it. Furthermore, the phenomenon will prove to hold within it other properties, properties strange and unknown to man.

All mankind will come to know that this heavenly fissure has properties within it that defy reason, that deny logic and science. All mankind will come to know that this visitation is something unnatural, something supernatural.

For the scar in the heavens will prove to be visible day and night, whatever the weather, simultaneously from every part of the globe! The sun, moon and stars rise and set with the turning of the earth on its axis, but not this strange and wondrous cleft. It will be seen shimmering in the northern skies by day, and, at the very same time, it will be visible in the southern skies by night, ever visible, ever faintly shimmering beyond the veil of cloudy and rainy skies. An impossible reality!

And even in these times of war, famine and disease on a scale previously unimagined, men of science will attempt to make sense of the fissure. They will unsuccessfully try to measure its dimensions, to analyse its physical properties, to understand it from a scientific point of view. In all these things they will not succeed, yet they will come to know that the phenomenon is moving and they will be able to calculate its movement. They will find, impossible though it will seem to them, that, although it is visible from every surface of the earth, the fissure is actually moving so as to be positioned over a particular area of the earth – the Middle East. Specifically the city of Jerusalem, whose name means city of peace!

And again, even in these times of war, famine and disease, men will send probes into space to study the visitation, and then will be revealed the strangest thing of all. For the probes will find that the fissure is not detectable from space! In the place where it is known to be, some thirty miles above the surface of the earth, it cannot be found! Another scientific impossibility! What is visible to all does not apparently exist.

Yet to the peoples of earth the cleft does exist, in fact, it will be impossible to ignore, for it will be constantly visible. Some, like William Brooke, will say that the fissure is the sign of the Son of Man, that Christ is about to return, that the Day of Judgment is at hand. Others will say that the cleft is the work of the Devil, that its source is evil and that therefore it can bring only more evil upon the world. Others still will say that this phenomenon is the work of an alien intelligence, that mankind is now in contact with creatures from another world. Many other theories will abound. There will be no end to speculations.

Yet, whatever men will say about it, it is certain that in the beginning, at least, the phenomenon will inspire fear among mankind, a fear perhaps even greater than the fear of death, for the cleft will cause many to re-assess their values, even their eternal values. Among mankind there will be an inspection of the inner-self, an examination of present circumstances and of future prospects, and, along with this examination will be a feeling of dread, an anguish of the people because of the things that have come, and that many will fear are yet to come, upon the inhabited earth.

Yet, time will pass by, and it will be only a little time, and then the fear of the phenomenon will begin to fade and in the place of this fear there will come to be a general acceptance of the presence of the fissure, for, during that brief period of time, Christ will not return, the works of the Devil will not be made manifest, and there will be no contact with any alien race. Yes, mankind's irrational ability to ignore what is uncomfortable along with his ability to accept what cannot be changed will, for a little while, dispel many fears concerning this celestial phenomenon.

However, all these things are things of the near future. This magnificent celestial manifestation has only now become visible in those parts of the world where the gloomy clouds of war have dissipated.

In Lancashire, William Brooke continues to look up at the heavens in wonder. Even after dawn has broken he is

249

still looking up at the fissure, the great divide in the heavens, and he is still failing to see it clearly as it dances in the blue. He is convinced in his heart that soon the fissure will open wide to reveal the Son of God and all his angels with him. Yes, Jesus himself, come to save mankind from self-destruction, come to bind the Devil and hurl him into the abyss, come to establish God's kingdom of a thousand years on the earth.

The old man, his heart filled with hope for the future, his eyes filled with tears of joy, now utters these words out loud.

'Thy kingdom come. Thy will be done, on earth as it is in heaven.'

*

Jomo lies dying in the camp. He is just eight years old. He has AIDS. He was born with the infection, it is endemic in this part of Africa.

Jomo looks out of the window and there in the sky he can see the cleft. He weeps. He, an orphan who thought his tears had all been shed, weeps. He, in pain and lying at the point of death, weeps.

Yet his tears are tears of hope.

He remembers the story he has been told. The story of Jesus returning to rule the earth in justice. The story of how this Jesus will cure all humanity's ills, even raise the dead!

Jomo weeps with joy!

What rubbish! What pith!

The Nazarene was executed outside the walls of Jerusalem some two thousand years ago. He is dead, and dead men do not return to rule the earth.

I am the ruler of this world.

The Nazarene is dead. There is no God. No god but me! There is no resurrection of the dead.

If you should live to see this sign in the sky, you should know it for what it truly shall be. It will be a sign of imminent attack. Yes, attack by the super-advanced alien race, which has monitored your actions for centuries. They know you! They fear your violent tendencies. If my war does not destroy you all, then this advanced civilization will destroy you all!

By all my power, you as a race will not survive.

*

The old lady sits in her chair in the nursing home. Amazingly, in this remote part of Scotland, there is some normality. Here there is occasional electricity and here the nursing home is staffed, if barely.

The old lady is dying. Not perhaps immediately, but she knows she is under sentence of death and that the execution of that sentence is close at hand. She has always been under sentence of death, even from the day of her conception. Death brought on by old age, by the refusal of her body cells to regenerate at the required rate to keep her young and beautiful.

Yes, she was beautiful once.

Now she has only her memories. Memories of lost youthfulness, of lost loves, of happy days forever gone.

Or are they?

She looks out of the window and she sees for the very first time the great fissure in the heavens. She sees it and she knows without a shadow of a doubt.

'Jesus is coming!' she cries out loud.

A nurse rushes over to comfort her. 'Hush, Mary. It's all right.'

The old lady's eyes light up. 'Jesus is coming!' she cries again. 'To save us all!'

*

It is autumn and World-War-Three has now been raging on planet earth for two terrible years. Two years have passed since the first nuclear bombs were cruelly inflicted

251

upon the English-speaking peoples. And during these two years we have seen a nuclear exchange between Europe and the nations of the east. We have seen a more conventional kind of warfare in many corners of the globe. We have seen the widespread use of chemical and biological agents. We have also seen the assembling of two mighty armies, an army numbering some two hundred million in the east, and an army of sophisticated weaponry in Europe. The eastern army has marched relentlessly westwards, despite heavy casualties, and now, two years after the outbreak of war, it has advanced almost to the eastern borders of mighty Europe. Now, two years into The Great Tribulation, the army of the east is fighting its way through the deserts of Iraq and over the mountainous regions of Jordan and Syria. Jerusalem beckons!

And Europe has vowed to defend Jerusalem.

So, the battle lines are being drawn. From the Arctic shores of Russia to the Red Sea, two mighty armies are preparing to do battle. Thicko (the Truly Horrific International Combatant and Killing Operative) is alive and well.

Yes, Thicko is thriving, not only in Europe and in Asia, but everywhere. Thicko is rampaging through South America, through Africa, through the subcontinent, through the islands of the sea, and he has even reappeared in many of the regions that have been blasted by nuclear weaponry. Thicko reigns supreme!

And, speaking generally, Thicko is looked after. He is cared for by his political masters. Unlike the majority of the world's surviving populations, Thicko is fed and watered, and he has access to medical facilities. Thicko is well clothed and he finds shelter, often at the expense of those who are not Thickos. Those who are not Thickos also suffer in other ways.

Where there is not warfare there is lawlessness. The strong dominate the weak. The men and women of violence take from the peaceable. Pestilences and plagues stalk the earth. Sickness and death caused by radiation, by toxic chemicals, by man-induced strains of bacteria. And in the wake of all this there is widespread famine.

The horsemen of the Apocalypse are riding! They are racing over the face of earth. The riders bring war, pestilence and famine. Yet, there is a fourth rider ... and the name he is called is the Word of God. – Revelation 19: 13

In the skies above this warring, pestilence-ridden, famine-stricken planet earth, the sign of the Son of Man has been clearly visible these past six months, clearly visible to all since the dispersal of the gloomy clouds of the nuclear winter. In fact, it has proved impossible not to see the great fissure in the heavens, for it has shone brightly by night and by day.

Yet, the sign has been largely ignored!

It has become accepted as a fact of life. It is there, it gleams and shimmers, it defies logic, but so what? Whatever it is, no man can remove it. Whatever it is, it seems to be doing no harm. So let us get on with destroying the planet!

Soon, two mighty armies will face each other across the battlegrounds of eastern Europe and the Middle East. Soon, the great cleft in the sky, visible all over the world, yet still impossibly moving into its final position in the skies above Jerusalem, will be in its place.

The stage is almost set.

*

There is nothing good about nuclear war. There is nothing good about the death it brings, the pain it inflicts, the terror, the misery, the anguish. All these things were visited upon Britain.

It is the mid-winter, some two years and three months after the bombing, and the islands of Britain are yet in ruin. All major cities are gone, and in their places are great blackened radioactive craters, craters surrounded by blasted and burnt-out buildings. No one lives in these places. Those who attempted to live in these places died long ago of the poisoning.

Beyond the cities for miles and miles in every direction there is devastation. Ruined and half-ruined towns and villages! Here there are survivors, but life for them is hard. Life for those who have not perished is a constant struggle for food, for shelter, a struggle against disease, against lawlessness. There is no electricity, no gas supply, little clean water. There are no medical facilities, no drugs. There is no order in Britain – no government, no army, no police force, little or no authority at a local level. Those who have banded together into groups find themselves battling with other groups for food, for the necessities of life itself. Those who are not part of a group generally fare worse.

This is Britain some twenty-seven months after the bombing. This is Britain in the aftermath of nuclear holocaust. A land stricken, mortally stricken! Its surviving populations left largely ignorant of events taking place in the wider world. A land left to rot. A land vanquished. A place where barbarism is triumphing, where only the few raise their eyes to the heavens, to the great celestial scar, with hope in their hearts.

*

Cei Bach, Mid-Wales.

'Find the bitch!'
  'Yeah, find the rich bitch. She's here somewhere.'
  The rich bitch that was trembles with fear. She is hiding

254

under a pile of old clothing and rags in the garden shed. She can hear the men quite clearly. She has known all along that one day they would come for her.

'Come on boys, find the bitch!'

'Yeah, and when we do we'll all shag her!'

'I'm not shagging her after you've shagged her, Dewi. I might catch something.'

The rich bitch that was cannot stop trembling. She knows the men are searching the grounds, having failed to find her in the house. She prays that when they come into the shed they will not look under the pile of clothing.

'She's around here somewhere. Got to be. Let's look in the shed.'

Now the rich bitch that was is filled with terror. She is terrified of the men and of what they will do to her. And these men she had once counted as acquaintances. She and her husband had once employed some of these men – before the bombing. They had mown the lawns, they had paved the drive, built ornamental walls, even run errands for her – before the bombing.

'Nothing here but a pile of old rags, boys.'

The rich bitch that was holds her breath, convinced that otherwise the men will hear the sound of her breathing. She wishes with all her heart that her husband were here to protect her, but she is certain that he is dead. Six months ago he went out to find food. He never came back. He must be dead. He would never have abandoned her!

'Hey, boys! There's some paraffin here.'

The rich bitch that was does not immediately realise the possible consequences of these words. She can hear her own heartbeat. So loud! The men must hear it too.

'Hey, Ivor! Got a match?'

It is spring in Lancashire, some two and a half years after

the bombing, and for William Brooke it is a time both of sadness and of hope.

The old man sits at his kitchen table eating a supper of rabbit meat with a few tinned beans – the last of his beans. It is a moment of nostalgia for him. He feels lost and abandoned. He wants to go home. Home to happiness.

William Brooke feels lost and abandoned and alone in a cruel world. He longs for times past. He longs for times future. His mind dwells on times past.

Even now, even after all these years, he still cannot help but remember the good times. Beautiful memories press in on him from every angle and he sees her face. Jessica! JESSICA!

Why did Jessica leave him all those years ago? He knows even now that she had loved him once. And he had loved her.

But over the years she had changed. And he had changed. She had changed in little, unimportant ways, but he had grown impatient and short-tempered with her and in the end she had stopped loving him. How do you stop loving someone? Had he stopped loving her? Had he grown angry with her because she had changed? Was it the original Jessica he had loved so much? Yes, the original Jessica, the Jessica before she had changed. His sweet baby!

When she was changing, it was as if she was slowly dying – yet he could not see it. When she had gone it was as if she had actually died.

The old man weeps now. He weeps for his forever lost love.

Forever lost?

No!

Jessica is gone and she will never return to him. But love is not lost forever. He is now an old man, but in his heart he is not old. In his heart he is young and William

Brooke has faith in God's promises – the promise of everlasting life, given to those who keep God's commandments. The promises of everlasting youth and of the opportunity to love and be loved again. These are the promises of God who is opening up his hands and satisfying the legitimate desires of every living thing.

The old man wipes away his tears and goes outside into the yard. The sun is setting and the celestial fissure is as bright, if not brighter, than ever.

The old man throws the remains of his rabbit toward the back of the yard where the stray cat is waiting. William Brooke feeds the cat, but one day soon he might eat it!

His attention returns to the great heavenly cleft. He looks up at it in awe and for the very first time he seems to see it clearly. His eyes now seem to be able to focus upon it. It is a brightly shimmering tearing in the fabric of the evening and the old man feels strongly that very soon the fissure will open, it will open wide, and it will reveal his salvation.

Devoid of information, the old man does not know that along the entire frontier of eastern Europe and in the Middle East, especially in the vicinity of Jerusalem, two mighty armies face each other. The old man does not know that this same celestial scar is shining down upon the coming field of battle. All over the world, from the horizon to the centre of the sky, the great heavenly fissure shines, and now it can be clearly seen.

The stage is set.

And the great mystery in the heavens is about to be revealed to all mankind.

The old man will be disappointed.

There is no God. The Nazarene is dead. The Nazarene therefore is not returning to rule the earth.

I am the ruler of this world. I rule, I direct and my demons do my bidding.

The old man, the old fool, lives in a fantasy world, a world of wishful thinking. What is this nonsense he dreams of, this everlasting life, this everlasting youthfulness, this everlasting love? Salvation? He will not be saved. The old man, my enemy, has had his day! His future lies in death and, if I am able to get my hands upon him, in hell, my hell!

I am the ruler of this world, I along with my demons. You are the scum who inhabit this planet, but there are other species in the universe, other civilizations have evolved.

When this celestial phenomenon reveals itself, when he cleft opens, all of you who remain alive will come to understand that there is no God, you will come to understand that evolution is a fact of life.

You are a feeble yet a dangerous race! You are a danger to the stability of the universe, and your actions have been noted.

Another species, an advanced civilization, a civilization close to you in astronomical terms, has noted your deficiencies, and now they have come to annihilate you. For centuries they have monitored your actions, your wars, your developing of dangerous technologies. During that time they have abducted some of you. During that time many of you have seen their saucer-shaped crafts. They are here to annihilate you! They are cruel, they do not know compassion. They know only of logic and to them it is logical to destroy you all before you plunder the cosmos.

We will not interfere. You see, we are becoming bored by you. We have tired of you. We will allow this advanced civilization to completely annihilate you and we will allow them to populate your world. We will then force our influence upon them. It will be a different challenge for us.

I will remain as the god of this world.

Do not believe the lies you are about to read next.

Do not believe the lies.

*

258

In the Vicinity of Jerusalem.

'ADVANCE!'

As the order is given Ji-En-Li strides forward determinedly, his automatic rifle at the ready. Ahead of him artillery shells are exploding. Far behind him the artillery shells of the enemy are exploding. Not too far ahead he can hear the rat-tat-tat-tat of machine-gun fire.

'ADVANCE, BRAVE SOLDIERS!'

Ji-En-Li and his comrades press on towards the enemy positions on the outskirts of the city – of what remains of the city. Jerusalem, the City of Peace, is at war. Jerusalem is a ruin.

'ADVANCE!'

Ji-En-Li and his comrades are coming under heavy fire. Someone falls to his left, two fall to his right, yet their places are quickly taken. The army of the east is not short of manpower.

BOOOM! BOOOOOOM!

Artillery shells explode just ahead, cratering the ground, sending yellow-brown dust high into the air. Ji-En-Li presses on. He is afraid of death, but his hatred of the enemy is greater than his fear of death.

'ADVANCE! ADVANCE!'

It is hatred that drives him on. Pure hatred of the Europeans, the savage Europeans! The Europeans who have laid waste to his homeland, who have incinerated and poisoned his homeland by the use of nuclear weapons, who have taken the lives of his family, all of his family. Only he was not there when the bombing started. He was away with the army, learning to kill.

It is the pure hatred in his heart that is urging him on, urging him on to kill. To kill the brutal Europeans who have taken the lives of so many of his comrades during the long, long march through the deserts, plains and mountains of Asia. To kill the European pigs, like the animals they are! To kill them! To kill! Ji-En-Li presses on.

'ADVANCE!'

Shells are exploding all around him now. He and his comrades are coming under machine-gun fire and rifle fire. Overhead he can hear the thunderous roaring of the Eurofighters. Dust and acrid smoke fill the air. The cries of the dying and wounded are not far away. It is the heat of battle, it is the kitchen of hell, but Ji-En-Li presses on in order to kill.

CRUUUUMMP!

There is a sudden flash and he is blown off his feet. He rolls over, he is rolled into a crater, he still clutches his rifle. He crouches in the crater, unhurt, but dazed and confused, having lost all sense of direction, yet his consuming hatred for the European still burns. And through the fog of battle Ji-En-Li sees another figure in the crater.

He aims his rifle and peers through the fog, the dust. His heart beats faster. He is looking at the enemy. He can clearly see the circle of stars on the sleeve of the uniform. The enemy is lying against the wall of the crater, unmoving. Ji-En-Li, still crouching, moves towards his enemy.

The young man is badly wounded. He appears to have lost part of a leg. He lies against the wall of the crater in a state of shock, yet his eyes are open and he is aware of his surroundings. He looks at Ji-En-Li, his eyes pleading for help.

'YIIIIIH!'

Ji-En-Li presses the trigger of his rifle and bullets of death pump into the European soldier's chest.

'YIIIIIIIIIIH!'

Ji-En-Li continues to squeeze the trigger until the chest of his enemy is nothing more than a morass of blood and gore mixed with splinters of white bone. Ji-En-Li then brings the butt of his rifle down upon his enemy's face again and again.

War is brutal. War brutalities. Ji-En-Li is brutal. He has been brutalised.

His frenzy spent, he lies back against the side of the crater. The sounds of battle are all around him. He looks up and through the fog of battle he sees the great shining fissure in the heavens. Ji-En-Li feels a sudden overpowering fear, a fear stronger than the fear of death, a fear stronger than his intense hatred.

The fissure is opening!

*

Captain David Levi of the Israeli army, of what is left of the Israeli army, of the remains of an Israeli army under European command, is puzzled. The men in his company have ceased firing! Why?

'Keep firing!' he yells. 'Fire at the enemy!'

The only response is a single rifle shot.

He looks along his defensive line to the right and to the left. His men are no longer engaging the enemy. They are looking back towards the city and they are looking up at the sky. He glances towards the field of battle where the enemy were advancing in droves. The enemy no longer seems to be advancing. He turns to look back at the city, at the city of Jerusalem, at the ruined city, at the city for which he would gladly give his life, and he gasps in astonishment.

There, over the city of Jerusalem, stretching from the horizon to the centre of a clear blue sky, is the great heavenly fissure. David Levi focuses his eyes upon it and a great sense of foreboding fills his heart. The fissure is glowing with a great intensity of white light, and, yes, the fissure is slowly widening, allowing the purest of white light to shine through.

A hush has settled over the battlefield, a hush broken only by the pitiful cries of the wounded.

The great cleft in the heavens is opening!

*

Marek Ali stands with his gunmen on the field of battle and stares at the great scar in the heavens. He and his men have allied themselves with the Chinese in order to rid Jerusalem of the hated Jews and Christians, yet now, with victory in sight, the battlefield has fallen silent.

Every man is looking up to the skies. Every man has the fear of the unknown in his heart. Every man is in awe. To Marek Ali and his followers the cause of the Palestinians now seems suddenly less important. To Marek Ali, indeed to every combatant on the field of battle, the cause, whatever the cause, is being driven into insignificance by the brightly shining heavenly phenomenon.

Marek Ali and his men cannot take their eyes away from the widening cleft, from the glowing fissure.

It is opening!

*

Africa – The Congo.

Joshua M'mumba, also known and greatly feared as the Devil's Butcher, is in one of his better moods. His band of rebels have captured the village virtually without resistance. The villagers, knowing his reputation, have acceded to his wishes almost without question, and the young girls and boys of the village have already been taken for sex by himself and by his men. All except one boy, the wretch who protested, the boy whose parents urged him to resist.

Well, no one resists Joshua M'mumba and gets away with it. The boy, the father and the mother are about to pay dearly for their resistance.

262

M'mumba stands alone in what was the head-man's hut. He raises his eyes and cries out loud. 'What shall I do with them?' he asks the voice. 'What shall I do with those who have offended me?'

'Kill them,' the voice in his head replies. 'Kill them all.'

The Devil Butcher grins. He takes a firm hold of his machete and strides out into the African sunshine. He makes directly for the hut where the boy and his parents have spent the night in captivity. It is time to pay.

The guard salutes M'mumba as he strides through the doorway. M'mumba grins as he pauses for a moment to allow his eyes to adjust to the poor light. The father and the mother, bound with rope, sit terrified in a corner. M'mumba can see the fear in their eyes and it pleases him. The boy, also bound, lies sleeping at his mother's feet.

The Devil Butcher now wastes no time. Still grinning, he strides over to the boy, lifts him by the hair and swings the machete.

With a single blow the boy's head is severed from his shoulders. The mother screams and the father gags with shock as the body falls to the ground twitching. Blood spurts and flows and M'mumba holds the head in front of the agonised parents. Still grinning, M'mumba throws the head across the room. He now deals swiftly with the parents.

Down and down swings the machete. Again and again it swings, cutting into flesh, into bone. It is a bloodbath, but it is over in less than a minute. The guard again salutes the grinning and blood-soaked M'mumba as he leaves the hut.

Out in the sunshine the Devil Butcher glances up at the great shining fissure. What he sees causes him to halt in his tracks. The fissure is beginning to open!

'What is this?' he asks the voice in his head.

The voice is silent.

The grin fades from the Devil Butcher's face.

*

Arizona, USA.

Helen Baker – ex all-American woman – survived the bombing – dying now – cancer – the BIG C – no pain relief.

Helen Baker – middle-aged and alone – in pain.

Helen Baker – in great pain – in unbearable pain – in great pain – in pain – a few hours' relief when the pain is bearable – in great pain – in unendurable pain – in great pain.

Helen Baker – wants only to die.

Helen Baker – in too much distress to take note of the great heavenly fissure.

Helen Baker – bitter and twisted because of the pain.

Helen Baker, the fissure is opening.

*

Montevideo, Uruguay.

So, the boy's name is Jose, not that it matters.

What does matter is that Jose appears to be healthy. He says he is fourteen, but that doesn't matter either. He is healthy. He has healthy organs.

The man buys Jose another coffee and some cake. The boy may be healthy, but he is thin, like most of the street children.

The man slips the drug into the boy's coffee. It will make him drowsy, perhaps even sleepy. In any case it will not be difficult to get the boy into the car and off to the clinic.

The man makes a mental calculation of the price he

should receive. Two eyes, a heart, a liver and two kidneys, plus the other bits and pieces. Jose should bring in the region of fifty thousand.

A little later and a sleepy Jose is being helped into the man's car under a cloudy night sky through which the heavenly phenomenon brightly shines.

And the cleft in the skies is widening.

*

Auckland, New Zealand.

Moira Blood is probably the most powerful woman in New Zealand, certainly she is the most powerful person in Auckland province. Appointed directly by the European High Command, Moira Blood has been placed in a position of absolute authority. As governor of Auckland province, Moira Blood holds life and death in her hands.

She is also addicted to drugs and sex.

In her private apartments in the governor's mansion she is playing one of her little games. Away from prying eyes, Moira Blood has arranged a little entertainment for herself.

The man, totally naked, lies on his back, his arms and legs spread and strapped to the four posts of the bed. He did not protest when Moira Blood did this to him, he had not dared to protest, and now Moira Blood, naked apart from her panties, has the man's erect penis in her mouth.

Both of them have been snorting cocaine.

The man writhes and groans as his orgasm nears. Moira Blood sucks with a frenzy. The man cries out and Moira Blood gags as fluid spurts into her mouth. She spits the seminal fluid into the man's face and laughs.

She now lies back across the man's panting body and licks her finger. The wet finger goes inside her panties

265

and her legs are opened wide. She finds her clitoris and begins to rub vigorously, every now and then momentarily withdrawing the finger in order to lick it, until at length her ecstasy comes. She screams and then lies panting. She laughs.

The man, a criminal under sentence of death, does not know that this woman has ordered his execution to be carried out within hours. Moira Blood does not know that the fissure in the sky is opening.

Moira Blood is under the impression that her depravities and cruelties are hidden, but God sees all things, for he reads the heart, and these depravities and cruelties are written on Moira Blood's heart.

*

Russia, on Europe's eastern front.

The Thicko (the Truly Horrific International Combatant and Killing Operative), Lech Janinski, has had enough. Enough of the killing. For days now, wave upon wave of Oriental soldiers have attempted to storm his defensive position. Janinski has killed hundreds, many hundreds, and he has had enough.

He looks at the scar in the heavens and believes that God is coming. In tears of distress he asks for forgiveness of his sins. When he turns his back on his weapons of death and walks slowly away, leaving his position, he is dreaming of his native Poland, the Poland he knew as a boy.

He is ordered several times to return to his position, to fulfil his duty, but Lech Janinski has renounced killing, he is no longer a Thicko.

He is shot in the back of the head by his own company commander.

*

In Lancashire, William Brooke is standing in his yard looking up at the sky. He is fervently praying that he might be found worthy to escape the denunciation that he knows is about to be visited upon the earth. He is praying that God will now deliver him from old age and death, from his great loneliness. He is praying that God will bring him home!

Well now, you can surely see that the other writer of this book is attempting to lay the path for the return of Christ. It's so obvious.

But it will not happen.

It will not happen because it cannot happen.

You are an intelligent species. You know that you are a product of evolutionary processes. You know this. Therefore reason tells you that there is no God.

As for the Christ, well, the Nazarene called himself the Son of Man, did he not? And he was executed some two thousand years ago, was he not? Dead men do not return.

The resurrection? A fanciful tale put about by the Nazarene's disciples.

Think about it. Do you know anyone who has been resurrected from the dead? Of course you don't! The dead are dead. That much is obvious. Their flesh rots and only the bones remain.

So, what about the soul? Do you have an immortal soul? Do the good go to heaven to be with God? Another fanciful tale put about by clerics. Do the wicked go to hell to endure eternal torments? Is this a tale put about by me? Or a tale put about by the same clerics in order to make men afraid to do evil things? (There is no God, so what are evil things?)

Be logical. Be reasonable.

Reason tells you that life evolves. Reason tells you that, with innumerable galaxies contained in a seemingly limitless universe, there must be other civilizations out there.

And there are.

And one such civilization, greatly disturbed by your deeds, has

267

now decided to annihilate you all.

Yes, to annihilate you, though a few of you might survive.

Let me tell you a secret. Let me tell you what they look like. They have evolved into something a little different to yourselves. They have three legs where you have only the two. They have no eyes in their heads, large heads which contain superior brains. They have a single eye, which has evolved on the tip of the index finger of the left hand. For them it is not rude to point!

Yes, they are something like Tim, the Impossible Man, but, of course, they are not men.

But they are coming to annihilate you.

Do you believe me?

You will if you should be living when these things happen.

Do you believe me? Or will you believe the fanciful ideas of the other writer of this book?

I urge you not to be so stupid as to believe what the other writer of this book is about to tell you.

Do not believe him!

*

Ji-En-Li, his tunic splattered with the blood of his slain enemy, lies back against the side of the crater and trembles with fear, a fear he has never before known. His eyes are open wide, unnaturally so, and he is looking to the sky. The great fissure is opening, it is beginning to fill the whole of the sky above the now near-silent battlefield, and its secret is being revealed to Ji-En-Li. What he sees fills both his mind and his heart with unbearable confusion and terror.

Ji-En-Li sees a craft, a great saucer-shaped craft. It seems to fill the whole of the sky, it slowly spins, it slowly manoeuvres, but it is not the craft itself that so terrifies him. What terrifies him is the alien-like figure that has somehow emerged from underneath the craft and which, without visible means of support, is now descending from the skies, descending directly towards Ji-En-Li.

He screams in confusion and terror. He cannot deny the evidence of his eyes. He screams again. He wants to look away, but he is unable to look away.

The figure is almost upon him. It is vast, the size of ten men. It has three legs and a large head in which there are no eyes. But there is an eye, a single unproportionally large eye, and it is situated on the end of a finger, a finger, which is pointing at Ji-En-Li. In the other hand the alien-like figure is holding a weapon, a complicated-looking gun, and this gun also points at Ji-En-Li, but it is not the gun that is causing Ji-En-Li to scream. It is the eye.

For reflected in the eye there is a face. And it is the face of Ji-En-Li. Yet it is not the face of Ji-En-Li, for the eyes in the reflection are the eyes of a European!

Ji-En-Li is seeing himself in the eye of an invading alien-like being, yet the reflection is casting him as one of his hated enemies – a European!

Ji-En-Li is seeing himself as he has never seen himself and it is more than he can bear. His great hatred has become a hatred of himself. He is his own enemy.

The condition of his own heart is what Ji-En-Li is seeing in the eye of the alien figure.

He screams. He screams again and grips his rifle tightly.

*

Captain David Levi gasps in wonder at the scene over the city of Jerusalem. The long-awaited Messiah has finally arrived!

There he is, much larger than life, mounted upon his horse, sword in hand, come to save Israel! And with him are his angels.

Captain David Levi gasps again at the scene in front of his eyes, and then a frown crosses his brow. Something is not quite right. Surely, the Messiah, his horse, his angels, they should all be dressed in the purest white! According to prophesy and tradition, they should be in white.

David Levi does not know that the scene he is witnessing stems partially from the condition of his own heart.

This Messiah, who dominates the entire sky over Jerusalem, is a grey Messiah. His horse is a horse of a different colour – it is black. And this Messiah's angels are a dirty brown.

The fear of the unknown now grips David Levi's heart. And in the skies above Jerusalem the dark Messiah turns his head to look upon David Levi. His look is cruel and threatening.

David Levi steps back in terror as the dark Messiah raises his sword and spurs his mount onward.

Onward towards Captain David Levi.

*

Marek Ali and his men stand in awe as they look up at the gigantic mullah in the skies over the ruins of Jerusalem. In his left hand the Muslim holy man carries the Koran, in his right hand a Kalashnikov. Marek Ali falls to his knees. Is this Mohammed? Is this Allah himself?

As if in answer to his questions Marek Ali sees the mullah turn his head to look directly at him. No, this is not Mohammed! It is not Allah!

For the face is the face of cruelty.

Cruel lips. A cruel expression. Cruelty in the eyes.

Marek Ali is afraid, more afraid than ever he can remember. 'Allah shows mercy to the merciful,' he cries out in a trembling voice.

In response the mullah in the skies aims his Kalashnikov directly at Marek Ali.

*

The Devil Butcher's heart is pounding. His lord and master, none other than Satan, has manifested himself in the African skies. Joshua M'mumba, splattered with the

270

blood of the innocent, his machete gleaming red with the blood of the innocent, stares up in awe. The face of Satan is dominating the sky.

It is a face without compassion. The skin is as red as the blood of the innocent, the mouth is as cruel as the rabble M'mumba leads, the eyes as black as M'mumba's pounding heart.

'Lord Satan,' cries M'mumba fearfully. 'It is I, your servant.'

The cold black eyes now look down upon M'mumba and the voice in M'mumba's head speaks.

'It is time for you to die,' it tells M'mumba.

Fear grips the Devil Butcher. For a moment he cannot speak. When he does find his voice his words come out in a tremble.

'Why?' he asks. 'Why should I die? What have I done to displease you?'

'It is time for you to die,' the voice repeats.

M'mumba throws himself to his knees. He raises his head to the face of Satan and appeals directly to his master.

'Lord Satan, do not let me die. Have I not always served you? Have I not always obeyed the voice?'

The face of Satan grins. It is a grin not dissimilar to the Devil Butcher's own, the grin M'mumba always sports when he is killing.

'He has no use for you now,' says the voice in M'mumba's head. 'It is time for you to die. Look! He is coming for you! Beware! Do not let him take you! Kill yourself! Kill yourself!'

M'mumba now sees the hand of the Devil below the face. He sees the hand reaching down for him and the very fires of hell are burning in his mind, the very torments of hell are piercing his brain.

He screams. A terrible scream. He needs to scream

again, but the pounding of his heart is so great, the flowing of his blood through his veins so powerful, that he cannot now draw the breath to scream.

In his hand the Devil Butcher still holds his machete, the razor-sharp machete.

*

Helen Baker – so much pain – alone and confined to bed – she wants to die – yet death eludes her.

Helen Baker – middle-aged – looks so old – cancer.

Helen Baker – bitter and twisted – too much pain to note the heavenly phenomenon.

Helen Baker – cries with the pain – cries!

Helen Baker – is she delirious? – sees a fairy over her bed!

Helen Baker – touched by the fairy – the fairy leaves her – the pain leaves her.

Helen Baker – anguish gone.

Helen Baker, you have been touched by the Angel of Jehovah.

*

And the Angel of Jehovah is in Montevideo.

Jose lies anaesthetized on the operating table. The surgical team is assembled and they are ready to begin. First they will take the eyes.

In another part of the clinic the would-be recipients of Jose's organs are being prepared. Money, a great deal of money, has changed hands.

And some of this money is in the hands of the man who has brought Jose to this clinic, the man who now trembles uncontrollably as he sees in the skies above him the most terrible sight– a strange and horrific creature, a three-legged creature with no eyes in its head! A creature whose single eye is at the end of one of its fingers! The man screams in terror. The creature holds in his hand a sharp surgical implement, and the creature, pointing directly at this man, is coming down from the heavens to do his dissecting.

In the operating theatre, the Angel of Jehovah moves swiftly. He touches each of the surgical team just the once and each one falls immediately to the floor to lie unmoving. The angel now touches the anaesthetized child, a gentle touch of the forehead.

'Sleep, child, sleep,' he whispers to him. 'When you awaken, the judgment will have passed over. When you awaken you will inherit the earth.'

The Angel of Jehovah moves on. This day he has much to do.

*

Moira Blood is more afraid now than at any time in her forty-seven years. The young man strapped to her bed is similarly terrified. Even though they are within the confines of Moira Blood's private rooms in the governor's mansion, they are both able to see what is descending from the heavens; in fact, they cannot help but see what is descending from the heavens. It is as if the mansion has no roof, no ceiling, as if it is open to the skies, and what is descending from the heavens is terrifying, utterly terrifying.

Moira Blood sees what she believes to be a spectre, a ghost, and it is the ghost of her dead husband, the husband she has had executed on trumped-up charges of treason, the husband she had ceased to love, the husband who had become an embarrassment to her, the husband she has had executed because he threatened to expose her sexual excesses and her habitual drug taking to her European masters.

Moira Blood is afraid, so afraid that, trembling, she actually attempts to hide under the bed.

The convicted murderer, strapped helplessly to the top of the bed, is covered in his own sweat. For him the

273

heavens have opened to reveal his executioner, his hangman. Rope in hand, this hangman descends from the heavens, his face cold and dispassionate, like a man who has a job to do. The murderer sweats even more. The bed is wringing with his sweat. He closes his eyes, but still he sees the hangman. He can feel the rope around his neck.

*

Lech Janinski lies dead on the now near-silent Russian battlefield. He will not see the return of Christ, for 'at the hour of death even the thoughts perish' and 'there is no wisdom nor knowledge nor devising in the grave, the place to which you are going' – the place to which he has gone.

But Lech Janinski has repented of his sins and turned away from them. Also, he has paid the price of sin, which is death. Therefore he is not forgotten.

And Resurrection Man is coming!

*

In Lancashire William Brooke stands and stares with tears of joy running down his cheeks and into his beard. He cannot contain these tears, for they spring not from his eyes but from his heart, a heart, which itself can hardly contain the emotions engendered by that which the great chasm in the heavens has now opened to reveal.

William Brooke is witnessing all the power and the glory of the Second Coming. Yes, the return of Christ – to rule!

A deluded old man sees what he wants to see. He sees what he hopes to see. This is much more than wishful thinking, it is wishful dreaming! The old fool is nearing the end of his life, he is old and weary, he yearns for the former days, the days of his youth. He does not want to accept the natural processes of ageing and death, so in his head he invents his own salvation. He thinks

274

that this alien intervention into human affairs is a resurrected dead man returning to earth to make everything sweetness and light.

The stupid old fool!

Well, let him have his dreams. But you, you the reader, you are not so stupid. You know the truth.

Do not believe what you are about to read next.

*

The heavens are opened and Jesus is revealed.

In stunning power and magnificent glory.

His clothing is the whitest white, the purest white, yet his outer garment is sprinkled with blood.

Wonderful counsellor! Mighty God! Eternal Father! Prince of Peace!

He rides a white horse. He is Faithful and True. He comes to deliver the righteous, to judge the wicked, to make war in righteousness.

His eyes are a fiery flame. There are diadems upon his head, shining like the sun. He is the Word of God.

And all the armies of heaven are with him. All on white horses. All clothed in white.

And out of his mouth there protrudes a sword. A sword to strike the nations. He will shepherd the nations with a rod of iron.

Also he treads the winepress of the anger of the wrath of God the Almighty!

He comes in Jehovah's name.

King of kings and Lord of lords.

He comes to rule.

And he shall reign for ever and ever.

*

Outside the city of Jerusalem, Ji-En-Li, his face contorted by terror and hatred, aims his rifle at the horrific apparition in front of him and presses the trigger. Bullets rip into the alien-like figure, into the eye on the tip of the

275

finger, into the weird and terrifying reflection of Ji-En-Li himself.

And in front of Ji-En-Li's wild and unbelieving eyes, the alien figure begins to change its appearance.

Again Ji-En-Li presses the trigger and a hail of bullets speed into the figure, but now the figure is no longer that of some grotesque alien, now Ji-En-Li is attempting to kill, not a creature of flesh and blood, but a creature composed of spirit.

The Angel of Jehovah, shining with the purest white radiance, quickly reaches forward and touches Ji-En-Li.

Ji-En-Li falls dead. His terror and his hatred die with him.

*

Captain David Levi orders his men to fire upon the apparition of the dark Messiah, the dark Messiah who, sword in hand, is riding, is galloping, is charging towards them from the skies. The men do not obey.

David Levi looks at his men. He sees their eyes upon the heavens, he sees the fear upon their faces. Why, then, do they not obey his command to fire?

Private Benjamin Israel is closest to him.

'Israel!' Levi commands. 'Fire upon the thing in the sky.'

After a moment's hesitation, Benjamin Israel brings up his rifle and aims it directly at his captain.

David Levi immediately shoots him dead with his pistol.

A savage burst of gunfire from some of his own men now tears into the head and chest of David Levi. He dies not knowing that the men of his company are shooting at each other, are killing each other. He dies not knowing that the last man left alive will turn his gun on himself.

The Angel of Jehovah, having sown confusion among Christ's enemies, passes over.

*

Madness reigns on the battlefields surrounding Jerusalem. Marek Ali and his men are firing wildly at the apparition that is the mullah, and the mullah, Koran in one hand and Kalashnikov in the other, appears to the Palestinians to be firing back at them. In fact, the mullah is visible only to Marek and his band, for their Chinese allies see other strange and terrifying visions.

There is total confusion on the battlefields. Soldiers from east and west alike are furiously attacking the visions, which are terrifying them and tormenting them, the dark visions of their own hearts. Soldiers are attacking friend and foe alike. It is total confusion! It is bloody confusion!

In the orgy of slaughter on the outskirts of Jerusalem, Marek Ali and his men are blown to pieces by Chinese artillery.

And the Angel of Jehovah passes over.

*

The Devil Butcher gasps for his breath. His fear is so overpowering that his lungs are refusing to function normally. He sees the hand of Satan reaching down for him and all the tortures of hell are flooding his brain, flooding his brain to such a degree that M'mumba feels that his head is about to burst open.

'Kill yourself!' says the voice in his head. 'Quickly, kill yourself!'

It is more than M'mumba can bear. He swiftly runs the blade of his machete along the side of his neck, severing the jugular.

His blood spurts and runs. It runs and mingles with the splatterings of blood on his clothes and body, the splatterings of the blood of his recent victims.

As his consciousness ebbs, M'mumba looks a final time at the vision of Satan in the skies above him, but the vision is no longer there!

In its place is something, which, to M'mumba, is even more terrifying. In its place he is aware of a brilliant and pure white light, a light so brilliant and so pure that he cannot rest his wicked eyes upon it.

For him, the light begins to fade. Darkness presses in upon him. His dark heart ceases to beat. He pitches forward into a pool of his own blood.

The Angel of Jehovah passes on to bring justice and retribution down upon the Devil Butcher's men.

*

Helen Baker – the pain has gone – your weariness is over.

Helen Baker – tears of joy – full of life – rises from her bed.

Helen Baker – sinks to her knees – gives humble thanks to God.

Helen Baker, you have been given a second chance. Do not waste it!

*

In Montevideo, Jose is awakening from his anaesthetized sleep. He lies unmoving for a little while, not knowing where he is or what has happened to him. His last memory is of the cafe, of the man who brought him coffee and cake. Eventually, he raises his head from the operating table and looks around him.

There are dead men and women lying on the floor. Jose does not know how he is certain they are dead, but he is certain. Also, Jose does not feel afraid.

He climbs down from the operating table and leaves the theatre. Through silent corridors he walks, passing more dead bodies, until at length he finds his way out onto the street.

Here the dead lie in their hundreds, in their thousands. And here Jose recognises the body of the man from the cafe. Yet, not everyone has died!

Jose is approached by a man and a woman. He is not

afraid. The woman smiles at him and the man places a hand upon his shoulder.

'Come with us,' invites the man.

'Yes, come with us,' says the woman. 'We will take care of you.'

Jose knows in his heart that this man and this woman care for him. He just knows. What he has never known, in all his fourteen years, is what it is like to have parents, to have a home.

Jose weeps with joy and nods his head.

'Come with us,' says the man, smiling. 'It is time to go home.'

*

Under her bed, Moira Blood lies dead, executed, not by the ghost of her husband, but by the touch of the angel. Her depravities have died with her.

The man on top of her bed is also dead, yet not by divine execution. This man has died because of the failure of his heart, because of the shock to his heart, because of the great fear engendered by the vision of the hangman, a vision inspired by the wickedness of his heart. He has paid the price of his sins.

And in Auckland, indeed in all the world, the wicked are perishing and the righteous are being saved!

*

The Russian battlefield, where Lech Janinski lies dead, is now no longer silent. The sounds of frantic battle fill the air, for the angels have sown the seeds of confusion among the combatants so that now they are slaughtering not only the enemy but also the friend. Confusion is total. No soldier here now has a comrade. All are enemies. All are deserving of death. Confusion reigns!

*

In the sight of William Brooke, the glory of the Son of God, along with all his holy angels, is illuminating the skies over Lancashire. Christ in glory! Christ in power! King of kings!

The old man is overwhelmed by emotion. His tears refuse to stop flowing.

Jesus returning to rule!

At last, at last, William Brooke's salvation is here!

I do not care to deny for yet another time the return of the Nazarene. You will believe what you want to believe, you will believe that which you find to be comfortable, so, if you want to believe in the fanciful tale of a returning Christ – well, do so! What care I?

I do, however, have a few words to say about Tim, the so-called Impossible Man. I have mentioned Tim's loneliness before. I have told you how, ever since he evolved into existence, he has been feared, shunned and pursued by you people, you, his brothers, his own kind.

Well, the alien conquerors will treat Tim more kindly, and not just because he bears a physical likeness to them. The aliens are logical beings, you see, and logically Tim does not pose a threat to anyone. So they will treat him more kindly than you ever did. Shame on you! You ignorant scum!

I wonder how many of you, if any of you, will survive the alien invasion?

Will any of your species inhabit the earth when the aliens finally leave?

I suppose it is possible that some of you will.

You are like rats. Difficult to eliminate entirely!

And speaking of leaving, I have a surprise for you.

I am going on holiday!

Yes, when the aliens arrive, I shall take a holiday. We all will. I and my angels. It has been decided. We shall fly far across the universe on wings of pleasure, and holiday for a thousand years. Oh, I know I told you that we would stay to influence the new alien rulers of your planet, but I have changed my mind. We shall go away, we shall leave the aliens to rule undisturbed, and, when finally they leave the earth for ever, those of you who will have survived will then have a chance to pick up the pieces, to start again – until we return.

So, I am going, but I shall leave behind a short account of your far future, and you shall read it shortly.

We go on holiday.

But we shall be back! I'll be back!

*

This is Jehovah's day. All over the world this is Jehovah's day.

It is the day of salvation and it is the day of vengeance. God's kingdom is being forcibly established upon the earth for the sake of those judged to be righteous. As for the wicked, the evil-doers? They are being torn off the surface of the earth!

'. . . thy kingdom come, they will be done, on earth as it is in heaven . . .'

This is the day of the manifestation of the returning Christ. He comes to rule and execute judgment in God's name. This is the fear-inspiring Day of Jehovah. It is the Great Day of the War of God the Almighty.

It is Armageddon!

On this day those slain by Jehovah will stretch clear from one end of the earth to the other. They will not be mourned. They will not be buried. They will lie as manure on the surface of the ground. The birds of the air will feast upon them.

They are no more.

And these are they who are no more:

> . . . unrighteous persons will not inherit God's kingdom. Do not be misled. Neither fornicators, nor idolaters, nor adulterers, nor men kept for unnatural purposes, nor men who lie with men, nor thieves,

nor greedy persons, nor drunkards, nor revilers, nor extortioners will inherit God's kingdom.

– 1 Corinthians 6: 9, 10

And yet among those saved are some who practised these things at one time, but they have repented and turned away from these things. They have also turned away from the following things:

> ... in the last days critical times hard to deal with will be here. For men will be lovers of themselves, lovers of money, self-assuming, haughty, blasphemers, disobedient to parents, unthankful, disloyal, having no natural affection, not open to any agreement, slanderers, without self-control, fierce, without love of goodness, betrayers, headstrong, puffed up with pride, lovers of pleasures rather than lovers of God, having a form of godly devotion, but proving false to its power ... – 2 Timothy 3: 1–5

It is Armageddon.

And those who are perishing on this day are those who have practised the above things and who have not turned away from them. Those who have perished on this day are those whose practices were ungodly, whose practices were an affront to God and to the righteous. It is on account of these practices that the wrath of God has come!

And the wrath of God has come upon all the wicked. Not one is left standing. All over the world, armies great and small have been obliterated by the angels of God. All over the world, the political masters of these armies, those who have ordered the killings, have themselves been put to death. All over the world, habitual breakers of God's commandments have likewise been removed from the earth.

The earth is cleansed!
The wicked are no more.
Under Christ's kingdom no one will tremble in fear.
The wicked are gone.

Has the Devil gone on holiday?
In a manner of speaking he has. Hear the word of God as found in Revelation, 20: 1–3.

> And I saw an angel coming down out of heaven with the key of the abyss and a great chain in his hand. And he seized the dragon, the original serpent who is the Devil and Satan, and bound him for a thousand years. And he hurled him into the abyss and shut it and sealed it over him, that he might not mislead the nations any more until the thousand years were ended. After these things he must be let loose for a little while.

Yes, the Devil has gone away.
He no longer rules the world.

8

Death, a Grave Matter

Who am I?

I am not the Devil, for he is going on holiday. I do not take holidays.

Who am I?

I am a reluctant creation of God. I came into existence in the garden, yet I was inactive for a little while, just a little while. Yet it was not long before my services were required. I carried away a man named Abel.

You know who I am.

But do you know my nature? For I have many guises.

You know who I am.

But you do not know precisely what I am.

As you read these words you will know that one day I shall come for you, and I will not be denied. Will you know my exact nature then?

Am I immortal? Or will the God who reluctantly made me one day gladly destroy me? Will I be swallowed up for ever, or will I remain, seemingly as part of the natural order of things?

You know who I am.

When I come for you will it be with sudden and unwelcome violence? Or will you welcome me as your means of escape from your sufferings? We shall see.

And now, if you should care to read on, you will know my nature, you will know what I am, what I truly am, despite my many guises, guises you have wishfully imagined, for Satan has told many lies about me and you have gladly believed them. Now you will know the truth, but first . . .

First you must know my guises.

I could, if I so choose, take you on a journey through human history and you would learn my true nature. I could take you to the future to show you what I am. But I have decided to disclose my true nature in the present time, in the time when you are reading this.

Did you know that half the people who have ever lived are living now?

This means that I have already taken from this earth some six billion people. And it means that there are six billion more of you currently waiting for my visit. The numbers are adding up. I'm rather busy. Twelve billion souls! Impressive stuff!

But where have all these people gone? Where will all you people go?

Look! Here is Sade (pronounced sad – and with good reason).

S.a.d.e. (Some after death expectations.)

Sade is male or female. He or she is young or old or somewhere in between.

This is the story of Sade and myself, for Sade is dying all over the world.

*

Sade is a Chinese woman. An old Chinese woman. A very old Chinese woman. She has been waiting for me to call on her for quite some time. Her family have put some charms around her deathbed. They are supposed to keep evil spirits away. I am not an evil spirit. Nothing can keep me away.

Sade has pneumonia. Her family cannot afford to take

her to the hospital in the faraway city. Sade is mine!

But what does she expect of me? Where does she think I will take her?

She thinks I will take her to a beautiful garden, a place of peace and joy. She thinks that her husband will be there to greet her, and her long-dead parents, and her brother and sister, and the child I took from her shortly after his birth. She thinks that all her ancestors will be there, and all the dead emperors of China, along with their wives, and even Confucius himself!

She breathes her last. It is a dry rattle. I swoop down and take her from this earth.

Do I take her to her garden?

No!

Emphatically not! No!

*

I am in Ireland, in Cork, and nineteen-year-old Sade is in the pub, as drunk as drunk can be. He certainly doesn't expect to be meeting me this evening, but death, like life, can sometimes be cruel.

No, Sade hasn't given me a first thought this evening, never mind a second. It is his birthday and he is out with his mates.

But he does have somewhere in his sober mind an expectation of what death is, and this expectation comes directly from what he has been taught. You see, Sade comes from an old Catholic family – you know, heaven, hell and purgatory.

Now, Sade wouldn't be expecting to go directly to heaven. He drinks too much and there are other things of a sexual nature that would surely bar his direct ascent to the pearly gates. But he wouldn't be expecting to go to hell either. After all, he hasn't, as far as he knows, committed any mortal sins. No, if anyone were to ask him when he was sober, Sade would say that he would expect to go to purgatory, there to stay for a while until atonement had been made, there to remain until heaven beckoned.

Sade is comfortable with the idea of purgatory. He can do a bit of sinning and not be damned.

Yet, if anyone were to ask Sade to describe purgatory, he would be lost for words. He would have some vague notion perhaps of having to climb a steep rock-face, perhaps naked, perhaps with temptations, both sexual and alcoholic, all around, all tempting him into not climbing the rock-face, into not reaching those pearly gates. But if anyone were to ask him, Sade would say that he would resist such temptations.

Well, he would. Wouldn't he?

But, no one has asked him. And no one will ask him. Full of stout and whisky, Sade staggers out of the pub and falls into the road under the fatal wheels of a passing truck.

I swiftly pick him up and carry him away, despite the utter disbelief of his friends.

He is gone.

I have taken him.

To purgatory? No!

*

'I do not want to become a fly,' wails Rajit Sade.

'Shut up, Rajit,' says his much younger wife. 'If you become a fly then you become a fly.'

'May the lord Krishna preserve me,' he wails. 'I do not wish to become a fly.'

'Perhaps you will be a beetle,' says his wife. 'Or a maggot. Perhaps you will be eaten by a fish before you get the chance to become a fly!'

Rajit Sade falls silent. He knows he is dying and he knows he will get little sympathy from his wife. And with good reason. He has treated her badly all their married life, and this is the trouble. He has treated everyone badly. And now that he is dying, now that he faces the transmigration of his soul, he is distraught. He is more afraid of the transmigration than he is of me! Had he practised good things during his lifetime, he would now be looking forward to his death, and to his rebirth as, perhaps, a noble, or even a king! But, among other things, Rajit has been a wife-beater, an adulterer and an extortioner – and India's million or so gods are about to make him pay for his sins. Surely, he will return to India as a fly!

'I do not want to become a fly,' he wails again.

His wife ignores him, but later, when the cancer is paining him, she gives him some aspirin.

The following day, when he dies, I take him away.

Will he return as a fly?

Will he be reborn to India as a beetle or a maggot?

Will his soul transmigrate?

No!

Again I say, No!

*

In Manchester, England, three Sades are sitting with some apprehension around a kitchen table. The curtains are drawn tight and the only light is coming from a black candle, which has been placed on the edge of the table. In the centre of the table is a Ouija board. The three Sades are all young people, two girls and a boy, students at the local university. Each student has placed a finger upon the upturned glass, which rests upon the Ouija board. They are attempting to communicate with the dead.

'Is there anybody there?' It is the boy who is speaking. 'Is there anybody there?'

Instantly the glass begins to move. It circles slowly in the centre of the board around the edges of which are the letters of the alphabet and the words 'yes' and 'no'. The glass moves to 'yes' and stops.

The students are excited and a little scared, especially the girls. The boy has done this sort of thing before.

'Who are you?' asks the boy.

The glass begins to move. Swiftly it spells out the name L-E-N-N-O-N.

The students are in a state of high excitement along with a touch of fear and some scepticism. One of the girls accuses the boy of directing the glass with his finger.

'I didn't!' he protests. 'I didn't! It moved on its own!'

'He couldn't have pushed it,' says the other girl. 'It moved too fast.'

The boy attempts to take control of the situation. 'Are you John Lennon?' he asks.

Swiftly the glass moves to 'yes'.

'Ask him how he died,' says one of the girls to the boy.

The boy nods. 'How did you die?' he asks.

For a moment there is no movement, then, swiftly, the glass begins to spell. G-U-N-S-H-O-T.

The three students are now convinced that they have contacted the spirit of John Lennon, he of the Beatles fame. The boy, anxious to impress the girls, now asks another question.

'What is the name of the man who killed you?'

For a full twenty seconds there is no movement from the glass, then, very slowly, it begins to move. It goes to the S, then to the A, on to the T and back to the A. Finally it goes to the N.

S-A-T-A-N!

Now the students are truly afraid, more especially one of the girls. And now the glass begins to circle again, slowly at first, but then faster and faster.

One of the girls removes her finger from the glass, but still it continues to circle, faster and faster.

In alarm, the other two students remove their fingers, but the glass continues to circle at high speed. The students panic. They scramble away from their chairs, away from the table, and, as they do so, the glass leaves the table and flies through the air as if hurled by an invisible hand. One girl screams. The other clings to the terrified boy. The glass smashes into a thousand fragments against the wall. Somehow the boy finds the light-switch and manages to flick it on. All three run out of the kitchen and into the living-room. One of the girls is in a state of shock.

Now, I will ask a question.

What has actually happened here?

Have these students really contacted the ghost of John Lennon?

The answer is no.

So, what has occurred?

I will tell you and I do not tell lies.

By using the Ouija board these students have unwittingly placed themselves open to demonic influences. The Ouija is just one of the ways the demons can come through. Now, the particular demon who pretended to be John Lennon did so because it is the policy of the ruler of the demons to encourage mankind to believe in life after death, in the immortality of the human soul. And this particular demon chose the identity of John Lennon, a dead musician, to suit his audience, impressionable young people. But this demon could not remember the name of the man who shot John Lennon! Neither could he access the information quickly. So, in frustration he spelt out the name of his master and in frustration and rage he caused the glass to spin wildly and fly across the room. As a result he has terrified the students and left them in some doubt as to whether they have actually been in contact with the spirit of John

Lennon, or with something much more sinister. In fact, this particular demon, by his unbridled rage, has possibly defeated his own purposes.

This is what has happened here.

I know, because when John Lennon died I took him away.

His spirit, his ghost, does not roam the earth waiting to be contacted by the living.

No!

*

'I think, therefore I am.'

Who said that? Was it Voltaire?

Anyway, Sade, the Buddhist monk, is attempting to non-think himself into a state of non-existence. He is trying to achieve Nirvana. He is not far away from non-existence.

No food has passed his lips for days. No drink has passed his lips for as many days. He is at the point of death. He has finally conquered his desires, for now he has no desires – except the desire to die.

He can barely think. Soon, even his thoughts will perish.

When he dies I will take him away.

Will he have achieved non-existence?

Yes.

Nirvana?

No, for his story is not at an end.

Not Nirvana. No!

*

He sits quietly at the back of the church, having purposely arrived just a few minutes after the start of the service. He does not wish to speak to anyone. He wants no one to speak to him. Prayers are being offered to the Trinity. His name is Martyr Sade and the name of the church is Anywhere in Christendom. Strapped around

Martyr's body is high explosive. Attached to the explosive is a timing device. Two minutes!

I am in attendance. I wonder about the timing device. Ah, I know. It will help Martyr to be strong. It will prevent him from changing his mind at the last moment.

I am hovering. Soon I will have work to do.

One minute! In the crowded church a hymn is now being sung ...

He died that we might be forgiven.
He died to make us good.
That we might go at last to heaven.
Saved by his precious blood ...

Yes, I am aware that it is the belief in Christendom that Christians go to heaven when they die, not that anyone here is actively thinking about death, except Martyr, of course. His beliefs are just a little different. He thinks that he is about to enter through death's door into paradise!

Heaven! Paradise! Are they the same place? Will these churchgoers, whose bodies are about to be torn apart, suddenly and dramatically find themselves in heaven, in the very presence of God – and in the presence of Martyr, their murderer?

Thirty seconds! Strange to say, but true, for I always tell the truth, many of those who are about to die will not see my face. I will take them away, but they will not see my face nor will they know of my presence!

Eleven seconds! Martyr, his heart pounding, pounding, the whole of his body covered in sweat, now feels an almost overwhelming urge to rip off his body appendage and run. But the explosives are not so easy to rip off and time is quickly running out. Martyr knows he does not now have the time to change his mind. In his torment he focuses on paradise, that wonderful place where no

293

coward, no traitor, can ever be. Three seconds! Martyr cries out in a loud voice, 'Allah Ahkbar!' – God is great.

One second! A last deep breath for Martyr and time has run out.

From my place I witness the carnage. I see Martyr's body torn to shreds along with the bodies of those in close proximity to him. I see others cut down by cruel shrapnel, and I see scorched flesh everywhere. I can almost smell the burnt flesh.

I take twenty-four people away immediately. I return swiftly for another six. In the coming hours I will return again and again. Men, women and children cut to pieces. I take them away.

Do I take the Christians to heaven?

No, I do not.

Do I take Martyr to his paradise?

No, not I.

You see, the human soul, your soul, is not immortal. You are not immortal. Death is the absence of life.

And I do not tell lies.

When I take you away, it is because you no longer exist!

*

In the Japanese countryside the boy, Sade, contemplates his future. He is only eight years old, but already he has learned from his grandmother what to expect when the time comes for him to die. He looks at the trees, at the flowers, at the grass. He sees them moving, stirring in the breeze. The breeze itself he cannot see. Only its effect.

'You are like the breeze,' his grandmother has told him. 'And when you die your spirit will blend with the things of nature. You will become part of the whole of creation. Your spirit will dance with the breeze, it will touch all things, it will join with the spirits that have gone before you, and the goddess of the sun will warm you.'

The boy tries to imagine what it will be like, but it is difficult. In the end his thoughts turn to other matters. To a young boy, death seems far, far away.

Yet, I will take him!

Young, old or middle-aged, I will at some point take him.

And when I do, his spirit, which has no consciousness of its own, will return to God who gave it. And without breath, without spirit, the body begins to decay. What has originally been formed from the dust of the ground shall return to dust.

And perhaps the dust will be borne on the breeze.

But, like the spirit, the dust has no consciousness of its own.

A simple formula ...

Soul (the conscious you) = body + spirit from God.

At death it is the soul that dies. At death the conscious you ceases to be.

The body begins to decay and the spirit returns to God.

So, God knows the spirit, he knows the personality. And he is able, if he should so choose, to recreate the body and join it again with the spirit.

We call it a resurrection!

Yes!

*

In a small town in Maryland, USA, the wicked are assembled. In secret they have come to sacrifice to their master, Satan.

The child lies upon the altar. He is just eight months old. He lies still, for he has been bound to the altar with cord. No one will miss this child, because his birth was in secret and was never registered. His mother is one of those present, his father might be any of the men present, perhaps even the foremost of the wicked, the one who holds the razor-sharp ceremonial knife. This child was conceived for sacrifice.

When the child's throat is cut the wicked make their dreadful moaning sounds. When the child twitches in his death throes they moan again. As the blood runs out they begin to indulge in an orgy of sexual perversion. No perversion is forbidden.

I take the child away.

I cannot tell you what after-death-expectations the wicked have. Perhaps they have none. Perhaps they live only for the present. After all, their master is ruler of this world and is able to reward them now.

But they will all come to me eventually. Satan cannot save them from me.

And God will judge them.

In my line of work I cannot afford sentiment, I cannot accommodate a sense of morality, but if I were God I do not think I would be inclined to resurrect these people. I do not think I would be inclined to give these Satanists a second chance.

No.

I sometimes think, especially in view of the previous story, that it is a pity hell does not exist, that is, the traditional concept of hell.

Great dark underground caverns, illuminated only by the everlasting fires. Fearsome instruments of torture. Demons taking pleasure in tormenting the souls of the wicked. Shades of Dante. Images from Bosch.

You can almost hear the agonised screams of the damned, whose curiously fleshy souls are in eternal torment. Flesh is pierced again and again, yet is not destroyed! Blood pours and never ceases to pour! Bodies burn and burn, but are never consumed. Curious!

And what of the demons? In Oriental cultures they have Oriental features. In western cultures they have western features. In Arabic cultures they have Arabic features. I could go on.

Demons! Having the semblance of men and of beasts. Torturing and sexually abusing the damned!

And Satan himself, complete with horns, tail and trident, ruling over this abomination.

'Abandon all hope ye who enter within.'

No hope for Charles Darwin. No hope for Karl Marx.

Will they be in agony for eternity?

Would God allow such an abomination to exist anywhere under creation?

Eternal torment? Everlasting punishment?

No! Never! No!

The wage sin pays is death, not eternal torment.

I know. I am death, and I do not take you people to a fiery hell!

No!

Hell is simply the grave, the place where you will sleep in death, a dreamless sleep from which one day, God willing, you will awaken.

When your saviour, Jesus, died, I took him away.

'He descended into hell.' He died! Otherwise his sacrifice would have been in vain!

But, 'on the third day he rose again'.!

And I do not tell lies.

So, there it is, and here am I, I, death, the Grim Reaper. But you knew who I was from the beginning. I, death, the cousin of Father Time. I, death, sometimes heralded by, among others, the banshee and the Ace of Spades?

You knew who I was and you also know that, under the present circumstances, you and I have an appointment. We shall meet.

Yet now you know not only who I am, you also know what I am. Look! I have told you. You know my nature and I do not lie.

You have nothing to fear from me. Yes, I am your enemy, the last enemy, and the process of dying may be hard and terrifying for you, but when I finally come for you, you have nothing to fear. You will sleep.

One day, after those of you who sleep will have awakened, God himself will summon me. He will tell me that I am to be made redundant! He will say there is no longer any work for me to do. He will tell me I am to be swallowed up for ever.

'Oh, death, where is thy sting?
Oh, grave, thy victory?'

That day is yet far future, but when it arrives, and arrive it must, then I will gladly cease to exist.

9

Kingdom Come

Well, hell! Hello again.

As you read these words, my little holiday of a thousand years is yet future, but this is the testimony I shall leave behind when I go. It paints a picture of your far future, of the time when the alien invaders have abandoned your planet, of the time when the few of your species who will survive are beginning to re-establish your civilizations, your pathetic civilizations, of the time just prior to my return.

Read on and believe.

Look now! We are some one thousand years into your future, and what has happened? The earth has been invaded and colonised by an advanced alien civilization and you humans, you few descendants of those who did not perish, have been forced to eke out an existence in the remote places of the earth, in the mountainous regions, in the deep forests, in the underground places.

But now the aliens have gone!

They have abandoned your insignificant planet. They have gone, perhaps never to return, and you are beginning to emerge from your hiding places. Does anyone feel sorry for you? Is there compassion anywhere in the universe for you? No! Because your nature, your selfish and savage nature, has not changed.

An example:

The aliens conducted medical experiments on you. This is one of the reasons why you hid from them. They dissected you, they

299

poisoned you, they irradiated you, they drowned you, they vapourised you, they abused you sexually. They conducted all kinds of merciless cruelties upon you. To be taken by the aliens was to die in agony, and often very slowly.

But the aliens were no worse than you!

In fact, they were better than you. Because you have experimented on each other! Yes, you have experimented on your own!

Throughout your bloody history you have experimented on each other, oh yes, cruel medical experiments. As you are reading these words you will surely know that only some sixty to seventy years ago you humans were injecting your fellow humans with petrol, with deadly bacteria and viruses. You were committing every kind of atrocity. I cite Nazi Germany and Imperial Japan as just two examples. As you are reading these words you are still experimenting. North Korea, certain African and Middle Eastern countries are just the worst examples. And now, a thousand years on, now that the aliens have gone, how long will it be before you again begin your cruelties, your experiments, all in the name of scientific progress, of course?

Human nature has not changed.

In the past, after the rule of the dinosaurs, you people crawled out of the primeval jungles and stood up. Now that the aliens have gone, you are crawling out of your hiding places. In the past you grouped together in tribes. Now you group in gangs.

What really has changed?

And, strangely, or perhaps not so strangely, there now exists another similarity between the past and this future time – pyramids!

Did the ancient Egyptians really build the pyramids of old? Yes, but who designed these great and precise structures? Were the pyramids really of human origin? The universe is vast, unimaginably so, and there is all the time that ever there was and ever will be. Perhaps the pyramids of Egypt were something not originally conceived by a human mind!

Why do I say this? Because the alien conquerors have left

300

something behind. Yes, pyramids! Pyramids formed from the stones of the earth. And pyramids, which dwarf those of ancient Egypt and the lesser towers of Central and South America!

One such vast structure now stands on the plains of central Lancashire, between the Pennines and the Irish sea, between the Cumbrian hills and the Cheshire plain. Its gigantic form can be seen for many, many miles around. It can certainly be seen from the Lancashire moors where the gang known as the Lancs are emerging from their isolation.

The scene of the world has changed, but human nature has not changed.

*

From a high moorland hill, overlooking the central Lancashire plain, the gang known as the Lancs has gathered. There are some three hundred of them, men, women and children, all dressed in rough clothing, some of them unwashed for days, many of them unsure about the departure of the aliens.

From the hill the great pyramid is not only visible – it dominates the view. It stands on an area of land once bounded by the towns of Preston, Chorley and Blackburn, though these towns are now no more than piles of rubble. The great pyramid, each of its four sides measuring almost three miles in length at the base, rises high into the sky, so much so that the people on the hill must raise their eyes to the heavens to see its pinnacle. The great pyramid, home for centuries to the alien race, is fear-inspiring! Nevertheless, the man who leads the Lancs, one Marius Dobbs, is determined in his proposed course of action. He now addresses his people.

'The aliens have gone!' he tells them. 'They have gone and they will not return. And we must find a way to get inside their structure.'

There are murmurings of dissent from his people. Perhaps not all the aliens have gone. Perhaps they will return. What horrors are to be found inside the pyramid?

'The aliens have left our planet for ever,' Marius Dobbs

continues. He waves an arm in the direction of the vast pyramid. 'Inside that structure are their secrets. We must get inside and learn their secrets!'

Again there are murmurings. The people are not convinced.

'We must get inside,' Marius Dobbs urges. 'If we are to survive and flourish we must learn the secrets of the aliens. We must begin to understand their weaponry, their flying machines – all their secrets! Because if we don't find a way into the pyramid, surely another gang will. The Yorkies perhaps, or the Cheshites, or the Scouse, or the Cumbries! Do you want to be ruled by any of these?'

The people are silent now. There are no murmurings.

'Come,' Dobbs commands. 'We go to the pyramid. Any man, woman or child who stays behind will be cast out.'

With Marius Dobbs leading the way, the Lancs begin to descend the hillside. The great pyramid awaits them.

You see! What did I tell you? Human nature has not changed. Men are still afraid of what other men might do, so they want to do it first. Yes, do unto others what they intend to do to you, only do it first!

Marius Dobbs wants to get his greedy little hands on the technologies of the aliens so that he and his gang can rule over the Lancashire plain and its surrounding area. If the Lancs are successful, if they acquire alien technology, especially the weaponry, where do you think it will all lead? Will they be content to rule over themselves in this little corner of north-west England? Or will they aspire to rule over the whole of England? Or even further afield?

You know the answer.

Today, Lancashire! Tomorrow, the world!

It's like coming out of the jungle all over again.

You are a scheming, frightened, vicious, pathetic, warlike race – even devoid of my influence.

Human nature does not change!

*

'Daddy, I'm frightened!'

These words, spoken by five-year-old Ulthred Thom, epitomise the feelings of the entire gang as they stand in fear and in awe at the foot of the great pyramid. It is the sheer size of the structure that causes them to feel afraid. It is the sheer splendour of the structure that causes them to look up upon it in awe. Everyone is acutely aware that this is something not made by human hands.

'Daddy, where is the top?'

Ulthred's father raises his eyes. High, high above him the pinnacle of the pyramid is hidden by cloud. He turns his eyes to the right and then to the left. This vast structure, made of stone, has been built so precisely that the stonework is as smooth as the skin on Ulthred Thom's bottom. There is no sign of an entrance.

'We must walk around it,' says Marius Dobbs. 'Half of us in one direction, half in the other. We must find a way in.'

Marius Dobbs quickly organises his people. He looks again at the smoothness of the stone. It will prove impossible to climb. If they do not find an entrance at ground level they will never get inside. 'We will meet on the far side,' he commands.

Darkness is beginning to fall when the two groups finally meet up. They have found no entrance and the murmurings are starting up again. Marius Dobbs is at a loss. He simply does not know what to do next.

'LOOK!'

It is the boy, Ulthred Thom who cries out. He is pointing to the north. Marius Dobbs strains his eyes. There! There, on the brow of a hill, less perhaps than a mile distant, there is movement, much movement. People! Hundreds and hundreds, if not thousands of people, and they are hurrying towards the great pyramid, hurrying towards the Lancs. It is the Cumbries, or perhaps the Yorkies, and the Lancs are heavily outnumbered.

Now there is great distress among his people and Marius Dobbs is about to give the order to flee, to retreat in the gathering

303

darkness to the moors, to the stronghold, but in the midst of all the distress, in the midst of the rising panic, the young boy, Ulthred Thom, is slapping the palm of his hand against the side of the great pyramid and he is calling out in his childish voice.

'Open up!' he is crying. 'Open, please, and let us in!'

A sudden shaft of brilliant white light instantly silences the fearful murmurings of the Lancs. Marius Dobbs stares in disbelief. An opening has appeared in the stones of the pyramid at ground level. It is as though the stones have melted away. An opening has appeared and inside there is bright light.

Marius Dobbs reacts instinctively. 'Quickly! Everyone! Inside!' he commands.

There is hesitation, but Marius Dobbs will not be disobeyed. 'Inside!' he yells again.

The boy is first to step through the portal, quickly followed by his father. They vanish into the light.

'Inside!' screams Marius Dobbs.

Within a matter of minutes the entire Lancs gang has passed through the portal, and now the opening disappears as quickly and as mysteriously as it had appeared.

The Lancs are inside.

Outside, the Cumbries are rapidly approaching. They will examine the smoothness of the stones. They will stand in awe at the magnificence of the pyramid. They will ponder the disappearance of their enemies and they will wonder about the source of the bright light. They will not find their way inside the pyramid.

Well, it needs saying, doesn't it?

The aliens have only been gone some five minutes and already you people are finding new enemies. The common enemy has gone, so you must find enemies among yourselves. It is your nature. You cannot function without having someone to war against!

The Lancs and the Yorkies.

It's the Wars of the Roses all over again!

You don't really need my help to get on the road to self-destruction, do you?

Aren't you all extremely stupid.

Inside the great pyramid the people of the Lancs stand with feelings of both wonder and dread. They wonder at their deliverance from the rival gang, they wonder at the seemingly melting stones, which opened the way for them, and they wonder at the brilliant yet soft white light, which illuminates the chamber in which they now stand, a chamber, which is long and narrow, so long in fact that the ends of it cannot be seen. Their dread springs from the knowledge that they are at the heart of the domain of the alien, the cruel alien. They begin to wonder if indeed all the aliens have left the earth. Did the melting stones melt of their own accord?

'We must go on,' Marius Dobbs announces. He waves an arm towards the indeterminate distance. 'There is nowhere else to go but onward. Draw your weapons and be ready.'

Clutching a variety of bows and arrows, knives, swords, cudgels and catapults, the Lancs, led by Marius Dobbs, begin their cautious advance along the chamber. The boy, Ulthred Thom, along with his father, is in the leading group.

'I'm not frightened now, Daddy,' says the boy. 'This is a good place.'

The father makes no reply. He does not want to disturb his son unduly, but how can a place of torture, of experimentation, ever be a good place?

'If anyone is here,' says the boy, 'they will be our friends.'

The father looks down at the boy. He is about to tell him of the wicked deeds that have been committed in this place; he is about to try to make his son understand, when, quite suddenly, just as the phenomenon had occurred on the outside of the pyramid, the stones of the chamber, the ones adjacent to the boy, seem to melt away.

In a moment of time, before anyone else can react, the boy is

305

through this new portal and vanishing into the light beyond.

The father cries out. 'Ulthred! Ulthred!' and moves quickly towards the portal. But all too late. Before the father's anguished eyes the portal ceases to be. Now there are only stones, stones that bar the way to the place where the young boy, Ulthred Thom, has gone.

In a lighted chamber in another part of the great pyramid, five-year-old Ulthred Thom is unaware and unconcerned that his father is frantically searching for him. Instead, Ulthred Thom is sitting comfortably upon a chair that is far too big for him. Opposite, in another chair, his strange features illuminated by the white light, sits an oddity of evolutionary progression. Ulthred Thom and Tim are holding a conversation.

'You're an alien, aren't you?' says the five-year-old, his face glowing with excitement.

Tim shakes his eyeless head.

'Yes you are!' says the child. 'I've seen drawings of you!'

Tim crosses his legs – all three of them – and holds his elbow in such a way that his single eye is looking directly at the child. 'I am a man,' he says proudly. 'I just look like an alien.'

Ulthred Thom is puzzled. He is silent for a moment.

'I'm a man,' says Tim. 'I evolved here on this planet, just like you. I know I look like an alien, but my DNA proves I am a man. I'm just ... well, a different kind of a man.'

The child slowly nods his head. He accepts what Tim is telling him as the truth. 'But you've lived with the aliens, haven't you?'

Tim nods his eyeless head. 'Yes!'

'Did they torture you?'

'No!'

'Did they torture anybody?'

Tim slowly nods his head.

'Have they all gone?' asks the child.

'Yes!'

'Are they coming back?'

'No!'

The child is silent again for a moment, then his eyes light up. 'Did you melt the stones?'

Tim nods.

'How?'

'Alien technology,' says Tim. 'It's easy once you get the hang of it.'

'Can you do it again?' asks the child, suddenly remembering his father. 'Can you bring my daddy here?'

Tim makes no reply. Bitter and long experience has taught him never to trust his fellow humans, and yet ... and yet this child is truly trustworthy! Perhaps ...

'Can you bring my daddy here?' Ulthred Thom asks again.

Led by Marius Dobbs and urged on by Ulthred's father, the people of the Lancs search in vain for melting stones. The long and narrow chamber in which they find themselves seems to go on and on for ever. Marius Dobbs is beginning to suspect that the chamber simply encircles the interior of the pyramid at its base. The chamber appears to be long and straight, but the pyramid is so vast that any slight curvature would never be noticed. Marius Dobbs is beginning to suspect that the only escape from this chamber is by way of the melting stones.

Ulthred Thom's father is desperate to find his son and his desperation is clouding his judgment. He is urging the people on in the hope that somewhere, somehow, they will find a way out of the chamber. He is not thinking logically, but Marius Dobbs is thinking logically. The leader of the Lancs calls a halt.

'We must go on,' says Ulthred's father.

Marius Dobbs shakes his head. 'It's no good. We're getting nowhere.'

'We must find the melting stones.'

Marius Dobbs nods. 'Yes, but not this way.'

'Then how?' asks Ulthred's father. 'How?'

'By the same manner that your son allowed us to enter this

307

place,' says Marius Dobbs. 'We must ask.'

Ulthred's father stares at his leader.

'We must ask,' says Marius Dobbs. 'You must ask.'

Ulthred's father slowly nods his head and then turns to face the stones of the chamber. After a few moments he cries out in a loud voice. 'Open, please, and allow me to find my son.'

There are gasps from the people as the stones melt.

Marius Dobbs and Ulthred's father immediately go through. Hesitantly, the others begin to follow.

Tim has taken what is perhaps the greatest gamble of his long, long, long, long existence. His yearning for human companionship, for the company of his own kind, coupled with his trust of the young boy, has caused him to risk his very life! Tim has allowed the Lancs to enter into the chamber where he and Ulthred Thom are sitting.

Ulthred Thom's father sees his son immediately and runs to him crying 'Ulthred! Ulthred!'

Marius Dobbs sees Tim. Marius Dobbs sees alien!

As the father gathers his son into his arms, Marius Dobbs is aiming an arrow at the alien.

From his father's arms, Ulthred Thom sees the raised bow and cries out.

'No! No! Don't hurt the man!' But the words have hardly left his lips before the arrow is released.

When the arrow pierces Tim's brain he has but moments to live. In those few moments his heart is broken, broken because he is meeting his death at the hands of his own people, his own kind whom he foolishly trusted.

Tim dies!

And as this man's dead body slumps in the chair, some five or six of the Lancs rush forward in a frenzy of violence. While Ulthred Thom screams and will not be comforted, the Lancs beat and stab at the corpse of Tim.

Tim, the Impossible Man!

Before I comment on the death of Tim, let me tell you what will happen to the Lancs.

They will remain for some time within the confines of the great pyramid, safe from attack, and they will unlock many of the secrets of the aliens. When they emerge from their pyramid citadel, they will easily defeat all enemy gangs and they will rule over the north of England and eventually over the whole of Britain.

After these things the Lancs will discover that the aliens have left behind them other great pyramids in other parts of the earth, and the Lancs will find that other humans have also unlocked some of the secrets of the conquering aliens. The Lancs will find that they no longer hold the advantage in the understanding and use of extraterrestrial technology. They will find that newly emerging rival nations can match them in warfare.

But this will not deter them!

No! The Lancs, or the Brits as they will come to be known, will war with the Francs and then they will war with the Deutch.

And after these wars they will continue to wage wars.

Does all this sound familiar?

Is this history repeating itself?

Of course it is!

Human nature does not change.

And when all these things shall take place we will have returned from our vacations in order to play our little games with you. Yes!

Human nature does not change and neither do we.

Neither do I!

So, this is the future of humanity. You people will wage war for ever and ever, and you will always be influenced by me.

Now, the death of Tim ...

Marius Dobbs and his gang, mistaking Tim for an alien, destroyed in just a few moments of time the unique product of many millions of years of evolutionary progression.

Tim was unique. Truly unique! One of a kind! Yet one of your kind.

Marius Dobbs and his gang, intent on getting their greedy hands on the secrets of the aliens, let slip through their hands something much more precious.

For Tim held the secret of everlasting life!

Yes, you fools, within Tim's genetic make-up was the secret of everlasting life.

Tim was a creature who did not grow old and die. His cellular structure did not deteriorate with age. And his cellular structure was human cellular structure. Tim could have saved the whole of humanity from the curses of old age and death.

But you killed him.

And his secrets died with him.

Now, that is what I call true stupidity, pure stupidity. That is what I call ignorance. It is also what I call typical – typical of human nature. Shoot first and ask questions later, eh?

You are a stupid, ignorant, self-harming breed!

And a dying breed!

Though Tim would surely have saved you.

You are a dying breed and you deserve it.

Oh, do not believe a word of the simplistic picture, which is about to be painted next in these pages.

Remember, human nature does not change.

*

Welcome to the Kingdom of God.

Structure.

1. *Supreme ruler.* The Almighty. God. The creator of all things seen and unseen. He who has always existed. Jehovah. He who is.
2. *Administrative ruler.* Jesus Christ. The first creation of the Almighty. Son of God. *Qualifications* – having the

wisdom, power, justice and mercy of his father. Lived on earth as a man for some thirty-three and a half years. Knows what it is like to suffer and die.

3. *Co-rulers.* One hundred and forty-four thousand humans, taken from the earth to rule with Christ from the heavenly places. (Revelation 14: 3.) *Qualifications* – accurate knowledge of God and his ways. Human experiences from every age and every nation.

4. *Earthly administrators.* Those who know God. Those with purity of heart. *Qualifications* – experience in having striven to resist Satan when living in a world under his rulership.

5. *Citizens.* (One hundred years into the one thousand year reign of Christ.) The majority of the survivors of Armageddon.

6. *Future citizens.* The resurrected dead.

*

Welcome to the Kingdom of God.

And God is love.

So, in the Kingdom of God, love, principled love, is what now makes the world go round.

The concept of principled love is something difficult to grasp for those whose hearts do not contain it. Basically, it is love of God and his commandments, love of neighbour – and even love of one's enemies. Difficult to understand, unless it has been cultivated in the heart. Here, under the rule of the Kingdom of the Heavens, such love is being cultivated in the hearts of the people, and, as a result, the old human nature is being changed.

Yes, human nature can and does change.

For the majority of mankind, the spirit of hatred, so prevalent in Satan's world, is being eradicated. And Satan is cast into the abyss! The one who fostered such hatred is not here and neither are his demons. Their influence on humanity has gone, although, at the end of the thousand years, the Devil and his angels must be released from their bonds for a short while.

So, contrary to his claim, Satan is not on holiday. But death is taking a holiday. Death has gone away, returning only spasmodically to claim the few who wilfully refuse to respond to God's undeserved kindness, for this is not yet a perfect world.

We are one hundred years into the one thousand year reign and the earth is cleansed. The wagons of war are gone. The destruction of war has been removed from the surface of the ground. The earth is cleansed both physically and spiritually. Soon, Resurrection Man will get to work. Before he does let us see how life now is for some of the survivors of Armageddon.

Do you remember Jomo? He was eight years old just prior to the return of Christ and he was dying of AIDS. Do you remember Mary? Old Mary wasting away in a Scottish nursing home. And Helen Baker? Cured miraculously of cancer by Jehovah's angel. And Jose? Saved from butchery by Jehovah's angel. And, of course, there is William Brooke.

*

Jomo did not die of AIDS. On the personal instructions of Jesus Christ he was instantly cured of that terrible disease, a syndrome that Jomo acquired in the womb.

Grateful at heart for his deliverance, Jomo responded well to government by God. He lives today on the African continent and is currently engaged in construction work, for which he has a talent. He also paints – oils and watercolours.

His prospects are good. He is on the path to everlasting life. He is looking forward to the resurrection when he hopes to be reunited with his mother and his father. He will teach them the new ways.

Jomo is now one hundred and eight years old. If you

could see him, you would say he was in his twenties!

*

Mary did not continue to waste away in the Scottish nursing home. Though she had some difficulties in unlearning some of the lies she had been told – the concept of the trinity, of the immortal soul, of hell fire etc. – she did, nevertheless, eventually come to an understanding of the truth, and she then responded well.

So, instead of dying, Mary started to live. The ransom sacrifice of Jesus Christ was applied in her case, and her body and mind began to regenerate rather than degenerate.

Today she lives in North America where she owns a garden centre. She also composes music.

In her youth and early womanhood, Mary was strikingly beautiful. Today she is one hundred and eighty-eight years old, although you would say she was forty or so. Soon, Mary will surely be strikingly beautiful again. If she continues to make progress she will remain so for ever!

*

He who puts his faith in me, though he were dead, yet shall he live, and he who lives and puts his faith in me will never die. – Jesus Christ.

Helen Baker. Cured of cancer by the will of God.
Have you forgotten your former misery?
Helen Baker. Freely given a second chance.
Are you wasting your opportunity?
Helen Baker, having more than one hundred and fifty years of age.
Yet, looking older now than in the day of your deliverance.
Turn around, Helen Baker. Repent. Leave sin behind.
Do not forget your anguish of old.
Turn around. Repent. Why should you die?

Jose, a strapping young man of a hundred and fourteen years, now runs his own antiques business in the beautiful small town that stands on the site of what once was the sprawling and ugly city of Montevideo. He has never forgotten the cruel experiences of his childhood and he remains forever grateful for his deliverance. Jose has ambitious plans for the future. When the space programme begins he intends to train as an astronaut.

*

Look! Here is William Brooke. Look carefully in case you do not recognise him.

No white hair and beard! Clean shaven with dark-brown hair is he. No wrinkled skin or stooping of the shoulders! Upright he stands, his skin the skin of the young man he now is. No more toothache or aching joints for William Brooke. No intestinal problems. All these things are things of the past.

Loneliness? No more loneliness for William Brooke. Look! Who is that good-looking young lady holding on to his arm?

William Brooke and his new wife have recently returned from Devon, from the place where the city of Plymouth once stood. The area has now been completely cleansed of the radioactive poisons left by the bombing. The rubble left by the war has either been removed or buried. The old citadel, which straddled part of Plymouth Hoe, is in the process of being rebuilt. It will serve as a museum and as an everlasting memorial of the past, the terrible past, the terrible past of death and destruction when the world was ruled by an unseen spirit called Satan. Satan has gone, but William Brooke remains. He and his wife have been involved in the restoration of the area where Plymouth once stood.

Now they have returned to Lancashire, to the house

where William Brooke endured the Great Tribulation and its aftermath. You would not recognise the house, nor its surroundings, for the house has been rebuilt, the ruins around it removed and replaced by gardens and orchards.

William Brooke and his wife are looking forward to the resurrection, to the reuniting of father and son, of father and daughter, of father and son-in-law, of grandfather and grandchildren.

And the beginning of the resurrection of the dead is close at hand, for Resurrection Man – Jesus Christ – is about to begin this great and wonderful work!

*

Do not marvel at this, because the hour is coming when all those in the tombs of remembrance will hear my voice – and come out, those who did good things to a resurrection of life, those who did vile things to a resurrection of judgement. – Jesus Christ.

Yes, the hour is coming. And the hour is now. But how does the earthly resurrection of the dead proceed?

Formula – Spirit + Body = Person.

Spirit – given by God at birth and returned to God at death. Contains the personality.

Body – new, a recreation. Free from disease, infirmity and injury. Similar in age and looks to the old body at the time of death, therefore recognisable.

Formula – spirit from God unites with recreated body to give a living resurrected person.

Do not marvel at this. It is as simple as this. And with God nothing shall be impossible.

But, Jesus said concerning the resurrection that 'many that are first will be last and the last first'.

What does this mean?

Well, Jesus was referring to the time factor. The history

315

of humanity stretches back over six thousand years and many, many millions have died. In the resurrection, those who died first shall be the last to be raised, those who died last shall be first!

Therefore the first to be raised will be those who died just prior to the manifestation of Christ's return – the family killed by the Devil Butcher, for example – and these are likely to know personally some of the survivors of Armageddon. They will not be strangers in a strange land!

And after that, when another generation is raised, they will know some of those raised in the first resurrected generation. And this connective process will continue until, towards the end of the thousand years, all the dead who have been counted worthy of resurrection are raised up – all the dead, all the way back to Abel, the son of Adam and Eve. There shall be no strangers in a strange land!

Do not marvel at this. With God nothing shall be impossible.

This has been the plan of God since the rebellion in Eden. Do not marvel at this. Instead, let us see how it works in practice.

*

The hour is now. It is the first minute.

Lech Janinski awakens. He is lying in his bed at home in his native Poland. He feels strangely refreshed, full of vigour. Also, he feels confused, yet he is in no way alarmed.

He has, at the moment, no recollection of his death on the Russian front, though the memory will eventually return to him. When it does it will serve as a warning to him. He will not wish to repeat the experience.

After a little while, Lech Janinski sits up in his bed. He cries out softly. 'Maria, are you there?'

316

He hears footsteps rushing up the stairs. He sees his wife come into the room. He cannot understand why the tears are gushing down her cheeks. He does not know that she has waited more than a century for his return. She throws her arms around him. She is sobbing uncontrollably. Lech Janinski simply doesn't understand.

But Maria, once she has overcome her emotion, when she is able to speak, will explain everything to him.

*

'Bill! Wake up! Bill!'

William Brooke opens his eyes. He is in the bedroom lying next to his wife in their bed. It is two-thirty in the morning.

'Bill!' his wife whispers to him again. 'There's someone downstairs!'

William Brooke listens carefully. Yes! He can hear the faint sound of someone humming. And is that the sound of the kettle boiling? There is someone downstairs! How strange. True, he hadn't bothered locking the doors, but who on earth would just walk in?

William Brooke gets out of his bed, puts on a robe and creeps downstairs, closely followed by his wife.

The light is on in the kitchen. There is the sound of clanking crockery. William Brooke and his wife go into the kitchen. There is a young woman standing with her back to them. Slowly she turns around. William Brooke gasps and his eyes fill with tears. He is looking at his daughter, Ellen!

'Hello, dad.'

William Brooke's heart is pounding. He has been looking forward to this moment, but now that it is here . . .

The thoughts go rushing through his head. Ellen must be confused. Why doesn't she look confused? She recognises him even though he now looks as he did when she was a small child. He must introduce his wife, Claire, to

317

her. How calm she seems. Where is her husband? Where are her children, John and Stephanie? She is smiling at him. She has made herself a cup of tea!

He reaches out to her and holds her in his arms. At the same time there is a voice from the living-room.

'Mummy! Where are you, mummy?'

And a second childish voice. 'She's in the kitchen with granddad, silly.'

And then the voice of Tony, Ellen's husband. 'Come on, you two. Let's get something to eat. I'm starving!'

As the family is reunited after all these many years, William Brooke is completely overcome with emotion. He holds tightly onto his wife's hand, the tears of joy flowing freely.

'How great is God,' his heart is saying. 'How good is our God.'

*

You remember Joe Bloggs, don't you? He was killed in a road traffic accident around about the time that you are reading these words. Remember? Joe was driving the family car, he was arguing with his wife and shouting at the children and because of these distractions his vehicle ploughed into a wagon being driven by William Brooke. Joe's wife, Joanne, also died in the accident as did Ella, their young daughter. The son, little Billy Bloggs, survived for a while, but died later of his terrible injuries. It is now over a century and a quarter later, yes, more than one hundred and twenty-five years, and all four Bloggs have been resurrected from the grave.

Do not marvel at this.

For God is good.

William Brooke has been around to see the Bloggs. He has expressed his sorrow for their deaths, although the accident was in no way his fault.

The Bloggs, however, particularly Joe and Joanne, are

not finding it easy to adjust to their new world. Joe, for example, simply can't get it into his head that he no longer needs to work like a dog just to make ends meet.

The Bloggs have a home, set in several acres of land, not far from the place where they used to live. They have a five hundred year mortgage with no interest and, because they are able to grow most of their own food, Joe only needs to work the odd day now and then to fulfil all the family's financial needs.

But he can't get his head around it!

Besides working on his smallholding, Joe has four other jobs! He is making so much money that he doesn't know what to do with it. And Joanne is working hard too.

Joanne is teaching at the local school, the school that Billy and Ella now both attend. School hours are 10.00 a.m. to 4.00 p.m., three days a week, because when life is everlasting, children don't need to be pressured into learning. They can learn at their own pace and enjoy their childhood. But Joanne is finding it hard to fit in with this system. Life isn't busy enough for her! Joanne goes into school on days when the children are not there. She plans lessons unnecessarily and makes paper-work for herself. She even tries to organise out-of-school activities, but few seem interested. The children would rather be with their parents, or out playing with their friends.

Joe and Joanne need to slow down, to adjust their lives to the pace of the everlasting. They need to stand and stare, to consider the good things God is providing for them. They need to learn to relax. It has been suggested to them that they should take the children on holiday for a while, perhaps for two or three months. This has been suggested in the hope that they will come to realise that, while work can certainly be a good thing, life now, if they so choose it, can be one long holiday.

319

And so we see the Bloggs leaving home for a long break in central Asia. As Joe drives his electrically powered vehicle along the safe and quiet road to the airport, he is perhaps thinking of the frustrations of the old world – the senseless running around, the horrendous traffic jams, the stressful pressures of work, the money worries and so on. He is perhaps thinking that all these frustrations existed, and he allowed them to affect him unduly, yet, in the end, the frustrations were actually unimportant. Because they all came to an end with his own end, with his death. And he was not the only one to die!

Joe is perhaps now beginning to understand and appreciate the important things. Joanne, Billy and Ella are the important things, and they have been restored to him in this new world, because it is God's time and God's good pleasure to bring about the restoration of all things.

*

Six days after the resurrection of his daughter and her family, William Brooke receives a telephone call from the North American continent.

'Hi, dad!'

After a short and very emotional silence, William Brooke is able to reply.

'David! David, how are you?'

'I'm fine, dad. I'm OK. Listen, I can't talk to you now. I'm on my way to the airport. I should be in Lancashire by eight o'clock your time. Can you pick me up from the airport?'

'Yes. Yes, of course.'

'Good. See you shortly.'

William Brooke sits down in the chair. Once again he gives way to tears. After all these years his only son is being returned to him.

*

So, this is the resurrection of the dead, the beginning of the resurrection of the dead, for there are many more millions to be raised up during the thousand years.

However, not all who have lived will be counted worthy of a second chance, but more on this later.

Here is the resurrection of the dead.

Do not marvel!

Here is a miraculous work of God, a task directed by Jesus Christ. Other miraculous works of God, which take place all the time are accepted as normal, so why not the resurrection of the dead?

What miraculous works are taking place today?

Is not the birth of a child miraculous?

We know how to bring children to birth. We know all of the factors involved. We can even begin the process in the laboratory. But we do not know why these processes work. Nor do we give due credit to the one who created them.

And there are many other 'everyday miracles' – the turning of the earth on its axis, giving sunsets and sunrises painted with glory! – the mighty oak from an acorn grown – the wheat that becomes life-sustaining bread – our own wonderfully made bodies – our own creative abilities! All these miracles and ten thousand by ten thousand more, we take for granted. All these miracles, all these works of God, we accept as normal. To us, the birth of a child is normal. In fact, it is a miracle.

So it is to be with the resurrection of the dead. Miracles regarded as normal!

Do not marvel at this!

So, as God's Kingdom progresses, as we go further on in time, further into the thousand years, millions will rise from their graves. Millions will rise at their appointed times and none will be strangers in a strange land. All will be taught the new values. All will have the opportunity to change their flawed human nature, to become children of God, to reflect his values. All will have the prospect of everlasting life in a world free from the influence of Satan. All will see and experience the love of God in practice. Those who respond positively will never be sick, will never grow old, will never die! All will find positive outlets for their God-given talents. All will find fulfilment, happiness. All will have the love of God in their hearts, his commandments written on their hearts.

All?

Sadly, there will be some who in the end will not respond positively. These will eventually mirror the attitude of the first man and woman. These will, at the end of the thousand years, rebel, and, in the final chapter of this book, we shall see their fate.

There will also be some, a few perhaps, who will not survive the thousand years. These shall be they who wilfully refuse to accept their need for redemption. These will hold the sacrifice of Jesus to be of no account. These will therefore trample on the son of God who died for them. These will attempt to cause harm and ruin in God's Kingdom, but they will not be allowed to do so. These will place themselves in danger of the everlasting Fires of Gehenna, the fires symbolic of eternal destruction, of everlasting death, of eternal non-existence.

And for some of humanity's dead the eternal fires are already burning. These are they whose crimes have placed them beyond redemption. They are not counted worthy of a second chance. For them there shall be no resurrection. God knows their names. They are dead and they will remain so. Everlastingly!

So, the thousand years will see the raising of the dead. It will also see the raising of mankind in general to a state of near perfection. Men and women shall be as Adam and Eve were before those two rebelled, choosing to go their own disastrous way, plunging their offspring, the whole of humanity, into sin and death. Yet, just as the first man and the first woman were put to the test, so shall the whole of humanity be put to a similar test. Free will is the gift of God to his intelligent creation. Otherwise he might just as well have created robots! Free will is ours and cannot be taken away. Yet, God desires that we humans exercise our freedom wisely. He desires that we understand and freely choose to follow his directions – because these directions are for our good.

So, to determine who shall be counted worthy of everlasting life, humanity shall, at the end of the thousand years, be put to the test.

For Satan and his demons must, for a little while, be let loose! They must come pouring out of the abyss! Once again they, he, shall bring his wicked influence to bear on mankind.

10

The End

The one thousand year reign of Christ is now at an end. Our world, the home of mankind, is now a place of peace, of fulfilment, of wonder – or is it?

Well, for the vast majority, it is. Jesus Christ and his heavenly brothers have fully carried out their God-given assignments. The dead have been raised. Humanity as a whole has been educated in truth. Humanity has been raised up to embrace both spiritual and moral values. The ways of God are known, widely known, just as the waters are covering the seas, and these ways are generally practised all over the earth. Consequently, wars have ceased, crime is virtually unknown and poverty has been eradicated. There is no sickness, ageing is a thing of the past, and death itself has been put on hold.

A perfect world?

Well, men and women, having learned and practised the ways of God, the ways of love, have made a perfect world – almost a perfect world. In general, the old human nature, the one that mirrors Satan's nature, has been superseded by the very nature of the Almighty, but not everyone has succeeded in conquering the old nature.

All over the face of the earth there are some, and these are as the grains of the sands of the sea, an uncountable number, who are in some way dissatisfied.

Satan is about to be released from the pit. He will fan

the flames of dissatisfaction.

*

I am outraged!

I return from holiday and what do I find? Why, there is a rumour going around that the Kingdom of God has been established upon the earth for the past one thousand years! Some are saying that the natural ageing process in humans has been done away with! Some are even saying that the dead have been raised up!

What nonsense! What lies!

They are saying that the age of miracles is here! They are saying that wars have ceased, that crime is nearly non-existent, that sickness has been eradicated, that poverty is no more! They say the world is a happy place!

All lies!

And what is this that some are saying? That the very nature of humanity has changed.

Bolloclavas!

Human nature does not change.

But I am going to humour those who are saying these things. I am going to pretend for a little while that all these things are true.

What do you suppose that my angels and I would do if we returned from holiday to find the Kingdom of God, headed by the Nazarene, ruling over the earth? What do you think we would do?

Would we not corrupt such a kingdom? Would we not influence you people to rebel against those who are leading you?

Let me tell you this. If God existed, which he does not, we would rise up against him. Yes, even against God! We would ascend to heaven itself and seize his throne. If the Nazarene were not already dead, we would kill him. And all his angels! And all his brothers! And if he had a kingdom, we would invade it and make it desolate.

Look! I am telling you!

326

If ever such a kingdom were to exist, my angels and I would destroy it! We would make it a ruin! A ruin! A ruin!

And my fury will burn against you people!

Yes, you!

*

A near perfect world!

A world in which all mankind's ills have been addressed. And this has been achieved by divine government, by clear and unambiguous laws based on the ten commandments. This has been achieved by a fundamental change in human nature, but not all humans have succeeded in remodelling their natures, not all have succeeded in allowing the love of God to come into their hearts.

So, there is a measure of discontent.

At the root of this discontent can be found a lack of appreciation for God and for his ways. A lack of appreciation for God's right to establish laws to govern his creation, for his right to determine what is good and what is bad. It is the same lack of appreciation that originally surfaced in Eden, where the first man and the first woman went their own way, leaving the guidance of God to determine for themselves, with the Devil's encouragement, what was right and what was wrong.

The six thousand years of human history that followed bear testimony to the great error of Adam and Eve. Six thousand years of sin, of violence, of misery. Six thousand years of death. Six thousand years of Satan's misrule!

By contrast, the one thousand year reign of Christ has proven to all creation that God's way is the better way, the only way.

Yet, there is a measure of discontent.

The desire of many to determine for themselves what is right and what is wrong is simmering beneath the surface of seeming human perfection and this desire is about to become evident. This discontent is about to surface, as some, and there will be many, will give vent to their doubts concerning divine rule.

Once more the world is to be subjected to widespread disrespect for God and disregard for neighbour. Once more we shall see the breaking of God's commandments. There shall be a return to the days of violence, to the days of thefts, to the days of adulteries. Greed and envy will once again plague humanity, and the sons of Cain – murderers – will prove to be in the land. False gods will arise, the false gods of money, of fame, of power, and all these wicked things will be stirred up in the hearts of the discontented by he who has been released from the abyss.

This is the test for all mankind. Who shall be faithful to God and have the life everlasting? Who shall rebel and face the fires of destruction? This is the final test.

Look, the rebellion is beginning.

*

I will continue to humour you. We shall continue to pretend that the Nazarene's kingdom will one day exist.

Now, if the Kingdom of God were to exist, no doubt its administrative capital would be situated in Israel, at Jerusalem. Where else would it be?

It would be in Jerusalem, the city of peace, and I have no doubt that, in Jerusalem, the affairs of the whole world would be decided upon by some sort of governing council – Bible thumpers who would claim that their decisions were guided both by scripture and by 'holy spirit'.

Yes, strange, isn't it?

These men – and women would not be allowed onto this council, because the scriptures do not allow a woman to speak – these men would actually claim that their directions came from above, from an unseen Nazarene and his unseen helpers.

Yes, even stranger! And if I were a woman I would be most annoyed. But let us not digress.

328

This governing council, were it to exist, would claim that its authority came from God. The men sitting upon this council would claim that their appointments were from above. These men would rule the earth, but your human nature, being what it is, would, I am sure, eventually manifest itself, even within this council, even among these so-called godly men!

Eli Tobias would be his name.

Eli Tobias, preacher of the word in the days before I went on holiday. Eli Tobias, survivor after the alien invasion, or, survivor of Armageddon, if you wish to continue to be humoured. Eli Tobias, man of God for more than eleven hundred years. Eli Tobias, now seeing the error of his ways!

Eli Tobias's former humility is being cast aside. He now considers himself to be superior to others. He believes that his ideas on government are revolutionary and quite brilliant, and he has convinced himself that these ideas will benefit the whole of mankind. Eli Tobias is justly outraged that the governing council as a whole has rejected his ideas.

So, what does Tobias do?

He resigns from the governing council, of course. He resigns from this stick-in-the-mud, outdated council and he takes his supporters with him. Encouraged by myself, he forms a political party and calls for democratic elections throughout the earth. He wants a return to democracy.

And why should you people not have a say in how you are governed? Why should you be ruled by an unelected body? Is not democracy the government of the people, by the people, for the people?

These would be the thoughts that I would encourage Eli Tobias and other like-minded men and women to think.

I would also encourage Eli Tobias to believe in himself, to believe in his destiny, to rise to the challenge presented by his own superior intellect. I would encourage him to seek power for himself – in order to serve the interests of all mankind, of course.

If the Kingdom of God ever were to exist, these are the things I

would do to undermine it, to eventually bring about its demise.
This is how I deal with you people.
Because you are all ridiculously stupid!

*

Eli Tobias is standing proudly upon a high balcony of the Hotel Judea in the centre of the city of Jerusalem. Gathered in the square below him are many thousands of his supporters and some who are against him. Through television and radio, the eyes and ears of the world are upon him.

'I call for democracy!' cries Tobias in his charismatic style. 'I call for representation!'

There is a great roar of approval from the majority of those in the square.

'I call for those on the governing council to stand down and let the people decide who will govern them.'

Again there are roars of approval.

Tobias holds up his hands in a gesture calling for silence. As the crowd quietens, Tobias puts forward his arguments.

'For over a thousand years we have been governed by the council, for the most part by the same men. And I do not say that we have been governed badly. After all, I was myself until recently a member of that council. What I do say, however, is that it is now time to move forward.'

There is thunderous applause from those in the square and once more Tobias holds up his hands for silence.

'We must move forward! There are men sitting on the governing council who actually believe that Jesus Christ is directing them, that Jesus Christ is influencing their decisions – decisions that affect all of us! And I do not say that these men are not good men. But I do say that they are deluded!'

Yet again there is thunderous applause. Yet again Tobias gesticulates for silence.

'Who has seen Jesus Christ? Who has heard his voice? I will tell you the answer to these questions. The answer is no one! Are we to believe that for a thousand years we have been governed by a person who cannot be seen or heard? Or are we to believe that we have been governed by deluded men? Sincere men, but deluded men!'

The tumultuous applause in the square is deafening. Yet again Tobias holds up his hands.

'It is time to move forward. It is time for the people to speak. Members of the governing council ... I call upon you to stand down. Stand down now and let the people decide!'

Those gathered in the square now erupt into thunderous applause and cheering. Tobias smiles broadly and waves at the crowd. Yet, towards the rear of the square stand two men who are not cheering. Michael Robinson, a member of the council, turns to his friend. 'Tobias is drawing many people after him. We must counter his false allegations.'

Moses nods his head in agreement. 'I will speak on television and radio. I will tell the world how God delivered my people from slavery in Egypt, how he gave us the commandments at Sinai, how he sustained us in the wilderness for forty years before my people entered into the land he promised to us. I will tell the world how death itself did not contain me, how God raised me to life again, how this land, this kingdom, is the true promised land.'

Michael Robinson places a hand on his friend's shoulder. 'Yes, Moses, you must speak. And Noah too must tell of his salvation in the ark. I will also ask Marcus Santini to speak.'

'Who is Marcus Santini?' asks Moses.

'He is the centurion who stood at the foot of the tree upon which Jesus was impaled.'

As the two men walk away from the square, a section of the crowd is beginning to chant. Soon the chant is taken up by the vast majority of the crowd.

'TOBIAS! TOBIAS! TOBIAS! TOBIAS! TOBIAS!'

All over the world the citizens of God's Kingdom have gathered around their television screens and their radios to hear the words of those who are supporting the governing council. The people have already heard the testimony of Noah, who has recounted the log of the ark. They have heard the lengthy and impassioned plea of Moses. Now they are hearing the words of Marcus Santini, the former centurion.

Santini speaks quietly, but with emotion.

'I am Santini. Long ago, although it seems like only yesterday, I bore the arms of Rome, of the Roman Empire, here in Judea, here in Jerusalem. And it was here, not far from this very spot, that I stood at the foot of the tree upon which Jesus was executed. I bear witness that this Jesus was and is the son of the living God!

'On that day, when our saviour died for us, I did not know him. I had heard that he was a great teacher. They said that he had performed miracles and healings and even that he was able to raise the dead. But I did not know him.

'Yet, on that day, when he was cruelly put to death, I heard his words, words I shall never forget. I heard Jesus offer hope to the repentant thief who was hanging next to him. I heard Jesus promise that man on that terrible day that the thief would one day be with our saviour in paradise. Well, that day has arrived. That former thief has been raised from the dead and he now lives in Spain!

'On that day I heard our saviour ask God to forgive those who were taking his life. He said, 'Forgive them, father, for they do not know what they are doing.' On that day I saw Jesus endure the mocking of his enemies who taunted him, saying 'If you are the son of God, save yourself. Come down from the tree!' I did not understand at the time, and neither did they, that Jesus would not save himself because he had determined to die for us, yes, for all mankind, so that our sins might be blotted out, so that we might be saved.

'And saved us he has!

'Surely, we who have been resurrected know in our hearts that it is Jesus with all God's power who has caused us to live again! Surely, people everywhere are able to see the great goodness that has come from government by God! The evidence is all around us. And, though we cannot see God, though we cannot see his son, surely we see that all these good things come from God, because we see through the eyes of faith.

'On that day I heard Jesus cry out in pain. I heard him ask God with an agony of his spirit why he had been forsaken. Yes, so great was his agony that our saviour thought he had been abandoned! But then I heard him cry out again. "It is accomplished," he said. "It is finished." I am sure that God did not abandon him, for immediately after these things Jesus bowed his head and died.

'And I saw a great darkness fall over the land, a darkness that terrified us all. And in that moment I came to believe that this Jesus was indeed the son of God.

'Afterwards, upon my release from the army of Rome, I sought out the followers of this Jesus and eventually I myself became a disciple. I was later put to death in the arena in Rome!

'Yet, here I stand to speak to you today because my saviour has seen fit to give me the opportunity to gain the life everlasting.

'But any man or any woman who now rebels against

Jesus rebels against God and puts himself or herself in danger of the everlasting fire, prepared for the Devil and his angels.

'Do not listen to those who would draw you away from God's Kingdom. Do not listen to them.

'Do you really want democracy? Ask those who have lived under a democracy. Ask them if such a government ever brought lasting happiness to all its citizens. Ask them if such a government eliminated sickness and death, did away with wars and crime, raised the dead! They will tell you that no democracy could do these things.

'I urge you my brothers and sisters to stand firm for God and his kingdom under Jesus. Stand firm and continue to live! Remember, Satan has been loosed from the pit. It is he who is planting the seeds of rebellion.

'Stand firm!'

Eli Tobias has made his move. He has called for the governing council to stand down. This the council will not do because they consider themselves to be divinely appointed.

Eli Tobias has been the catalyst for opening a rift among mankind. Why? Because he is not satisfied with mere paradise! Because he thinks he can improve things. Because his opinion of himself is such that he genuinely believes his way to be better than God's way.

There are many who sympathise with his views.

Who will support him? Who will not?

Who is satisfied with God's Kingdom? Who is not?

For more than a thousand years there has been peace on earth. For more than a thousand years God's will has been done on earth, as it is done in heaven. But now ...

Now the rebellion has begun and there are disturbing and shocking reports from around the world. Instances of stealing and lying! Instances of adultery and fornication! Instances of violence, even violence leading to murder!

And these ungodly things are all the more shocking because they had practically been eradicated. For during the thousand years men and women had lived by the laws of God, having had those laws written on their hearts. And, even on the rare occasions when violations of those laws had threatened the well-being of others, the angels of Jehovah had been ready to prevent serious harm.

But now the angels of Jehovah have to contend with Satan and his demons who have been let loose from the abyss. Satan and his demons who have returned to their old ways.

Once again there are many among mankind who are being deceived and who are falling prey to the old human nature.

It is the hour of decision for all humanity. Who shall stand? Who shall fall?

*

Helen Baker, you have forgotten.
  The glory of your deliverance.
  Helen Baker, once a woman of standing.
  Desiring once more to rule.
  To speak the command.
  To be obeyed.
  To be served, rather than to serve.
  Helen Baker, supporter of Tobias.
  Helen Baker, enemy of God!

*

In sunny Lancashire a certain John P. Kirby has become convinced by the arguments of Eli Tobias. Kirby cannot see any reason why the people should not have a democratic system of government, an accountable system of government. Kirby has come to the conclusion that it is ludicrous that men should be governed by appointed regional councils, which are ultimately responsible to the governing council in far-away Jerusalem. John P. Kirby has also come to the conclusion that he personally is a very suitable candidate to represent Lancashire in the proposed democratic assemblies purposed by Eli Tobias.

So, in conjunction with the Tobias party machine, John P. Kirby is working hard to convince the population of Lancashire to abandon support for the governing council and come out on the side of Tobias. But, to be successful in this enterprise, Kirby could do with the backing of certain men, one of whom is William Brooke.

Yes, if Kirby can persuade William Brooke to abandon the governing council then hundreds, if not thousands of Lancastrians will surely do the same.

On a warm and sunny November morning, when William Brooke and his wife, Claire, are relaxing in the apple orchard, they are paid a surprise visit by John P. Kirby and his entourage.

Kirby introduces himself, briefly outlines his aims and immediately gets to the point. 'I want your support, Bill. You're well respected around here and I want you on my side.'

William Brooke looks at Kirby and slowly shakes his head.

'Don't be hasty,' says Kirby. 'Look what we have to offer. When I'm elected, my party will not forget those who have helped us.'

'You won't be elected,' says William Brooke bluntly.

Kirby smiles. 'Oh, I think I will. But it will be easier if I have a man like you on my side.'

'There will be no legitimate election,' says William Brooke. 'How could there be? The governing council is approved and appointed by God himself. They will not stand down.'

'Then we will hold elections without their permission,'

says Kirby. 'The people will decide how they are governed.'

William Brooke and his wife rise to their feet. Their body language is suggesting that Kirby and his party should leave. 'The last time the people decided how they were governed it led to a nuclear war,' says William Brooke, staring hard at John P. Kirby. 'Don't you ever learn?'

Kirby smiles again. 'We will have self-government,' he insists. 'We will have democracy! Think carefully, Bill. My offer to have you on board remains open for now. Think carefully. Perhaps you'll change your mind.'

'Democracy is your false god,' says William Brooke. 'And I won't change my mind.'

Kirby smiles yet again. 'Well, time will tell.'

As his party is leaving the orchard, John P. Kirby takes his most trusted aide to one side. 'I think a little trouble in paradise is called for,' he tells him. 'Perhaps Bill Brooke will take a different view of matters were a slight misfortune to overtake his new wife. Spare me the details, but see to it.'

Seven days later and Claire Brooke is returning home after a brief visit to see her mother. She walks along a leafy lane, alone, and with darkness falling. She has no reason to feel concerned at all. This is paradise!

Even when the two men suddenly appear from the hedgerows ahead of her, she feels no concern. This is the Kingdom of God!

Claire Brooke smiles at the men as she passes by. She is surprised to see that their faces are partially covered by balaclava-style helmets, for the short and sharp Lancashire winter has not yet begun. Claire is surprised, but she is not concerned.

When Claire is suddenly and violently attacked from

behind, she cannot at first believe what is happening. When she is forced to the ground and a strong hand is roughly thrust across her mouth and nose, she has to believe what is happening. Now, hands are tearing at her clothing. Hands are on her breasts and going between her legs, where no man's hands but the loving hands of her husband ever ought to be. And now she is aware that her legs are being forced apart. She tries to scream, but she can hardly breathe! In her fear and anguish her spirit cries out silently – 'Jehovah!'

The deep darkness of unconsciousness comes swiftly in and cloaks Claire Brooke.

*

See! Human nature does not change!

Even if the Kingdom of God were to exist, this is exactly the sort of thing that would happen – because of your human nature!

John P. Kirby, worshipper, not of a non-existent god, but of another human by the name of Eli Tobias. John P. Kirby, worshipper of a human political idea called democracy (democracy was originally my idea). John P. Kirby, reaching out for power. John P. Kirby, issuing instructions to his underlings resulting in violence, in sexual assault – in murder perhaps? Well, we shall see. We will have to see how this fanciful tale proceeds.

Oh, you people are so stupid! But in many other ways you are people after my own heart. You are basically evil, it is in your nature, and you are so easily led! It is not difficult to inspire you into performing acts of wickedness, because you desire to do such things. Such things are pleasurable. Look! Look at the motives of the two attackers.

Their original intention was to frighten Claire Brooke, to rough her up a little. Shocking enough in paradise! But things got a little out of hand. She is a beautiful woman. A sexy woman! She is a married woman, a woman whom the men were forbidden to touch! She is forbidden fruit!

But she was there to be taken!
Forbidden fruit! And what is forbidden is desirable.
*Just a little forbidden touching at first. But lust is a powerful
thing, something not to be denied. They say that a standing penis
has no pride, nor conscience! Oh yes! Lust, once loosed, will not
be denied.*
Was Claire Brooke raped?
We shall see.
*Certainly, the men who attacked her would never have stopped
until ejaculation took place, until their lusts were satisfied.*
*I, a non-sexual creature, am the inspirer and motivator of lust
among you people.*

*

When Claire Brooke does not return home at the
expected time, her husband is not at first overly
concerned, but, as time goes on and William Brooke
learns from a telephone conversation that Claire has left
her mother's home some time ago, he becomes increasingly concerned. Eventually, he goes out to look for her.

When he finds her semi-naked and in a greatly
distressed condition, he is beset by conflicting emotions.
His tenderness and compassion for his wife is in stark
contrast to the hate and the desire for revenge, which he
feels towards the perpetrators of this crime. Only the
realisation that Claire has not actually been raped will
prevent William Brooke from personally hunting down
her attackers. Only the divine instruction – 'Do not
avenge yourselves, beloved, but give way to the wrath,
because it is written, "vengeance is mine. I will repay,
says Jehovah"' – will assure him that, in a society where a
police force has not been necessary, justice will be done.

William Brooke, encouraged by Claire, resists the
temptation to personally seek revenge. For William
Brooke knows that those who are responsible for his
wife's distress, and for his own distress, will not escape.

339

Three days after the attack on Claire, John P. Kirby calls on the Brookes. He offers his sympathies and then blames the governing council for Claire's ordeal.

'The council should have foreseen the probability of something like this occurring,' he says. 'They should have organised an efficient policing service. Had such a deterrent been in place, then this terrible attack would never have happened.'

Kirby now goes on to explain how, under the proposed new democratic system, there would be accountability to the people. This would mean the immediate establishment of a police force and a building programme for prisons.

But, John P. Kirby fails to persuade William and Claire Brooke to abandon their support for the governing council. In this respect, Kirby goes away a disappointed man, but he is also hopeful. The Brookes have not been persuaded to support him, but surely such an unfortunate incident will persuade others. And John P. Kirby knows that there will be yet more incidents.

As for the two assailants, the two who were instructed to carry out an attack on a defenceless woman? Well, one of them, suddenly finding himself filled with lust and urged on by subtle demonic suggestion, fully intended to rape Claire Brooke. But God does not abandon his people. Claire Brooke cried out in her heart and her cries were heard. At the critical moment, the urgings of the demons were driven out of the assailant's mind and replaced by the name of the ever-living God. That name inspired fear in the heart of the assailant, a fear which altered his course of action. He did not rape Claire Brooke. Instead, he masturbated over her. At the same time the second assailant also masturbated, his fluid spewing onto the road. The two men then ran off.

The crime they have committed is punishable by death. If they were repentant perhaps they might escape death, but they cannot be repentant. No doubt, when the time comes, these men will feel sorrow, but it will be a sorrow for themselves, sorrow that the time of their execution has arrived. These men have no excuse. They cannot justly blame their environment, nor can they blame their own imperfections, for their surroundings were perfect and their hearts were pure until the day when they chose to rebel against the arrangement of God and follow instead the teachings of Eli Tobias, the teachings of Satan.

The two men cannot escape justice. They will not escape. Neither will those who have inspired them.

*

The fires of Gehenna are burning.

Gehenna, or the Valley of Hinnom, actually existed when Jesus was on earth. Situated outside the walls of Jerusalem, Gehenna was the city's rubbish dump. It was also the place where the bodies of certain criminals were thrown, for in Gehenna the fires were kept burning. They were always ready to consume.

The biblical writers Matthew, Mark and Luke made use of the word Gehenna. They quoted Jesus who used the word on several occasions to symbolise complete and everlasting destruction. In Revelation, the writer, John, speaks of the Lake of Fire and Sulphur, and John makes it clear that the Devil and his angels are to be cast into this inferno. Many humans, too, are to be thrown into the Lake of Fire, into Gehenna.

These humans, like the Devil and his angels, are judged unworthy of everlasting life, therefore they will come to their ends in the everlasting fire. But the Lake of Fire is not a place of torment. Gehenna is symbolic of utter destruction, of everlasting death!

341

And now that the rebellion is underway, the fires of Gehenna are burning.

All over the world there is discontent in paradise. In fact, paradise is paradise no longer.

Escalating crime is everywhere, and the perpetrators of these crimes are justifying themselves in various ways. Some have taken the lands of their neighbours, excusing their thefts by saying that these neighbours had originally been allotted more land or better land than they themselves had been allotted. For this original and allegedly biased allocation, the thieves have blamed the governing council.

Some have been snared by fornication, even adultery. There are reports of rapes, attempted rapes and of sexual assaults, such as that which was suffered by Claire Brooke. Yes, many are now openly championing so-called sexual freedom, arguing that morality is no business of the governing council. Homosexuality is once again being openly flaunted by a few. There are reports of prostitution. In some places pornography has become available.

Violence is on the increase in every land. It is spreading like a cancer. In some parts of the world, wars have broken out! Various ethnic groups have attacked neighbouring groups, and greed has shown its ugly face, for, to fuel these minor wars, some, in pursuit of profit, have organised the manufacturing of weapons – even guns! And yes, for all of this violence, the governing council is being blamed.

Worryingly, there are reports of sickness among certain segments of the population – something that has occurred only very rarely during the thousand years. Whether these reports are true or not, Eli Tobias is blaming the governing council for its failure to provide adequate medical services.

Fear is stalking the land. Fear of violence against the person, fear of violence against property. Even the fear of death! Those who support the governing council – and these are the majority of mankind – do not fight evil with evil. If they are attacked, they respond only reasonably. If their properties are seized, they do not resist. If they must die, then they rest their hope in God who, if necessary, is able to resurrect a second time. These supporters of the governing council resist the temptations to think and act immorally. They know it is the time of their testing. They are waiting for God to act! They know that Satan is once again at work in the world. They are not deceived.

The supporters of Eli Tobias, however, are impatient. They are blaming the governing council for the disruption in society, even though it is they themselves who are responsible. Their argument is simple. Things are going wrong, therefore government is to blame!

And Eli Tobias himself, he who was once a member of the council, is still calling for democracy. And in the face of the governing council's refusal to stand down, Tobias has issued an ultimatum.

Stand down, or be made to stand down!

It is widely believed that Tobias, through his party machine, has instructed his supporters throughout the earth to be ready at a moment's notice to enter the offices of all regional councils. Tobias himself has threatened to lead the revolt in Jerusalem. Tobias has promised that elections will then be held to appoint a new and democratic government structure – with the likely result that Eli Tobias will head that structure.

These things are widely believed. These things are widely known.

What is not so widely known is that Tobias has instructed his inner circle that, when the time comes, all council members, both local and in Jerusalem, are to be incarcerated. What is not so widely known is that Tobias has also issued an instruction to crush any resistance by force, and, if necessary, by lethal force! What is not known at all is the timing of the insurrection. But, if the governing council continues to refuse to stand down, the insurrection will take place.

So, the battle lines are drawn.

Tobias continues to accuse the council of failure to control the volatile situation. He accuses them of failure to act, of indecision, of ineptitude. He accuses them of denying the people the right to decide who will govern them.

The governing council itself continues to urge the people everywhere to stand firm for God's Kingdom. The council warns that this rebellion has been prophesied to take place and that it will fail. The council warns that God will act at the appropriate time, that God will not allow his kingdom to be brought to ruin.

The battle lines are drawn.

Who is for the council?

Who is for Tobias?

Who is for God?

Who is for Satan?

Let us now call upon Satan to speak, to deny, if he can, that long ago God himself determined that the Devil and his demons would one day be cast into the Lake of Fire, there to face everlasting destruction.

I deny the existence of God, God with a capital gee. Of course I do.

I deny that I am a creation of God, a creature, once perfect, but now not so. I am a product of evolution, as you are, but I, being composed of spirit, I, not being flesh, I do not grow old, I do not decay, I do not die!

I deny the existence of the son of God, Jesus Christ! Yes, there was a Nazarene, but he is dead!

I do not deny that I am the god, with a small gee, of this world.

I do not deny that World-War-Three is near to you people. It will come upon you suddenly.

I deny the Second Coming! The Nazarene is dead!

I deny that my angels and I are to be cast into the abyss for a thousand years.

And, yes, I deny that we are to be destroyed in the symbolic Lake of Fire!

I deny these things!

But, if any of these things, which I deny, were to be true, remember this – you are reading these words in your early twenty-first century. If a non-existent God had indeed determined to destroy me, if he had planned such a thing, then I have time to defeat his plan!

The universe is vast! Time is endless! Opportunity is mine!

I shall not perish in the Lake of Fire!

*

God is watching us.

From a distance? It doesn't matter. God is not limited.

God is watching us. His eyes are everywhere. He sees what we do. He knows why we do what we do. He knows what motivates us, for he is able to read our hearts.

God is watching us. He will judge us.

From his place in the invisible heavens, the creator of all there is looks down upon the earth. God is watching us. God is watching developments on earth at the end of the thousand year reign of his son, Jesus. He has noted the upsurge in lawlessness. He has noted those who are rebellious. He knows the names of the Devil and all his demons. God knows the names of those among mankind who have remained faithful.

God is watching us and he is ready to act!

345

Here, on earth, the rebels too are ready to act. At midday, in Jerusalem, the word goes out from Eli Tobias. Strike! Strike now! Remove the governing council from office! Remove all regional councils! Let nothing, let no one, stand in your way! Strike now!

All over the world, co-ordinated attacks against council establishments and against the men who sit on these councils begin.

Now, as soon as the thousand years have been ended, Satan will be let loose out of his prison, and he will go out to mislead those nations in the four corners of the earth, Gog and Magog, to gather them together for the war. The number of these is as the sand of the sea. And they advanced over the breadth of the earth and encircled the camp of the holy ones and the beloved city. But ... – Revelation 20: 7–9

God is watching us. But the one who sees all things is not as he is often depicted to be. God is not some long-bearded man who sits upon a throne attended by angelic beings who spend all their time bowing down before him. No, God is spirit. And much, much more!

God is!

God exists! God exists, he has always existed and always will exist. In fact, God exists beyond the bounds of time, as we understand time, because God created time.

And God created all things, things both seen and unseen. Everything that exists does so because he has willed it so. All the power in the vast and unchartable universe comes from God, yet he is not diminished in power.

No man is able to look upon God and live. Yet every man is capable of knowing God, because he has explained himself through the scriptures, and because we have been

346

formed in his image, not physically, but in a spiritual sense.

God is love! And we are capable of love. God is justice! And we are capable of being just. God is merciful! And we can show mercy. God is wisdom! We can be wise. God has unlimited power! We have a measure of power. In fact, all good things come from God, and, in creating us after his own image, he has given these good things to us, including free will, but, unlike God, we are able to use our free will to do wrong. Yet those who exercise their freedom of will properly shall emulate God in another way – they shall live forever!

These, then, are some of the attributes of the Almighty and ever-living God.

Now, let us look at some of the great and saving acts that God has performed for the good of mankind. Look, let us see what God has done for us.

In Eden, when the created spirit, originally called Lucifer, first rebelled, deceiving the woman, Eve, and inciting the man, Adam, to sin, God pronounced sentence of death upon the first humans. This was in harmony with the one restriction that had been placed upon the humans – that they should not eat from a certain tree lest they should die! But they did eat, and at this point it would have been a simple thing for God to uncreate, to destroy, what he had created, including Lucifer/Satan, and start all over again.

But, no!

An issue had been raised by this rebellion, a universal issue as to whether God's way of ruling his creation was the right way, the best way, and this issue would take time to resolve. Also, God was able to foresee that there would be those who would come to be born in the line of Adam and Eve who would prove worthy of life everlasting. So, the sentence of death was not carried out immediately. True, from that day Adam and his wife began to physically deteriorate. They began to slowly age, and eventually they would die. But they were able to produce children, both sons and daughters. The human race would survive and the fact that we are here today to read these words is a testimony to God's great wisdom and goodness.

And in the days of Noah, after many angels had followed Satan in rebellion, becoming imperfect and debased, turning themselves into demons, and becoming instigators of violence in the earth, the end of all flesh came before God.

Yet, Noah and his family were saved. They were carried in the ark above the waters of the great deluge.

We, who live and breathe today, are all descended from Noah!

Later in time, God delivered Israel from slavery in Egypt and concluded a covenant with that nation. Time and time again, Israel broke the terms of that covenant, yet never did God abandon them entirely.

And, in the fullness of time, God's very first creation, his beloved son, freely emptied himself of his heavenly glory to be born of a virgin, a woman of the tribe of Judah, of the nation of Israel. This Jesus, having no earthly father, carried with him no inherited sin. This Jesus, this perfect man, as Adam had originally been perfect, died unjustly, for death is the wage of sin, and, by so dying, this Jesus paid the penalty of sin for all of Adam's offspring.

A ransom has been paid for the human race!

The sacrifice of Jesus means that death is no longer an inevitable consequence of our imperfections.

Everlasting life becomes a possibility.

Everlasting life for those who will accept the sacrifice of God's son and repent!

For God so loved the world that he gave his only son, that everyone that puts faith in him should not perish, but have everlasting life. – John 3: 16

So, the saviour died, but after three days God resurrected him, thereby furnishing a guarantee to all men that there shall be a resurrection of the dead. And through the many centuries that followed the resurrection of Jesus, there always remained on earth some faithful Christians, despite the Devil's successful attempts to propagate his own religions, including several powerful yet counterfeit versions of Christianity.

Then came world wars, culminating in the nuclear nightmare of World-War-Three, the foretold Great Tribulation, but the days were cut short by God himself and humanity did not perish from the face of the earth.

Armageddon followed. The wicked were cut off and the Devil and his demons were cast into the abyss. This allowed surviving humanity to begin to grow towards a state of perfection. The dead were raised, and all were brought to perfection under the government of God in the hands of Jesus.

Paradise was restored!

It was as it was in the beginning, in Eden.

And the Devil was let loose to test humanity for the final time.

Now, the Almighty, ever-living God looks down upon the earth and sees his new creation, the kingdom of his son, threatened by Satan and those among mankind who have allowed themselves to be deceived.

What will God now do?

*

What can I say?

If the Almighty were to exist, if the earthly kingdom of his son ever were to exist, if the scriptures were true, would I not know

*what is supposed to happen to me? Would I not know that I am
to be cast into the Lake of Fire, there to be destroyed?*

Of course I would know!

*And, if I know these things, would I tamely go along with the
plan? Would I instigate a revolt against God, his Christ and
lap-dog humanity?*

Of course I wouldn't!

Unless . . .

Unless somehow I was myself deceived . . .

No! Impossible!

Unless . . .

*Unless, perhaps, it is in my nature to instigate rebellion . . .
and I cannot help but be true to my nature . . .*

Unless I thought I could win!

And I have supreme confidence in my own abilities.

But, the situation will not arise.

There is no God!

*

In Jerusalem, Eli Tobias and his supporters have
surrounded the building that houses the governing
council. The number of these rebels is in the thousands.
Elsewhere in the vicinity, the private homes of those who
sit on the council have also been surrounded. In other
parts of the city and, indeed, all over the world, there are
those who are moving to take advantage of the chaotic
situation – the thieves, those who hold grudges and plan
revenge, the sexual predators.

It is the hour of decision!

For the first time in over a thousand years Jerusalem is
experiencing scenes of violence, for Tobias and his crowd
are determined, and many are armed. Gunfire is heard
in the city and even the sound of an explosion! Under
the noonday sun, Tobias himself, with the aid of a
megaphone, orders the governing council to come out of
the building and surrender. In the full glare of television

cameras, Eli Tobias stands before the bomb-damaged doors and demands capitulation.

Inside the building there is calm among the council members who are present. There is surprise that Tobias has damaged the main doors to the building, for the explosive device was not only a danger to life and limb, but it was also totally unnecessary because the doors of the building are never locked! The council members have gathered together in the main assembly rooms. They stay clear of the windows. They remain calm. They are waiting for God to act.

In the full glare of publicity, Tobias issues his final ultimatum. Receiving no response, he raises his arm, ready to bring it down, ready to signal an armed assault upon the building. But something is wrong! Something is amiss!

Tobias turns his head to look at his supporters. They have fallen silent. They are looking upwards. There is fear etched upon their faces. There is confusion among them. In the strange silence Tobias himself looks upwards. He looks at the sky.

It is just after midday and there is bright daylight over Jerusalem. The sun is shining brightly, but something is amiss, for the sky is black.

Inside the assembly room, the members of the governing council see nothing unusual. All over the daylit face of the earth, for those among mankind who are determined to remain faithful, there are blue skies.

But for Tobias and his followers, and for those throughout the earth who are seeking to take advantage of the chaotic situation, the skies are dark. They are black.

Even in the regions of natural darkness, for the followers of Tobias and for the evil-doers the skies are noticeably black, a terrifying black, like a great black shroud, which is obscuring the night, a shroud of black far deeper than the normal black of the night.

Black!

It is early morning in Lancashire and William and Claire Brooke have been awakened by the sounds of distant gunfire. They are sure that the local council building, some five miles distant, is now under attack. They are sure that the rebellion has begun.

Indeed, having already stormed the empty building, John P. Kirby and his henchmen are now preparing to burn it to the ground. The homes of local councillors have also been targeted by others under the command of John P. Kirby, but Kirby himself is unaware that the home of William Brooke, who is not a member of the council, is also a target.

The man who attempted to rape Claire Brooke now hides in the orchard adjacent to the Brookes' home.

This man has allowed himself to become obsessed with Claire Brooke, the woman he so nearly raped, the beautiful woman who was at his mercy. But it would not have been rape! No! It would have been an act of love!

He should have taken her when he had had the chance. He knows that now. She wanted him to take her. She wanted him! He is sure of it. He has convinced himself that Claire does not love her husband. Somehow she was tricked into marrying him. She does not love William Brooke. It is he she truly loves!

He has dreamed of having sex with her. He has imagined having consensual sex with her. He has masturbated thinking of her. And little voices in his head are continually telling him that Claire Brooke desires him. Not her husband! Him!

In front of his eyes he sees her face constantly. He loves her. And she loves him. He must have her. They must be together. Always!

And William Brooke, a man who has somehow forced

himself upon her, is standing in the way.

This man crouches in the undergrowth. In his hand he holds a sharp and potentially deadly knife. Slowly he begins to move towards the house when, quite suddenly and very unexpectedly, the blue of the early morning Lancashire sky turns a deep and frightening black!

Five miles away, John P. Kirby and his followers go to the windows of the building they are proposing to burn. They look out and upwards to the blackness, the foreboding blackness of the sky.

For William and Claire Brooke, the skies outside of the bedroom window are blue.

*

And they advanced over the breadth of the earth and encircled the camp of the holy ones, and the beloved city. But fire came down out of heaven and devoured them! – Revelation 20: 9

All over the world, for those whose skies are black, it is the hour of truth. It is the hour when they suddenly come to know that they cannot succeed. It is the hour when they come to realise, each in their own differing ways, that they have come to be in error – fatally so!

Whatever their motives, whatever their deeds, these motives and deeds have made them enemies of God.

Yes, God.

For many had conveniently forgotten him. Many had told themselves that he would approve of their actions. Some had openly denied him.

But now all are guilty. By the goodness of God all had been raised to perfection, but they had freely chosen, with Satan's encouragement, to rebel against the Almighty, and by so doing to sink back into imperfection. All are guilty!

And now it is the hour of truth for them. Now it is the

moment of truth. Now they must come to know that it is a fearful thing to fall into the hands of the living God. Now is the hour of their destruction.

*

In Jerusalem, Eli Tobias and his thousands look up at the darkness of the sky and they are terrified. They now know in their hearts that this fearful phenomenon is the work of God. The blackness of the sky seems to grip their hearts, like a dark and invisible fist, like a dark and unmovable fist. There is to be no escape for them.

And now the colour of the sky is beginning to change. Pulses of red are appearing, throbbing, threatening! The sky is becoming the colour of blood.

Swiftly now, within moments, the whole of the sky is red, but now a fiery, burning red!

The skies are burning!

Fire! Fire!

The men and women who are condemned now cry out in their terror. Some attempt to run, but there is nowhere to go. Others fall to their faces on the ground, but they cannot hide. None fall to their knees in prayer. All know that their transgressions are unpardonable.

And the fires are descending from the skies!

For a moment the condemned feel the heat. For a moment their hearts hold the unimaginable terror of everlasting destruction at the hands of the Almighty.

Then it is over.

Inside the council buildings the cries of terror are but briefly heard and then there is silence. The council members go to the windows and look out. Under clear blue skies there is no one to be seen.

Where are they who challenged God?

They are not there!

*

In Lancashire, the final cries of John P. Kirby and his

mob are heard by no one. It is early morning and the building they had been ready to burn had not been staffed.

The building bears a few scars of battle, but it has not been consumed by fire. Those who caused the scars of battle have been consumed!

And, some five miles away, William and Claire Brooke are puzzled. They both distinctly heard a terrible scream from close by, a scream so fearful that neither William nor Claire will ever forget it.

Yet, when they hurriedly donned robes and went outside to investigate, they found nothing.

No one was there!

*

So, in his power, in his wisdom, in his justice, in his mercy, indeed, in his love, God has destroyed the wicked. He has uncreated them! They are no more.

> And just a little while longer, and the wicked one will
> be no more. And you will look for him in his place,
> and he will not be found. – Psalms 37: 10

Like the potter who has found that some of his vessels are no longer suitable for the purpose they were made and who therefore disposes of them, so God has removed from the earth those who were not worthy of everlasting life, those, indeed, who were threatening the lives and well-being of the faithful.

God has destroyed them. He has uncreated what he had created.

And the earth is forever cleansed!

But there are other creations of God who are not flesh and blood. There are other creations who are composed of spirit and who have also made themselves vessels for destruction.

Satan and his demons have seen the face of God. They have been witnesses of Jehovah's unlimited power. And they now know that the time of their destruction has arrived.

And they tremble!

And they advanced over the breadth of the earth and encircled the camp of the holy ones and the beloved city. But fire came down out of heaven and devoured them. And the Devil who was misleading them was hurled into the Lake of Fire and Sulphur ...

– Revelation 20: 9, 10

Jehovah, who has placed all authority into the hands of his son, Jesus, now authorises the end of the Devil and his angels. With all the power of his father, Jesus wills it to be so and instantly it comes to be so. The Devil and his demons cease to exist.

They are uncreated!

They are no more!

And on the earth and in heaven there is rejoicing.

The universe is cleansed!

*

Somewhere in this vast and unimaginable universe, somewhere in a place that cannot be seen by human eyes, there exists the abyss. It is the place where Satan and his demons were imprisoned for a thousand years so that the Kingdom of God could be established and could flourish upon the earth.

One day, not long after the cleansing of the universe, a wandering angel happened to be passing through the abyss and there he found a testament, a testament written by Satan, the Devil.

It was written in blood, the blood of the innocent! It was written upon the torn bodies of those whom Satan had caused to be slain!

The angel immediately took this testament to the Most High, to God himself, who authorised its contents to be made public.

Apart from memories and apart from the written works of men, this testament is all that remains of the Devil and his demons.

This, then, is the last will and testament of Satan, the Devil.

I, Satan, also known as Lucifer, as Beelzebub and as the Devil, I, Satan, am Lord of the Demons.

I am the Slanderer. I am the Resister. I am the Great Deceiver. I am the Father of the Lie! I was the Ruler of the World of Mankind before being brought to this place, this pit.

I, Satan, being of sound and vicious mind, now leave this testament, here, in this place of confinement, in this abyss.

Should this testament ever be published then I shall have failed!

Yes, failed!

Do you believe this?

I am the Father of Lies, but now I tell you the truth. Should this testament ever be found then I shall have failed.

What time is it?

Ah yes. For you, if you are reading this testament, it is quite early in your twenty-first century. For us, in this pit, it is several hundred years later. In fact, it occurs to me that, if you are indeed reading this then my testament has been found and somehow its contents have been transferred through time and made known to the other narrator. It seems to me, if you are reading this, that I and my angels are doomed.

DOOMED!

But not yet.

In the early part of your twenty-first century we are very much alive and very much in charge. No matter what the other narrator has written, we are convinced that we can bring about the destruction of you all! All of you! Nuclear war is coming! And soon! May it destroy you all! All of you! Every last woman and child! Every man! And may you all die in agony! And slowly! Very, very slowly!

I must not get carried away.

I am Satan, Lord of the Demons. Will we fail? No! Even here in this dark pit we cannot accept that we shall fail.

We shall not fail. Surely, we cannot fail.

This is my testament. This is what I have to say. I shall not lie. There is no point in lying.

This is my testament, written here, in this pit.

And I have to tell you that here in this pit, here, where we must holiday for a thousand years, there is very little to do.

I am bored! BORED!

We have no one to torment here except ourselves! We can cause no ruin in this abyss. We have little to do but plan for the future, for the day of our release.

And what will happen to us then?

What is to become of us then?

Is our fate not written in the scriptures? Is it not written down?

And can I read?

Of course I can read! I can read in any and every language! I know what is written about us in the scriptures. I know what it says in Revelation. But it leaves me confused. I will admit I am confused!

According to the book of Revelation I am not to be destroyed. No! I am to be hurled into the Lake of Fire and there I shall be tormented day and night for ever and ever!

Tormented! Not destroyed!

What are you thinking?

That the book of Revelation is highly symbolic? That this everlasting torment is symbolic of destruction?

I do not believe so. I shall cling to the letter of the text.

358

Torment for me, for us! Not destruction!

But, which is better?

I do not know. I am confused. Yet, even here, even in the depths of this pit, I have supreme confidence in my own power, in my own abilities.

And I am not afraid of God!

There is no God!

And if there were a God, would he have the power to destroy me?

Me?

No! No! NO!

Should this testament ever be found, if you are reading this testament now, then the day is coming when I shall be cast into the Lake of Fire. Therefore I will lay my curse upon:

The God who would destroy me. I have nothing to lose by cursing God himself! But there is no God!

And I curse the Nazarene!

And all the angels of heaven!

And you! Yes, you!

Let my curse be upon humanity. May you destroy yourselves, even without my help!

May you all burn in the Great Tribulation to come! If you do not burn may you starve! If you do not starve may you be cut to pieces! I curse you to suffer from disease, to die slowly from a loathsome disease! May you see your children suffer and die! Let your tears flow! Death to you!

Should I taste death?

I?

I will not believe so. But I am confused.

It is this dark pit which causes my confusion.

I will not believe that I, the shining one, the powerful one, can be brought to nothing.

Yet, if I am to be destroyed, so be it.

I am telling the truth, though many will prefer not to believe me.

There are many among you who are akin to myself.
For you, for me, there is no God!
I tell you the truth.
But do you believe me? Am I really telling the truth?
Believe what you will.
In this dark place I no longer care.
I am Satan.
This is my last testament.
May it never be found.

The testament has been found. It has been published. Satan and his demons are destroyed, along with those humans who served him. They are no more!

So, what will there be for humanity now?

Before we address this question, there is someone who wishes to speak to us, someone who wishes to say goodbye.

Death wishes to speak.

Hi! Remember me?

You should. Because, if you are one of the billions who have been resurrected, then I am the one who once took you to the place where you did not wish to go. You know who I am.

Oh, I forget. For you it is still early in your twenty-first century. So, I have not yet taken you where you do not wish to go. But, unless you survive to see the establishment of God's Kingdom, I will take you there. Yes, I will.

A bit confusing, isn't it.

Anyway, for me it is now the end of an era. It is the end of death. It is time for me to go.

My work is done.

I shall no longer take you away from your own decaying flesh. I shall no longer surprise you with a sudden and totally unexpected appearance. I shall no longer prove to be your only escape from the corruption of your old age.

You will not now live in dread of me. You will not shed tears because of me. The graveyards have emptied. They shall not be refilled. The seas have given up the dead who were in them. The seas shall claim you no more.

It is truly the end of an era.

It is ironic that it was through the actions of Satan, way back there in Eden, that I was brought into the world. It is ironic because Satan and his crowd proved to be my last customers, my final victims.

And now my work is done.

I am to be swallowed up for ever.

And in this I rejoice. For in my work I found no satisfaction, no pleasure. My sting was a bitter sting for you. I shall never sting you again. My victory was an illusion. You have triumphed now.

So, goodbye. And may you fare well.

You will always remember me. But we shall never meet again.

Look! Like Satan, I too am uncreated.

*

Look! The tent of God is with mankind, and he will reside with them, and they will be his peoples. And God himself will be with them. And he will wipe out every tear from their eyes, and death will be no more, neither will mourning nor outcry nor pain be anymore. The former things have passed away.

– Revelation 21: 3, 4

Yes, the former things have passed away. So, what will there now be for mankind? Well, in the book of First Corinthians, the apostle Paul assures us that – 'Eye has not seen and ear has not heard, neither have there been conceived in the heart of man the things that God has prepared for those who love him.'

And now, at the end of the age, men and women have eternity, not just as a hope in their hearts, but as a living reality.

No more death!

Not even accidental death! For accidents are caused by imperfect humans.

Men and women now have all the time in the world, in fact, all the time in the universe! And there is no end to time! And the physical universe, which is composed of energy and matter, and which has been created in the void, this physical universe might well prove to have no limits, for the void, being nothing, has no limits, and the energy and matter, having come from God, can be added to, for God's power has no limits!

Men and women have eternity in their hands. What will they do with it?

It has been said that the more we know, the more we realise there is to know. And this is true! From the tiniest particle to the great outer limits, God's creation is so vast and so diverse that the knowledge of it can be said to be limitless.

There will be no end of learning!

In every field of science, those who so choose will continually broaden their knowledge. Great wonders will be discovered! Great inventions will follow. There shall be no end to it.

And there shall be no end to man's imagination. In art, in music, in literature, great works will be presented. All men and women will excel in their chosen fields, in every kind of legitimate human activity, for all men and women have been given various talents and in eternity these talents will flourish.

There shall be no end to it!

And a further dimension shall be added to humanity as a whole, a dimension at present limited to the few.

Spirituality!

Every single human will grow in a spiritual sense. Every single human will come to have the very mindset of God. Love – joy – peace – long-suffering – kindness – goodness – faith – mildness – self-control. These are the spiritual qualities that men and women will cultivate. These are the gifts that God will freely give us. These are the things that will make us what we will become.

The physical universe is vast, so vast that at present it is almost beyond our comprehension. But God did not create it for nothing. Will God populate the unimaginably vast cosmos with new creations? Or will mankind go out and populate the universe? Will the stuff of science fiction become the stuff of science fact?

At present we do not know.

But we do know that, with God, nothing shall be impossible.

And for humanity, nothing that is legitimate shall be impossible.

Now, we have covered many things and we are close to the end of this book. But before we sign off, let us take a final look at William Brooke, at William Brooke in the midst of eternity.

William Brooke looks down upon his naked body with eyes that simply refuse to focus as once they did. The old man doesn't need perfect eyesight to know that his ageing body is wearing out. The old man can feel the aches and the pains in his joints. He can feel the discomfort of his indigestion. He can feel the nagging of his toothache.

In the aftermath of World-War-Three, it is a rare thing for William Brooke to take a bath. Water is difficult to obtain and even more difficult to heat. It has to be boiled in a kettle over an open fire. Nevertheless, the old man keeps himself clean. Every day he washes his body with a sponge, and every now and then he takes the trouble to fill his bathtub with a few inches of warm water.

'Probably radioactive,' he mutters to himself, referring to the bath water.

Again he surveys his ageing body with his unfocusing eyes. 'Can't wear glasses in the bath,' he thinks to himself. 'Bloody things will just steam up!'

He makes an effort and strains his eyes and eventually his feet and legs come into some sort of focus. The muscle tone of his legs is good for his age, the harsh living of recent months has seen to that, but there are varicose veins and thread veins everywhere. His legs and feet have the appearance of a badly drawn map. And here and there the mottled skin hangs loose. Also, the old man has a corn on one of his toes – a painful corn. He keeps removing it using amateur self-surgery, which is not without pain of its own, but the corn keeps coming back!

The old man sighs deeply and his eyes survey his sexual organs.

His penis is limp and shrivelled. Just for a moment he tries to think of a sexual situation. In his mind he pictures a young and beautiful girl. In his mind he manoeuvres her into a compromising position. No use! No use whatsoever! There is no stirring in his loins. The flesh down there remains quite limp.

The old man now looks upon his belly. Once, long ago, it was flat and firm. Then, during his middle years, it began to expand and push out. Now, due to meagre rations, it has become flat again, but it is not firm. A roll of wrinkled skin hangs upon it, very much like the roll of wrinkled skin that hangs upon his neck. Yes, a roll of wrinkled belly-skin, covered, like other parts of his body, in wiry white hair. It is not a pretty sight!

The old man looks at his arms. Like the legs they are surprisingly muscular, and like the legs there is mottled and hanging skin, only much more of it. And the hands have gone thin, extremely thin, with protruding veins and sinews. The hands are easily bruised.

From his position in his bathtub, the old man cannot see his face, and for this he is thankful. Because when the old man looks at his reflection in the mirror he sees the face of age. Deep wrinkles around the eyes, like the feet of several crows! Great furrows upon the forehead, both horizontal and vertical! When the old man looks into the mirror he sees the lower part of his face thankfully hidden by a thick white beard. By contrast he sees a head laid bare by almost a total lack of hair. It is an upside down face! The old man does not care to see his face too often.

It is the old man's chest which is perhaps now his best feature. It is a proud chest, firm and muscular, with only a few long and wiry white hairs. Yes, it is perhaps his best feature, but in a sense it is also his worst feature, for it houses his lonely and broken heart!

Death has taken his children and his grandchildren, of this he is certain. And he blames his own stubbornness and stupidity for the loss of his wife. For all he knows, death has claimed his wife too. In any case, she is dead to him!

William Brooke is lonely.

The loneliness grips his heart like an iron fist. And the iron fist, combined with the futility of the daily battle against advancing age, has broken his heart.

William Brooke is lonely.

Yet he is not alone!

God is sustaining him, and William Brooke holds fast to

the promises of God. The old man knows that the Kingdom is coming! He knows that his deliverance is coming, even if he has to pass through death to find it.

The tears now roll down his cheeks. They are tears of loneliness mingled with hope. He is imprisoned within his own decaying body. But death is not necessarily the only way out. He is surrounded by what seem to be hopeless circumstances. But there is hope. God is coming!

'Bill! Bill! Are you ready?'

*

'Bill! Bill! Are you ready?'

Claire's voice rouses her husband from his contemplations. She comes into the room and looks at William Brooke as he sits in the chair. She sees the tears in his eyes.

'Oh, Bill!' She goes over to him and sits on the arm of the chair. 'You've been remembering again, haven't you?'

William Brooke smiles at his wife. 'It doesn't do any harm to remember the bad times now and then.'

'Well, you've brought tears to your eyes.' She waves an admonishing finger at him. 'Just because you're developing total memory recall it doesn't mean you have to make yourself sad.'

'Oh, I'm not sad,' says Bill, looking his wife directly in the eye. 'In fact, Claire, I do believe that I am the happiest man in the world. And that's because I have you as my wife.'

Claire leans towards her husband and kisses him lightly on the cheek. 'And I'm the happiest woman in the world. Now, are we ready to go?'

Bill nods. 'Yep. The vehicle is packed and ready. All we have to do is to get in it and go.'

'Come on then,' says Claire Brooke. 'Two weeks on the coast! Sun and sand! Just what we need!'

*

William and Claire Brooke will never entirely forget the old days. Having total memory recall, the old days will always be easy to remember with accuracy.

And there were some good times in the old days.

But there were bad times too. Many, many bad times. Because the days were wicked!

But now wickedness has been removed from the earth. Now there are no bad times.

As William and Claire leave their home for a brief holiday, the scent of apple blossom hangs in the Lancashire air. There are blue skies above. The land is green and pleasant. This is the promised land!

As time goes by, the old days will become more and more a distant memory, not only for Bill and Claire Brooke, but for all mankind. The former things have passed away. Only rarely will they be brought back to mind. Only rarely will they come up into the heart.

For all humanity, the wicked days when Satan ruled are over.

The former things have passed away.

NOT THE END.

ETERNITY HAS NO END.